T0361600

"There's no place like Rivenlea in Lindsay Franklin's magical portal fantasy, *The Unraveling of Emlyn DuLaine*. Readers will unravel alongside these whimsical characters as they swoon over story boys, soar with wyverns, and sail into classic stories teeming with nostalgia and wonder. Franklin's brilliant nods to literature will have fans of Oz and other beloved tales flipping the pages for more. Filled with unexpected friendships and twists that are sure to leave readers guessing, this un-putdownable novel is an instant modern classic!"

—SARA ELLA, award-winning author of The Curious Realities, *Coral*, and the *Unblemished* trilogy

"Franklin has crafted a sparkling adventure full of mystery and shifting reality. I loved traversing familiar and strange worlds with Emlyn DuLaine, a character who is relatable, charming, and perfectly sarcastic."

—RACHELLE NELSON, author of *Sky of Seven Colors* and *Embergold*

"Franklin has created a love letter to the voracious reader. In *The Unraveling of Emlyn DuLaine* she provides a fun, flirty, yet perilous jaunt through the fantasy realm of Rivenlea and some classic stories as Emlyn tries to save her sister in a literal literary adventure. She tackles tropes in YA fiction and twists them to rev up the merrymaking, only to then leave the reader wanting more by the end. This book was so enjoyable—the only downside is waiting for book two!"

—JASON JOYNER, award-winning author of *Launch*

THE
Unraveling
OF
Emlyn
DuLaine

Books by Lindsay A. Franklin

The Weaver Trilogy
The Story Peddler
The Story Raider
The Story Hunter

The Rivenlea Sphere
The Unraveling of Emlyn DuLaine

Devotionals
Adored
Beloved
Sunny Days Ahead
Embracing Imperfect

THE RIVENLEA SPHERE | ONE

THE Unraveling OF Emlyn DuLaine

LINDSAY A. FRANKLIN

For Genessa, my sister,
who is sunshine and freckles
and story time and make-believe.

MY SISTER IS DEAD.

That's the only explanation I can think of, anyway. Why else would I be sitting here, at the police station downtown on a Wednesday afternoon, when I should be doing my calc homework or studying for my physics test? My sister is dead— and they want to question me about it.

Again.

My knee bounces incessantly, and I hear Mom's voice in my head. *Emlyn, would you stop, already? You'll jackhammer through the concrete.*

If only I could jackhammer through the concrete. If only my anxious twitching could open a hole in the floor large enough to swallow me. Then I wouldn't have to sit here, waiting for Detective What's-His-Name to come in and grill me about Camille.

Could be worse, I guess. Mom could be in the room with me rather than just in my head. I know she's on the other side of the two-way glass, ready to listen to everything I say, everything they say to me, but at least I can't see her fretful gaze and that disapproving line between her brows.

That line has taken up permanent residence in the seven years since Camille disappeared, and I'm honestly not sure if it's on account of her missing daughter or her disappointing daughter who was left behind.

"Miss DuLaine."

I startle at the sound of Detective Whatever's voice as he strides into the room, all business and armed with file folders.

The files catch my attention—mostly due to their pathetic thinness. To be expected, I suppose, when someone vanishes without a trace. No evidence. No reports or analyses or leads to follow up on. The thinness of those folders represents my family's many unanswered questions—and the thinness of our bonds to each other since Camille left. Left us alone, side by side, absent the glue who used to hold us together.

"Miss DuLaine?"

I startle again and look up. He's staring at me, and I realize immediately he's asked me a question I've failed to answer.

Already.

"I'm sorry, Detective . . ." I search for some kind of name tag, but I don't see one. He's not uniformed, instead wearing a dress shirt and tie—well-matched, fashionable, quality fabric. I briefly wonder if his wife dresses him—is he married?—and how much money a detective in a largish city makes and whether or not he's one of those men who spends money on expensive haircuts.

I meet his gaze and realize I've done it again. "I'm sorry, what?"

He smiles, not unkindly, but it's a little condescending. Like I've accidentally amused and annoyed him in one fell swoop.

Join the club, sir.

"Detective Garcia. That's my name."

His detective badge hangs from his neck and lies on top of his tie. It looks weirdly heavy. "It's the most common surname in California."

He sits at the table across from me and smiles again—easily this time, obviously trying to put my awkward, tense, ball-of-anxiety self at ease. "Is it? I didn't know that."

I nod, feeling my lips press into a tight line, but I can't seem to relax them. As if the signal between my brain and my body has been short-circuited.

"Miss DuLaine, thank you for coming down here today."

"Did I have a choice?" My question sounds sassy, but I don't mean it that way. I don't mean to back talk, but couldn't they have told me over the phone?

Hello, Emlyn, good to speak with you again—your sister's body has finally been found. You can now return to pretending you've moved on with your life. Take care!

How hard would that have been?

Instead, here I am, sitting in this awful chair. They could at least spring for comfortable chairs. If you have to deliver terrible news to dead peoples' family members, you could at least let them sit somewhere comfy while you do it.

But then it occurs to me that suspects probably sit in these chairs too.

My stomach suddenly turns to iron. Then liquefies. Then reforms in not quite the right spot inside my torso.

Am I a suspect?

Detective Garcia immediately morphs into a mythical supervillain—like some weird amalgamation of Lex Luthor and the Joker, wearing an expensive tie and banal smile as he plots my painful and unnecessarily complicated demise.

I close my eyes, willing the thought from my imagination. When I open them, all that's left is the expensive tie and banal smile.

"I'm sorry," I choke past my Saharan throat. "I'm a little anxious."

I can hear my therapist laughing from across town.

"That's okay." He places his file folders on the table and opens one. "I'm sure it's not the easiest thing to talk about."

"I didn't kill her," I blurt.

"Excuse me?"

"I did not kill my sister. I was only ten when Camille disappeared."

"Yes, I know." He raises one eyebrow and pauses. "Perhaps we'll wait for my colleague before we get started with the interview."

Interview? Is this an interview, an interrogation, or informing next of kin?

Then it all snaps into place.

"You're a cold-case detective."

He looks mildly surprised. "Yes. Very good, Miss DuLaine."

"You haven't found Camille's body. Or any new evidence at all. I'm just here to give another statement."

Every nerve in my body begins to spark. It starts at my scalp and tingles across my shoulders, moving throughout me, all the way to my toes in a slow, excruciating wave of dread.

There's no new information. No body, no evidence, no leads. Just like before. They are simply here to rehash everything—to rip open the wound, pull off the scab, revisit the very worst day of my life in sharpest detail.

Detective Garcia is greeting his colleague as she glides into the room—Dr. Crawford, the ID badge on the lanyard around her neck says—and I know immediately she's a shrink. I can spot them a mile away—kind, yet clinical, warm enough to get you talking, cold enough to remain detached from whatever trauma you're about to spew at them.

I immediately resent her close-lipped smile, even though I know I'm being unfair.

"Hello, Emmy," she says. "Can I call you Emmy? I read in your file that you prefer it. Though you were a child then. Perhaps you prefer Emlyn now?"

"Emmy's fine." Said absolutely no one ever.

"Emmy." Dr. Crawford smiles sadly, understandingly. "I know this is difficult. But this is actually a good thing—your sister's case being transferred to the cold-case unit. That means Camille's disappearance is going to get fresh eyes, fresh attention. Detective Garcia and his colleagues are going to work really hard to get you and your family some answers. I'm sure you miss your sister a lot."

My walls slip into place around me—the emotional fortress that is my most familiar domain. I don't like being told how to feel, what I must be thinking.

I mean, she's right, but that's beside the point. She doesn't know me. For all she knows, I'm a self-centered brat who doesn't miss my sister at all.

"It was a long time ago," I say.

"Can you tell us what you remember?" Detective Garcia leans forward and fiddles with a recording device. "I'm going to record our conversation, if that's okay."

I have to wonder why they phrase it that way. What if it's not okay? Am I allowed to say no? I already know the answer, and I'm annoyed they always pretend you're in control of something when you're not.

"We're not really in control of anything," I accidentally say aloud.

"Pardon?" Dr. Crawford's pen pauses over her notepad.

"Nothing. Sorry." I know she's about to scrawl new diagnoses for me there.

"Can you start from the beginning?" Detective Garcia asks.

The rehearsed story slides out easily.

"It was seven years ago. I was ten. Camille was twelve. She and I were playing at the park down the street from our house. We were on the swings first, then Camille wanted to do flips on the bars. She did gymnastics. She was good at that stuff. I wasn't—I'm not—so I sat nearby under a tree and told her a story."

"A story?" Detective Garcia interrupts.

"Yes. That's my thing. Was my thing. I liked to write stories."

"But not anymore?" Dr. Crawford presses.

"No." This is not part of the rehearsed story, so I don't add more.

Detective Garcia tilts his head. "What happened next, Miss DuLaine?"

I feel Mom watching me from the other side of the glass.

Stick to the script, Emmy.

"I got to the fun part of the story. It was about a magic library."

Dr. Crawford smiles. "Magic library?"

I squirm, a little defensive. "What ten-year-old book lover doesn't want to visit a magic library?"

"Sure." She writes something on her notepad. "I'd want to visit one now, honestly."

I don't answer. I'm waiting until it's appropriate to get back to the script. Detective Garcia nods at me, and that's my cue.

"I had a good idea. I turned to write it down in my notebook—I always carried one with me. That distracted me for a minute, and when I looked up . . ." I pause, my brain tripping over the script.

I don't like to lie.

"It's okay, Emmy." Dr. Crawford urges me forward with her sad, understanding, close-lipped, unfairly irritating smile. "What did you see when you looked up?"

"Camille was gone."

"How long do you think you were writing in your notebook?" Detective Garcia asks.

I wasn't.

"Maybe a minute?" My leg is bouncing again.

"Wow." Dr. Crawford leans back in her chair and sighs. "It's such a cliché that someone's life can change in a minute, but yours really did, didn't it?"

"Yes." What else should I say to that?

Detective Garcia is studying my face. "Miss DuLaine." He smiles. "Emmy."

Uh-oh. He's first-naming me. "Yes?"

"You know, any information you can provide will help us with your sister's case."

Mom's gaze burns harder from the other side of the glass.

"Yes, I understand," I say.

"We're not judging you," Dr. Crawford adds. "We just want the truth."

"Any detail you remember could be helpful." Detective Garcia tilts his head the other direction, his gaze never leaving me. Dr. Crawford's smile is gone, and slight frown lines have appeared around her mouth.

They know I'm lying.

But they don't understand why. I have to lie. Everyone has told me for seven years the truth is wrong. What else am I supposed to do?

Stick to the script.

"Emmy?" Detective Garcia's expensive tie is staring at me. His badge is judging me. His recording device waiting to accuse, convict, and sentence me.

"She . . ." My tongue is Death Valley. My throat is the Gobi. "Camille vanished."

"You mean you looked up and she was gone?"

"No. As I told my story, I was watching her, not looking at my notebook." I imagine Mom screaming from the other side of the glass—though I've never actually heard her scream before. "I watched her unravel."

"Un . . . ravel." Detective Garcia's black eyebrows rise so high they nearly disappear into his hairline. "What do you mean by 'unravel'?"

I mean exactly what it sounds like—and this is why I always tell the lie, like I've been trained. "I mean that one second my sister was there, turning flips on the bar. The next second, she dropped to the ground and"—I struggle to get the words out, knowing how ridiculous they sound, knowing there's a reason I haven't said them aloud for years—"she ribboned away."

"Ribboned?"

"I don't know how else to say it." I fight to erase the frustration from my voice but lose the battle. "I mean it literally. I watched her hands and arms and legs and body—her face—shred to ribbons, unravel into strips, and then disappear."

Echoing silence booms through the room.

"Miss DuLaine." Detective Garcia places his palms on his

open file folder. "If something like that had happened to Camille, there would have been blood evidence at the park, surely."

"I don't mean it like that." I rub my forehead, a familiar headache beginning to pulse behind my eyes. "I don't mean her flesh was shredded." Dr. Crawford winces. "It was like she was made of fabric, and the fabric came apart at the seams, turned into strips, and then vanished into thin air."

They're staring at me.

"That's what I saw." I fixate on an imperfection in the tabletop. "I know it sounds . . . stupid." I avoid the word "crazy" because it's not my favorite.

"Emmy," Dr. Crawford says softly, "I believe you."

My eyes snap up. "You do?" Suddenly, I love her sad, understanding, close-lipped smile.

"I believe you are not lying to us right now. I believe you honestly think you saw that happen to Camille."

I hate her sad smile.

"Emmy, sometimes when we experience something traumatic—"

"Our minds create a reality that's easier to accept than the trauma we actually experienced?" I finish for her. "I know. I've heard that before. But do you honestly think it's easier for me to sit here and tell you I watched my sister unravel and disappear than it is to say something that makes reasonable sense?"

Dr. Crawford places her notepad on the table. "Emmy, my hope is that you and I will be able to work together to uncover whatever is buried beneath this manufactured memory."

"You're not listening."

"Remember, anything you witnessed in those moments when Camille disappeared will be helpful to the detectives working on your sister's case. This is very important."

"You . . . you think I don't know that? You think I don't wish I could provide something more helpful than 'my sister ribboned away' or even 'I looked down, and then suddenly she was gone'? If I could offer anything—*anything*—to help close Camille's case,

I would. Of course I would." I look at them both, wondering what they must think of me. Either that I'm crazy or some sort of deranged psychopath—those seem to be the only two options. Suddenly, I'm on my feet. "I told you the truth. I told you what I saw, and if you think I'm making it up, I have nothing left to say."

"Miss DuLaine, we—"

"No. We're done. I already know it's my fault. Whether you want to believe the truth or the script, I'm to blame."

"Script?" Poor Dr. Crawford looks very confused.

"Either I saw what I think I saw, and I have nothing useful to tell you—no information, no leads you can follow, no help to give—and Camille's case remaining unsolved is my fault. Not to mention the fact that I might be insane. Or else everything my therapist and my parents have been telling me for seven years is true—I got distracted, looked away, and didn't see how it happened. Didn't see who snatched her, where she wandered, or anything else of value."

"Emmy, please sit—"

"Don't you see? Either way, it's my fault. And now it's been seven years, and Camille is probably dead. We all know that's true."

"Miss DuLaine," Detective Garcia begins, "we didn't mean to suggest—"

"Don't feel bad." I grab my bag and sling it over my shoulder. Tears sting my eyes, but my internal walls are still up. They keep me from any outward displays of emotion.

Except anger.

"Look, Detective Garcia, Dr. Crawford. I appreciate the attempt. But we all know Camille is dead, and whatever happened in that park, it would be better for everyone if this case went from cold to nonexistent."

MOM'S FURY BILLOWS AROUND ME

like a cloud. I consider cracking the window, like that might vent some of her rage into the air rushing past us as we jet down the freeway toward home.

My knee bounces, and my fingers tap a frenzied rhythm against my armrest.

"Emlyn, would you please." My mom has a talent for finely dicing her speech so that even normal words hit my skin like little blades.

"Sorry."

I wait for the tinderbox to explode, but it doesn't. We sit in passive-aggressive silence so thick I could practically skate across it.

The mental image—gliding gracefully over my mom's expert-level passive-aggression, prepping for an Olympic jump—makes me snort.

"Is something funny?"

"No. Just about to double lutz on our communication issues."

"What?"

"Nothing." I turn to the window and watch the shoulder zip by.

Weird that it's called the "shoulder" of the road. Imagine a shoulder that ran the entire length of your body. There's probably another name for it. I scan my memory, recalling someone saying "breakdown lane" once. That's a better name. More accurate description.

"After all these years, Emlyn."

There it is.

I pause. Chew on her displeasure for a moment. "'Breakdown lane' is better than 'shoulder,' don't you think?"

"What?"

"Nothing."

"Could you pay attention for one second?"

"I am."

"Then did you hear what I said?"

"What?"

Mom sighs. I'm being difficult on purpose, I know. But so is she. What is the point of rehashing all of this? I said what I said. I can't take it back now. I could pretend, but what good has that ever done any of us? How has it made anything better?

It hasn't. Not ever.

I chew the inside of my lip, buying an extra three seconds. "Sorry. You must feel like you wasted a lot of money on my therapy."

"That is so rude."

She's not wrong.

"Why would you say such a thing?" Her voice takes on the shrill pitch it gets when her feelings are hurt—or at least when she's about to tell me I hurt her feelings. She waits a beat. "You are so hurtful."

"Sorry."

"Are you? I'm not sure that's true."

"What do you want me to say, Mom? My memory is what it is."

"Emlyn." She sighs again, seeming to gather every shred of energy, every scrap of willpower I haven't yet obliterated with my tiresome existence. "Seven years of therapy. You've worked on this with Katelyn, haven't you?"

"Yes."

"And yet still, when being questioned by the police, of all things, you revert to this ridiculous childhood imagining?"

"Weren't you listening at the station? Dr. Crawford says I'm traumatized, not ridiculous."

"That's not funny."

"Isn't it?"

"No. Emlyn, this is important. I have never been more embarrassed in my life."

I'm sure that's not true—I've had way worse outbursts than today's, and we both know it. But I let her keep going.

"They are investigators, Emlyn, and to say something so absurd to them is humiliating. For you as much as me."

"I'd think more for me, since I'm the one who said it."

"And yet you're not embarrassed in the least! It's like you have no sense of . . ." Mom trails off, like she can't find the word.

"Shame? I have no sense of shame?" I can hear my therapist laughing again.

Mom draws a deep breath and flips on her signal to take our exit. "No sense of propriety. This was an inappropriate time to repeat that story. At some point, imagination turns to dishonesty, and dishonesty is wickedness. Repeating that story crossed into dishonesty a long time ago. You were a child when it happened, but you're seventeen now."

I don't bother pointing out the irony here. There are layers.

I'm being accused of dishonesty for telling the truth. Because the truth sounds unbelievable. Fantastical. And, yes, ridiculous. But it's what I saw.

Unless . . .

A gremlin of doubt tiptoes into my mind. What if Katelyn and Dr. Crawford and every psych I've talked to in the last seven years are right? I can't process what I saw the day Camille disappeared, so I've created a new narrative. I believe I really saw it, but I didn't. Something else happened, and it's blocked from my mind.

And yet it's all so clear. The surprised *O* of Camille's mouth, her sharp intake of breath, the wideness of her eyes as her body unraveled.

"Imagination can become a stumbling block, Emlyn."

Mom never loved my natural inclination toward storytelling. It bordered too close to lying. I don't point out that I haven't written a single story since that day. Even though Katelyn told me I should—to help me heal, to help reconnect with my "artist's heart," as she called it.

I have been unable to convince her my heart shriveled up and died a long time ago. If I ever had one.

"You absolutely must get past this," Mom continues. "For all our sakes."

"But especially yours?"

"No, especially *yours*!" I can practically hear her teeth grinding from the passenger seat.

"Right."

An out-of-place detail catches my attention as we drive up our street. The neighbors' yard. Something's not right. What is it?

They haven't pulled in their trash cans yet, and their Christmas lights are still up, even though it's May. But none of that is unusual for them. Then I notice the beds of nasturtium out front.

The big bed of flowers had just bloomed, and I swear they were like flames this morning—reds and oranges and sunny yellows.

Now they look . . . white? Could they have replanted? Why would they? Is there a white variety of nasturtium? Probably. But it still doesn't make sense.

As we approach, my forehead creases deeper. Because I can see now the flowers aren't white at all. They're murky and depressing, like the flat gray sky when the marine layer settles over my patch of SoCal suburbia.

Or like someone has sucked out the color through a straw.

"Weird."

"Excuse me?" Mom's needlelike words pierce me back to

awareness. We're still awkwardly trapped in the car together, both probably wishing we were anywhere else.

"Nothing. Sorry." I glance over my shoulder at the neighbors' yard one last time.

"What ever are you looking at, Emlyn?"

I consider mentioning the weird flowers. Mom's better with plants than I am. Maybe she knows something.

But I turn to her, and she's practically glaring, waiting for me to say something offensive or disappointing.

"Nasturtium."

"What?"

"Never mind."

The gloomy, brooding flowers match my mood, so I let it alone for now. I hop out of the car at my first opportunity, then slam the door behind me with satisfying finality.

My sister is dead, and to be honest, most of the time I wish it had been me instead.

3

"DINNER IS IN AN HOUR,"
Mom calls down the hall after me.

"Okay." I get a second chance at a good door-slam. Not enough to draw my dad's attention, but enough to let my mom know I'm feeling . . . things.

The moment I'm alone in my room, my anger drains. Like a plug somewhere in my toes has been pulled, and every drop of the frustration and snark and irritation I immerse myself in for protection runs out in a pool around me. I'm left exhausted. Empty. Hollowed, like a fractured eggshell relieved of its insides.

I draw a breath and lean against my closed door, as though I'm too fragile to move.

Sometimes it feels that way.

I flip on my light switch. The LED strip lights lining the seam where my wall meets the ceiling come to life—bright purple to match my galaxy bedspread.

Camille is dead.

Today is the first time I've said it aloud to anyone. My sister is dead.

I close my eyes. Try to picture her.

A flash of honey-gold hair swirls through my memory. Her carefree laugh in response to some dumb joke I've made. Her eyes—sparkling blue.

My eyes snap open. Blue green? Or blue gray? Or clear, crystal blue?

I push off my door and go to my nightstand to grab the framed picture from beside my bed. But Camille's eyes are closed in this photo. She and I are little—maybe nine and seven. She has her arms around me, and we're laughing. Laughing so hard, our eyes are closed. I'm curled in on myself, my face barely visible to the camera, and Camille's head is tilted toward the sky, uninhibited in her laughter, soaking up every moment of fun, every moment of life.

Because that's how she was.

And I'm curled up like a constipated turtle, because that's how I am.

She would have laughed at that.

I smile a little and set the frame back down. But the fact remains—I can't remember exactly what my sister's eyes were like. I can't remember exactly what her voice sounded like, can't force it to mind the way I used to be able to when I imagined she was still beside me on our adventures.

I sink to the floor and lean against my nightstand. After a moment, I reach under the bed and pull out a treasured shoebox, filled with my Camille things. A bracelet she braided for me out of Mom's embroidery floss. (Mom scolded her, but only a little.) A folded piece of paper I don't bother to open. It's a feature I printed from a local news website—Camille's disappearance made headlines for a couple days when it happened. But a missing child case with no leads can't really compete in the twenty-four-hour news cycle of a largish city. With no new info to keep the clicks coming, Camille quickly faded from relevance, and I was left with my sad little printout as evidence our community once shared in the heartbreak.

At least for a second.

Camille's seventh-grade school picture—wallet size—rests somewhere near the bottom of the box. I pull it out and examine it. It's not the same as seeing her eyes in person. No photo can capture the sparkle. The life. The way her eyes twinkled when she laughed or when we shared a sisterly joke.

But they're definitely blue green, I decide.

In the very bottom of the box is my notebook. The pocket-size one I had on me that day. The one where I jotted down my notes about the magical library and the dragons and the characters in beautiful clothes. With all their hair colors noted in detail. Camille always asked about hair for some reason, so every strand was accounted for. None of my story people ever had to wonder about their hair color, texture, highlights, lowlights, or battles with frizz.

Camille insisted I document it all.

I smile, and tears trickle out with it. Because grief is like that, shifting the context of all your memories. It sneaks up on you in the middle of a happy recollection, tinging everything, casting a shadow, robbing you of everything that used to be good.

A once-joyful moment is now a moment lost, a time you can't revisit. A person you can't see or touch or feel.

Or even fully remember anymore.

I place my hand on the notebook. "I'm sorry, Camille. I should have written you down. Every detail."

For seven years, I should have been writing Camille so I'd never forget exactly what she was like.

Before I can think better of it, I'm grabbing a pen. Opening that notebook.

Inside, a child's imaginings lay preserved in time.

Friendly dragons. Overpowered superheroes who can do the most ridiculous things, like shoot lasers and fire from their hands. Enchanted forests that serve no purpose except to delight a ten-year-old—a girl who dearly wanted to stroll through a grove of trees filled with glittery leaves and strange fairies and magical pools of water.

I flip to a fresh page and stop, pen poised above the paper.

What to write?

A memory floats back to me—Camille up on the bars, flipping backward as she giggles at my plot twists.

"You need a boy, Emmy," she'd said.

"What? Ew, no."

She laughed. "I mean in your story. A story boy."

"Still ew, and still no."

"Oh, come on."

I'd sighed. Camille had some obnoxious new interests since she'd entered junior high. "Fine. What kind of story boy?"

"A swoony one."

"Obviously."

"But make him kind of sensitive—sensitive and swoony."

"Is there any other kind of story boy?"

"He should be chivalrous."

I glanced up at her, eyebrow arched.

"It means courageous but courteous. Chivalrous, like a knight."

"I know what it means. I don't know how to spell it."

"So, like, he's the hero, but he's nice still."

"He's the hero? Then I bet he's a little bit of a jerk."

Camille frowned disapprovingly. "Emmy."

"I'm just saying. Are the popular boys at *your* school nice?"

She'd sighed at me. "Some of them, yes. But anyway, *you're* writing him. You can make him whatever you want. Heroes can be nice."

"Fine, so he's swoony, chivalrous, and a little bit of a jerk sometimes because he knows he's good-looking and it's gone to his head." I smirked up at her. "He has dark-blond hair. And brown eyes."

She grinned. "What's his name?"

"Um . . . Larry?"

Camille snort-laughed. "No."

"Lar . . . Laramie."

She shook her head and did another flip. "That's weird."

"It sounds fancy."

"I think it's a city in Wyoming."

"I'm keeping it."

"Okay. As long as you make him more nice than jerk. Deal?"

"Deal."

"Good. Now tell me about these dragons."

I'd done so. I had started telling her about the dragons and then the magical library. Ten minutes later, she was gone.

I flip to a fresh page in my notebook and gently press pen to paper.

A shiver tiptoes down my spine. Camille's ghost whispers in my ear.

What comes next, Emmy?

An adventure through the enchanted forest? A trip to the magical library? Maybe a ride on a friendly dragon?

No. The story boy, of course. Because that's what Camille had asked for. The hero who is mostly nice.

Laramie . . . who needs a last name. Shayle, I decide, because it's perfectly ridiculous and Camille would have hated it. (It's a rock, she would say; sedimentary, I would reply.)

He is what comes next.

My pen begins to glide across the paper.

"Shayle, huh?" Laramie brushes sweaty, dark-gold hair from his forehead with the back of his hand and grins. Sunlight beats down on his face, and tall grass brushes about his knees, just hitting the tops of his boots. But otherwise, the scene is blank, like he's standing in an empty field in the middle of nowhere.

It's my story sandbox where I bring my characters so we can get to know each other.

I lift a shoulder. "I'm the storyteller. Do what you're told."

He draws a sword from the scabbard at his hip and assumes a fighting stance. "And what would that be, exactly?" Another grin. "Rescuing maidens? Slaying fire-breathing beasts?"

"Don't be silly. The dragons there are friendly."

Laramie's forehead puckers a moment, then smooths. "The dragons here," he says, glancing around at the nothingness. "And where is here?"

"Rivenlea," I reply without hesitation, because of course

that's where he's from. That's where he is. The storyworld of my childhood.

A blanket of grief suddenly envelops me, encircling my shoulders, squeezing my chest, flattening me into the floor.

Laramie's expression changes—falls, deepens, presses in toward me, until I can feel his gaze as if he were actually in the room with me. "Miss, are you all right?" He reaches out his hand, as if he might brush away the tears I don't dare shed.

I stare back at him, Camille's chivalrous story boy, and hunt for words. "My sister—" A lump in my throat cuts me off. I swallow hard, forcing it back down. "My sister and I used to play there."

"Here? In Rivenlea?"

"Sort of." A smile breaks through my shroud of sorrow. "It's hard to explain, and you wouldn't understand, story boy."

His eyes lock with mine, the tiniest smile pulling at one corner of his mouth. I notice the dimples in his cheeks then, and the strong cut of his jaw, just showing signs of stubble. The way his broad shoulders stretch his shirt ever so slightly, and the definition of his biceps when they catch the sunlight.

My stomach cartwheels.

"Wouldn't I?" he says.

I will my internal organs back into their proper positions. "Wouldn't you what?"

His smile grows. "Understand."

Oh. Right.

I glance down at my notebook. I've filled two pages with notes about Laramie and his chocolate-pudding eyes and mischievous dimples.

Can dimples be mischievous? Because his are. It says so in my notes.

"Okay, Camille," I mutter. "I get it now."

If only I could actually say it to her. If only I could show Laramie to her—see what she thinks and ask what I should change.

The name, for one, she would say, and of course I would refuse.

I lean my head back against my nightstand and blow out a long, slow breath, because my therapist, Katelyn, is forever telling me to "breathe through the hard moments, Emmy." So I try. I really do. Pulling in and releasing slow, steady breaths, as though that will actually make it hurt less.

But something isn't right. Something is wonky, and it's not just my therapist's advice or my lame attempts to implement it.

My LED light strip. Wasn't it purple before? Purple to match my galaxy bedspread. Now it glows cool white—colorless.

Dad must be tinkering with the smart bulbs again. He's forever tweaking those things and accidentally messing up my light design.

I consider pulling up the app and switching it back, but I lack the energy to dig in my bag for my phone.

So I glance back down at my notebook and reconjure the picture of Laramie Shayle in my mind. But this time, he's not alone. Quite against my will, someone else is there.

A woman—probably late twenties—stands beside him, her eyebrows raised, her dark river of hair accentuating high cheekbones and a no-nonsense expression.

"Are you coming, or what?" she asks. "We haven't got all day."

I frown at her. "Are you talking to me?" This isn't how it works. I'm the one who gives the commands. I'm the one who steers the conversation.

She is breaking the rules of the sandbox.

I can feel her exasperation across the cosmos. "Who else?"

"I . . . I'm the storyteller." It sounds extraordinarily feeble, even to my own ears.

"Well, then." The woman narrows her gaze, and I swear actual flames dance in her dark eyes. "Why aren't you telling the story, Emlyn?"

I gasp and snap the notebook closed. The characters never

know my name. Not unless I tell them. And I'm sure I've never met this woman—in my imagination or elsewhere.

My skin prickles, sparks of anxiety flitting across my face and arms, skittering all the way to my toes.

Maybe that's enough writing for today. Maybe this is something I should ease into a day at a time.

Or . . . a month at a time. A year?

A quarter past never?

I stand, preparing to find a safe spot in my desk where I can tuck the notebook. Possibly forever.

That drawer—the one where I shove old homework and scraps of paper I've scribbled ideas and questions and thoughts on. I open the drawer and begin to slide the notebook inside.

"Why aren't you telling the story, Emlyn?"

I hear the dark-haired woman's voice as though she's standing right next to me, and I have to choke down a scream. I retract from the desk like it's on fire.

But then I hear her voice again: "Are you coming? We've already been waiting for ages."

Without thinking, I chuck my notebook across the room. I want it as far away from me as possible, as quickly as possible.

It skids under my bed. I hear a soft plunk as it hits the wall on the other side.

There. That'll teach it.

But a split second later, I freeze. The swirled purple and blue and pink and black of my bedspread are gone. It has been replaced by a plain gray comforter.

Except, as I look harder, I can make out the faint pattern of the stars and dust and space gas that make galaxies look swirly.

And there is the ghost of that grape juice stain from two years ago. That slight pull in the fabric where I caught my bracelet last week.

And I realize my colorful bedspread has not been replaced with a plain one. Instead, the color has somehow drained away from my actual comforter, leaving a hollow shadow in its place.

I'M ROOTED TO THE SPOT,

cycling through my options.

Scream. Run. Call my shrink. Call the authorities. Call Dad. Call Mom.

The options get less enticing as the list continues. But I can't seem to stop the scroll of words running through my brain, nor can I settle on what to do. What is the proper response when the color begins to drain from one's room?

I stand there, thinking of every possible action, while doing exactly nothing.

If that isn't a metaphor for my life, I don't know what is.

A wet, snorty grunt interrupts my musings. It sounds like a pig with a deviated septum. Or a dog with severe hay fever.

Maybe that is the better metaphor for my life.

I blink really hard, as if that might hit the reset button on my brain.

But a moment later, another grunt sounds. It's coming from under my bed.

I close my eyes again, forcing my nausea to subside. There is no way I am actually hearing this noise. How could I? We don't have pets. And even if we did, what kind of pet would make that sound?

Another grunt—louder this time, and I can't ignore it.

There's only one thing to do. I tiptoe toward the bed and slowly lift the drab comforter. I peek into the void, telling myself I will see absolutely nothing, and the delusion will be beaten back into submission.

A pair of glowing sapphire eyes stares at me.

I yelp and scramble away from the bed in a mess of flying limbs and acute terror.

Because that pair of sapphire eyes is now thundering toward me.

A creature the size of a Shih Tzu charges me, a blur of midnight-blue scales, leathery black wings folded back, and a spiked tail poised for striking.

My body flounders as my brain pounds the truth at me—a truth too strange to comprehend. Dragon. Dragon!

Tiny. Weird. Dragon!

A tiny, weird dragon that stretches its mouth wide as its sapphire gaze focuses on my arm.

It's going to bite me.

I grab the first thing I lay hands on from my desk—the novel I've been reading—and lob it at the charging mini-dragon. It glances off the dragon's scales, barely fazing it.

Next, I hurl a stack of math notes. And then a handful of colorful pens. And then my AP US History book.

But the dragon's leathery wings unfurl, and it launches itself over my defenses, beyond all the school supplies within my reach, and sinks its teeth into my forearm.

I let loose the scream I've been holding in, expecting a wail that will draw the neighborhood, a screech that will peel paint from the walls and separate light from dark.

Instead, I produce a hoarse shriek.

But as the tiny, regrettably sharp dragon teeth sink into my flesh, I realize I know this dragon. I know it because I created it. Many years ago, I wrote it into one of my stories—this specific dragon, though much, much larger.

I'd written one for Camille too. Hers was aqua and pale

yellow, like the water and sand on a tropical beach. Mine was dark and midnight because . . . well, obviously.

And here it is, my own dragon, doing its very best to gnaw a chunk out of my forearm.

Pain lances up to my shoulder, and panic threatens to overwhelm me.

But then I remember something crucial.

The truth of it beats back the panic and infuses steel into my spine.

I am the storyteller.

I created this dragon, so I ought to be able to command it. But it needs a name . . .

"Frank!" I blurt the first name that comes to mind. "Frank the Dragon, I demand that you stop."

Frank freezes. Baleful sapphire eyes look up at me, and he cocks his head to one side, my arm still firmly trapped between his jaws.

"Frank—drop it. Drop it now."

He glances down at my arm, then meets my eyes again. He does not let go of my flesh.

"I mean it. *Let go.*"

I feel rather than hear him sigh. But he releases my arm, and blood oozes to the surface immediately. Then he sits on his haunches like a cat, studying me intently.

I study him right back, my eyes narrowed. "You're cute. Don't get me wrong. But this is it, right? You're the evidence that I have, indeed, finally lost my mind."

Frank makes a noise midway between a snort and a purr.

"I'm hallucinating."

Frank chortles.

I *must* be hallucinating.

"Okay, great. Thanks for nothing." I glance at my bed, then at Frank. "You stay there. Don't move."

I can't quite bring myself to turn my back on this mini-dragon while I go investigate under my bed. I'm not sure what

I'm hoping to find—a portal or a dragon factory or the empty eggshell Frank just hatched out of—but I have to at least check.

I pull up the bedspread again, take another glance at Frank, and peek under the bed.

Nothing. There's nothing—no evidence that a dragon has just charged out from there.

Except the notebook.

I stare at the notebook for five long seconds. And then I notice the page it has fallen open to. Ten-year-old notes about Frank, alongside some scribbles about Camille's tropical dragon. I'd written down their descriptions and sketched a couple of lopsided creatures that might be construed as dragons, if you squinted really hard. But how could . . . It just doesn't make—

I let out another hoarse cry when I glance up to find Frank hovering inches from my face, trying to peer under the bed with me.

I glare at him. "Can you not do that?"

He snuffles.

I reach under the bed to retrieve my notebook. I immediately snap the book shut and shove it in my back pocket, half expecting Frank to disappear when I do.

He doesn't. He extends one leathery wing, then the other, eyeing the webbing like he's inspecting stitching on a new garment. Then he turns to me and snorts.

"Where did you come from, Frank?"

My imagination, of course. It's the only explanation. I simply must be hallucinating this creature next to me.

Except a drip of blood on my laminate flooring begs to differ.

Frank has, very clearly, torn a number of little holes in my arm. I prod the wound, just to check if it hurts.

It does.

I squeeze it to see if it bleeds more.

It does.

"Okay, little dragon. I am not amused. But we are going to assume you're a figment of my imagination."

He blinks his reptilian sapphire eyes.

"I'm sorry. Don't mean to be rude. But I'm sure you understand. Now, I can't explain why I'm bleeding if you're not real, except that I must have scraped my arm on something."

Something tooth-shaped.

I shove the thought away. Force myself to act like everything is fine. Because . . . I really need it to be.

Another drop of blood hits the floor.

"I'm going to go wrap this up, and when I get back, I expect you to be gone, okay?"

Frank huffs, and a tiny bit of white smoke curls from both his nostrils.

"Don't even think about it."

I pivot and stride to my bedroom door—decisively, as if I haven't completely lost it. I pull the door open like I mean it.

I march down the hallway toward the bathroom feeling slightly better about my life choices, until I hear the click of dragony claws against the laminate.

Frank is following me.

I ignore the bodily presence I sense behind me as I begin to pull first aid supplies from the cabinet—mild soap, antibacterial ointment, sterile bandages, and tea tree oil for good measure. Because who even knows what's in dragon saliva.

A scrape, I remind myself. It's just a scrape. I begin to clean and wrap my wound that is definitely not a dragon bite.

Frank headbutts my leg.

"Stop that."

Frank headbutts me again, then snorts.

I'm about to scold him, but then I hear it. Footsteps headed this way. Careful, deliberate, passive-aggressive footsteps.

Mom.

Despite the fact that I've just spent the last five minutes telling myself this dragon isn't real and he didn't really bite me, I scoop Frank into my arms. He looks up at me uneasily, seeming to understand we're both in danger.

Mom's footsteps pad closer, and I can tell she's about to turn the corner in the hallway. When she does, we'll be in full view.

Without another thought, I shove Frank into the cabinet under the sink and slam the door.

Mom turns the corner a heartbeat later. Her frown impales me, even from a distance. "Emlyn, please don't slam the cabinets."

"Sorry."

Frank snorts. Barely muffled by the cabinet door.

Mom halts in the hallway. "What was that?"

I can't stop my eyes from darting to the closed cabinet door. "Nothing."

Frank burbles.

Mom's eyebrows pinch together. "I heard that."

I clutch one hand to my stomach. "Sorry. I'm so hungry. Is dinner ready?"

"It's been ready. That's why I came up. I've been calling you."

"Sorry. I didn't hear." Three apologies in the space of a minute? That has to be a record.

Frank unleashes a noise that could not be mistaken for a person's stomach on any planet—a huffing, snorting, grunting chuff. If my stomach ever makes that sound, I will seek medical attention immediately.

Mom's eyebrows shoot up. She's not buying it either. "Emlyn! What on earth is that noise?"

"I . . ."

I have no idea what to say.

Mom steps into the bathroom, apparently unconcerned about all the first aid supplies on the counter or the two large bandages on my arm, and goes directly to Frank's hiding place.

Though "hiding place" might be a stretch. Because Frank decides at that moment to let out another huff, and white smoke ghosts out from under the cabinet door.

I briefly wonder how hard it is to strangle a dragon.

But then I remind myself—Frank can't possibly be there. He

can't actually be under that sink. If he's a delusion, as surely he must be, we are in no danger. Mom will pull open that cabinet door and be met with bottles of cleaner, a bag of cotton balls, and some extra rolls of toilet paper.

Not a dragon. Obviously.

My arm throbs. Frank's smoke is beginning to billow about the bathroom tiles. A crash sounds from within the cabinet.

"Emlyn!" Mom snaps, like I've carelessly knocked something over, even though she can see me standing here, touching nothing.

"Sorry."

"What are you hiding in here?"

"I–"

She yanks open the cabinet door.

And is met with nothing unusual. Bottles of cleaner. A bag of cotton balls. Toilet paper.

There is no dragon inside the cabinet, and my nerves seem to flare with heat and cold at once. My stomach drops.

Where is Frank?

I'm not sure if I'm more concerned about the fact that Frank is missing or the fact that I actually expected him to be there. My mind feels split down the middle.

Mom leans over and peers into the cabinet, her frown deep. "What's going on in here?"

My tongue feels like sandpaper. It scrapes across the roof of my mouth as I try to form words. "Nothing. I was just bandaging my arm."

Mom glances at my arm but doesn't ask. She's still frowning as she reaches out and rights a bottle of tub cleaner that has fallen over.

Been knocked over?

No. Because there is no dragon. I try to wipe the image of that white smoke from my mind. Try to will the scent away from my nostrils.

Mom closes the cabinet door and straightens. She looks

concerned, but I can't track why. Is she concerned about her cabinet? About me? My arm or my mental health?

But all she says is, "Dinner is ready. Come down now, please."

"Sure. I'll just"—I glance at the mess of first aid supplies—"put this stuff away. Be down in a few."

After one more hard look, Mom nods, then turns and retreats.

I wait until I hear her footsteps hit the squeaky bottom stair. Then I drop to my knees and yank open the cabinet door again.

Nothing.

I start pulling out bottles of cleaner and rolls of toilet paper like a maniac. Because somewhere, deep in my soul, I need Frank to be in there.

Deep in my soul? Probably more like deep in my stomach, which is working itself into a proper pretzel. Either way, I keep tearing apart the bathroom, searching. And, if we're honest, hoping. Hoping that I haven't lost my ever-loving mind.

But Frank isn't here. I'd have seen him immediately if he was. Spiky tears poke at my eyes because I've had about enough of this day, but I pull out the bag of cotton balls anyway. I'm nothing if not thorough.

And there awaits a tiny dragon, covered in midnight-blue scales and standing about three inches tall now. Glowing sapphire eyes stare at me unblinkingly. One dragony claw is held to his lips that I swear are curled into a smug smile, as though telling me to *shh*. He has nestled himself among my bottles of nail polish. One color matches his scales perfectly.

I don't know whether to laugh or cry. Or squish him in my fist.

"Frank?" I whisper.

He weaves through the nail polish bottles toward me, grunts wetly, then climbs onto my outstretched palm.

I draw him to my face, note the weight of him in my hand, inhale the scent of smoke still lingering on his scales. "Are you really here?"

He bites my thumb.

I only just stop myself from dropping him. "Don't do that!"

His innocent sapphire eyes stare. Dinner is getting colder by the second. Mom will come back soon.

"What am I going to do with you?"

Frank reaches out his forelegs and wraps them around my thumb. He begins to pull, and I become immediately aware that even three-inch dragons are strong. Frank has succeeded in subluxing my thumb by the time I realize he's trying to pull me somewhere.

I leave the disaster all over the bathroom floor and obey the pocket-size reptile, who seems to be directing me back to my room. But when we reach my doorway, Frank gestures forward, pointing his snout toward the stairs.

"Bad idea, little buddy."

Frank grazes his teeth along my palm.

"Ouch!" I glare at him. "You can't bite me every time I annoy you."

Frank sinks his teeth into my finger.

I swallow a yelp. "Fine," I whisper. "What do you want?"

He points his snout toward the stairs again. Then gestures his foreleg at the front door.

Oh no.

I hear Mom close the silverware drawer with a medium-size crash.

She is not pleased.

I bite my lip and throw caution to the wind.

Gripping Frank securely in my palm, I fly down the stairs. "Be right back!" I shout in the direction of the kitchen.

"Emlyn?" Alarm sharpens Mom's tone.

"Don't wait for me!"

"Emlyn!"

I breeze out before she can stop me. But the second I pull the door closed behind me, I realize I have no idea what I'm doing or where I'm going.

Need to ask my dragon, obviously.

I uncurl my hand and find . . . nothing.

The front door swings open. "Emlyn Aveline DuLaine!"

I whip around.

Mom's cheeks are red, and I can practically hear her blood pressure rising. "What on earth is wrong with you today?"

My mouth opens soundlessly. It closes shakily. I don't know what to say. More importantly, I don't know where my dragon is.

Something squirms against my backside. My spine stiffens, and I suck in a breath. Because I am one hundred percent sure there is a tiny dragon wiggling into my back pocket, and I am equally sure he just nipped me.

Unless a giant wolf spider has made its way into the back pocket of my jeans somehow. The idea takes hold in my mind, and suddenly I'm picturing a bunch of hairy spider legs waving out of my pocket, and I can't suppress a shuddering snort.

I sound like Frank.

"Emlyn, are you sick?" Mom reaches for my forehead.

"I'm okay, Mom." I dodge her hand. "I just need to . . . check something."

"Wha—"

I don't let her finish. I turn and run, because my mom does a lot of things well, but running isn't one of them.

She calls after me, but I don't stop. I put my head down and run as hard as I can.

Sprinting toward nothing. And if that's not a metaphor for my life . . .

Well, you know.

5

CALCULATIONS ABOUT PRECISELY

how angry my mom will be when I return home are not going well. This is worse than the time I hung up on her when she called from the store, and my punishment for that rudeness was pretty stiff. (Lots of extra chores and grounded for two months from all electronics, except my laptop for school.)

I haven't run away since I was six years old. This time, it isn't the least bit cute. There's no tiny suitcase full of stuffed animals and pretend credit cards I made out of cardboard. And this time, Camille isn't here to follow me to the park, where I was determined to live under the play equipment, and convince me to return home so Mom and Dad wouldn't be sad.

"Emmy, if you don't come back, Mom won't have anyone to help her in the garden. I'm bad at it," Camille had said, kneeling beside me.

It wasn't true, and I was vaguely aware of it, even at the time.

"Dad will be so sad. You're the only one who thinks he's funny." She'd wrinkled her nose and smiled.

Also not true—we both always laughed at his dorky jokes.

I had focused on the little tower of wood chips I was stacking. "They don't even like me. They wish I was like you."

Camille added a wood chip to my stack. "That's not true."

I shot her a look.

"They just don't know you like I do," she said softly.

"They're my mom and dad."

"Yeah, but you don't talk to them like you talk to me."

She had a point. But it was because they didn't understand me—they never really had, and now, eleven years later, it's only gotten worse.

"What do they always call you?" Camille had asked.

I'd rolled my eyes. "Their miracle baby."

The memories swirl around me now—almost visible, like wisps of smoke—and I realize I'm not running anymore. I've stopped, and when I look around, bile crawls up my throat.

I'm at the park. The one near our house. The one where Camille and I always played. The one I haven't visited in seven years.

My gaze snaps to the monkey bars, and my stomach clenches. I blink, and Camille is there, flipping on the bars.

I blink again, and she's gone.

My hands rest on my knees as I lean over, heaving. My stomach is empty, so nothing comes up, except the bile already burning my throat.

A soft thud next to me snags my attention. Frank has jumped down from my jeans pocket. He doesn't seem bothered by the fact that my body is trying to vomit up my feelings. Or even like he notices. He's gesturing onward, straight into the park.

Straight into my worst memories.

"I can't," I choke.

I see her unravel. Her surprised face. Her gaping mouth. Her body as it unwinds, shreds, disappears.

Her wide blue-green eyes—asking a question, pleading for help, crying out.

I drop to my knees, unable to hold myself up anymore. The notebook in my pocket presses against me.

Frank snorts, pointing his little head toward the bars.

"I can't, you insufferable reptile." Sweat breaks out across my entire body, and my lungs squeeze. The hyperventilation is coming on.

Frank chuffs impatiently.

Camille's eyes unravel.

Frank grunts.

Camille screams.

I grasp my head with both hands. That scream never happened. Those terrible few moments when I lost my sister were silent. My imagination is trying to change the story, and I need to get my thoughts under control. Reel it back in, Emmy.

"Well? Are you coming?" the dark-haired woman's voice intrudes. "We've been waiting for ages."

The wind picks up around me, and my breathing becomes frantic. There isn't enough air in all of California to fill my lungs.

I look up and see that Frank is the size of a Shih Tzu again. Someone is going to notice him, but I can barely muster the brain cells to worry about that right now. He stands on the precise location where my sister vanished.

"Frank." The word scarcely registers over the rushing wind. "Frank!" My parchment-dry throat isn't helping matters.

Frank's wings and ears flap as he looks back at me. I squint and lean forward, trying to force my vision to correct itself. To obey. To show me what's actually there.

Because the gateway I'm seeing now can't possibly be real. It's barely visible, shimmering like it's made of heat waves—a transparent arch just behind Frank, over the exact spot where Camille unraveled. He's still paused there, sapphire eyes beckoning.

I can't.

He snorts, disgust clear. But he doesn't try to convince me again. He spreads his wings and jumps through the gateway.

I inhale a gasp—then watch the dragon ribbon into bits and vanish.

The wind kicks into a gale. The trees edging the park bend

under the force. I stare at the spot where my imaginary dragon stood a moment ago.

He's gone now. He's gone, and I could simply turn around and run home. Fight the wind, face Mom. It wouldn't be pleasant. But I could do it.

My nerves prickle. Ice trickles down my spine.

Because in that moment, I realize the most awful truth. This is the closest I've ever been to finding out what happened to Camille. For the first time in so many years, it feels like the answers dance just before me, within grasp.

I take a step toward the gateway, still shimmering transparently.

What if . . . ?

The hope is almost too sharp, too painful to bear.

But what if—what if I could not only find out what happened to Camille but actually *find Camille*?

What if she's still alive?

I shake myself. I need to run away, go back home. Be responsible and sane. Instead, I take another step forward. And then another. And then I'm running toward the gateway before I can change my mind. I'm running toward my last, painful, desperate, foolish hope of finding my sister alive.

A whirlwind hits me so hard it throws me the last few steps to the gateway. My hair whips against my face like stinging branches. I close my eyes against the cyclone, but then I feel it happen. I feel my body disconnect from itself, my seams part, my fibers unwind.

And I'm sure my mouth is frozen in a surprised *O*.

My shredded body ripples through the air, tumbling and floating at once, falling into nothingness.

Until I feel the strips of myself knitting back together, becoming solid, taking shape. And then the presence of something large is rushing toward me.

The ground.

Oh well. It was fun while it lasted.

I land awkwardly on my back, and the air is knocked from my lungs. But I don't smash my head. A miracle.

I pause. Force a painful breath.

I'm almost sure I'm not dead. Tall grass waves over me, a purplish-blue sky spans far above.

But then my vision is blocked by a silhouette. A dark cascade of hair pops into view. High cheekbones. No-nonsense expression. Now-familiar voice.

"Well. It's about time."

6

"YOU'RE SUPPOSED TO STAY

in the sandbox." It's the only thing I can think of to say to the dark-haired character who keeps intruding into my consciousness. How in the world is she here, through the portal into . . . wherever this is?

Her eyebrow rises. "Excuse me?"

I try to sit up. And fail. My body feels like it weighs nine hundred pounds. "Oof."

"Indeed." The woman crouches beside me. "Are you injured?"

"Just emotionally."

She cracks a wry smile. "It's good to see you, Emlyn."

"Is it?" I don't bother to try to understand—the fact that she knows my name, seems to know *me*. Not until I can get some air into my lungs and some blood back to my brain.

The sky above us darkens. A dragon thirty times the size of Frank in Shih Tzu form soars across the purple-blue expanse. I try to yelp, but the sound gets strangled somewhere in my throat. Because I recognize those midnight-blue scales gliding through the sky.

Frank is ginormous.

One glance at my bandaged arm drives home the fact that Frank could swallow me in one bite now if he wanted.

Let's hope the nugget of fondness I feel for him goes both ways.

The woman follows my gaze. "Ah. You brought the wyvern back. Well done."

Wyvern? "I . . . think the wyvern brought me, not the other way around."

Frank turns a flip, seeming to enjoy his return to what I hope is full-size. But in the next moment, he catapults toward the earth like a meteor. The ground shakes beneath his clawed feet as he lands somewhere nearby.

I manage to prop myself up on my elbows in time to watch as he shrinks to the size of a pony and trots toward us. He sidles up beside the woman and snorts—a much larger sound than it was back in my bedroom.

"My, Frank," I manage. "What big nostrils you have."

"Frank?" The woman's eyebrow rises again.

"I named him."

"Her."

I finally manage to sit all the way up. "What?"

"This wyvern is female."

The exasperation in her voice nettles me—as though determining the anatomy of wyverns or dragons or whatever is a basic skill one learns in elementary school.

She shakes her head. "You have so much to relearn." She extends her hand down to me.

I accept her help, and she pulls me to my feet.

But as soon as I have my footing, I recoil from her grip. Heat courses through her hand, like she's running a high fever.

"Something wrong?" she asks as I snatch my hand back. Flames and amusement dance in her eyes.

I blink and then gape. Her eyes look normal again—dark brown, not unlike my own.

I'm jarred from the moment a second later by a stiff headbutt against the right side of my body. My legs nearly buckle beneath me, but I retain my balance. "Frank."

He—*she* chortles.

"Francesca?" I offer. "Frankie?"

She growls, then huffs out a cloud of smoke large enough to obscure me and the dark-haired stranger.

I cough. "Never mind. Frank it is."

She seems satisfied, resting back on her haunches, her head cocked to one side.

I turn to the stranger and finally take in her whole appearance. She's taller than I am, but that's no great accomplishment. Her silky hair is pin straight, falling over one shoulder in a glossy near-black cascade. She's almost entirely covered in black leather. Pants, a vest that looks like body armor, bracers covering her forearms, a utility belt fit for a hobbit going on a very long adventure—and ready to meet an orc or two—and tall black boots. Her inky cloak stretches to the ground, the hood pulled back and resting at the nape of her neck. The only color on her ensemble comes from a deep red scarf at her throat.

I wouldn't want to meet her in a dark alley.

Her lips quirk as she watches me dissect her, standing there in an open field. An open field I finally recognize.

The nerves across my shoulders tingle. I'm pretty sure we're standing in my character sandbox. And that I've completely lost my mind.

I clear my throat. "I would introduce myself, but it seems you already know me."

"We've been waiting a long time."

"So you've said." I feel the weight of my notebook in my back pocket. "But I can't imagine what you mean by that."

Another wry smile. "I'm Rhyan Doyle."

"Uh. Okay." I'm not sure if this is supposed to mean something to me, but it doesn't. "I'm Emlyn. You can call me Emmy."

She extends her fire-hot hand again. "Pleasure."

I take it, shake, and try to pretend her fingers aren't almost too warm to touch. "So . . ." I take another long look at the huge field of tall grass. Giant evergreens line the horizon. I think I see another dragon winging through the sky far away. "What is this place?"

"Rivenlea," she says simply, as though that explains everything.

Or anything.

"Right." Annoyance pinches my voice. "The world I made up when I was five."

A noncommittal shrug. "If you say so."

My patience is beginning to fray. "I do say so. Rivenlea is not a real place. I've been writing stories about Rivenlea since I could manage a pencil."

"Well, not exactly. You stopped writing stories about anything some years ago. Did you not?"

Shots fired. And that one hits me hard.

"My sister died," I say, but even as it leaves my mouth, I know it's not the correct counterstrike.

Because I don't know that Camille is dead—not for sure. Yesterday, I'd have said it was certain, but today? Today, everything is flipped upside down, and I don't know what to believe anymore.

All I can do is lean on the facts. Camille disappeared, and the infinitesimal chance she might actually be alive and I could still find her is what prompted me to follow a disagreeable wyvern, or whatever, through a portal into . . . my own imagination.

A headache is blossoming. And I get the sneaking suspicion Rhyan can see right through me.

She shakes her head. "Whatever you say."

I suddenly don't care about selecting the correct counterattack in this argument. The pinprick of hope in my heart opens to a wide, painful chasm. If any of this is real—and that's a big if—then it's my only chance to possibly find out what happened to my sister. So I ought to engage with this world as though it is real. At least until I get some answers.

"I'm doing a thought experiment," I say to Rhyan.

A small grin cracks her face. "Of course you are."

I ignore the spark of weirdness that ignites in my chest—this woman I can't remember who acts like she knows me—and forge on. "I am assuming you're real."

"Why, thank you."

"Just for the time being."

"Sure."

"Until any of this starts to make sense." I pause. "Do you know Camille?"

The sharp planes of Rhyan's face soften somehow. "We'll get to that. First, you should meet the rest of the Novem."

"The what?"

She pulls a chunk of dried meat from one of the pouches on her utility belt and offers it to Frank, her brow crinkling thoughtfully. "Have you really forgotten everything?"

Because I have resolved to at least pretend like this is actually happening and I'm not hallucinating, I scroll through my brain, trying to remember everything I ever dreamed up about Rivenlea. I have never, to my remembrance, made up anything called a Novem. I never made a character named Rhyan.

But as I gaze once again at the tall, waving grass and the blank canvas of the place where I'm standing, I'm sure it's my sandbox. And she *said* it's Rivenlea.

Plus, there's Frank the female dragon, standing beside me, licking her scaled lips, and I know I made her up years ago.

"I'm not sure what I've forgotten," I say truthfully. "But I think I might have fallen into my own head somehow."

"That seems impossible." Rhyan swipes a recurve bow I hadn't noticed before from the grass, and I jump back. She chuckles. "I dropped it when I ran over to make sure you weren't dead."

"Oh."

She sweeps her cloak back and pulls an arrow from a pouch secured at one hip. "Come. Your wyvern is hungry."

I glance at Frank. Her sapphire eyes stare at me accusatorily, as though I really ought to have noticed.

"She's not mine, exactly," I say in a feeble attempt to defend myself.

"Isn't she?" Rhyan turns and strides toward the evergreens in the distance. "She seems to believe she is."

And you did make her up, my traitorous thoughts remind me.

Stumbling on my still-unsteady feet, I follow after Rhyan, trying to keep pace with her long strides. "Can't Frank feed herself?"

"She's just a baby, Emmy."

The image of Frank soaring through the sky pops to mind. Ginormous Frank gliding through the atmosphere like a flying school bus is a baby. Got it.

I cast a sideways glance at the bow and arrow in Rhyan's hand. "What are you going to do?"

"Teach you about Novems."

"With that?" Concern pitches my voice higher.

Rhyan glances at her weapon with amusement. "No. I'm going to teach you about Novems while I find a snack for your baby."

We reach the edge of the trees—an expansive forest that blots out the sky and obscures vision of all else—and Rhyan stops. "Wait here. I'll be right back."

"Wai—" But before I can even get the word out, she's pulled her red scarf up over her mouth, flipped her black hood onto her head, and slipped into the trees.

I stare after her for a moment, then turn to Frank. "This is your fault."

She gurgles and headbutts my shoulder.

"Ow." I roll my shoulders to try to loosen them. That fall may or may not have happened in my imagination. But the soreness is all too real.

I plop myself onto the grass, and Frank curls up beside

me, a deep rumble reverberating in her reptilian chest. She blinks at me.

"Don't try to be cute now. You brought me . . . here. To the forest of my insanity." I stare at the trees. They seem every bit as solid as any trees I've seen when I wasn't hallucinating.

Maybe it is real? Maybe somehow this forest actually exists, and maybe I'm actually sitting here in this present moment.

But then the blue dragon beside me snorts, and I'm reconsidering my logic.

Rhyan appears a few minutes later, a rabbit skewered with an arrow clutched in one hand. My empty stomach heaves.

She eyes me. "Are you quite well?"

I try not to look at the very dead floof in her hand. "I don't eat furry things. I'm a pescatarian."

Her lips twitch. "I see. Might want to look away."

I obey without hesitation and refuse to let my imagination guess what she might be doing. Though I can't help but picture her in a cloak made of rabbit fur or puppy fur or kitten fur.

"There," Rhyan says, and I turn to find the dead bunny still in her hands, but at least the arrow is out now. I ignore his twitchless little nose and try to focus on what she's saying as she squats and begins to clean her arrowhead. "A Novem is a unit of nine—nine members of a special ops team assigned to missions together. Each member is uniquely equipped to serve the team, complete the mission, and restore order."

I stare at her for a moment. "Okay. Restore order to what?"

"We'll get there." She pauses from her work long enough to shoot me a wry look. "Oh, and you're the long-lost ninth member of our Novem. Did I mention that?"

"Very funny." But she holds my gaze a moment longer than is comfortable. "You are kidding, right?"

"I rarely am." She rises, the bunny carcass in hand again. "The Novem belongs to me—I'm your commander." She spares me an amused glance. "And I'm a Flare."

Before I can ask, her hand ignites.

Flames leap from her palm and swallow her fingers, the rabbit, and my voice. I stare in mute shock as the small fire roars a few moments longer, then dies with a faint *pop*.

Rhyan tosses the broiled meat straight up into the air, and Frank rises onto her hind legs. She snags the rabbit midair on its way down, then happily crunches the ill-fated bunny with a meaty squish and crackle of bones.

If I weren't so stunned, my stomach would probably heave again.

"You're our Dragon," Rhyan says.

I turn to Frank shakily. "Congratulations," I manage.

"That's a wyvern."

"What?"

"Not a Dragon." Irritation clips her words again. "I wasn't talking about her. *You* are our Dragon."

I stare at her. "Um." Glance down at myself, looking every bit the normal teen in my jeans, Converse high-tops, and a faded black T-shirt with an *Alice in Wonderland* quote on it: "Who in the world am I? Ah, that's the great puzzle."

I look back at Rhyan. "Dragon?"

She shakes her head and sighs. "We'd better meet the others." A nod at Frank. "Would you mind?"

Frank grunts, then trots away from the trees, doubling in size as she goes. Not quite as large as a school bus, but big enough to carry both me and Rhyan on her back.

Which seems to be Rhyan's plan. She's slung her bow across her back, returned her cleaned arrow to its quiver, and used Frank's bent foreleg as a stepstool to glide onto the wyvern's back.

She extends her feverish Flare hand down to me. "Coming, Dragon?"

"You are obviously confused," I say, but I take her hand and let her assist me as I scramble awkwardly onto Frank's back.

She laughs as I clutch her cloak in a death grip. "So, so much to rediscover."

Including Camille's whereabouts? Maybe. The flame of hope flickers brighter.

And with that, Frank unfolds her leathery wings and springs off her powerful hind legs, propelling us toward the answers to all my questions, the satisfaction of the deepest desires of my heart. Everything I've longed for the last seven years.

Or else toward certain doom.

I can hardly tell the difference anymore.

I SHOULD OPEN MY EYES.

I know, okay?

I'm soaring through the air on the back of a literal wyvern-dragon-whatever, flying over what can only be described as a new world—at least to me. I should open my eyes.

Instead, my face is buried in Rhyan's back, her cloak clenched in my fists, and I've definitely screamed once.

More than once.

Okay, many times. I have screamed many times, because Frank the snake is dipping suddenly, brushing the tops of trees with her claws, winging through turns far too sharp for my taste. My stomach has dropped into my sneakers, bounced up my throat, and plummeted again, thanks to Frank's flight path.

And she seems to be enjoying herself, which only adds to my dismay.

That treacherous reptile.

"Emmy." Rhyan gently nudges me. "Look."

I crack open one eye. To our left, a sea stretches into eternity. Frank is following the uneven coastline, and I'm reminded of road trips up the Pacific Coast Highway in California, staring at the blue expanse of the ocean.

Except this water is black as pitch.

"Is it . . . oil?" It's the only association I can grasp—the only thing that makes any sense.

Except it doesn't. Not really. A sea of oil? Rhyan and any other Flares would have to be very careful when they went swimming.

"No," she says. But she doesn't offer any further explanation except, "You'll visit someday, then you'll see."

I'm just about to allow myself to open both eyes and maybe unclench my muscles when Frank dives suddenly.

I guess we've begun our final descent.

Frank crash-lands—at least it feels like it—five seconds later, and I nearly topple off her back. Rhyan lets out a small whoop, and I can only assume she finds this enjoyable. She hops down with ease and reaches back to help me shakily struggle off Frank. As soon as we've dismounted, Frank shrinks to dog size. She heels to me, like we're going for a walk and she's a well-trained dragon.

Wyvern.

Whatever.

My feet don't feel quite solid beneath me as I try to convince myself I truly am standing on the cobblestone path where Frank has landed.

Except, I wonder . . . *am* I actually standing here? Because I recognize this place. I know this stone path winding through redbrick buildings, the cast iron streetlamps punctuating the greenbelts and hedges. The wooden shop signs announcing the wares and services in branded lettering. The evergreens ringing the complex, the flowering shrubs lining the path.

Even the bustle of several strangers, going about their daily business, strums a familiar tune on the strings of my heart.

"Castramore," I whisper, the single word heavy with disbelief.

Rhyan's eyebrows rise. "You know it?"

"I wrote it."

Her smile quirks. The disbelief I feel is reflected back at

me in her expression. "Castramore has been the epicenter of Rivenlea for centuries."

"Yes."

A young woman is leaning out a second-story window, hanging wash on the line, laughing and shouting at a teenage boy dangling out a window across the alley. "Jason! Didn'ya get the wash from your mum?"

The boy named Jason flashes an impish grin. "She'd have to catch me first if she wants me to do some chores." He swings out just a bit farther, finds a divot in the mortar between bricks, and Spider-Mans up the building toward the third-story window. "See ya, Denica!"

Denica shakes her head and continues about the laundry like a responsible person as Jason wriggles through the open window of some unfortunate neighbor.

"Yes," I say again, barely able to process what I'm witnessing. "Castramore is the epicenter of Rivenlea. And I wrote it." I made up the characters Jason and Denica for a Rivenlea short story I'd been writing at the time.

"They get married when they finish growing up," I say vaguely, watching the teenage version of my childhood imagining Denica hang otherworldly laundry on a line that can't exist in a world of my imagination. What in the name of pharmaceuticals is happening here?

Rhyan's gaze drills into me—I feel it boring holes, but I can't seem to rip my eyes away from the mundane, yet wholly fantastical, scene.

"Are you all right, Emmy?" she says at last.

I finally turn. Blink. "I honestly don't know how to answer that question."

Genuine concern fills Rhyan's expression. "There's no denying you have a special connection to Rivenlea. But believing you created this entire world is taking it a bit far, don't you think?"

My cheeks heat, burning in so much humiliation it makes me

wonder if I might be a Flare. "I didn't mean . . . That is . . ." But I'm exactly zero percent sure what I mean. I guess I did suggest I was the story god of Rhyan's world, and maybe that's a little presumptuous.

But how are some elements of Rivenlea—an entire city block, even—so familiar? As if she can hear my thoughts, Frank headbutts my leg, reminding me she is yet another piece of this bizarre puzzle I imagined. I have the proof in my back pocket, scribbled in an old journal. Childhood musings jotted down a lifetime ago.

"Shall we meet some of the others?" Rhyan nods down the cobblestone street, toward a large building a short distance away. "They'll be anxious to see you. We've been waiting so long."

"As you've said." I absently pat Frank's head, and she flaps her ears and grumbles a gentle purr.

Gentle for a wyvern.

We follow Rhyan down the street. Jason is now dangling from the third-story window by his fingertips as the occupant of that apartment screeches and tries to smack him with a broom. Denica looks mildly concerned, but others have poked their heads from their windows to watch the scene with amusement.

"Oy!" a girl with long blonde hair calls down from two stories above Denica's window.

Denica turns her gaze upward. "Oy, Andi!"

Andi. Another one I created and used as a filler character in a short story about the magical forest.

"Is it true he's escorting you to the ball?" Andi nods to Jason, who has just slipped one hand out of the way in time to escape a rap from the broomstick.

Denica shakes her head and clucks her tongue. "If the fool can stay alive long enough!"

I hear the neighbors' chorus of laughter for a moment before we're out of earshot.

"He'll live," I say.

"What?"

"Jason. He'll live."

"Oh." Rhyan pauses. "Well, I guess he always does."

"They get married eventually." My shoes *skitch* against the stones as I pull to an abrupt stop. "Oh!"

We've just cleared the busy streets of downtown Castramore, and a large building has come into full view. Despite the familiarity, despite the fact that I visualized bits of it, imagined elements, dreamed up snippets, the sight still steals my breath.

The building is constructed of redbrick, striated with half a dozen rows of paneled glass windows, their beveled diamond panes casting back rays of midday sun. Turrets stand guard at the corners, their conical tops dressed in dark shingles, the spans between connected by a series of pointed gables.

Ivy snakes the exterior walls, and the Rivenlite evergreens are interrupted by trees of other varieties, awash in early autumn color. Red, gold, orange, as though they've joined Rhyan in becoming Flares, their hands and arms alight for the season.

Or forever. For all I know, it's always autumn in Rivenlea. It is my favorite season, after all. And I'm quite sure I made up this place.

"Emmy? Are you coming?" Rhyan stands framed in the huge wooden door, propped open.

Last time Rhyan invited me to hurry up, I responded by following a wyvern into a portal of my own thoughts. I glance at Frank. She seems completely unconcerned about the havoc she's wreaked by showing up under my bed and trashing my bathroom cabinet.

She bats her wyvern lashes and scampers off after a colorful butterfly.

"She'll be fine." Rhyan nods. "She'll wait for you."

Right. Because she's already been waiting for years. Supposedly.

I stand in the shade of the massive building—immobile, indecisive. Because I already know what's inside.

It's Ambryfell. Home of the Rivenlea library.

I DON'T RECALL MAKING A

choice to follow Rhyan. I'm not sure exactly how I crossed the threshold into the place I was dreaming of when my sister disappeared. Yet somehow I find myself trailing after Rhyan, following the slight warmth of her wake.

Outside, Ambryfell is a fortress of redbrick. Inside, gray stone reigns, giving me the impression I'm traversing the halls of a medieval castle.

Dungeon? Torture chamber? Possibly. I don't have much choice but to continue scurrying after the Flare who says she's the leader of my . . .

"Hey, what were those things called again?" I skip a few steps, trying to erase the advantage of her longer stride.

"What things?"

"The teams you mentioned before. You're the Flare."

"Yes, and you're the Dragon." I don't bother arguing with her. "Novem," she answers. "The teams are called Novems."

"Right. Which exist to restore order to . . . what, exactly?"

"This." We have crossed the foyer. Rhyan pauses in front of a pair of wooden double doors, grins, then pushes them open.

I hesitate. Can it actually be? The library I wrote all those years ago?

Rhyan gestures me forward. "Come on, Dragon."

I follow her into my childhood fantasy.

Except the Ambryfell library is more than even I could have imagined. Vaulted ceilings soar overhead, beyond the reach of the lanterns and torches illuminating the immediate areas.

Shelves upon shelves, as far as I can see, enough to satisfy the most voracious library patron, the loneliest, most bored, most in-need-of-continual-escape reader.

In other words, me.

But these shelves aren't filled with books as I expect them to be. My Ambryfell was filled with books, albeit magic ones. But these shelves are full of spheres—clear glass orbs—hovering over the shelves, glowing faintly in a kaleidoscope of colors and patterns. Movement swirls within the spheres, but none is close enough for me to make out any detail.

There's plenty to occupy my attention right in front of me, however, as the foyer of this vast chamber is filled with odd lights of its own.

I feel Rhyan's eyes on me and glance over. She's wearing a satisfied smile. "What do you think?" She indicates the thing in the foyer.

I stare at the glowing, pulsating dots of light. An interconnected web of circles?

"They're spheres too," I realize aloud. "Little ones."

"Representations of spheres." Rhyan points. "This is the sphere map. It shows the placement of our pillar spheres. Very useful when we build gateways. It also alerts us to breakdowns in the pillars. Not all spheres are pillars, of course. We have constant patrols circling the library to note anything amiss in the other spheres. Less crucial, but still important. The map doesn't house the actual pillar spheres, of course. It's just a map, so when we gateway, we dive into the real spheres." She gestures vaguely to the shelves behind us.

I stare at her blankly. "Cool." None of this means anything to me.

She laughs. "You asked me to explain."

"Explain, not throw me headfirst into a wall of jargon."

"Fair enough. This is why I leave the real explanations to Rizak."

Before I can ask, a man appears from behind a row of shelves, a sphere in one hand and a polishing cloth in the other. "Did someone call me?"

Rhyan nods to me. "Rizak, this is Emlyn." A meaningful look passes between them. "Our Dragon."

I wish she'd stop saying that. "You can call me Emmy."

Rizak stuffs the cleaning cloth into the pocket of his trousers and gives me a warm smile. "Hello, Miss Emmy. I'm Rizak, Keeper of Spheres."

The librarian.

Rizak is middle-aged, or at least appears to be. For all I know, he's immortal. He's got a wiry build and a pleasant face—friendly eyes and that warm smile. If I liked people at all, I think I'd like him.

"The missing Dragon, here at last." Rizak shakes his head as if in wonder, awed by my presence.

I want to sink into the floor.

"I . . . I'm not a Dragon. But I brought a wyvern."

Rhyan snorts.

Rizak looks briefly puzzled, then brushes it aside. "Well, I suppose you'll want a tour?" His friendly eyes fill with hope, and I almost admit I do like him.

"That would be wonderful," Rhyan answers for me. "The basics, if you don't mind."

"Sure." He lifts the sphere he's still holding. "Let me just put this one back where it belongs."

I peer at the orb and take a step closer, in spite of myself. "There are strands floating inside." As I watch, the strands weave themselves together and pop into the shape of a tiny stone turret wrapped with red roses, continually blooming and closing and blooming.

"Ah, this one again." Rhyan leans closer to the sphere, squinting down at it. "What is it this time?"

"Love Triangle gone south. As usual." Rizak sighs and holds the stone turret orb up to the light. "Someday he'll learn, I suppose, that he can't rewrite it, no matter how he wishes to. But Novem III will have to set him straight this time, I'm afraid."

I glance at the shelves of spheres as Rizak disappears among them to replace the turret sphere. Spheres instead of books.

And Novems are special ops teams assigned to missions . . .

"You fix stories," I say to Rhyan, the truth suddenly very obvious. Plain. Like I should have realized ages ago. "The spheres are stories. They break, then you fix them. Somehow."

"Very good, Miss Emmy," Rizak says, reappearing on cue. I wonder if he always does that. "Definitely a Dragon, no matter what she looks like."

I'm not sure how offended I should be.

Rhyan catches my gaze. "You don't look like most Dragons," she explains.

I still can't decide if I'm offended.

Rizak gestures to the sphere map. "This is Rivenlea," he says, pointing to a large golden sphere anchoring the center of the glowing cluster of orbs. "These are the pillar spheres." He indicates the many smaller silvery orbs circling the golden one, each connected by a thread like spider silk to the Rivenlea Sphere.

"Pillar spheres?"

A smile warms Rizak's kind face. "The stories that shape culture. The stories that echo through centuries, told and retold from generation to generation. Stories with themes that speak to the human experience."

"Classics," I say.

"Pillars," Rhyan corrects.

I fight the urge to roll my eyes. "Okay. Pillars." I examine the map. There are several hundred pillars represented there, but Ambryfell contains thousands and thousands of spheres. Maybe millions, depending on how large this fortress is. "What about the spheres not on the map?"

"Ah!" Rizak gestures for us to follow him down one row of shelves. "Few spheres make it onto the map, that's true. But every story has a sphere."

"*Every* story?"

"Every story ever published."

So there are definitely millions of spheres in Ambryfell. I'm halfway down one aisle, and I feel engulfed. Surrounded on all sides, swimming in a sea of spheres. Drowning in them.

"We patrol them constantly," Rizak continues, "but there are so many, oftentimes we don't notice a rogue story for a good long while."

"Leaves a terrible mess for the Novems when a story goes off its rails for too long," Rhyan adds.

I pause in front of a sphere—glowing aqua and full of water. The flash of a scaled fin catches the light, then disappears just as fast. My skin prickles, and my breath catches. "It's beautiful."

"It's beautiful when it's behaving." Rizak plucks another sphere from a nearby shelf and pulls out his polishing cloth once again.

Inside a nearby crystal-clear sphere, a tiny, shabby, stuffed bunny bangs his fisted paws on the glass. His stitched mouth doesn't move, but his fists pound silently, and I can only imagine he's screaming on the inside.

"*The Velveteen Rabbit,*" I say, wanting to back away from the poor creature's distress but finding myself rooted to the spot. Riveted to the scene before me.

Rhyan shrugs, the title clearly meaning little to her, but Rizak beams. "Yes! Very good. Oh, how delightful to have someone else familiar with Earth's stories."

"He's trying to escape." I could swear the little button eyes have grown wider, pleading with me. Begging me to release him from his spherical prison.

"We've assigned Novem XII to that one." Rizak replaces the sphere he's been polishing. "He'll be right as rain soon enough."

"And what will the Novem do, exactly?" I try to push out the mental image of someone shaking the glass orb until the Velveteen Rabbit is too senseless to protest. Or a Flare setting the story on fire.

"They will travel into the sphere and set things right."

Rizak says this matter-of-factly. Like it's normal. Expected. As though it makes any sense whatsoever.

"We fix what's broken," Rhyan explains. "It allows the story to reset, every beat right back where the author intended."

My mouth drops open. I know I'm gaping stupidly.

But I can't help it.

"Stories, Miss Emmy, are what bind us. Stories hold us together and help us think through problems, work through emotions. They take us on adventures, allow us to escape, but even more than that, they help us see the universe more clearly. Through stories, fantastical though they be, we see reality in greater detail."

"Okay." I plunk down on the floor right there, because I need a minute. "Okay."

"They're important," Rizak continues, "because without story, the universe begins to crumble."

"Literally," Rhyan says. "Our work holds not only the spheres, not only Rivenlea, but Earth in its happy stasis."

My gaze jerks up to her. "Happy stasis?"

"Yes. When we keep the stories in order, Earth remains in order."

I frown. "Have you . . . been to Earth?"

"There's no bridge to Earth. No portal between there and Rivenlea." She shoots me a pointed look. "Save one, infrequently used."

I leave that statement alone for now, though approximately four hundred questions bloom in my mind.

I'm still stuck on Earth's "happy stasis."

"Rhyan, Earth is . . . hard." I'm not sure how else to phrase it. "There isn't a 'happy stasis' or perfect order. It's broken."

"Well, nowhere is perfect," she concedes.

"It does take us time to identify the breaks sometimes, as we've said," Rizak adds.

They don't understand what I'm trying to say.

"I'm sure," Rizak muses, "there are snags in the fabric, if you will, when stories start to go rogue. But the Novems always set them right. And Earth becomes restabilized." He smiles, warm and filled with peace. "Earth always gets her happily ever after back."

They believe this—*truly* believe it. Even Rhyan—sharp, no-nonsense Rhyan—believes this is the truth of my world.

Planet.

Sphere.

Whatever.

I don't know how to tell them. How do I explain about war and poverty and violence and all kinds of bigotry? About hatred and death, malice and destruction. How do I explain grief? Or pain?

With every second that passes, I feel surer I must have fallen into a fantasy. No real people—Flare, Dragon, human, or otherwise—could be so naïve. Could they?

But what if they're correct? What if the problems of Earth only exist because there's trouble within the spheres? Maybe the things I see as Earth's brokenness wouldn't have such a foothold if the stories behaved as they were written.

"Emmy?"

I startle. Both Rhyan and Rizak are staring at me. I'm still on the floor.

"Oh." I climb to my feet. Trying to make sense of all the new information being thrown my way.

Light glints off a sphere right at my eye level. A pair of carrot-red braids swirls inside. I glimpse a straw hat.

Emotion I can't identify swells in my chest. Tears prickle my eyes. "It's Anne," I say around the tears I'm too embarrassed to shed. Because I could never explain what that story meant to me as a child—not even if I wanted to, and I certainly don't right now.

Rhyan is blank again, but understanding crosses Rizak's face, and I wonder if he knows every sphere in Ambryfell. Or perhaps just the pillars.

"A perennial favorite," he says.

I hardly hear him, for now I'm moving through the aisles, gazing at spheres everywhere. In one, a boy sails by in a swirl of glittering pixie dust.

Peter Pan.

In another, two girls whisper and giggle in an attic brittle with cold and neglect but warmed by their shared imaginings.

Becky and Sara Crewe—*A Little Princess.*

And there's the pillar that's inspired who knows how many other spheres. A blonde girl slips down the rabbit hole after a white bunny in a waistcoat.

Alice.

I stop and lean against a shelf, careful not to disturb the levitating orbs. Imagine knocking over the sphere containing the actual living, breathing version of *Alice's Adventures in Wonderland.*

"This . . . can't be real," I whisper. I have to stop talking like it's real.

But I feel the woodgrain beneath my fingers. I'm aware of my heart speeding up. My breath failing to fill my lungs. The very real, very familiar panic edging my consciousness, blackening the corners of my thoughts.

Have I ever panicked in a dream? Had an anxiety attack while staring off into space, imagining things?

Maybe. But I've never had a dream quite like this.

"I wrote some of this place," I murmur, my gaze traveling the length and breadth of the aisle. "But certainly not all of it."

"It's real, Emmy." Rhyan's voice is gentler than I've yet heard it. "And you are part of it."

My resolve wavers.

"I can show you," Rhyan offers. "I can show you the Novems in action. And then maybe you'll believe."

"'Alas, Alas, if your mother knew, her loving heart would break in two,'" I say more to myself than Rhyan or Rizak, staring at an orb filled with geese.

"Pardon?"

I ignore Rhyan's question but turn to face her. "Okay. Show me."

WE LEAVE RIZAK TO HIS

sphere polishing and walk out of the library—Rhyan with calm purpose, me in dazed silence.

"One quick stop." Rhyan turns down a hallway. "If I know him, he'll be in the study."

We pass approximately twelve million doors, but Rhyan doesn't enter any of them, and I begin to disagree sharply with her concept of a "quick" stop. She turns another corner, then finally selects one door of many—black-stained wood with an arched top and iron strap hinges that look like they weigh a ton.

"This one," she says, pushing it open.

I follow her inside.

"Canon!" she calls out, and I almost duck.

But she's addressing the man seated at a desk, surrounded by maps and charts and journals. The room is lit by glowing stones set in small alcoves all about the walls.

He looks up, slightly bewildered.

"Captain Doyle," he says to Rhyan as he jumps to his feet.

He looks to be about Rhyan's age. With his short-cropped dark hair, pale skin, and angular features, they could be siblings, but the man's eyes don't dance with flames. Instead, the light of the glowing stones reflects strangely, almost as though there are mirrors behind his dark eyes.

But perhaps it's a trick of the spectacles he's wearing.

Sure. We'll go with that.

He's staring at me with those strange eyes. My voice is lost somewhere inside me because a faint glow appears in each of his fingertips as he comes around the desk to extend his hand to me.

"Canon Egbert," he says. Then with a small shake of his head, as if trying to clear it of smoke, "If you don't remember."

I didn't write this man. He isn't one of my characters. Like Rhyan and Rizak, I don't know him, by face or name.

But even in Rivenlea, I suppose it's expected to shake a person's hand when they offer it.

I take his hand and give it a hearty shake. "Emlyn DuLaine. People call me Emmy."

Canon's eyes widen as he stares down at our clasped hands, then he shoots his gaze to Rhyan. Rhyan covers a laugh with a phony cough, and I know I've done something wrong. But I have no idea what.

Canon extricates his hand from mine. "Rhyan has not schooled you in Rivenlite protocol, I see."

My face is an inferno.

Rhyan just shrugs. "There wasn't time for all that nonsense."

He visibly bristles at the word "nonsense." But then he carefully places a pleasant smile on his face and addresses me. "Gentlemen bow to ladies upon first meeting."

I mentally note that Rizak did not bother with this formality, but I see no reason to annoy the guy with the weird mirror eyes and glowing fingers.

He extends his hand again, and I take it—tentatively. Maybe his fingers are electrified.

Unlike my hearty handshake, Canon's touch is delicate, as though I'm made of whipped meringue. Then he dips a courtly bow over my hand.

"A pleasure, Miss DuLaine," he says.

I stand there like a dolt until Rhyan nudges me. "Oh. A pleasure, Mr. . . . Canon."

"Egbert," Rhyan whispers.

"Old Germanic name," I say before I can stop myself from spewing this useless tidbit.

"Oh," Canon says as he rises. "Old Germanic? Do you mean German, like the Brothers Grimm?"

"Yes," I say. "Sort of. I mean, yes. Like the Brothers Grimm. Those . . . pillar-sphere-makers. I guess," I add lamely.

Canon raises an eyebrow at Rhyan.

She shrugs again. "She's been on Earth a long time, Canon. Give her a break."

"Well." The mild smile reappears. "Welcome back to Castramore. When a gentleman takes your hand, it is polite to incline your head to him as you introduce yourself or in greeting one another."

"But if he's bowing, he won't see that, so what difference does it make?"

Rhyan snorts, but I sort of wish I hadn't said it. Wasn't I going to try not to annoy this man?

"Those are cool," I blurt, pointing to the stones set in the alcoves on the wall, groping for anything to change the subject.

Canon glances at the alcoves. "Glowstones. Mined from the caves in south Rivenlea. Inexhaustible sources of light. Terribly useful."

"And green."

He frowns, then glances again at the stones, which look like regular rocks hewn into pointed cylinders, pulsing softly with warm white light. "They are not green."

"No, I meant environ—never mind."

"I've promised to show Emmy the Novems," Rhyan says, cutting through the awkwardness.

"Ah, very good," Canon replies. "Shall I escort you ladies to the yard?"

Rhyan accepts for us both.

Canon leads us back through the maze of deserted hallways. We reach the main foyer, and I'm about to head toward the front doors, but Canon instead turns us down another hallway.

We make our way toward the back of this fortress and out another large double door, and if I was expecting a lawn or garden or anything else one might describe as a "yard," I was quite mistaken.

Instead, the yard is more like a coliseum of stone steps ringing endless ranges, pitches, and training blocks. Racks of weapons and shields dot the fields.

And the whole place is filled with people. Buzzing like bees in a hive.

Or possibly hornets in a nest. Who can tell?

Archers loose arrows toward targets. Swordsmen and swordswomen spar, and one woman in particular catches my eye. She evades a strike from her competitor by flipping off a stack of hay bales and catching her opponent in the back a split second before he can react.

I'm about to ask what the long, shallow trough full of water is for, but before I can open my mouth, a Flare with a silver buzz cut fires up his hand. He thrusts it into the trough, and the liquid ignites.

Okay. Not water.

I gape for a moment, but he's not finished. He withdraws his hand and throws an arc of fire at the woman standing across the pitch from him. She catches the flame in her hands, then chucks it at a target—a small pile of hay and sticks surrounded by stones. She hits her mark, and the kindling sparks.

"Flares," Rhyan announces unnecessarily. "Working on their accuracy."

"For what?" I squeak.

"Missions."

The only thing I can think of is the Velveteen Rabbit trapped in a bonfire.

I nearly grab Rhyan's arm but restrain myself. "You don't hurt the characters, do you?"

Rhyan gives me a look, but she doesn't answer right away.

Alarm sparks. "Do you? I need an answer on this."

"And if I refuse to answer, you'll do what exactly?"

"I'll write you out of this story," I respond without thinking.

If this really is my story, somehow growing a life of its own, I may have just threatened to murder a character.

She considers it a moment, something dancing in her eyes—amusement or fire. "Fair enough," she says finally, gesturing to the dozens of sparring partners filling the yard. "We don't hurt the characters, exactly. Not long-term, at least, and we do favor nonlethal methods whenever possible. Everything we do is in service of putting the story right. Getting everything back to the beginning."

Once upon a time. But it doesn't sit right in my gut.

I let it go for now. "Okay. So what is all this?"

"This is the yard, where Novems train."

The two Flares have lit several more of their stone-ringed targets. "So those two are from a Novem of Flares?"

"No. There is one Flare per Novem."

"Each member of the Novem serves a different purpose," Canon puts in. "Each has their own gift, and each brings the benefit of that gift to their team."

I watch two young men beat the tar out of what appears to be the Rivenlite version of a punching dummy—a linen bag stuffed with something. "And what's their gift? Brute strength?"

Canon frowns at me, and I sense I've been offensive.

"Sorry," I say hastily. "Just a joke."

"One of them is a Muse. The other is a Bolt. Most Novem members are trained in various combat techniques in addition to honing their specific gifts."

"Where do I opt out?" Is it like PE at school? Do I need a note?

Rhyan looks vaguely amused but chooses not to argue with me.

Canon, on the other hand, is regarding me like I've said something scandalous. "Everyone has to train."

"I haven't decided whether I'm staying."

His eyebrows rise higher, and I realize they are a direct

indicator of his level of inner hysteria. "Not staying?" he says, as though I've just told him I plan to eat a newborn puppy for dinner. "You must."

"Must I?" I turn to Rhyan. "I have no choice?"

"There's always a choice." She folds her arms across her chest, studying me.

Canon's eyebrows tick up. Between the two of us, Rhyan and I might be able to make those eyebrows simply fall off his forehead at some point. "There isn't a choice. Emlyn is our Dragon. Novem XVII simply cannot be without our Dragon." His head turns to Rhyan. "Do you doubt Emlyn is our ninth?"

"Not at all." Her gaze slides to me. "But *she* does."

I mirror her stance. Challenging her—or faking it as best I can without my knees collapsing. "I don't know exactly what's happening here, but I do know I made up some of the things I'm seeing. Actually made them up, from my head, when I was little. I don't know how, but the most reasonable explanation is I've had a psychotic break. Second most reasonable explanation"—I pause, knowing how stupid it'll sound—"is I've fallen into my own story, but my story has grown a life of its own."

Rhyan watches some of the sparring Novems. "Can I offer an alternative suggestion?"

No.

"Sure."

"What if you didn't create those stories when you were little? What if you were remembering them?"

At her words, every nerve in my body wakes. A rolling wave, a body-wide chill.

"You're suggesting I've been here before." I can't decide whether or not that's a question. I know it's what she's saying, but I can't wrap my mind around it.

She doesn't answer directly. "How about we make a deal?"

"Terms?"

Her fiery eyes meet mine. "We teach you what the Novems are all about. Let you meet the rest of the team. You've seen Ambryfell yourself. Sleep on it and see how this all looks in the morning. Spend a day here. Then you can decide whether or not you'll stay."

Canon's eyebrows are about to take flight. He opens his mouth to object.

But Rhyan holds up a hand. "Stand down, Novemite Egbert."

His mouth immediately shuts, and I remember Rhyan is his superior. At least I think she is. My knowledge of Novem chain of command is squidgy, but he did call her Captain Doyle.

Protest works its way up my throat and fights to control my voice. I want to tell Rhyan I will absolutely not entertain any more nonsense. To please take me back to whatever portal will return me to my regular life so I can check myself into some sort of facility and face my mother's wrath, because somehow even that feels preferable.

But just as I am about to give voice to my most strenuous objections, I catch sight of a woman with long green braids and pale seafoam-colored skin. As if the sight of her weren't strange enough, the next moment, she's punching her right arm into the earth, the delicate limb disappearing up to the elbow.

Surely she's injured herself—broken her wrist, at least. But she doesn't seem distressed. In fact, her eyes are closed, as if in prayer. Her lips move, and I can't tell if she's speaking softly or singing.

Either way, at her command vines begin to sprout from the ground. Runners climb up a waiting trellis. I hadn't noticed the trellis before, but there are several others lined up—and a few other greenish-skinned people standing nearby.

The vines snake up the trellis, completely blanketing it. Before I can take a breath, the vines flower. Blue buds like starbursts explode everywhere, and the green-skinned people gasp and clap and cheer.

"Morning glories," I say numbly.

"What?"

"Nothing." I face Rhyan. "You have one day. Teach me about the Novems."

CANON EGBERT BOWS POLITELY

to every person we pass as we stroll between the training fields. Rhyan's hooded might-mug-you-in-a-dark-forest ensemble appears to be training attire, as the other Flares are dressed similarly. Canon is wearing something more casual—deep forest-green trousers, a cream-colored shirt, and tall brown boots.

The jeans and T-shirts of Rivenlea, maybe? My actual jeans and T-shirt feel incredibly conspicuous.

He stops before a corner of the training field that has a series of circular mirrors of varying sizes and heights angled toward each other, and lifts a hand in greeting. "Good afternoon, fellow Bolts."

About a dozen people turn to us, curiosity evident in their vaguely mirrored eyes. They're all wearing fitted brown leather jackets, but my focus is snagged on their gloves. The fingers are missing tips.

And all the Bolts' exposed fingertips are glowing bright white.

"Canon." An older Bolt woman bows her head. "A new friend?"

"Our ninth." Pride laces his voice and his smile, and I'm equal parts touched and annoyed. I honestly can't remember the last time someone was proud of me, but it also seems like Canon is certain I'm staying. And that's obnoxious.

"Emmy," I say quietly. "Emmy DuLaine."

"Canon thought Emmy might like to see what Bolts do." Rhyan gestures toward the series of mirrors.

The Bolt lady steps back. "Be our guest." She and the others move well away from the mirrors.

Canon claims the center of the ring, flexing his fingers, but I honestly can't imagine Canon's supernatural power being very exciting. Maybe he's going to give a riveting recitation from a dusty history tome. Or show me a super fancy spreadsheet.

Before I have a chance to dream up the nerdiest gift possible—magnification eyesight to examine specimens without a microscope?—Canon spins, drops to one knee, thrusts his hand outward, directing his gaze toward the largest mirror. White-hot beams of light shoot from the fingertips of his right hand and from his eyes, gathering into one single beam that slices into the largest mirror, then reflects off them each in turn, bouncing all around the circle, hitting every mirror before the beam strikes a short stone wall off to one side. The stones are covered in tiny black dots, the ghosts of previous beams.

I hadn't noticed it there before, but I see now that Canon has directed this beam through a thin cord stretched vertically in a weighted stand in front of the stone wall.

Surely he had a one in a million chance of slicing through such a tiny target. I can't stop my mouth from falling open, and somewhere in a corner of my mind, I repent of thinking Canon was the stodgiest person in Rivenlea.

I mean, that may be true, but the guy can shoot lasers out of his hands and face. That has to count for something.

Rhyan grins at me. "Bolts. Terribly handy for . . . slicing things. Repelling baddies."

"Breaking into safes," I say, then immediately regret it. "I'm not actually a bank robber," I clarify.

Rhyan merely shrugs. "Or breaking into safes. If the mission demands it." She nods to a cluster of green-skinned people.

"Harmonies. Useful for healing the land, terraforming barren planets, listening to the earth. Bringing dead things back to life."

I watch as one Harmony makes a patch of hot-pink flowers sprout from the earth to supportive applause and celebratory hugs from the other Harmonies nearby.

"A sentimental bunch," she remarks.

"Oh, then I'm probably a Harmony."

Rhyan snorts—maybe she's already used to my humor—and beckons me to continue on with my tour as Canon helps his fellow Bolts reset their practice field.

One section of the yard is set up with extremely large nets stretched between huge poles, as though some giants might use the area to play volleyball.

But there are no giants in sight. Only a group of men and women wearing bronze breastplates and greaves, leather trousers or skirts, and gleaming gilt helmets. Whips and golden ropes dangle from their belts.

As if they don't look enough like Greek gods and goddesses, one of the young women squats as though winding up her muscles, then springs into the air. She soars preternaturally high, and at the crest of her jump, a pair of feathery wings unfolds, and she glides toward a target on the far side of the field.

I stumble back a step and instinctively yelp.

Rhyan laughs. "Gryphons," she says, her attention on the flying woman and her comrades. "Useful for aerial missions. Scaling unclimbable walls. Rescuing trapped characters."

My eyes are glued to the flying woman vaulting through the air. The Gryphon turns a flip, then catches a draft being directed her way . . . from the hands of a girl dressed in a gauzy aquamarine gown. Her sleeves flutter in the breeze of her own creation as she works, first in concert with the soaring Gryphon, then against her, shifting her focus to trying to ground the winged creature.

I let out a cry of dismay when a strong gust knocks the Gryphon off course, causing her to tumble into an outstretched net, but Rhyan merely nods to the girl in the blue dress. "Zephyrs. Wind warriors—useful for controlling the weather. Battling through unruly seas. Creating wildfires. And also helping Gryphons in their training."

The Gryphon is being rescued from the net by a male Zephyr and two other Gryphons, and I realize the offending gust was a training exercise, not an attack.

Still seems dangerous.

I wonder if people can die in Rivenlea. I still can't decide whether or not this world is real, and I wonder if these Novemites can get injured by the very real-looking swords they're using. Or tumble from the sky and break their arms. Or set their hair on fire.

I side-eye a couple Flares shooting streams of flame toward each other.

"You know about Flares," Rhyan says, following my gaze. "We tend to captain the Novems, though not always. Fire is our weapon of choice. We can ignite as an offensive or defensive maneuver. Rather useful in a variety of circumstances. Very destructive when we team up with a Zephyr."

She draws my attention to another group, and I can't for the life of me figure out how what they're doing qualifies as training. They lounge around a fire pit, one strumming a guitar, some of the others singing a song, some others talking and laughing over the music.

"Muses," says Rhyan.

"What's their superpower—hanging out?"

"Looks that way, doesn't it? But don't underestimate them. They're the keepers of story magic."

My eyes widen. "Keepers of story magic?"

"That's right. You'd be surprised how often it's the magic system that goes awry. Too much handwavium in most stories. Far too much."

I stare at her.

She sees my confusion and smiles. "You saw the heart

of Ambryfell. You saw the spheres. I'm trying to show you what's true." She motions to the group of loungers. "They are our resident tricksters. Wicked clever pilferers, sneakthieves, pickpockets. Handy with tools. Great at rebuilding broken magic systems."

A group a bit farther afield appears to be sparring with normal swords, engaging in normal combat. I watch them closely, waiting for something to—

The swordsman I'm watching suddenly morphs into a tree. The boy he's fighting slams into the trunk. He staggers backward, the air obviously knocked from his lungs.

Treeman morphs back into a human and strikes out at his winded opponent. Who turns into a shield at the last second before the sword strikes him. Treeman spins, attacks again. Shieldboy shifts again—this time into a giant molded jelly.

Treeman's sword slices straight through him, and I gasp.

But those near Treeman and Shieldboy have burst into peals of laughter. Treeman extricates his sword from the jelly, shaking his head. Shieldboy—or Jellyguy in this moment—shifts back into a human, a giant grin on his face. He appears unharmed.

Rhyan rolls her eyes, but she's smiling. "Echoes. Able to shift into the form of anything they've ever seen. I probably don't need to explain how useful they are."

No, indeed.

If I could choose anything, what would I shift into?

A plate of cookies. No, a mug of hot coffee. A giant sub sandwich, three kinds of cheese, extra tomatoes and onions. No, a bowl of mashed potatoes, big pat of butter and fresh-cracked black pepper.

I might just be hungry.

"Sentinels," Rhyan says, startling me. She has mistaken my distant gaze for focus on yet another group of Novemites. "Training with our Dragons."

My heart stops. Hiccups. Restarts again, punching a breath up my throat.

Dragons. What everyone keeps insisting I am.

The Sentinels are fairly easy to spot. There's a row of them turned to stone.

"Impenetrable," Rhyan observes. "They're our guardians. Our protectors. And our gateways onto the mission field."

Not sure what that means, but I catalog it away for later. "And the Dragons?"

"Come closer. Tell me what you see."

I sidle up beside her and focus on the Dragons. They're sparring with each other but not throwing punches. Their movements are small, precise, and effect—

"Ah!" a Dragon cries out, her opponent having leveraged her shoulder joint just so.

"It's a game of angles," I say to Rhyan. "Leverage. Putting pressure on the joints in just the right way so as to require relatively little force."

"And cause maximum pain," Rhyan adds.

Yes, there is that.

"Oh." Realization hits me in the face. "They're . . ."

Rhyan waits for me to finish, but when I don't, she supplies, "Scaled."

Glittering reptilian skin catches the setting sunlight. It's subtle. You might not notice it if they were standing in the shade, but as the sun hits them full on, you can't miss it. Dragons in shades of iridescent blue and purple, green and red.

But even from a distance, it's impossible to miss their eyes. Empty black or white voids stand in place of irises, pupils, and anything else . . . human.

"Salem," Rhyan calls, and to my horror, a gorgeous shimmering blue creature turns to us, her white orbs locking on me.

I feel her gaze crawl inside my mind.

The Dragon called Salem strides toward us, gliding as though her thigh-high, spike-heeled boots are as comfortable as sneakers. Her mane of pale silver hair is woven into a complex braid that reaches past her hips.

Her gaze is still locked on me.

I feel the plainness of my T-shirt and jeans next to her black leathers. The ordinariness of my shoes next to her Wonder Woman boots. The mundaneness of my brown curls beside her silver locks. The everydayness of my human skin compared to her glittery scales.

The complete and utter humanness of Earthling Emlyn beside the otherworldly Rivenlite Salem.

And she sees it too.

I feel her disapproval. Her disdain. Her puzzlement. She looks through me, all the way to my backbone, which is feeling less solid by the millisecond.

After an excruciating moment, she turns to Rhyan. "Captain Doyle?"

"This is Emlyn DuLaine, Novem XVII's Dragon."

I reach out my hand, then note that Salem has a humanlike hand, except for the black claws at the end of each of her fingers. She takes my hand, and I catch her cue just in time. We bow our heads to each other.

"People call me Emmy," I say, "but my mother calls me Disappointment."

Her lips quirk, but those cold eyes tell me nothing as she drops my hand. I'm not sure if she's smiling or sneering. "I can imagine."

Sneering.

Rhyan slices through the tension with her assertive, matter-of-fact, impossible-to-deter voice. "Emmy will be training with you and the other Dragons at some point."

"Will she?" Salem's pale silver brow rises. "We'll see." Then she turns and leaves.

After a moment of silence, I say, "That went well. Made a great impression, I did."

Rhyan waves a hand. "Dragons are prickly."

"Excuse me!"

"Ah, you admit you're a Dragon?"

I glare, and she laughs. "I was just speaking up for my good friend Salem," I say flatly. "We're besties."

"Right."

I glance at the group of Dragons, who are now listening to Salem and openly staring at me. "But seriously, Rhyan. You can't honestly believe I'm one of them."

"Why's that?"

I stare down at myself. I can't believe she's making me spell this out. "Look at me."

She shakes her head. "The fact that you dissected their method of grappling before even noticing they have literal scales on their faces tells me all I need to know. You're a Dragon."

I sigh. "Does anyone ever win arguments with you?"

"No." She looks to the group of Dragons, who are *still* staring at me. "Dragons possess double sight. They are our mission strategists."

"Double sight?"

"They see what is, to the rest of us, unseen. Moods, feelings, truth."

No wonder it felt like Salem was crawling through my mind. She kind of was. I shudder.

"It sounds unsettling," Rhyan admits, "but double sight is incredibly useful on missions. They are able to see broken story structure—and, more importantly, how to fix it."

Observing things others miss. Fixing broken stuff. Intuiting things.

It all tracks with my personality, I guess. But Rhyan seems to be avoiding the obvious. "You have noticed I'm human, right? You do realize I am a single, solitary human surrounded by superheroes?"

"We don't use the term 'superhero.'"

"Does that make it less true? You have the ability to set your hands on fire. There are flames in your eyeballs. Canon shoots lasers out of his face. I watched an Echo turn himself into jelly. Literal, actual jelly. You can't possibly stand there and tell me I belong here. Not with a straight face, anyway."

"You belong here," Rhyan deadpans, unblinking.

"Ha."

"I can prove it," she says more seriously.

My curiosity is piqued, in spite of myself. Can she? Can she actually prove it in a way that will satisfy me?

Somehow I doubt it, but I'm interested in letting her try.

She gestures back toward Ambryfell. "Come. I'll show you."

I try not to make eye contact with anyone as we pass the Novemites, many more of whom have noticed our presence. Rhyan inclines her head occasionally—super casual, as though nothing is wrong.

But of course something is wrong.

I'm wrong.

We're nearly to the doors, nearly safe from curious eyes, but before we can reach shelter, a form shimmers before me. Nothingness winks into somethingness, and my heart tries to flee my chest.

A squeal escapes my lips as I grind to a halt. But not fast enough to avoid crashing into the figure before me. It takes me one second to realize the figure is a solidly built boy.

I've fallen into him in such a way that I'm awkwardly, mortifyingly grabbing his arms to steady myself.

I send approximately thirty thousand signals to my brain to move somewhere—*anywhere*—but my treacherous body betrays me, and I stay there considering sinking into the ground, considering punching the boy who somehow materialized before me and practically forced me to grab his arms to steady myself.

Which . . . I am still doing.

My brain and body finally connect, and I jump back as if burned, and for all I know, this wall of a boy is a Flare and he *has* burned me, and who invited him into my personal space, anyway?

But of course he's not a Flare. He's an Echo.

"Please, forgive me," he says. "I didn't mean to startle you."

I try to speak, but a sound like a gopher getting sucked into a lawnmower comes out instead. Because I recognize his voice.

And it's not a distant memory of some random character I dropped into a scene ten years ago to fill out my fictional cast. It's not Denica or Jason or Andi or the other dozens of people I've created over the years.

It's my story boy. Camille's story boy.

Laramie Shayle, the boy I just wrote to fulfill my presumed-dead sister's request for a little swoon, is standing before me in the very attractive flesh.

11

LARAMIE'S CHOCOLATE-PUDDING

eyes lock on me, and his mouth curves into a smile. Warm, kind—enticing.

I fling that thought into the dirt. Stomp on it, kick it, pound it into dust. The audacity of my very own story boy appearing in the middle of my day, the middle of my mental breakdown, is not to be tolerated. I do not have time for this complication.

"How dare you," I say aloud, not fully intending to.

"Huh?" He looks genuinely confused, and who can blame him? I'm losing it.

"You . . . I . . ." What do I say? "I wrote you."

Heavens, Emmy, not that. Whatever you say, don't say *that*.

His brows rise. "You wrote me?"

"You're . . ." Stop speaking, Emmy. "You're my story boy."

Oops.

A playful grin teases the corners of his lips. "Oh yeah? How does the story end?"

Rhyan clears her throat loudly, conspicuously, and I'm not sure if she's annoyed with me or him. Probably both. "We were just on our way to the Taenarum," she tells him.

"Shall I join you?" Laramie asks.

Yes, I think. "No," I say. "Absolutely not."

Somehow this makes his impish smile grow, and I feel

perfectly ready to disintegrate as he looks to Rhyan. "Captain Doyle?" he asks.

He'll take his leave now, surely, whatever Rhyan says. Because for all that I cannot believe he has the nerve to appear like this, as though he were a real person, his manners perfectly adequate.

He's a *polite* abomination.

And then, I reason, once we get away and he goes about his business, I will probably never have to see Laramie Shayle again. There are at least two dozen Novems training here at this moment, and who knows how many more living and working in Castramore. Laramie can blend into the background of this twisted tale and never darken my proverbial doorstep again.

"Yes, come with us," Rhyan says to my utter horror. "And perhaps a proper introduction first."

Or perhaps I could die first.

"Laramie Shayle," she continues, "this is Emmy DuLaine, Rivenlea's long-lost Dragon."

I bristle and consider contradicting her. But what does it matter? After this awkward exchange to punctuate a humiliating introduction—and after we go to the Taenarum, whatever that is—I never have to see Laramie again. Who cares if he thinks I'm a Dragon?

Laramie takes my hand and bows. Presses his lips gently to the tops of my knuckles, meeting my gaze for half a heartbeat.

Melting my knees into puddles and dousing me from head to toe in a bucket of emotions I can't sift.

I glare at the literary cliché standing before me and mostly hope I never lay eyes on him again.

Because everyone hates Insta-Love. I am certainly included in "everyone," and if I could get my flip-flopping stomach and galloping heart to understand the fact, that'd be great.

"Emmy, Laramie is our Novem's Echo."

I still, my breath caught. "But . . ." What objection can I possibly give? "That's . . ."

Laramie smiles. "Yes?"

I glare at him. "That's fine," I finish lamely.

"Glad you approve." Rhyan's eyes glint with equal parts bemusement and amusement.

"They don't mean the same thing," I say aloud.

"Pardon?" Laramie says.

"Bemusement and amusement," I say. "People think they do."

A smile flickers on Rhyan's face, and I see that she connects the dots of my thoughts—what she was projecting, what I observed, where my mind wandered, to the definitions of those two words, and how I spoke my thoughts aloud as though anyone else could see what's happening in my mind in the interim.

Unexpectedly, warmth flashes inside me at being understood. For the first time since Camille disappeared.

But then, before she voices it, I see what she's about to say: "Dragon."

"Human," I point out.

"Double sight," Rhyan insists.

"Reading people's facial expressions is not a superpower." I glance at Laramie, and when he catches my gaze, I swear he has entire constellations in his eyes for all they twinkle.

My internal organs promptly liquefy.

"To the Taenarum?" he asks.

"Please," Rhyan says, allowing him to hold the door open for us.

I stride past him, attempting to pick up the shreds of my dignity and refusing to inhale the woodsy scent of his cologne.

Aftershave?

I slide a furtive glance his way, and he catches me looking at him.

Because of course he does. His Cheshire Cat grin stretches impossibly wide, mischief and nonsense dancing in his hot cocoa eyes.

"Emlyn?" Rhyan's voice cuts into my mortification, and she grabs my elbow and steers me down a hallway. "This way."

Laramie's presence presses against my consciousness. He keeps a respectful distance, but I can feel his gaze on the back of my head. I hear his thoughts racing, wondering at this strange new addition to Rivenlea. I sense the weight of his very existence in the same hallway, sharing the same space as me.

How dare he . . . exist.

No, my own brain corrects me. *How dare he make me feel out of control of my emotions.*

"Emmy." Rhyan snaps me out of it again.

I realize she's stopped in front of a small open doorway, and I've somehow barreled past without noticing. My face roasts as I retrace a few steps to Rhyan and . . . Laramie.

Why did I name him that? Camille was right. What a ridiculous name.

I dare a glance straight into his eyes, refuse to flinch or blink or blush. "It's a city in Wyoming."

He nods, as though he has any idea what Wyoming is. "Emmy, Wyoming. I like the sound of that city. Perhaps one day I'll visit."

"I—no." If only I had a net to capture the butterflies flitting through my brain. "No. That's not right."

"I can't visit?" His face falls in feigned disappointment. "Shame." His grin returns, a thousand-watt smile that could probably replace a glowstone, should the need ever arise.

The butterflies take flight, along with my common sense, and I briefly wonder if the need will ever arise.

I force myself to break eye contact before Rhyan's sharp call beckons me. Again.

We're in a small alcove, scarcely big enough for three, and Rhyan's warmth makes the space uncomfortable. I inch away, only to find my shoulder brushing Laramie's.

A bolt of electricity darts through me, and I would wonder if he's a Bolt. Except I know he's not.

And it's not that kind of electricity.

I drop-kick the Insta-Love out of my brain and my heart, into the darkness. I force myself to be attentive to Rhyan's words.

"The Taenarum," she says, "is down here. Watch your step."

She descends a tight spiral staircase and is out of sight in a heartbeat.

Laramie offers his hand—and another atomic smile.

My gaze is glued to his outstretched fingers. Every cell in my body screams at me—what they're saying, I couldn't tell you. "No, thank you." I turn and follow after Rhyan quickly so I don't have to see how my refusal lands on him.

Is he disappointed? Indifferent?

Which is worse?

I don't allow myself to wonder, instead trailing Rhyan down the staircase—down, down, down, until I'm sure we'll reach the core of the Earth soon.

Or the core of Rivenlea.

The core of Rivenlea is probably made of glitter and stardust, or maybe meringue and rainbows.

Rhyan pauses at the bottom of the stairs before I am aware of it. I untangle myself from her cloak and realize we're in a basement of some sort.

Except it's more like a cave, carved directly into the stone that must serve as the foundation of Ambryfell.

The walls glow, casting stained glass reflections all over the floor, the ceiling. And Rhyan's arms as she stretches them wide.

"The Taenarum," she says.

"The place where you're going to prove things to me," I murmur, taking in the source of the colored lights.

Jewels. The walls are filled with tiny hollows, and set within the hollows are jewels that radiate like glowstones but have the clear, polished look of cut gems.

"Watch your step, Em," Laramie says, reaching out his hand. He glances at my beat-up shoes. "I'm not sure those boots are safe here. It's slippery."

Indignation rises in me. That he's given me a nickname. That he called my sneakers "boots." That he's worried I might slip.

That I've turned into the universe's most irrational creature in his presence.

I'm so annoyed, I grab his hand and let him help me.

That'll show him.

But he's not wrong. The stone floor is slippery, and the tread on my shoes is worn. More than once, I'm grateful for his strong grip.

"Do you see?" Rhyan watches me looking at the stones as we move through the chamber.

"They're in clusters of nine," I say.

"Novems."

"Em, look closer."

I bristle again at the nickname, yet I don't hate the way it sounds on his lilting Rivenlite accent.

I lean toward the glowing jewels and see what he's pointing out. Words. There's a word etched in every stone set in a hollow.

Including the only one in the Taenarum not glowing. The one we've stopped in front of.

My gut knows the truth before my brain processes it. These aren't simply words etched in the stones. They're *names.*

And the only unlit stone has the name *Emlyn* carved into it, clear as the payment terms on my therapy bills.

I stare at it and try to erase it with my mind. I fail entirely.

"It could be another Emlyn," I say weakly, taking in the other names around the circle, recognizing only Rhyan, Canon, and Laramie.

Rhyan's stone glows red. Canon's is clear like glass. Laramie's casts a forest-green hue across his cheek.

"Sure," Rhyan says, a smile tugging one corner of her mouth. "And you landing in Rivenlea is mere coincidence?"

"Maybe Frank got the wrong Emlyn." I stare hard at the Emlyn gem. "Gemlyn," I mutter.

"I thought you wrote Frank," Rhyan points out. "How does that work?"

"I haven't plugged the plot holes yet, okay?" I turn to her. "This is your proof? A stone with my name carved in it? You could have had it carved an hour ago, for all I know."

"Touch it," she says, her smile taking on slight smugness.

Knowing I won't like what's about to happen, I go ahead and touch the gem.

The moment I do, the stone lights up. Opalescent purple. Unlike the others—pearly, filled with storms of different colored lights reflecting off the opaque surface. Not a crystalline jewel like everyone else's. The one oddball.

Figures.

But Rhyan seems unbothered by the difference. Her face is aglow, her smile now devoid of any smugness. "This is why I'm sure, Emmy. This is why I have no doubt."

She runs her hand along the circle of nine, now complete and glowing, even with its one odd purple stone.

Our Novem. *Her* Novem.

Her voice drops, speaking more to herself than to me or Laramie. "We've been waiting for a year and a half. And you're here at last."

12

GIVING LARAMIE SHAYLE

license to worry about the security of my footing was a mistake. I can scarcely breathe or move or take two steps without him ensuring my path is safe.

"A year and a half means I was expected when I was sixteen," I say to Rhyan, briefly acknowledging Laramie as he holds a door open for me.

"All Novemites report to Ambryfell on their sixteenth birthdays." She quirks a smile my way. "Except you."

"But how did anyone know I was turning sixteen in the first place?"

"Your stone appeared in the Taenarum nursery on the day you were born, of course."

"But that's impossible. I was born on Earth. Why would a stone appear here in Rivenlea?"

Rhyan stops walking as we enter the foyer of Ambryfell and turns to me, jaw firm. "Because that's how it works. Future Novemites' stones appear in the nursery on their birthdays. Sixteen years later, they report, and the stones are set in the active cavern of the Taenarum."

"Except mine."

"No, it was set," she says and heads for the front door. "But you never showed up."

We cross the threshold of Ambryfell, stepping out into the setting Castramorian sun.

The moment we do, a blue-black blur slams into me, knocking me backward. I lie there a moment, stunned.

Then a familiar, if somewhat unwelcome, face pops into my view.

"Frank," I huff.

The wyvern snorts a puff of smoke over me but then nuzzles her scaly snout into my outstretched palm, and I can hardly stay angry.

A sharp whistle diverts Frank's attention, and she abandons our snuggly reunion.

Laramie—the source of the whistle—is using some sort of sign language Frank seems to understand. Laramie lowers his hands, and she sits back on her haunches. He sweeps his right hand in a downward motion, and Frank responds by sprawling on her side.

He strokes her scaled belly. "You've trained her well, Em."

"I didn't train her," I grumble. "She . . . came that way."

"Well, then I guess all the praise is hers." Frank rolls over onto her back and stretches her forelegs toward her head so Laramie can scratch her armpits. "What a smart girl she is," he coos.

"Stop it." I brush off my jeans and straighten. "She doesn't like you."

Frank begins to purr. Loudly.

Laramie grins. "Is that so?" He pats Frank's lizard cheek, and the traitor soaks up every drop of his attention. "She doesn't seem to mind."

Frank's purr sounds like a lawnmower.

"Emmy, you're bleeding." Rhyan is examining my scraped arm. The bandage from my wyvern bite has come off, and truly I'm a mess.

Was it just a few hours ago Frank showed up in my bedroom and took a bite from my arm?

I watch the story boy of my imagination become my pet wyvern's favorite person in all universes.

Curiouser and curiouser.

"We should get you home," Rhyan says.

I startle. "Home? The day isn't up yet. We said twenty-four hours, right? There's got to be at least twenty-one left."

"Not that home. Your home in Rivenlea."

Relief is followed immediately by heat in my cheeks. Because I have not decided to stay. That's not what I meant. It was just too soon, and—

My inner protests are cut short by Laramie signaling Frank to stand, and I can't help but be impressed by how good he is with her. How easily she minds him.

"I could train you," he says, catching my lingering gaze.

"To roll over? I'm good, thanks."

He snorts. "To command your wyvern."

"That's not the kind of relationship Frank and I have. We have mutual respect. No commands necessary."

Frank responds by headbutting me in the chest hard enough to induce a cough.

"I see." Laramie doesn't press the issue. "Shall I take her to the hive?" He flashes a grin. "Frank, not you, Em."

"Yes," Rhyan says, "you get the wyvern settled, and I'll see Emlyn to her cabin."

Cabin? That could either be delightfully cozy or the setting of a slasher flick. Not much in between with a cabin.

But before I have a chance to ask, Laramie Shayle is scooping my hand into his, sweeping my fingers to his lips in a gentlemanly kiss. A kiss that shines a spotlight on my awkwardness—the fact that I'm plainly human, wearing basic Earthly clothes, an absolute fish out of water in this strange world with manners I don't understand. Manners I'm not sure I want to understand, and a boy I'm not sure I want to know.

A story boy I absolutely made up in my pocket-size journal.

"Miss DuLaine, it was the most acute pleasure to meet you."

I try to look away from him, but I'm held in two pools of hot-cocoa flirtation and chocolate-pudding mischief and disconcerting self-confidence.

With a ribbon of sincerity running through it.

Is that possible?

"I hate marshmallows," I say.

His lips curve. He's still holding my hand. "Do you?"

"In my cocoa."

"I'll remember that," he says, as if anything I say makes sense. As if he could track the strange jumps of my mind and the gaps between what I think and what I say.

If he can do that, he probably is my soul mate.

He spares me another long glance, then tips his head to Rhyan. "Captain."

Laramie sends some invisible signal to Frank, and the two of them stroll away. The tiniest sliver of me goes with them.

I can't stand it. How could Laramie Shayle climb out of my brain, off my page, into my life, and turn me into an Insta-Love cliché?

I spend at least forty-five seconds telling myself it's affection for Frank, not attraction to Laramie, simmering in my gut right now.

It could be true. I do somewhat like that wyvern, against my better judgment.

"Emmy?" Rhyan is waiting for me, getting impatient.

I snap my mind back to the matter at hand and push thoughts of Laramie and Frank and Insta-Love from my mind. I'm in a committed relationship with my neuroses, thanks very much.

"Oh, sorry. I'm coming," I hurriedly reply and follow Rhyan east through Castramore. If east is even a thing in Rivenlea, and if I have my bearings right and the mental map of this place I'm beginning to construct is accurate.

An internal voice that sounds a lot like Rhyan tells me my map is definitely accurate, since I'm a Dragon.

We travel through rows of shops and narrow townhouses

and apartments. Wooden signs outside the shops swing in the gentle breeze. The sun sets behind the tallest of the trees edging the town.

Rhyan draws attention wherever we walk. People nod, bow, smile, wave. She returns their attention without slowing her pace, moving through the dinnertime bustle like a practiced celebrity. Maybe she is a celebrity—a Novem captain.

My captain for the next twenty-one hours.

Is this what it's like for the Novemites? Are they celebrities in Rivenlea? Do they command stares and whispers and excitement wherever they go?

If so, this gig is looking less attractive by the second.

I keep my head low and pretend I'm invisible—just like at school.

Rhyan turns down a deserted alleyway and beckons me after her. "Sorry," she says when we're well away from the curious onlookers. "I should have warned you the streets would be busy this time of day. Suppertime."

"Is it always like that? I mean, does everyone know who you are?"

She gives a slight shrug. "I suppose. You get used to it."

Pfft. "Maybe you get used to it," I say aloud.

Cobblestones bleed away to a packed-dirt path. I see evidence of horseshoes, and I'm vaguely surprised they don't just ride wyverns everywhere around here.

I mean, why wouldn't they?

But I don't raise the question and only traipse after my captain.

For the next twenty-one hours.

The dirt path skirts the edge of Castramore, winds down a gentle slope, then flattens back out as we head toward the trees. Nestled along the forest's perimeter are a number of tiny cabins, so earthy and unpolished that if you squint, they almost disappear among the tree trunks.

"Home," Rhyan announces.

"You live here too?"

"Most Novemites do. Some move into Ambryfell or get married and settle into apartments in Castramore, but most of us are here. We live together, train together, work together, and play together, for those inclined to play." She tosses a grin my way. "Save the worlds together."

A shiver rattles me, and I can't source it. Is it the idea that Novems are saving the world, giving Earth her "happily ever after" that doesn't actually exist?

Or is it the idea that some of the Novemites marry each other and settle in Castramore?

I roll my eyes at myself.

"This is you." Rhyan stops in front of a cabin set a bit back into the trees.

I freeze, struck by this space. I breathe in the damp, cool forest air. Broken green light filters through branches clothed in life—leaves resting on the edge of summer and autumn, waiting for their moment to light like Flares, then fall for the year. The scent of pine and decomposing brush and peace and stillness fills my awareness.

I could live here. At least for the next twenty and a half hours.

"Your housemate ought to be back from training. I sent word." Rhyan prepares to knock on the bark-covered front door of the cabin.

But before she does, the door creaks open, and an angel stands before us.

13

SHE'S PALE AS AN ASPEN,

or nearly so, her porcelain skin making it impossible to tell how old she is. She could be a hundred, or she could be twelve. Her swathe of waist-length, blonde hair is plaited and draped over one shoulder.

She seems half changed out of her gear—golden greaves cover her shins, but the breastplate I saw on others of her kind is nowhere to be seen. She's still wearing her leather skirt and a simple tunic.

But I especially notice her light blue eyes—curious and kind. Wondering and waiting.

For me to say something, probably.

"You're a Gryphon," I declare unnecessarily. The white feathery mass poking up from behind one shoulder was all the announcement anyone should have needed.

She smiles. "That is true."

"Emlyn, this is Wistlee, your housemate," Rhyan says. "Wistlee, I trust you'll get Emmy settled. See you for supper?"

"Yes, Captain."

Rhyan steps back, then stops and says, "Glad you're here, Emmy. We've . . ." She grins. "Well, you know."

"Thanks, Rhyan."

And then she's gone, and I'm standing there with an actual winged creature in the small entryway we apparently share.

A familiar feeling creeps over me—a bit how I used to feel around Camille. She was my opposite in every way. Camille smiled; I scowled. Camille was wide open; I was closed off. Camille sought out life; I guarded against it.

Being next to Wistlee is like that, but worse. She's perfectly otherworldly. Ethereal. Like a golden sparkle catching full sunlight.

And I'm an abyss of sarcasm and emotional trauma sucking the oxygen from the room.

But Wistlee seems unruffled, or at least unaware of the stark differences between the two of us. Her face is serenity. "I have the kettle on. Would you like tea?"

"Sure."

She turns toward the small stove near the front of the cabin, and I stifle a gasp.

She's a broken angel.

The feathery mass visible over her right shoulder is, indeed, a Gryphon wing. But along her other shoulder blade, a black clump of tissue is folded in upon itself.

"Don't be troubled," she says, not turning back around as she busies herself with the water. "It is not painful."

She senses me staring at her. Knows I'm looking at her broken wing.

I want to sink through the floorboards.

"I'm sorry," I say.

"No need to be." She pours steaming water over strainers filled with tea leaves. "It is not very troublesome."

"I meant for staring. I'm sorry for staring."

"Oh." She turns slightly, a hint of a smile on her lips. "But everyone does."

"Even here?" I resist the urge to look closer at the wing. Is it damaged? Malformed?

Or simply different?

"Yes, especially here." She faces me fully now, letting our tea steep in the mugs on the countertop. "Gryphons are meant to have two feathered wings. I am quite the unpleasant rarity."

"That's not true," I say immediately.

She tilts her head, waiting for me to explain myself.

"I mean . . . being different doesn't automatically make you unpleasant."

"It pleases me to hear you say so." The expression in her blue eyes shifts ever so slightly, and I realize I've misjudged something.

But I can't quite grasp what.

Wistlee, the golden, sparkling angel looks serene, peaceful, beautiful, perfect. And I've assumed that, as such, she couldn't truly understand a person like me. That she couldn't *be* a person like me. Someone who's been through the wringer and come out the other side a little worse for wear.

But that isn't true, is it? We can never tell a person's journey just from looking at the outside.

I decide I like Wistlee, the Gryphon with one wing.

"It is a wing," she says, as though she's reading my mind again. She pulls the strainers from our mugs and discards the tea leaves. "Would you like to see?"

I'm not sure if it's ruder to accept or to refuse. "If you're comfortable with it," I say finally.

She smiles. "If I were not comfortable with it, I would not have offered."

The golden Gryphon girl has excellent boundaries. My therapist would be so proud.

Wistlee turns toward the counter again, but this time, it's to give me a full view of her back. She unfolds the white feathery wing first. It stretches all the way to the front door. The glowstones placed about the cabin pick up on the faintest golden sheen amid the white.

It's spectacular. Majestic. Unlike anything in creation I've ever seen.

And then she unfolds the other wing.

I step forward, almost involuntarily. Leathery flesh stretches across a bony framework. Midnight black. Pulled taut, almost grotesque, yet not. There's an elegance to the design, a beauty to the intricate structure.

"Like a bat's wing," I murmur.

Wistlee glances over her shoulder at me. "You are not repulsed?"

"Why would I be?" I resist the urge to touch the membranous wing. "It's beautiful in its own way."

She smiles, retracts both wings, then takes our mugs from the counter to the small table in the common living space. "That is kind of you to say. I'm afraid not everyone agrees, but perhaps it's enough that you think so."

"Does it work?"

She laughs—a sound like the tinkling of bells. "Oh, but you are a Dragon! For that is the chief concern of a Dragon: does it work? And the secondary concern?" she prompts, waiting for me to fill in the blank.

And strangely, I know how. "Secondary concern: can it be improved?"

She laughs again. "The Novem will be pleased to have a Dragon at last. Even if they do not have a functional Gryphon."

"Oh. It doesn't work." I fight to keep my disappointment for her off my face.

But she must hear it in my voice. "Do not be troubled. A Gryphon who cannot fly is useful in other ways, one hopes."

"Does it bother you—not being able to fly?"

"It did once. Perhaps it still does. But this is my reality. I cannot grow another feathered wing, and without it, I will not fly. It would not do to become consumed with that which I cannot change. Would it?"

I nod mutely, then after a moment say, "Does Rhyan . . ." But I don't know the right words. Is she bothered by it? Does she care? Does she treat you differently?

None of that seems appropriate to say.

Wistlee sips her tea before responding. "Captain Doyle has always been kind to me. She insists I have other uses, and she assures me not all missions require the use of an aerial."

"Well, that's good." I'd have thought less of Rhyan if the answer were different.

"Captain Doyle took me in when I was banished."

"Banished? Who banished you?"

"'A Gryphon who cannot fly is not a Gryphon.'" Her thin smile doesn't reach her eyes. "That is what my father said at the time."

It occurs to me there's a whole unfamiliar society here—cultures I don't understand, and I don't mean in the sense that I don't know when to bow or curtsy, or when not to shake hands. As I look once more at Wistlee's folded wing, the truth hits home. She is actually a different species, and I know nothing of her kind, their customs, their norms.

"World-building," I mumble.

"Pardon?"

"Nothing." I have to remember I've agreed to assume for one day that this place is real and I haven't fallen into my story.

"I'm sorry your father said that to you," I say truthfully, unsure what banishment means for a Gryphon like Wistlee and how deeply it would affect her. Or how expected or normal that is.

"Thank you. I have hope I will be able to redeem myself, despite what the others say about me."

"To prove your worth?"

"To find my identity. My path cannot be the same as other Gryphons, to be sure, so my quest is to discover who I am and what my purpose is."

I smile at her. "Same." I take my first sip of tea and nearly spit it out in surprise.

It's not bad. Not at all. But the flavor explodes in my mouth in such a strange way—somehow fruitier than juice and creamier than milk, yet containing neither of those ingredients. I stare at the trash bin where Wistlee discarded our leaves, tempted to rifle through and find them.

What in all the worlds was she steeping?

"Do you dislike it?" The slightest crease has appeared on her brow.

"No. Not at all. I just . . . It's not like Earth tea."

Her eyes brighten. "I should like to ask you many questions about your home and yourself."

Another sip of tea gives me a moment to think. "Earth is less colorful than Rivenlea." The drab flowers and disappearing blues and purples of my bedspread come to mind for the first time in a while. Now they pick at my consciousness, insisting I not forget. Demanding I search for answers.

Perhaps answers that are not summed up as, *You're clearly losing your mind, Emmy.*

"I like to tell stories," I say suddenly.

Wistlee pauses with her mug halfway to her lips. "Do you?"

"Yes. Stories like the . . . spheres." I'm not quite sure how to phrase things. "It's been a while since I've told a proper story, but I started writing again this afternoon."

Wistlee cocks her head to the side, waiting for me to continue.

"I created Laramie Shayle."

She straightens. "Laramie Shayle is our Echo."

"Yes. But I wrote about him in my notebook just a few hours ago. I originally made him up when I was ten because my sister wanted a swoony story boy."

I might as well throw it all out there and give Wistlee a reason to reject me right now, a reason not to be my friend. An excuse to write me off. Best to get it done quickly before I'm really invested.

Wistlee carefully sets down her mug and looks at me. "I do not know what 'swoony' means."

A laugh escapes me, and with it, some tension dissipates.

"Swoon-worthy?" Her expression is blank. I rack my brain for a different descriptor. "Attractive."

"Oh, yes, Laramie Shayle is very attractive."

For no reason my cheeks heat. "I suppose."

"I do not find him particularly attractive for myself, as he is not of my species"—I choke on my tea—"but he is an excellent example of a well-formed humanoid specimen."

I dab the dribbling tea off my chin. Clearly, I, too, am a well-formed humanoid specimen. Should I ask how that works, exactly? Which species are considered "humanoid"? If a regular human had interest in Laramie—which I absolutely do not—is that some gross cross-species taboo?

But it doesn't matter. I'm only here for another nineteen and a half hours.

"It's not so much his attractiveness that concerns me," I begin.

"Are you certain? Your face has turned very red."

My cheeks get hotter. "Yes, very certain. It's the fact that I wrote him."

Wistlee laces her porcelain fingers together and looks down at them. "That is strange. Laramie has been in Castramore as long as I have. I do not know his origins or family history."

"Backstory," I mumble. "I've wondered if time moves differently here. Or else . . ." I pause. Do I risk sounding completely crazy and possibly offensive? "Maybe 'here' doesn't really exist."

Wistlee doesn't even blink. "Those are reasonable conclusions to draw, given the facts from your perspective."

My mouth opens slightly.

"I cannot provide you with answers, Emmy, but I can tell you a few facts from my perspective."

I try to tame my eagerness. "Please."

"As far as I'm aware, Rivenlea has always existed. And my clan, though I am no longer considered part of it, has existed in Rivenlea for centuries. I have studied the genealogies, as family histories are deeply important in Gryphon culture." Her eyes are soft and kind, curious not skeptical, as she asks her next question. "Do you believe you wrote Gryphons too?"

"No," I tell her firmly. "Rivenlite Gryphons are totally new to me."

She nods. "Very well. I wondered if perhaps you were creator of Rivenlea."

I stare at her. "You don't find that idea . . . insane?"

"I don't see why it would be. Rivenlites, of all people, should understand that every world has a creator. Every sphere was imagined by someone, and I don't see why your world or my world should be any different."

I could hug her.

But I keep my wits about me for once and sit there like a normal person. "What do you think about me having imagined some parts of this world? Is that possible?"

"Perhaps. I don't see how it could be, but perhaps. I do not have answers for you Emmy, but if you would like help seeking them, I am here for you."

A lump the size of the Statue of Liberty works its way up my throat.

I have a friend?

Suddenly, I have never missed Camille more than I do in this moment, but I'm thankful for Wistlee.

I am about to mention my missing sister and the answers I'm seeking in this strange place. But Wistlee speaks first.

"Do you consider Laramie Shayle to be a suitable mate?"

My tea mug slams to the table far harder than I intend. "*What?*" She opens her mouth, but I cut her off before she gets a chance to say something that makes me want to disappear. "Never mind. I understand."

I stare into my mug. My tea swirls in eddies of mockery. The mug is laughing at my distress.

"I . . . no," I say at last. "He's impossible." In more ways than one.

"I do not know what you mean by that."

"He shouldn't exist." I drop my head into my hands. Another headache is forming. "But even if he does exist and I didn't create him, I feel like I'm trapped in a YA novel."

Wistlee waits for me to elaborate. I know I'm speaking in terms that must not make sense to her.

"I don't feel like myself around him," I venture. "I become that obnoxious YA protagonist who immediately falls for some guy she doesn't know because he's . . ."

"Swoony?"

My gaze falls to the dregs of tea settling in my mug. "I refuse to be an Insta-Love cliché. It's ridiculous. And it's not the way life works, even if it's like that in books."

"I believe—"

But I don't get to find out what Wistlee believes, because there's a knock at our door. She moves to stand, but I hold up a hand.

"I'll get it," I say.

In three paces, I've cleared the distance to the front door. I pull it open.

Before me stands a lanky boy with a cut jawline, perfectly straight nose, and a shock of silky black hair falling over one keen brown eye. His mouth curves, his eyes narrow, not in a complete smile but a warm, friendly expression that invites a person in. Initiates trust. Forges connection.

"Hey," he says. "I'm Phen."

"Of course you are," I huff. "Not today, Love Triangle!"

And I slam the door in his face.

I STARE AT THE CLOSED DOOR

and rethink my life choices.

"Oh, Emmy." Wistlee rises and moves to the door.

Before she can correct my mistake for me, I yank the door back open. A bewildered Phen is standing there, brow furrowed, mouth slightly open.

"I'm sorry," I splutter. "I don't know what I was thinking."

I was thinking that two handsome boys with winning smiles in a YA novel can only mean one thing. And I absolutely refuse to Love Triangle. I will not.

Not on top of Insta-Love.

But Phen isn't tripping over himself to bow before me and kiss my hand. He isn't raking his eyes over my face like I'm his one true love, arrived at last after so much waiting and a veritable lifetime spent apart.

He's leaving all that nonsense to Laramie Shayle, and thank goodness.

"Is it safe?" Phen ducks his head and peers inside our cabin. "Am I likely to be executed on sight?"

A black hole of shame swallows me. "I'm so sorry."

He quirks a half smile. "Don't worry about it. I'm going to assume that wasn't about me."

I step back and allow him access to the cabin. "No, it wasn't.

I'm so sorry." If I apologize eighty-seven times, perhaps he will forget this someday.

Hopefully within the next nineteen hours.

Phen shakes the hair from his face. "Phen Fydell. I hear you're our Dragon."

So Phen is a member of our Novem. That explains why he's come. He wanted to meet the new girl.

And she slammed the door in his face.

"I'm an idiot," I say aloud.

Phen shrugs. "That's not what I hear."

I almost laugh. "Thanks. But I'm afraid to ask what you have heard."

"Your level of fear should be entirely dependent on who I've been talking to. Hey, Wistlee," he adds, then plunks himself on our couch.

I guess he's comfortable here, and I wonder if he and Wistlee are close friends.

"Hello, Phen." Wistlee busies herself in the kitchen, cleaning up our tea. "Is it suppertime already?"

"We're late, actually." His gaze follows Wistlee as she whisks through a doorway at the back of the cabin. "Everyone will assume you and Emlyn have been getting ready."

Suddenly, I can feel my sneakers, T-shirt, and jeans again. I'm probably supposed to be wearing something else.

"Emmy," I say.

Phen turns back to me and nods. "Not Emlyn."

"Emlyn is okay. But you can call me Emmy."

He smiles. "I will, then."

"Emmy, would you like to wear a dress to dinner?" Wistlee appears in the doorway again, holding up two dresses—one emerald green, the other sapphire blue—simple but gorgeous, like they've been yanked off the rack of a fantasy novel.

Which I'm pretty sure they have.

"I couldn't borrow your clothes, Wistlee." For one, I'm significantly shorter than she is. Second, surely her dresses have slits in the back for her wings. Third, I would absolutely spill mustard or whatever on myself at dinner, forever ruining her perfect fantasy novel dress, and I can't have that.

"Oh, these are not mine. They were made for you."

I stare at her. Stare at the dresses—that do indeed appear to be my size, now that I look at them, and are, in fact, in two of my favorite colors.

Wistlee studies me. "This troubles you."

I shift. "Somehow, I'm getting used to it. To things. Sort of." The emerald-green dress whispers my name. "Will everyone else be dressed up?"

"It is customary for Novemites to dress for dinner."

Only then do I fully notice Phen's dark trousers, polished boots, and white shirt. Not altogether different from what most of the men wear to train, but certainly cleaned up and presentable.

Unlike me in my ratty jeans.

"I'll change." I take the green dress and head through the door Wistlee indicates.

There are two of them at the back of the cabin, and I assume this room is mine and the other is hers.

The room is furnished simply with a scrubbed-wood bed, trunk, and night table. The bed is piled with knitted blankets so cozy-looking, I want to dive in and sleep for approximately two weeks.

Instead, I peel off my Earth clothes, fold them, and place them in a neat pile on top of my shoes. Mom would be so proud.

An uninvited pang shoots through my gut at the thought.

Those emotions are too complicated to entertain, so I busy myself checking the trunk for shoes. A pair of leather slip-ons rests at the bottom—exactly my size—next to folded garments of various colors and fabrics. A pair of boots sits in one corner of the trunk.

For training.

My heart skips. Will they expect me to train? Surely they will, and I can only imagine the ensuing catastrophes.

I slip the emerald dress over my head and rearrange my curls, attempting to smooth the frizz without much success.

A knock sounds at the door. "Emmy, are you well?"

"Almost finished." I try not to think about how dirty and sweaty and tired my face probably is. I try to forget I'm about to see Laramie again and face the whole of Rivenlea, for all I know, and I pull open the door to Wistlee and Phen.

"You look lovely," Wistlee says.

"For a humanoid," Phen adds.

I fake a glare at him. "Thanks."

He holds up a hand. "I'm humanoid."

Wistlee looks a vision in an ivory dress with brown leather accents. As I expected, her clothes are clearly designed to accommodate her wings.

I wish mine were designed to accommodate my awkwardness.

The three of us make our way out of the cabin and set out through the trees, retracing the steps I took with Rhyan not long ago.

"What are you?" I ask Phen, knowing it sounds a little rude, but not knowing how else to phrase it. "In the Novem, I mean."

"Sentinel."

"The guardians, right?" I recall the stony protectors from the yard.

"That's right. The captain taught you some things already, then."

"Yes, she gave me a tour of Ambryfell earlier."

"I saw."

My stomach clenches. I can't shake the feeling I've been paraded around in front of everyone for inspection.

"And Sentinels are humanoid?" I ask, remembering his comment. He certainly looks human.

Except for the whole turning to stone and creating portals thing.

He nods. "Sentinels, Muses, Flares, Echoes, Bolts, and Zephyrs are humanoid."

"But not Dragons," I say, and it's not a question. I recall Salem and her otherworldly scales and empty eyes.

"Not Dragons." Phen glances at me. "But you look humanoid."

"Not humanoid," I counter. "Actually human. If I belong in Rivenlea at all, I'm supposed to work in a shop, probably."

"Nothing wrong with working in a shop."

"No. And yet, here I am. Everyone insisting I'm a Dragon and belong in a Novem."

"It is a puzzle." Phen shrugs. "But you're in the Taenarum. There's no doubt."

"I have doubts, but does anyone care about my doubts?" I'm vaguely aware that I'm whining.

"Why should they listen to you? You're just a human."

I stop short and give him a look. But when I do, I see the humor dancing in his eyes. The twinkle. The quirked lips. The good-natured sarcasm simmering in his words.

I like Phen Fydell much more than I want to, because goodness knows I don't know what to do with *one* friend, let alone two.

15

PHEN AND I CATCH UP

to Wistlee and begin to climb the hill, but my shoes are slipperier than I expect. I keep stumbling, but between Phen's quick reflexes and Wistlee grabbing my hands and pulling me toward her, I don't slip down the hill. Instead, I crest the rise to find Laramie standing a few paces away, surrounded by a large knot of strangers, all openly aghast at Phen's hands on my elbows and back.

Annoyance bubbles up, but I'll only make a fool of myself if I say something.

I lift my chin and refuse to notice how well Laramie cleans up, striding past as though I don't see him.

"Miss DuLaine?"

I half turn. "They're slippery," I say. I'm referring to my shoes, but I might as well be talking about my feelings.

We're several paces past Laramie and his group, all of whom are ogling me.

"The mating rituals of humanoid species are strange, indeed," Wistlee observes as we head toward Ambryfell. I almost stumble again.

The streets are quieter now. The lamps have been lit in the deepening dusk. Home fires glow in most of the windows we pass, and I imagine stews bubbling and bread baking in brick ovens. But who knows what Rivenlites eat. I'm just guessing.

My stomach growls. "This is not a mating ritual," I say absently, most of my attention focused on the idea of warm bread slathered in butter.

"You didn't see the look on Laramie's face," Phen points out. "I think I've offended him."

"He'll live." I pause as Wistlee holds open the door to Ambryfell. "Who were all those people he was with?"

"His friends." Phen takes the door from Wistlee and holds it for her as she enters after me. "Other Novemites. He's really popular."

"Naturally."

Wistlee and Phen lead me through the hallways of Ambryfell once again, and I expect to lose my way immediately. But the dining hall sits a short distance down a hallway to the right of the foyer.

If the library is the heart of Ambryfell, the dining hall looks like a lung, full of breath and life, bustling bodies and animated conversation.

A kaleidoscope of Novemites sits among long rectangular tables, stretching the length of the hall. Some appear to be clustered within their Novems—one of each type, at least from what I can tell visually. Others are clustered in groups according to their types. A band of Gryphons eyes us as we enter, and I get the distinct feeling their piercing gazes are on Wistlee, not me.

And there's Rhyan, toward the far end of the hall, standing behind a bench and waving to get our attention.

"Cap wants to sit together," Phen says, leading us in her direction. "Probably wants you to meet everyone."

I follow my new friends—a word, a concept, a feeling still foreign—toward our commander. I smooth my dress of invisible wrinkles, then toy with the end of one of my ringlets. Change my mind and flip it over my shoulder instead. Search for pockets my dress doesn't have, wishing I could still my hands and my mind and my racing heart.

"Welcome, my little Novemulus." Rhyan smiles and gestures toward the open bench space around her.

We take our seats. "Novemulus?" I whisper to Phen.

"Just a nickname. We're the babies," he explains. "At least, I assume you are. You look to be—what, sixteen?"

"Seventeen," I counter, pulling myself to my full, unimpressive height. "And a half."

He grins. "Still the babies."

"Oh." I pretend to be interested in the baskets of bread in front of us—and I *am* interested, don't get me wrong. "How old is . . . everyone?"

"The Novem is late teens, mostly. Rhyan's more like a hundred, I think."

Wistlee shakes her head at him. "She's thirty-one. As is Canon."

"Laramie is nineteen," Phen casually remarks.

Somehow, I'm relieved when Rhyan interrupts. "Emmy, I'd like you to meet the rest of your Novem." She motions across the table to a couple strangers.

A black-haired boy with a wide grin and sparkling eyes waves at me. Rhyan introduces him. "Rivit Kiran, our Muse." Then she gestures to a girl with bright green eyes and sandy blonde hair. "Marella Calum, our Zephyr."

Marella acknowledges me with a nod and a breeze that ruffles my hair. This sends a slight chill across my shoulders, prompting a giggle from Marella and a smile from Rivit.

"They're a thing," Phen whispers to me.

"It's obvious you've met Phen Fydell, our Sentinel," Rhyan continues. "And of course there is Wistlee, our Gryphon."

My gaze bounces involuntarily to the Gryphons across the dining hall who were casting judgy glances at Wistlee as we entered. She either doesn't notice them or pretends not to.

Or perhaps she, with her excellent boundaries, truly considers it none of her business what others think of her.

I give an inward sigh.

"And here's our Harmony." Rhyan gestures to a willowy woman with mint-green skin who approaches with Canon by her side. A fern-green braid reaches all the way to her waist.

As she gets closer, I see subtle markings on her arms. Tattoos, perhaps? They're pearlescent white, catching the light every so often, in a pattern like leafy vines.

Not tattoos, I realize. They appear to be her veins, scarcely visible through her skin.

"Faela Bratus," she says, taking my hand in hers. Her skin is surprisingly warm. She bows elegantly, and I try to return the gesture, except I'm sitting. So I only accomplish an incline of my head.

At least Canon looks semi-pleased with my attempt.

"Where is that boy?" Rhyan mutters to herself, then turns to me. "Well, I suppose you've met him already." She raises her voice. "Everyone, this is Emlyn DuLaine, our Dragon. Here at last."

For the next eighteen hours and fifteen minutes.

"You can call me Emmy," I manage, but I can't seem to make my voice loud enough in this crowded hall.

"She doesn't look like a Dragon." Marella's piercing eyes narrow.

"Perhaps not." Rhyan unfolds a napkin and places it on her lap, deliberately unconcerned. "But she is one."

"We'll see." Marella's gaze is pinned to me.

I meet her gaze. Because what else am I going to do? Tell her she's right, and I'm really just here to maybe find my sister then get back to my boring unDragony life as quickly as possible?

"Emmy, may I sit beside you?"

Laramie's familiar voice startles me. How did he slink into the dining hall, shed his entourage, and sneak up behind me without my notice?

I blame Marella.

I swivel on the bench to meet his chocolate Labrador eyes.

Labrador.

Lhasa Apso.

Labradoodle.

"I'm a cat person," I mumble.

One of his eyebrows lifts. "Me too."

"I thought you were a wyvern person."

He shrugs, a smile creeping over his face. "What can I say? All animals like me."

"Well, I don't like you, so you may want to reexamine your theory."

"Did you just refer to yourself as an animal?"

This conversation has already run away from me somehow.

I clear my throat. "No, you may not sit beside me. Those spots are taken." With Wistlee on one side and Phen on the other, I feel secure in this statement.

"I don't mind!" Phen's voice is seventeen degrees too bright.

"Phen," I hiss.

But he's already popped up and is making his way around to the other side of the table so he can sit across from me and Wistlee instead. He scoots onto the opposite bench beside Rivit with a grin on his face.

I glare at him.

"Your dress is beautiful," Laramie says, loudly enough that anyone caring to eavesdrop certainly could.

And I'm mortified to discover some faces I kind of recognize from his crew of friends. They're seated nearby and *do* appear to be listening.

Laramie uses a pitcher to fill my water glass first, then his. It's a wonder he meets those targets, as his gaze is still focused on me, a bit of a smile twisting his perfect lips. "Rivenlea agrees with you."

Inescapable snickering sounds from the next table over, and I begin to wonder if Laramie does this all the time. Is he a hopeless flirt or actively humiliating me on purpose? He'd seemed kind earlier, much to my annoyance.

My brain flicks through the possibilities, but I don't even really know Laramie. Only what I jotted in my notebook and observed this afternoon. How can I tell what's real?

The only thing that's certain is I will *not* become a disgusting cliché.

My voice drops in one last desperate appeal. "Can't you see you're embarrassing me? And yourself?"

"Am I?" His voice lowers to match mine—quieter, even, as he leans in closer, his breath brushing against my ear, skittering across my neck.

A response tries to form, but my brain must be on hiatus.

"Am I really?" Laramie asks again, leaving *just* enough space between us to remain on the correct side of propriety. And not a hair's breadth more.

"I . . ." is all I can manage.

He smiles. The dimple in his left cheek appearing, his eyes twinkling. Clearly enjoying the fact that I'm tongue-tied, enjoying the effect he has on me. Enjoying the attention of all his friends watching us.

Death to Insta-Love, and death to the girl who swoons for this boy.

Before I can scrape together a rational thought, I jump up from my seat.

And in the process unsteady the bench. The stars would have to align just so, the weight perfectly imbalanced at just the correct angle, unless physics are now staging a revolt against me too.

For a moment, Wistlee, Rhyan, Canon, and Laramie teeter backward, and I'm afraid I have managed to knock them over. But then they all correct at once, instinctually. The bench slams back into proper position, hitting my legs and knocking me forward into the pitcher of water. I stay there for at least six seconds too long, sprawled over the table like a fool.

After a moment of stunned silence, snickering rises throughout the hall.

Wistlee's hands find me then, and she gently collects me from my humiliation and sets me on the bench beside her. She hands me a napkin for the water droplets, then passes me a bowl of vegetable stew, shaking her head. "Very strange mating rituals, indeed."

That's when I notice Laramie Shayle has vanished.

16

"I LOOK LIKE AN IDIOT. I'M NOT
coming out."

"I'm quite sure you look fine," Wistlee says through my door.
"It's just clothing."

Just clothing.

Wistlee and I have had breakfast in our cabin already. We're
supposed to report for training soon. Best I can tell, it's around
eleven in the morning, which means Rhyan has approximately
six hours left to show me this is real, I belong here, and staying
in Rivenlea is definitely what I ought to do. Despite making a
complete fool of myself at dinner last night.

This outfit is not helping.

The high-heeled, thigh-high black boots. The leather trousers
and vest. The sleeveless shirt beneath the vest showed off the
other Dragons' iridescent scaled arms. My extremely regular
human arms are less impressive.

It all looked fine on Salem and the other Dragons. But on me?

"I look like I'm playing dress-up."

"May I come in?"

I sigh. "Why not?"

Wistlee glides into my room, eyeing me carefully, her brow
furrowed. "I do not see the problem."

"This is . . . not how I dress."

"Perhaps not on Earth. But your clothing is quite suitable for a Rivenlite Dragon."

I don't bother telling her I'm not really a Dragon. Instead, I gather up my courage, wave away my self-consciousness, and steel my nerves.

I promised Rhyan an entire day, and I'm no liar. A fool playing dress-up, sure. But not a liar.

I nod to Wistlee. "Okay. Let's go."

The yard is buzzing with as much activity as yesterday. But this time, Novems are clustered together, training by team not type. Wistlee and I find Phen quickly. He's waving his arms wildly at us, so he's hard to miss.

"Sleep well?" he asks us both, and I take a moment to appreciate that he cares. He's kind, this Sentinel Phen.

I soak up the feeling of having a friend.

But I can't say that aloud. No need to telegraph the fact that I'm seventeen and haven't really had a friend since my sister disappeared.

Camille and I used to joke that we had a special sister sense. Like the connection between twins, except we were two years apart. Camille was joking, but I secretly wondered if it was true.

If I reached out to her here in Rivenlea, using whatever sister connection we may have had, would she hear me? Is this where she's been all these years?

"Emmy!"

I nearly startle out of my skin. Phen and Wistlee are both looking at me with concern. I've clearly been zoning.

"Sorry. Just thinking."

"Welcome, everyone," Rhyan is saying now, and I realize our circle has filled out completely, all the other members of our Novem present.

I refuse to acknowledge our Echo, visible only in my periphery.

"This is the first true day of training for Novem XVII, now that we're complete." Rhyan looks my direction, and my cheeks respond by lighting themselves on fire. "Emmy's most obvious gap will probably be in physical combat."

"*Most* obvious?" Marella arches an eyebrow. "I'm not sure about that." She casts a pointed glance at a nearby Dragon.

I'm suddenly very aware of my outfit again.

"Emlyn's most physically visible gaps are not the same as her actual limitations," Canon interjects, and it could almost be a compliment.

"Fair enough." Marella concedes. "But are we going to talk about the fact that she looks like an Earthling? We're supposed to have a *Dragon* on our missions. Isn't that what we've been waiting for?"

"Give her a chance, Ella." Laramie's voice. "She hasn't even had a day of training."

He's sticking up for me?

Marella shrugs. "I'm just saying what everyone else is thinking."

I keep quiet because she's probably right.

"I was not thinking such things." Wistlee pointedly unfolds both her wings. "If Emmy is not accepted as a full and equal member of this Novem, perhaps I should not be either."

No hint of doubt flickers in her words, her stance, her eyes. But she's expressed it openly to me, so I know it's there, behind the show of strength. The words spoken in my defense.

"I didn't mean that, Wistlee." Marella has the decency to look abashed.

"That's enough, all of you." Rhyan steps into the center of our uneasy knot. "This is my Novem. I say who's supposed to be here, got it?"

Marella folds her arms across her chest with a gust of wind, but she bites her tongue.

It's going to be a long day.

"Emmy, you'll work on swordplay with Laramie first."

Before I can form any kind of objection, Rhyan has moved on to pairing up the rest of Novem XVII. In a matter of seconds, everyone else has moved away to their own spaces.

I have no choice, so I finally look at him.

He's standing there with two wooden practice swords in his hands. Despite the fact that he just stood up for me, his eyes aren't warm.

Today, he's stony enough to be a Sentinel.

He tosses me one of the wooden practice swords, and I only just catch it. An apology forms on my lips, and I almost get it out. But he speaks first.

"Come to learn something useful, have you?"

Annoyance sparks in my gut. It begins to thaw my embarrassment, replacing it with my familiar prickliness. "I'd hoped to. Maybe I should find a different teacher."

"All the useful learning is happening right here, love."

My knuckles whiten around the wooden hilt. "As if there's room for anything inside that pretty head of yours besides your ego."

He smirks. "You admit I'm pretty."

"I admit nothing." Except I already have.

Laramie spins his wooden sword in his hand, and I can't fully squash my humiliation. He was embarrassingly attentive yesterday, and seeing him climb off my own page into the flesh— the nerve.

But this guy, haughty and combative, is worse. All my fears are confirmed. Any attentiveness was just an act. Now that I've embarrassed myself in true YA protagonist fashion, he's lost all interest.

And I hate how much that stings.

Enough to make a few tears prickle behind my eyes.

Fury sparks—indignation that he could make me feel anything besides annoyed. "Well," I demand, "are we going to start this? Or are you afraid of getting dirty?"

"More concerned about you losing your footing in those

things." He nods to my boots. "You could only just keep yourself upright yesterday in the most mundane footwear."

If I whack him across the head with this wooden sword, would that be bad form? "Just show me what to do with this thing before I stab you with it."

He grins and softens a little, and I chide myself for being relieved. "Hold it down the hilt farther, closer to the cross guard."

I adjust my hands. "Like that?"

"Yes. Now straighten your wrist but keep it flexible."

I try. Apparently I fail.

"No, like this." He moves behind me.

I nudge him back. "Go away." But there's no bite to my command.

He holds up both hands in surrender. "Sorry. Thought we were having a productive training session."

I mull that over for a second, because of course he's right. "Okay, you can come back."

He dips into a bow. "As you wish."

A few hours later, I have to admit Laramie is a good teacher. I've followed him through a few basic sword strokes and learned a little footwork.

"So I'm ready to spar now, right?" I am completely sarcastic, because I'm the worst one in the yard by many miles.

But it's still somehow embarrassing when he responds with a snort. "Ah, no, little one. Not even close."

Little one? I glare at him. "Oh yeah?"

"Yes."

Why is that so offensive to me?

Because you don't want Laramie—or anyone else—to think you're not a true member of the Novem, my own mind accuses.

"Yes, Em," he says again. "You would get destroyed. You're only just learning."

His words are sane and completely true. Yet I still find myself saying, "Okay, let's go, then!"

He shakes his head and laughs. "Gladly."

My sword blocks his first strike a half second too late, and the force of his attack reverberates through my arm with a nervy ripple. I shove him away with all the strength I can muster.

But he's bigger than I am. Bigger and stronger, and far, far better at this.

What in the world was I thinking?

My paltry attempt at a strike I just learned is easily dismantled by Laramie—the one who taught me the strike. He counters with a fancy combination. I stumble. He pulls in closer and sticks his foot behind my ankle, sweeping my wobbly feet from beneath me.

I land on my backside in the grass.

A chorus of laughter erupts around us, and I'm mortified to discover we have an audience. That seems to be a hazard of hanging around Laramie Shayle. He's standing over me now, and I can't decide if he's grinning or gloating.

My muscles ache. But it's my pride that's most bruised. How could I have been so stupid?

"Red is your color, Em."

I glare. "I'm wearing black."

"I meant your face." He winks. "Better luck next time." Then Laramie strides away without helping me up.

At least he didn't call me "little one."

"Emmy," Rhyan calls.

I've only just brushed the grass and dirt from my trousers. Is she going to scold me for challenging Laramie?

She probably should.

Instead, she approaches saying, "I'm going to have you work with Salem and the other Dragons for a while."

As if this day couldn't get any worse.

"And the rest of the Novem will be observing."

It just got worse.

"Why?" The panic is clear in my voice. "Why does everyone else need to observe?"

Rhyan is beside me now. Understanding flickers in her eyes. "I know it's awkward. But you're not a biological Dragon. It's important Novem XVII understands how best to work with *our* Dragon."

I can't argue with the logic.

But I want to.

Instead, I swallow my pride—a lumpy, spiky pill—and nod.

Rhyan leads me to a cluster of Dragons. They cut a stunning silhouette, grouped together like they're posing for a superhero movie poster, scales glittering in the sunshine, empty eyes boring into me like I've offended them.

I probably have. And who can blame them? How would I feel if some random human showed up in my superpowered world and claimed to be just like me?

A dorky wave is my stellar opening. "Hey, Dragons."

I'm doing great.

Salem, positioned in the middle of the Dragon cluster, heaves a sigh. "Captain Doyle."

It's not a question, but I hear the plea within. *Must I really?*

Rhyan is unrelenting, and I get the feeling that's standard for her. Her "Thank you, Salem" carries a weight of meaning.

Salem draws herself up. "Very well. Aleigha?"

A Dragon with lavender scales and silver hair steps forward, a sphere in her hand. She holds her palm flat, and the sphere begins to levitate.

"Tell me, Emlyn." Salem's empty orbs are turned on me. "What do you see?"

I feel the eyes of Novem XVII, the eyes of all the Dragons, the eyes of all the worlds on me.

"I see a sphere." I'm hesitant, even though that's clearly what Aleigha is holding. The sense that I'm missing something key grows.

"Look closer."

As I peer into the glass ball, tiny figures come into focus. "I see a door. Nearly concealed by vines. A little girl discovering this place for the first time." I squint. "A sick boy in bed. It's *The Secret Garden.*"

"Jordith?" Salem motions a male Dragon forward. He has pale blue scales, black mane and eyes, and a sphere floating over his hand.

Clearly I'm supposed to read this one too.

I lean forward. A series of pages flash within the sphere. Letters, diary entries, telegrams.

"It's epistolary." I watch another moment, and a Victorian man with a long white mustache appears. A splash of blood. *"Dracula."*

"Jaynem?"

A Dragon with golden-yellow scales and cream-colored braids holds out a third orb. To her credit, she offers a friendly smile. Perhaps not all the Dragons despise me.

"I see women in Regency Era clothing," I say. "A handsome man with a serious face. One woman reading a book." A smile spreads across my face. "Her hem six inches deep in mud. *Pride and Prejudice.*"

Salem passes her hands beneath the three spheres, transferring them from Aleigha's, Jordith's, and Jaynem's control to her own. She lifts them up to eye level. "Do you know what I see?"

"I'm sure I don't."

"I see every beat of these stories. From the opening lines to the inciting incidents to the midpoints. The climaxes, the denouements, all the way to 'The End.' I see the invisible scaffolding that holds these spheres in place. Were I to jump into one of these spheres, I would see the moments that are broken. Exactly what needs to be fixed. Precisely where everything went wrong. That is the function of a Dragon. Our *raison d'être.* It's what we bring to the Novem. Our entire purpose."

Her white eyes rake over me, and I can guess what she sees here—inadequacy. "You're no Dragon," she scoffs. "However much some may wish it."

This last statement is directed at Rhyan, though Salem stays fixed on me. The other Dragons swivel to look at the captain, and Rhyan opens her mouth to say something.

"I'm not useless," I cut Rhyan off before she can speak. The knowledge that I've been judged incompetent burns in my chest. "You're right—I'm not a biological Dragon. I can't physically see the structure you see. I won't be able to tell my Novem the things you can tell yours."

"You admit you don't belong?"

"Maybe I have something else to offer," I say. "You can see the scaffolding of these stories, but I feel their hearts. Their very human, Earthbound hearts.

"I can tell you about the rebirth found in Archibald Craven's garden—and why it mattered. Why healing after abandonment and trauma has resonated with readers for centuries. I can tell you why writers still retread the well-worn theme of good versus evil in their work. I can tell you why those literary battles resonate with us, in the world at large and within our own hearts."

I plunge on. "I can tell you why a witty love story about mistaken first impressions still hits here"—I tap my chest—"after centuries of cultural change and technological progress. It really shouldn't still apply, it shouldn't make sense to us or be relatable anymore, and yet it is. You may see these stories in a way I can't, but I can *feel* them in a way you can't. Because they were written for me—for humanity. You Rivenlites say stories hold us together? I am part of that fabric. These stories are knitted into my heart, my very being."

Resounding silence has me rethinking my monologue. "I . . ." My voice shrivels. "I'm not useless. I have something to offer too."

Before I can regret my speech too much—and before I can determine how it's been received—I turn on my heel and stride back to Ambryfell.

Rhyan's time is just about up.

17

SHELVES OF SPHERES

stretch before me. Endless stories, spanning the entire breadth of human history.

At least, according to Rizak.

I can't possibly know them all, of course. So maybe I don't really have much to offer my Novem, anyway.

It doesn't matter. I'm not staying.

Training today only confirmed my instincts. I don't belong here. And Rhyan hasn't told me anything useful about Camille. Maybe I can ask a few more questions, see what I can find out, and then go home.

If I can even get home.

Surely I can. There's some sort of portal. I got here, after all. Maybe Frank has to fly me somewhere, since I fell from the sky. Maybe we have to go back up to get home.

If she'll let me, I'll smuggle Frank to Earth. If she promises to stay small, I can probably hide her from Mom.

"You look troubled, Emlyn."

I whirl around at the man's voice, expecting Rizak.

A middle-aged stranger's face greets me instead. He has dark hair and blue eyes, currently filled with pity.

"I'm figuring out how to get home." May as well speak the truth. What difference does it make? "Who are you?"

He bows. "Hadeon Exan." His grin spreads wide and friendly. "But just Hadeon is fine."

"You can call me Emmy," I say. "How did you know my name?"

"Oh, everyone knows you. Word spreads fast in Castramore. Besides, it's not every day someone drops into our sphere."

"Has it ever happened before?"

"Only once that I recall."

My nerves spark. "But it *has* happened?"

Hadeon gives a slow nod. "Yes, it has. Though that was an unfortunate matter."

My breath catches. "Please, can you tell me anything about it? Was it a girl? A blonde girl with blue-green eyes named Camille?"

He cocks his head, his sympathy washing over me like a breeze.

No, wait—it's an actual breeze.

"You're a Zephyr," I realize aloud.

He smiles again. "You've learned some things in your short time here."

"I guess." But I'm not going to let him duck away from my questions. "Please. I'm looking for my sister. Do you know if anyone like the girl I described has ever been here? It would have been about seven years ago."

"If you seek answers to your questions, you'll probably need to stick around, don't you think?"

I frown at him. "I am definitely in a novel. That's the only reason anyone would be so frustrating and withholding for no good reason."

Hadeon chuckles. "You're not entirely wrong. And you're not entirely right."

I'm ready to throw him through this shelf of spheres. "Who are you, anyway? Where's Rizak?"

"I'm just one of many guardians patrolling the spheres." He

glances pointedly at the area. "You happened to be plotting your exit from Rivenlea in one of my rows."

My sigh is heavy as lead. "I feel like today has been two weeks long." I plunk onto the floor and rest my head in my hands.

Hadeon huffs as he lowers to the floor beside me. I peek at him in time to catch a grimace. "Not as young as I used to be," he says with a wink. "These bones are tired. Too many years sphere-diving, I'd wager."

"You were in a Novem?"

He nods. "Most born with the gifts are at some point. I have two fully human parents, so their baby Zephyr was quite a surprise."

"I can imagine." I sigh again. "I'm in the opposite position, you know."

"So I've heard."

"I should probably go home to Earth. If there's a way."

We sit in silence for a few moments. A soft, melodic hum rises from the spheres. A chorus of theme and meaning.

And probably some plot beats, to Salem's point.

"If I stay, she'll probably smother me in my sleep."

Hadeon's face puzzles. "Your housemate?"

The thought of Wistlee—and an ensuing thought for Phen—sends a pang of regret through me. I don't actually want to leave them. Not yet.

"Not my housemate. She's great. It's a Dragon who is not fond of me."

"Ah, yes. Well, Dragons are prickly."

I dart him a glance, and he just grins.

"And I'm pretty sure the Zephyr in my Novem agrees with her."

"Zephyrs are very changeable, you'll learn." He casts a puff of wind in my direction.

I have to smile at that. A moment of silence passes between us. "So, what was your best mission?" I ask.

"The best?"

"Or most memorable."

"Ah." He tilts his head back, staring past the spheres on the shelf in front of us. "I will tell you that story another time, perhaps."

I eye him. "But only if I stay."

"It would be hard to tell you otherwise. It works exclusively one direction. The stories created on Earth appear here. Not the other way around."

My breath falters. "And if I leave, there's no guarantee I will ever be able to get back."

"Isn't that the way of it?"

Indeed.

"Emmy." He pats my shoulder. "You don't know me from any other Rivenlite you might pass on the streets of Castramore. You have no reason to trust me. But there is one thing of which I can assure you."

I look at him.

"The answers you seek are here in Rivenlea, not back home." His blue eyes twinkle. He gives my shoulder another pat, then heaves himself up and continues his patrol of the long, lonely aisle.

Camille. He's talking about Camille.

I'm not sure how much time has passed when Phen's voice breaks into my awareness. "Emmy!"

I turn to see him bolting down the aisle of spheres.

"I found her!" he shouts over his shoulder, and I'm tempted to shush him. It is a library, after all.

Wistlee, Rhyan, Canon—every member of Novem XVII rounds the corner. Even Marella. Even Laramie, who hangs back at the end of the aisle, casually propped against the shelves, as if the matter at hand doesn't much concern him. But his face is red, his chest heaving.

He has clearly been running.

"Emmy." Phen skids to a stop beside me. I accept his offered hand and pull myself up. "Are you all right? We've been looking everywhere. Rhyan was really worried."

It's hard to picture the unflappable Captain Doyle being worried about much. The idea warms one corner of my calcified heart.

"Sorry," I say to her and Phen and the others as they approach. "I didn't mean to scare you. Just thought I'd—" But the explanation dies on my tongue.

I was in Ambryfell so I could view the spheres one last time before leaving.

And now I don't want to.

In that way she has, Rhyan seems to correctly guess at least part of what I'm thinking. "You're going to stay."

"For now."

"Good." Satisfaction glows in her eyes. "I know Salem can be . . ."

"Prickly."

"That's one word for it," Rhyan says wryly. "She's not as bad as she seems. But I let her know exactly how I felt about what happened today."

My smile is genuine. "Thank you."

With that, I follow the other members of Novem XVII out of the library and into the clear evening air. I don't mention meeting Hadeon. Nor do I tell them I've got a side quest and that my side quest is actually *the* quest. I don't tell them I won't give up my search for Camille until I have all the answers I seek.

If anything has become apparent, it's that I will have to be relentless in excavating information about my sister.

And I'll have to do it alone.

18

THE NEXT MORNING, I PLACE

the entirety of my allowance on the counter—every bill and coin Rhyan gave me the previous night. "My size on Earth is six and a half, but I don't suppose that will help you much."

The Castramorian shoemaker stares at me blankly. "No, miss."

"I need real shoes."

"Real shoes?"

"Non-ridiculous ones."

"She means comfortable shoes, sir," Wistlee translates for me.

I hold up my offending Dragon boots. "My feet are still swollen from wearing these yesterday. Probably the other Dragons don't mind, but I do not have lizard feet. I need comfortable boots, good for missions and training and whatever else. No heels, nothing pinchy or weird. Can you do it for this?" I scooch the pile of Castramorian money across the counter, offering the lot if the shoemaker will accept the job.

I need him to.

"This . . ." He glances at Wistlee. "This is a bit too much, miss."

"Okay, just take out what you need."

Rhyan said it was spending money. Novems have homes, clothing, and food provided for them. Anything extra we want comes from our allowance, and what my feet want most in this world is different boots.

The shoemaker extracts two of the bills and a small assortment of coins. "This should cover it. I will let you know if the leather costs more."

"Thank you."

He glances at my Earthly sneakers and doesn't fully conceal a grimace. "Shall we get you measured, then?"

Twenty minutes later, Wistlee and I are headed over to the yard for training. Phen is waiting for us by the front doors of Ambryfell. "How was your shopping trip?"

"You make it sound like something frivolous." I sweep past him as he holds open the door. "I assure you it was entirely practical."

Phen raises his brows at my high-tops, paired inelegantly with my Dragon training attire. "I can imagine."

"Do you think Rhyan would let the three of us work together today?" I mutter quietly to Wistlee and Phen. No other option seems particularly appealing.

"Captains are not in the habit of accommodating their Novems' personal relationships." Wistlee offers a sympathetic smile. "If Captain Doyle wants you to work on your swordsmanship, she'll have you work with her best."

And that's you-know-who, of course. Why couldn't he be good at literally anything else? Gymnastics or software engineering or playing the trombone or sourdough baking or untying complicated knots. Anything except swordplay.

But as Rhyan gathers us together, the barely concealed excitement sparking on her face tells me she has something much more interesting than our training assignments to share.

"Novem XVII, I've got excellent news."

Canon's wide smile tells me he already knows. The others perk up immediately, and they clearly sense what's coming before my brain catches up.

"We've been assigned our first mission," Rhyan announces.

"Oh!" Faela gasps and clasps her green hands together. "At last!"

"Where?" Rivit asks above the excited buzz. "Where are we going, Captain?"

Phen's beside me, and something about the vibes rolling off him pulls my attention. He looks pale—a little nauseous, even. I discreetly grab his elbow and give it a little squeeze.

"As soon as the Elder Council gives us their final approval, we're being sent to . . ." Rhyan trails off to ramp up the suspense, delaying satisfaction as long as she can before the Novem riots. A smile breaks on her face. *"The Wonderful Wizard of Oz."*

The news is met by a variety of shrugs, albeit happy ones, from the rest of the Novem, and I realize I'm the only one who knows the story. Surely it's a pillar, somewhere on the sphere map in the library. But I'm realizing most Novemites don't spend too much time studying stories. And why should they? If Dragons are able to physically see story structure and identify what's broken on sight, why spend energy learning stories?

Except that stories are amazing.

I remember Rizak's words about the importance of story for humanity—how story holds us together, shapes us, instructs us—and I can't help feeling like the Rivenlites have missed something. Something crucial.

Stories hold space for us in our broken, messed-up world— space to escape, to grow, to grieve. But Rivenlites believe our world is perfect, if only we can put stories back into their boxes and force them to behave.

"It must be a horror story by the look on Emmy's face," Laramie's voice wanders into my thoughts.

The Novem is staring at me. They gather that I know the story, but they've misinterpreted my expression.

They have no idea. It's not Oz that's freaking me out, it's their worldview.

I collect myself and clear my throat. "No, it's a good one. A favorite when I was young." I turn to Rhyan. "Do we know how it's broken?"

"The distress is visible just by looking at the sphere, but it's hard to know specifics until we jump in. That's why we train for everything, yes?"

"Yes, Captain!" choruses everyone except me.

I've been missing cues since I was forced to appear onstage in my third-grade play.

"To that end," Rhyan continues, "Faela, Wistlee, and Marella, I have a project for you to work on. Phen, you'll practice gateways today."

Phen goes from "a little nauseous" to nearly Faela's hue.

If Rhyan notices, she doesn't say anything. "Emmy, you and Laramie will work on your combat skills again. You'll need to utilize every possible minute of battle training before we leave."

I'm about to protest that Oz isn't really that kind of book. It's not like we're hopping into the *Iliad*.

But the thought of flying monkeys screeching across the sky has me rethinking that. Could I cut one out of the sky if I needed to? The idea makes me queasy.

And so does the idea of training with Laramie, but here he is again, holding the wooden practice swords. Everyone else has trickled over to their assignments, but I'm standing here thinking about flying monkeys and wondering how Homer would describe Laramie's eyes. Surely he would have something more beautiful to say than "pools of chocolate pudding."

"You look angry," Laramie observes casually.

"Just thinking about Homer."

"Who?"

"My boyfriend."

He flinches, and I'm not proud of the satisfaction it brings me. "You have a boyfriend?"

"No. Homer's been dead several millennia."

A slight frown is his only response.

"Now *you* look angry," I say.

"Why would I be?" He tosses one of the swords to me. "Ready?"

I block his first strike with my wooden blade. He neutralizes my counter easily, but I skip over his attempt to trip me—the move that won him our match yesterday.

His eyes glint. "You do learn quickly, Em."

I'm pleased enough to overlook the nickname. Maybe even pleased enough to *like* the nickname.

But then he says, "You're still terrible, but you're not making the same mistakes twice. It's a good sign."

I volley my best glare at him, but it only makes him laugh and launch a new attack. Despite my terribleness, I hold my own for several minutes. I know Laramie is going easy on me, but the slightest bit of sweat has broken out across his forehead, so at least I'm making him work a little.

He even sweats perfectly, glistening just enough to look rugged and masculine but not enough to look unhuggable. I tamp down the urge to smash his chiseled YA hero face.

The distraction costs me, and I take a smack to my calf from the flat of his blade. I yelp and hop back. Mischief glitters in his eyes, and I try to imagine it's malevolence instead. It would make it easier to concentrate on punishing him for that strike.

And yet, even my imagination can't manage it. He's an imp, not a villain.

I attempt the combination he taught me yesterday, and Laramie has to dodge away. Before he can pivot and regain his advantage, I launch the combo again, this time from another angle.

If only I had more tricks up my sleeve—some unexpected move to pull out and surprise him. But I have to work with what I've got. So instead, I use my speed—and the fact that I have comfortable shoes today—to try to keep him off-balance.

Making full use of what I learned from the five years of ballet I endured as a child, I stay light and mobile, blocking his strikes and launching a few of my own when possible. Though this is clearly my weakest skill, somehow I find myself behind Laramie's unguarded back for half a second.

But half a second is all it takes.

I put all my anemic strength behind a flat whack, braced for the satisfying smack against Laramie's back. My sword meets—

Nothing.

Laramie has vanished.

My momentum takes me forward into the void, and I stumble and fall awkwardly to the ground, triggering a flashback of my first dinner in Rivenlea.

I pause on all fours for a moment, trying to understand what happened. My sparring partner has vanished into thin air. And in his place is . . . something lying in the dirt.

A rose. It's a rose with sunshine-yellow petals and flares of red around the edges.

"A circus rose," I puff into the dust I'm lying in, still groping to understand what I'm looking at.

But the next second, the rose pops back into its true form— Laramie Shayle, sitting cross-legged on the ground and grinning at me puckishly. "Nearly had me."

I scramble to my feet, almost too angry to find my footing at first. "You . . . you cheated!"

Laramie shrugs and hops to his feet. "Did I?"

"Yes!" My voice has risen enough to draw attention, but I don't care. "You can't just shift into something else when I'm about to land a strike."

"Says who?"

"Says me! Says . . . I don't know, the rules of engagement? Common decency?"

He laughs. He laughs in my face. "You're overreacting."

I draw myself up to my full height. "Are you actively trying to convince me to smother you in your sleep? Do you want me to poison your dinner? Because I will. Tell me I'm overreacting again and find out."

His grin only widens. "It would be unwise for an Echo—or

anyone, for that matter—not to use all the tools at his disposal when engaged in combat. Don't you agree?"

"I don't have such tools," I seethe.

"That isn't my fault."

In this moment, I want nothing more than to win this argument. I can't say why, and I know I'm not going to. Because Laramie isn't exactly incorrect. But it still feels like he cheated to gain the advantage.

I choose silence and glare daggers into his face instead.

He shakes his head. "You did well. The flower was for you."

"The flower *was* you."

His expression suggests I'm amusing.

We're still being watched by several onlookers, and I decide I've had about enough. "Good day, Mr. Shayle."

He bows dramatically. "Your Majesty."

19

"YOUR MAJESTY," I MUTTER
to myself as I go down the hallway toward the library. "Well,
off with his head."

I pause and consider what I've just said. I'm not the villain
in this story, am I?

Laramie scrambles my brain. I can't think straight when
I'm around him, and maybe I did overreact. But he annoys and
incites me on purpose, and that's at least as bad.

And the man is mercurial. One minute turning on the
charm, the next cold as a snowflake, the next like one of the
little boys on the playground pulling the girls' pigtails because
he's too unevolved to simply say, "I like you."

When he annoys me on purpose, is that what he's trying to
say? Or does he do it for sport?

Probably the latter.

Once in the library, I head straight for the sphere map. I cut
out of training early without asking Rhyan. Probably shouldn't
have done that. But I didn't much want to hang around amid the
whispers and stares and giggles. And I definitely didn't want to
hang around Laramie anymore.

"Stupid circus rose." The circus part feels accurate.

I scan the sphere map, looking for my target. It has to be
here. It's a classic—a pillar, as the Rivenlites would say.

There. To the left, a little lower than halfway down. A glowing representation of a sphere filled with smoke. I peer closer. The smoke is rising from the ruins of the Emerald City.

My breath hitches.

This story and Baum's other Oz tales were childhood favorites of mine. The oddity and whimsy and wonder unlocked my young imagination and inspired me to dream up some truly fantastical story elements of my own.

At the time, I was unconcerned with the conventions of story I came to understand and analyze as I grew older. Though I was no longer writing my own worlds, I was consuming, critiquing, cherishing the worlds of others. Things like world-building and continuity mattered.

But in my Oz years, all that mattered was imagination. And that was a precious thing.

What would the Novem find when we traveled there?

"I heard about your assignment."

I turn to find Rizak, the librarian, standing nearby. "Hi, Rizak. Yeah, I guess we're getting ready to go to Oz."

"An unusual sphere, that one."

"You could say that again." I smile at the childhood memories.

We stand in companionable silence for a few moments, watching the sphere map glow. "Shouldn't you be in training?" Rizak asks finally.

"Probably."

He chuckles. "Well, take your time. The library is open to all." Then he disappears back among the shelves, pulling his polishing cloth from a pocket in his trousers.

Unease stirs in my gut as I watch *The Wonderful Wizard of Oz* smoke ominously for several more minutes. Will I even be able to help my Novem once we're there?

"Psst."

My head swivels around at the whisper. Hadeon Exan

stands partially concealed down one of the aisles of spheres. He beckons me over.

I glance at the door back into the main hallway of Ambryfell but then walk toward Hadeon instead.

"Fancy meeting you here again," he says.

"It's where I come whenever I've been embarrassed at training. Apparently."

"Well, in that case . . . I have a secret for you." He glances around conspiratorially, then lowers his voice. "There's a very quiet, very secluded spot where no one will ever be able to find you."

I cock a brow at him. "Except you, I suppose."

"Good point." He smiles. "Interested?"

I'm curious, at least, so I say, "I could be."

"This way." He beckons me down the aisle.

I distantly wish I'd told Wistlee and Phen where I was huffing off to. Not that I'm worried Hadeon will kidnap me. But this is still an unfamiliar place with unfamiliar people. The buddy system is never a bad idea.

And I do have a couple of buddies now.

But I couldn't be going anywhere too weird. After all, Hadeon doesn't seem to be leaving the library, merely heading deeper among the shelves.

We take multiple turns, and I'm not sure I'd be able to find my way out except that the sphere map glows in the foyer. The glow emanates all the way up to the ceiling, and it appears to be visible from everywhere within the cavernous room. I could at least determine the right direction to go.

"Here," Hadeon says at last. He indicates the comfiest-looking pile of cushions, pillows, and knitted blankets fluffed into a corner. It looks like the perfect place to read or think.

Or brood, in my case.

"This looks lovely," I say.

He spreads his arms wide and smiles. "It's all yours. Back to my rounds now."

Then I'm left alone with the soft hum and gentle glow of the spheres. I settle into the mound of comfort and draw in a deep breath. I try not to think about flying monkeys or a ruined Emerald City. And try not to obsess over what we'll find when we hop into Oz.

A soft *ting* pulls my attention toward a nearby shelf. I crane my neck, trying to see if I can identify which sphere made the noise.

Ting-ting.

I sit up. Some sphere has gone its own way, breaking from the melodic, harmonious hum of the others. Doing its own thing. Tinkling like a little bell amid the symphony strings of the other spheres in the library.

For some reason, that makes me smile.

But I can't figure out which one it is, and the tinkling sound has stopped for the moment. So I settle back into the pillows and cushions and blankets and attempt to relax.

Ting-ting plink.

I shoot back up, scanning the shelves, searching for—

There.

I scramble out of my knitted cocoon and go toward the shelves to the sphere flickering in an offbeat, discordant way. The sphere swirling with a pattern that looks . . . exactly like my bedspread.

I only just stop myself from pulling the sphere off the shelf and peering into it. Maybe I'm not supposed to touch them. Perhaps some sort of alarm will sound if I do.

I look around, hoping to see Rizak or Hadeon, but I'm entirely alone in this little corner of the library. I inch as close as possible to the shelf without touching anything, noting every detail of the sphere plunking its little tune.

Frank. A tiny representation of her, but Frank, just the same. Her miniature self sails through the skyspace of the sphere, turning flips alongside a sand-yellow and turquoise wyvern.

My breath stills. Camille's wyvern.

The one I wrote for her years ago when I would have called it her dragon. The two creatures fly figure eights around each other, soaring and sailing and swooping.

I peer closer.

At the very bottom of the sphere, a tiny figure stands.

I know her immediately. How many times had I described her red-gold hair and perfect freckles? How often had I made up some adventure for her to embark upon or a quest to undertake, only to get bored partway through and send her off in an entirely different direction?

It's Princess Brielle Song, my most enduring main character. And there nearby is her mother, Queen Veronica. They're best friends, of course, because I'd written the idealized mother-daughter relationship I wished I had.

My brain can't quite crunch through what I'm seeing.

Why are they here? I'm still not entirely sure I haven't fallen into my own idea notebook—that Rivenlea isn't somehow my own creation.

But following the rules of Rivenlea, as they've been explained to me by Rizak and Rhyan, this sphere should not be here. Published stories, Rizak said. Every story ever published. And my childhood musings were, mercifully, never published.

So why is this sphere here?

And, more to the point, why does it feel like everywhere I turn, my creations and my very existence are breaking all the rules?

20

"YOU STAND HERE," PHEN

explains, "and call her."

"I don't know how to call her." I stare up at the mountainside rising before us, pocked with cave mouths like a giant piece of honeycomb. Appropriately named the hive, this is where the wyverns live. "Do I just shout her name?"

"Most wyverns respond to whistled commands," Wistlee says.

Laramie's ability to easily speak to Frank comes to mind, and I almost wish he were here.

Almost.

I attempt a feeble whistle. "There's no way she heard that."

Wistlee emits a shrill sound that nearly makes my ears pop. "I am not sure if Frank will respond to me, but perhaps." She smiles.

"Thanks." I rub my ear and watch the caves, hoping Frank will make an appearance. Seeing her tiny form in the sphere a week ago has made me anxious to check on her at the first opportunity. We've been training nonstop, and breaks have been few and far between.

While we've been busy with mission preparation, I've been mulling things over, considering my options. I decided to talk to Wistlee and Phen. To do that, we needed to get away from the listening ears of others. The caves are a solid twenty-minute walk from Castramore. At the moment, we're completely alone.

"So." I gaze at one yawning cave mouth. "I found something in the library last week."

Wistlee and Phen exchange a glance and wait for me to go on.

"It's a draft, I guess, though even calling it that seems like a stretch. They're my characters and creatures I used to play with all the time. I never actually finished a full story, I don't think. Maybe some short stories."

Phen frowns. "And you found what, exactly, in the library?"

"A sphere."

"A . . . real sphere?" Phen's brows furrow. "In the library? In Ambryfell?"

He's obviously as bothered by it as I am.

"That shouldn't be possible, right? I'm not missing something important?" I turn to my housemate. "Wist?"

"No, indeed. That should not be possible."

We stand in troubled silence for a moment.

And then I'm run over by a big rig.

At least that's what it feels like. I'm flat on my back in the dirt, coughing to try to draw breath into my lungs. Two large, scaly, clawed feet rest on my chest.

"Frank," I puff weakly.

Frank aggressively nuzzles my neck and face, shoving her snout against my cheek, snorting into my ears.

"Ugh, that tickles." But I can't stay mad at such an affectionate reptile. Even if she might be secretly trying to kill me.

Wistlee gives Frank a sharp command, and Frank backs off my chest, resting on her haunches instead. It allows me enough space to sit up. I make eye contact with my wyvern, and I'm honestly not sure who's the pet and who's the owner here.

Phen helps me to my feet.

I recall us to our conversation as I stroke Frank's snout. "This is concerning, right? I'm not overreacting?"

I bristle at my use of that word. Blasted Laramie.

"No," Wistlee says immediately. "You are not overreacting. The rules are . . . Well, they are supposed to be rules."

"And it seems like I'm breaking all of them." Frank pushes her flank into me, so I start patting her side. She rumbles out a smoky purr. "I'm a Dragon who's not a Dragon. An Earthling in the midst of Rivenlites. Things I wrote live here. But not everything that lives here is something I wrote. My childhood story scraps are an actual sphere in the Ambryfell library. A wyvern climbs out of my notebook. My sister . . ."

I don't know how to finish that one. Because I only suspect Camille somehow ended up here, and no one will tell me anything useful.

"None of it makes sense," I finish, sidestepping the Camille connection for now.

"I think you should ask Captain Doyle," Wistlee says. "She would have some insight to offer, surely."

"Or maybe Canon?" Phen suggests. "He's always reading and researching and studying things. He's also Novem XVII's liaison to the Elder Council. Maybe he knows something."

"No." I'm not sure why I respond with such force. I pat Frank in silence for a few moments and try to puzzle through it.

"They don't seem to believe me," I say slowly, unraveling my interactions with Rhyan and Canon over the last ten days. "I tried to explain some things about Earth, and Rhyan didn't grasp what I was saying. Canon keeps implying I've met him before and simply don't remember, but I'm sure I haven't. And when I asked about my sister, Rhyan was cagey. I tried again yesterday, and Rhyan said now is the time for mission training, not questions about Camille."

They're staring blankly, and I realize I haven't told either of them anything about Camille. And I need to. But I don't know where to begin. I take a breath.

"My first brush with Rivenlea was seven years ago. I was telling my sister a story, writing notes in my notebook. And she just ribboned away. She unraveled in front of my eyes and was gone. I haven't seen her since."

Phen grimaces. "Oh, wow. That's hard, Emmy."

"How dreadful." Wistlee's eyes are filled with compassion. "I'm sorry."

"Thanks." I attempt a smile. It's strange to tell that story and not have my sanity immediately questioned. "Frank brought me to the exact spot where Camille disappeared, and there was the portal to Rivenlea. When I came through the portal, the same thing happened to me. I felt myself unravel, then knit back together. Surely it's all connected. Camille is here . . . don't you think?"

"It seems possible." Wistlee is speaking carefully, and I wonder if she's afraid I'm about to lose it.

She doesn't know that ship sailed long ago.

"I don't think I've heard of another Earthling appearing in Rivenlea before." Phen looks at Wistlee. "Have you?"

She shakes her golden mane. "Not that I'm aware of. But it would not be the first time the Elder Council concealed sensitive information from the populace. It could have happened and we were none the wiser."

"Fair," Phen agrees. "I still think we should talk to Rhyan or Canon."

"No," I insist. "At least not yet. I sense I'm going to need to build an airtight case before I get those two to believe me. Right now, all I have is a pile of questions."

"Then what about Rizak?" Wistlee suggests. "He is a neutral party, and if anyone would know pertinent information about a sphere in the library, it's Rizak."

The idea turns over in my mind. I'm still not thrilled for some reason. Probably something about that "happily ever after" conversation I had with him and Rhyan.

But I like Rizak. Instinctively, I trust him. My gut says he's on our side, even if he's clueless about Earth.

I massage Frank behind her floppy ears. "Okay. We can ask Rizak what he thinks. In a few days."

Phen shakes his head. "Emmy. We could be leaving for our mission any moment. Whenever Rhyan says it's time, we go. We shouldn't waste a few days if you want to find out what's going on."

My breath shakes. But I know he's not wrong.

"At the end of this journey," Wistlee says gently, "there could be answers about your sister."

She unknowingly echoes what Hadeon said to me a week ago. I've still avoided mention of meeting Hadeon, and I wonder if I've had a reason to do so—albeit subconsciously.

"Okay," I say at last. "Let's talk to Rizak."

21

RIZAK STARES AT US,
his mouth hanging open.

"Rizak?" I try to catch his gaze. "Are you okay?"

"I just . . ." He shakes his head. "After all this time, I finally have an answer about that curious sphere, and yet it still doesn't make any sense. Very strange, indeed!"

That doesn't sound promising.

"Are you saying you don't know why it's there either?" I venture, hoping he'll reassure me but knowing he won't.

"I'm afraid not, Emmy. But chin up! That doesn't mean I cannot help you." He pats my hand. "We will figure this out together, yes?"

I nod, hoping he's right. Wistlee lays a hand on my shoulder, and Phen offers a smile.

"Emmy, tell me everything you can about that sphere. We'll start there."

I close my eyes, combing over each detail etched into my memory. "Two of my characters were inside. The princess who starred in many of my adventures and her mother, the queen." My eyes pop open. "Does Rivenlea have a queen?"

"No, we have an Elder Council."

"Elected or appointed?"

"Appointed."

"By whom?" Can't say why I'm asking. Just collecting data. One never knows what might be relevant.

"By . . . the council." Rizak frowns, and I wonder if he's never considered this before.

"So, the council appoints itself? Of course. What could go wrong?" I shake my head, moving on. "Okay, so no royal family in Rivenlea." My eyes close again. "Frank and Camille's wyvern—let's call him Steve—were in there."

The two wyverns soar through the sky in my mind, over the tall grass of my imagination sandbox.

"They were in the sandbox."

"A sandbox?" I open my eyes to Rizak's confused expression. "A box of sand?"

"No, my imagination sandbox. It's the empty field where I would put characters and creatures and ideas when I wanted to play with them. To be honest, most of my writings took place in the sandbox because I didn't know how to plot a story when I was ten. I rarely got to once upon a time, let alone the end. And that's kind of the point."

"Rizak, sir, why are Emmy's scraps of story here? They oughtn't be." Wistlee seems off-balance. Like a little portion of her mind is coming undone at the breaking of this particular rule.

Rizak sighs. "It is puzzling." He turns to me. "Emmy, tell me about some of your other ideas. The ones you can't see in the sphere."

The question catches me off guard. I'd made a point to set aside storytelling years ago, consuming the stories and ideas of others instead. I hadn't cracked open any of my notebooks for years prior to the day I jumped into Rivenlea.

But I rack my brain, knowing if I focus, some well-loved idea from the past will float to the surface.

It does.

"Glitter trees."

Phen's eyes widen briefly, and he seems to be holding on to a laugh. "Glitter trees?"

"I was six years old," I retort.

"What ever is a glitter tree?" Wistlee asks.

It's exactly what it sounds like.

"I imagined a forest where the branches are composed entirely of glitter."

Why? Because glitter is sparkly, obviously, and a six-year-old needs no other explanation or reason.

And that's just as it should be.

"What else did little Emmy dream up?" Phen asks, eyes dancing.

"Um." I elect not to tell him about my most embarrassing ideas. "There were talking mushrooms."

Phen doesn't even try to hold on to his laugh this time.

"I was little!" I protest, but then I'm laughing too.

"The real question," Phen says, "is what in the world a mushroom has to talk about."

I'm about to tell him exactly what little Emlyn imagined mushrooms had to say, but my gaze snags on Rizak. He's not laughing along with the rest of us. In fact, his color has drained.

"Rizak?"

He shakes his head, as if clearing cobwebs from his mind. "Forgive me. It's just . . ."

We wait for him to finish, but he seems to be lost in his thoughts somewhere.

"Sir?" Wistlee leans forward to catch his gaze.

"Oh, I am sorry." He wrings his hands, his frown growing deeper. "There is more than one mystery in Rivenlea, that is certain."

My hackles rise. "Explain." I catch myself just in time to avoid rudeness. "Please?"

"There is a forest. Not near Castramore, though not exactly far, either. Just far enough to be considered a distance."

Remind me never to ask Rizak for directions.

"The forest has been sealed off using means available to council and only council. For the protection of the populace."

After a moment of silence, Phen speaks. "Sir, what in the worlds are you talking about?"

Rizak's hand-wringing intensifies. "Oh dear. This is most troubling. And puzzling. The Silvarum."

We stare blankly in response.

"The Forest of Ideas. That's what they call it." His eyes shift to me. "And now I believe I know why."

My heart begins to race. "Why has council sealed it off?"

"For the protection of the populace," Rizak repeats. It's like he's reading off a propaganda pamphlet.

"But why? Is it dangerous for some reason?"

"I'm sure I don't know, Miss Emmy. There are many unexplained, uh, features of that forest. Council thought it better to limit those allowed in."

"Is anyone ever allowed in?" I press. Suddenly I want nothing more than to see what's inside that forest.

"Some, yes. Some people even live in there. The forest requires care, of course."

Phen, Wistlee, and I share a glance. Do forests usually require care? They seem to do pretty well when left to their own devices.

"Rizak, how can we get into the forest?" I ask.

"The Silvarum?" He draws back, aghast. "Oh, I'm not sure that's a good idea."

I hate to scandalize the poor librarian, so I try to soften my tone. "If we were to insist?"

Rizak draws a deep breath. "Well, we must petition the Elder Council, in that case. I will file a request."

"A request for entrance into the forest?"

"No. Dear heavens, no. A request for an audience. If approved, you will be able to petition for entrance to the forest at the next regular meeting of the council. Unless their agenda is already full, in which case they will schedule you for the next-next council meeting, or perhaps the next-next-next meeting. Things do get busy at times."

I die inside.

My veins suddenly seem to crawl with fire ants. Itching. Tickling. Burning with the need to be anywhere but here. Doing anything but this. Making some sort of progress, finding some answers.

"Thank you, Rizak," I hear Wistlee say, and it sounds like she's speaking through water. "Please do put in the request. We will check back with you for more information in due time."

In due time.

I die a second death.

Phen and Wist seem to sense my distress—the fact that I'm about to implode—and they gently pull me away from Rizak and the sphere map, toward the exit.

My mind is spinning, buzzing, and flaming at once. I force a few deep breaths, trying to calm my nervous system and make my higher reasoning click in again.

We round the corner into the hallway outside the library, and there strolls Laramie Shayle, headed straight toward us.

22

LARAMIE OFFERS ME

something between a glare, a smirk, and a smolder, and I distantly wonder if he learned that expression in some YA hero training program.

"Rhyan sent me to look for you three. You missed supper."

That's why my stomach feels hollow—and slightly twisted, full of dragonflies, vaguely nauseous.

I'm just hungry.

Laramie turns to Phen. "Faela set some food aside for you." Then to Wistlee. "Perhaps you wouldn't mind giving Emmy and me a moment?"

"Sure," Phen says far too quickly. And he's still sort of laughing.

I will stab him later.

Wistlee locks eyes with me. Reads me. Makes sure I'm okay.

I send her a silent message—it's fine. Laramie is annoying, but it's fine.

She inclines her head toward us both. "Emmy, we'll meet you in the dining hall."

I nod.

Laramie waits several long moments until my friends are fully out of sight, out of earshot. "Would you feel more comfortable in the library?" he asks.

"No." My answer is quick—immediate and instinctual. For some reason, the idea of Laramie finding my illicit sphere that shouldn't exist fills me with mortification.

He wouldn't, of course, if we merely stepped into the library's foyer to have whatever discussion he wants to have. That sphere is buried on the lowest shelf of some distant bookcase in a weird corner of the room.

But still, the hallway is fine.

"Fair enough. I thought we should talk about what happened."

My brain is still stuck on the impossible sphere and the Silvarum and Elder Council red tape. Is that what he means?

He must read panic in my eyes. "Goodness, Em, but you are dramatic."

It takes me two seconds to realize he meant he wanted to discuss what happened between us in training last week—the *cheating*—but my nerves light up in indignation.

How dare he call me dramatic.

"I thought you were talking about something else, first of all. And second, I am *not* dramatic. You cheated, and it's not okay."

Rhyan had not paired us up in the days since, and I wonder if she sensed I needed a break from Laramie and his reindeer games. Or perhaps Laramie needed some real mission training and couldn't afford to spend all his time babysitting me and my inferior sword skills.

"I understand why you feel that way," he says. But the twitch of his lips makes me question his sincerity.

And it hits me suddenly that this is my main problem with Laramie.

It's impossible to tell what's real with him. What's genuine, and what's grandstanding. What's true, and what's showboating.

He's a shapeshifter in more ways than one.

"You're glaring at me like you wish to peel the skin from my body," he says.

"I'm considering it."

"That's very violent of you."

"Sarcasm. If you plan to converse with me much, I suggest you get better at detecting it."

"Oh, I plan to have many conversations with you, and I think I've already got a pretty good read." He unleashes a full-wattage grin.

I roll my eyes. "You don't know me at all."

"Don't I?"

I know I shouldn't, but before I can stop myself, the words are just pouring out of my stupid mouth. "Try me."

His gaze flicks to my face, then my sneakers, then back again. Sizing me up. Judging me, deciding who I am.

He smirks. "Everything about you says 'go away.' You've spent your life making sure everyone knows their presence is not wanted, their attention is not sought." The smirk loses most of its smugness—unfolds into another disarming smile. "Everything about you is carefully constructed to keep people out."

My heart constricts, squeezes shut. Just how I've kept it since the day Camille disappeared. "And yet, here you stand. I've built a wall, brick by brick, to keep people out, but here you are. Still. Why not disappear again, like you did that first night?" I fight to keep any indication of my pain from the question.

But I'm not sure I've succeeded.

The mockery melts from his expression. "I thought . . ." His gaze warms. "Well, I'll leave if you ask me to." But he takes a tentative step closer. "Say the word, and I'm gone."

The scent of peppermint invades my senses. Like gum. Do they have gum in Rivenlea? Does Laramie chew gum?

Toothpaste.

It must be toothpaste.

It's definitely peppermint toothpaste.

My brain is toothpaste.

"But if you don't want me to leave . . ." he begins, but he doesn't finish his thought. He just takes another step closer, and all I can think is *toothpaste.*

I draw a tiny breath. Inhale oxygen that I will exhale in a demand he leave. Insisting he go. Declaring what I know to be true—that he and I could never, ever be a thing, for heaven's sake. He's a book boy I dreamed up for my sister's amusement, and who even wants a boyfriend anyway when there are at least two quests to worry about?

"Stay," I whisper.

And then my true fear crashes into my toothpaste brain, splattering peppermint and impostor syndrome everywhere.

How could anyone ever love you, Em?

Laramie morphs in my imagination. His jaw becomes thrice as chiseled. His eyes harden. He turns into a dashing villain, a toxic love interest, a controlling, narcissistic antagonist rolled into one horrid package with washboard abs. I imagine him saying the words to me, the rejection forming on his lips, the cutting pronouncement slicing into my heart.

And yet, poking through that terrible imagining is the truth. The knowledge that, whatever annoyances and irritants Laramie throws my way, he would never—not in a million years—say those words to me. Even if he shifts on me, disappears on me, he'd never say *that.*

This book boy may be a little arrogant, a little changeable, a bit hard for me to read. But he is not cruel. He might even be . . . kind.

And the way he's looking at me right now is melting my backbone. Unknitting my muscle fibers. Dissolving my cells.

He is the hydrofluoric acid of romance.

He takes one more step toward me, and there's hardly any space between us at all. He reaches up. Finds a loose curl that's somehow escaped my ponytail. "You lost this."

"No, I didn't," I murmur. "It's right there."

He grins.

I'm afraid if I open my mouth, the dragonflies in my stomach will escape. But I do it anyway. "Are you sorry for cheating?"

Our noses are nearly touching. "No," he whispers.

"Do you promise never to do it again?"

"No." His grin widens. "But at least next time you'll be expecting it."

He winks. Tucks my hair back behind my ear.

"See you tomorrow, Em."

He slips past me, leaving behind a cloud of peppermint and uncertainty.

"Toothpaste?" Wistlee asks. "Emmy, I'm afraid I don't understand."

"Neither do I," I mutter. The memory of my weak knees in that hallway is beyond embarrassing.

And yet, not wholly unpleasant.

"You know what it is?" I say.

"I'm sure I don't."

"He makes me feel backward. Like I can't think straight or say the things I mean to say. Like . . ."

"You are not in control?"

"Exactly."

"Mm." Wistlee bites her lip.

I brace myself. "What?"

"Well, have you ever wondered why you must be in control at all times? Perhaps that is not the healthiest impulse."

"Wait a minute. This is supposed to be about why Laramie is terrible. Don't flip the script on me."

"Is it?" Wistlee smiles. "I guess I missed that."

Time to change the subject. "Hey, Wist?"

"Yes?"

"There's something I haven't told you."

"Oh?"

"I . . . met someone."

She furrows her brow at me. "Emmy, why do you look so sheepish? You are not required to have feelings for Laramie. It is perfectly acceptable if you met someone else." But then she goes slightly paler than usual. "Oh. Is it Phen? That could be awkward."

A laugh bubbles up. "No! I didn't mean I *met someone*. Not like that."

I stop just short of admitting any interest in Laramie.

"I meant there was a man in the library. A retired Zephyr."

"Oh." Wistlee's blue eyes widen. "And I take it this meeting was instructive in some way?"

"I guess." I fold my legs beneath me on the couch. It's late, and I know we should go to bed. This day has felt weeks long. "His name is Hadeon Exan. Do you know him?"

"I don't think so."

"He's one of the people who patrols the spheres in the library."

And then I relay to Wistlee everything I can recall of what Hadeon and I have discussed. Spheres, missions, how I should not return to Earth. I tell her it was he who showed me the cozy thinking spot in the library where I saw my unexplained story sphere.

"I think . . ." I venture slowly, knowing what I'm about to say will probably not go over well with Wistlee. "I think I want to ask Hadeon if he can get me into the Silvarum."

Wistlee stares blankly for several seconds. "Oh, Emmy, no."

"I don't know what else to do. You heard what Rizak said. The next-next council meeting, with a maybe attached to it. I can't wait that long!"

"I certainly understand the impulse, but . . ." Wistlee pauses. "I think it best to wait for Rizak to speak to the Elder Council. Do we really know who this Hadeon Exan is?"

The question strikes me. It hasn't occurred to me that people in this little fantasy bubble might be anything other than what they say they are. "I guess not," I admit. "I only know what he's told me. But, to be fair, I've only been here ten days, so that's technically true of everyone."

"Yes, I suppose. But at least with Phen and myself and the rest of Novem XVII, *we* have known each other for years. So you have my word about Phen, Phen's word about Captain Doyle—"

"Marella's word about Laramie," I throw in, pulling an unpleasant face.

Wistlee shoots me a look. "I only mean to say Hadeon is unknown to us. Perhaps you ought to be cautious."

"Maybe Phen knows him?"

But there's no reason why that would be true, and I see that response forming on Wistlee's lips.

"Let's just say I want to get in touch with Hadeon," I say quickly. "How would I go about doing that here in Castramore?"

"If he's a citizen of Castramore—and anyone employed at Ambryfell would be—he will be listed in the town registry."

"Where is that?"

"The post office. If you leave a letter addressed to him there, they will be able to get in touch with him." Wistlee's forehead creases. "But, Emmy, I strongly urge you to speak to Captain Doyle about this first."

"I will. I'll ask her soon, okay?"

Wistlee nods. "Good."

And I'm not lying, exactly.

I will speak to Rhyan about this at some point. Probably soon. But I'm not setting aside the idea of contacting Hadeon, asking him to meet me in the library by that cozy corner he showed me.

Because something deep inside tells me he can help me understand why I, a random Earthling, am somehow breaking Rivenlea.

23

I TRIED TO BE PATIENT.

Honestly.

I made it through another week of Oz training, avoiding lingering thoughts of the Silvarum, my illegal sphere in the library, and my puzzling connection to this strange world. I forced myself to wait patiently for word from the Elder Council, taking the advice of Wistlee and Rizak, both of whom I trust. Becoming an expert in my new favorite game, Dodge the Echo, has helped keep me occupied.

But word from the council hasn't come, and I can't wait anymore. I need something—a nugget of news, a shred of information, a micron of hope that someone can answer my questions and help me find my sister.

And that's why, in the dead of night, I'm putting on my sneakers.

Because I'm a sneak. Ignoring Wistlee's advice, breaking at least a couple of rules, and throwing caution to the wind.

If only I were a Muse and could slip silently through the darkened streets with ease. But I'm not. I'm an anxiety-ridden quasi-Dragon who despises the dishonesty of what I'm doing.

I'm not lying, per se. But somehow it feels like it.

A sound from the common room startles me. I still. Is Wistlee awake?

Silence blankets the cabin again, and I decide it must have been the house settling. Or perhaps a talking raccoon trying to break in and scold me about my life choices.

Speaking of talking raccoons tiptoeing into places they don't belong, I tuck a sealed letter into my cloak and slip outside as silently as possible.

I dart through the paths between cabins, then the streets of Castramore. My breath puffs out in clouds of condensation and consternation, but it only takes me a few minutes to find the building with the symbol of an envelope branded into the wooden sign swinging above the door.

The post office.

I pull my letter from my cloak and check the name I scrawled on the envelope one last time.

Mr. Hadeon Exan.

I push it into the mail slot carved into the front door and pray it'll reach him by breakfast.

I am a terrible person.

My face must look green, and my expression must reflect the misery I feel. Wistlee has asked me approximately forty-seven times if everything is okay this morning. And now my head is buried in a bowl of porridge as I try to avoid meeting her gaze over breakfast in the dining hall.

I don't have the heart to tell her the truth. That I sneaked out in the dead of night to deliver a note to Hadeon, asking him to meet me this afternoon.

My eyelids feel like they weigh twelve pounds. I needed at least three more hours of sleep.

And I need a bucket of bleach to scrub away my guilty conscience.

The fact that I can feel Laramie's smoldering gaze on me from a few benches over is not helping matters.

"Wow. Emmy, you look terrible." Phen plunks down beside me, having grabbed three warm biscuits from a basket on his way. His plate is piled high with enough breakfast fare to impress the entire football team at my school.

I shoot him an icy glare. "Thanks."

"Didn't you sleep?" He demolishes a piece of bacon in two bites.

I move my bowl farther away. "That smells gross."

"You don't like bacon?" I might as well have said kittens are ugly and ice cream is nasty.

"I'm a pescatarian," I say, swatting away the strip of bacon he's now nudging under my nose.

"So, fish you'll eat, but this smells gross?" He shakes his head. "You're weird."

He's not wrong.

Wistlee is still watching me. Has she figured out I ignored her advice to wait for word from the Elder Council? Does she know I'm a sneak?

"We should report to the yard soon," is all she says, eyeing Phen's mountain of food. "Captain Doyle asked us to report early, remember."

"Oh, that's right." Phen starts shoveling food into his face at triple speed. "Just gimmie a sec," he mumbles around an entire biscuit.

Wistlee sighs and shakes her head. Farther down our table, some Gryphons politely dismantle their respective breakfasts with proper silverware and impeccable table manners.

"Humanoid males have unusual etiquette," Wistlee observes.

We both eye Phen.

He glances up, another biscuit in one hand, a sausage link impaled on a fork in the other. "What?"

"After training, I'm going to head into town and check on my boots," I blurt, spitting out my prepared excuse in such a way that everyone must surely know I'm fibbing.

But Phen is too focused on his food to notice anything amiss. He swallows a massive bite. "Want company?"

Wistlee waits for my response, watching carefully.

I swallow hard. "No, that's okay. I doubt they're done yet. Just want to check."

Phen shrugs. "Sure. We can meet up later."

"Yes." Is Wistlee secretly a Bolt? Because her gaze is burning holes into me.

I'll tell her. I'll tell her tonight—confess all Hadeon tells me during our meeting today, if he even got my message in time. I just can't confess yet. What if she makes me promise not to meet him? What if she simply *asks* me not to?

I wouldn't be able to tell her no. The fact is, I know I'm being reckless, and I don't want anyone to dissuade me.

Wistlee doesn't voice what we both know she's thinking. She lets it be, leaving me to make my own stupid choices and sit with the consequences.

And I will somehow have to get through this training session with the sick knowledge that I am the very worst friend resting in my stomach.

THOUGHTS OF HOW DISHONEST I

am have finally relegated themselves to the back of my brain.

At least for now.

Because I'm standing in the cozy little corner of the library that Hadeon showed me, trying my hardest not to stare at my sphere. My notebook burns in my hand. Maybe he didn't get my message after all?

But then there's a tap on my shoulder.

I whirl to find Hadeon behind me. "Sorry, I didn't mean to startle you."

"Not your fault." I release my tension in a stream of breath. "I'm jumpy."

"I see." He holds up my note. "What's this all about, Emmy?"

"Where do you live?" I blurt, then wince at my invasiveness. "I mean—sorry. It's just . . . my friend pointed out I don't know anything about you. Not really. If I'm going to ask for your help—if I'm going to take your advice—I should know something about you. So if you'll forgive the question, where do you live, exactly?"

His face projects puzzlement, but he answers without hesitation. "I live in Castramore, as I have for twenty years. Ever since the time came to join my Novem. I used to live in the barracks where you live now, then I moved into an apartment in town after I retired. It's two floors above the apothecary, if you want specifics." He smiles. "And my favorite color is blue."

"Oh, okay." I have no clue what to do with this information. Hadeon is no longer a floating head who randomly appears in the library sometimes and tells me things, now that I know something to anchor him.

"Backstory," I say absently.

Does it change things? Would Wistlee think this is okay now? Or would she still advise me to talk to Rhyan?

The latter.

Concern puckers Hadeon's forehead. "Are you well, Emmy?"

"Not really." Then I make a decision. I point to my sphere like I'm accusing it. "That shouldn't be here. It's not allowed."

Hadeon peers at it. "That sphere?"

I flip open my notebook to a page I'd found last night. It contains a scrap of a scene between Princess Bri and Queen Veronica. "See? That's them. They're . . . there."

I'm barely making sense. Exhaustion and frustration obscure my ability to communicate, and I am the very worst liar. The moment I see Wistlee, I'm going to tell her what I did and go straight to Rhyan.

This was stupid.

But Hadeon looks properly troubled by the sphere, just like everyone has. This rekindles my resolve to at least make the most of this clandestine meeting, since we're here.

"I asked Rizak about it," I tell Hadeon. "He wasn't sure what it meant, but he wondered if it was somehow connected to the Silvarum." I watch Hadeon's face closely at the mention of the forest.

He doesn't disappoint.

His eyes pop wide. Mouth opens slightly. "Yes, of course." He rakes a hand through his dark hair—graying a bit at the temples.

My voice drops. "Rizak says he will petition the Elder Council."

"For an audience?"

"Yes. For an audience so I can ask them about this." I point to the sphere. "And request entrance to the Silvarum."

"Mm." Hadeon's eyes narrow. "But you were not pleased with this solution?"

"No." Guilt pinches me. "I thought . . . Well, I wondered if you might know a way I can get into the forest myself. Not to do anything bad," I add quickly. "Just to investigate. To see if I can figure out what's going on. Like, why am I connected to Rivenlea in such strange ways? And why do I seem to be breaking all the rules?"

And, most important of all, where is my sister?

But I keep that question to myself.

"I need to understand what's happening, Hadeon. I need to understand who I am."

Hadeon's eyes mist. He draws a deep breath. "Ah, Emmy."

"What is it?" Concern sharpens my senses and makes me forget I'm sleepy and irritated.

"Your determination. Your rawness and vulnerability. You remind me—" He pulls up short.

"I remind you of what?"

Hadeon hesitates, then speaks. Resigned. "You remind me so much of her."

The words knock me back. I grip the bookshelf to steady myself. "You know her," I whisper. "You know my sister."

He seems to just barely hang on to unshed tears. "I knew her. And you're the spitting image, truly."

My brain speeds up, like images and thoughts and memories are flashing through on fast forward. Hyperspeed. I can't slow them down enough to grab hold of any one thing to express it.

"You knew her," is all I can manage. "You knew Camille."

Hadeon doesn't answer directly but blows out another deep sigh. "There's someone who can help you. Getting into the Silvarum is beyond my capabilities. But I know someone who can help you learn more."

Answers, so long out of reach, dance before my fingers. I want to reach out and snatch them before they have a chance to slip away.

Again.

Always.

Instead, I capture Hadeon in my gaze. I refuse to release him until he makes good on his promise. "Take me to them."

25

I POSITION MYSELF IN

Hadeon's shadow as we walk through the streets of Castramore. I keep just a half pace behind his long stride, hoping I will be able to duck away from prying eyes, should we pass any.

Wistlee and Phen could be about. For all I know, they're trying to find me at the shoemaker's shop—where I told them I'd be—because they're good friends. The best. Kind and concerned with what's going on in my life, even though we've practically just met.

Guilt works its way up my throat, and regret meets it there.

I shift my focus to the back of Hadeon's head. Breathe in the cooling Zephyr breeze he produces as he moves.

He'd be very useful in the summertime.

"Hadeon Exan!" A woman's head appears in the service window of a shop. "Been a while." Her cinnamon curls are piled atop her head, though one ringlet has escaped and plastered itself to her sweaty neck.

A bake shop. She's surrounded by mountains of muffins, a cascade of cookies, a bevy of brownies.

"Mokah," Hadeon says, slowing to a stop in front of the window. "Nice to see you." His breeze kicks up, and he intentionally directs some into the sweltering bake shop.

She must have a dozen ovens working in there.

"Likewise." Her gaze shifts to me, and something about her soft blue eyes, rosy cheeks, and smattering of freckles says, "Let's be friends." She smiles. "And who is this?"

"This is Miss Emmy DuLaine. The—"

"Dragon for Novem XVII! Of course!" I'm startled by her enthusiastic reaction. "I've heard all about you. I'm Mokah Snick, resident baker of Castramore." She pauses. "Well . . . one of them, anyway."

"The best one," Hadeon insists.

Mokah's cheeks flush pinker. "Oh, you. Here, have some cookies." She passes six cookies out the window into Hadeon's waiting hands. Each is studded with a different color candied fruit, a sparkly rainbow of confections.

Hadeon sneaks a wink at me.

"Nice to meet you, Ms. Snick," I say.

"Call me Mokah, please. Everyone does. And don't you forget, Novemites get free treats in the afternoons following training sessions. Hadeon never outgrew the habit."

Hadeon takes a bite of a cookie filled with gems of pale yellow fruit. "I do not even have the manners to apologize. How could I, when the treats are so delectable? Surely you don't blame me."

Mokah huffs, but she's still smiling. "Lovely to meet you, Emmy. Don't be a stranger. And bring your friends!"

Guilt stabs again at the mention of my friends. "I will."

Hadeon and I continue on our way, and Hadeon passes me a cookie with red berries in it. "You won't regret it."

The berries taste like a cross between a strawberry and a raspberry, but with the structure of a cranberry—better for baking. The cookie is buttery, crisp on the outside and delightfully chewy inside.

"I do not regret it," I say between tiny bites, savoring every morsel.

I'm several bites into my cookie when Hadeon stops suddenly in front of a shop. The sign announces *Teyra's Tinctures: Apothecary.*

"My front window," Hadeon says, looking two stories up to

a window above the row of shops. "In case you wondered if I wasn't speaking the truth."

My face burns. "Sorry. I . . ."

"I'm just teasing, Emmy." He reaches for the knob to the apothecary's front door. "I mean, that really is my apartment. But we're here because I want to introduce you to Teyra."

Teyra. She must be the one who can help me learn more about the Silvarum.

Sparks begin at the top of my head and dance all the way to my toes.

Camille. Where is Camille? Where is my sister?

"Emmy?"

My brain reconnects with my body, and I realize I'm still standing on the cobblestone path outside, frozen. Unable to move for fear of what I might discover. Or what I might fail to discover.

And if that's not a metaphor for my life . . .

I force my feet to behave and move toward where Hadeon is standing. Toward answers.

He opens the door, and an old-fashioned bell jangles. I step past him into the shop, and Hadeon follows.

We enter a single room stuffy with the scent of burning incense and so packed with hundreds of tiny glass bottles and pots filled with various live plants, I can hardly see the shelves they're lining. Nearly all the light from glowstones and the large front window is filtered through glass, colored liquids, and leafy plants, casting a kaleidoscope across the floor and Hadeon's face.

"Teyra?" Hadeon calls. "Are you in?"

I peer closer at the nearest collection of colored liquids. The handwritten labels have words in a language I've never seen with characters I don't recognize. I suppose you'd need to be an apothecary to decipher them.

"Hadeon?" A green face peeks up from behind a countertop I didn't notice because it's so covered in miscellany. "I didn't hear the bell!"

And no small wonder. Her head is wrapped tightly in a plum-colored turban, and I imagine it muffles the sound somewhat.

Teyra's gaze trails to me. Stops. Widens.

Her emerald eyes swallow me. I wait for Hadeon to break the spell and tell her why we're here, who I am.

But something nudges the truth forward in my mind. She already knows. I don't know how, but Teyra already knows who I am.

"Emlyn DuLaine." She gets to her feet and puts her pale green fingers over her heart. "We meet at last."

Whispers of the Chosen One trope swirl around me, and I'm not amused. How does she know me?

Hadeon finally speaks up. "Teyra has been anxious to meet Rivenlea's newest Dragon," he says quickly, but I don't miss the meaningful glance he darts at Teyra. Like she ought to rein it in.

Like Emmy is getting a little suspicious.

I'm about to request an explanation, but Teyra gets there first. "Yes, yes. How exciting that Novem XVII is finally complete. Captain Doyle has been waiting ever so long." Her emerald eyes fill with tears.

My gaze narrows. "Close with Rhyan, are you?"

Teyra's response is to start heading around the counter toward me. She's taller than I expect. Willowy and graceful. "The captain and I have done business before, but it's not that." She puts her hands on my shoulders and holds me at arm's length. Inspecting me. "It's the completeness, Emmy. Can I call you Emmy?"

"I . . . yes."

"Novem XVII has been incomplete for so long. And to finally have the missing piece fall into its perfectly fitted place is . . ." She puts her hand to her heart again and bows her head. Overcome.

I try not to recoil at the bald display of emotion. I remind myself I don't know or understand Harmony culture. I don't even know or understand Rivenlite culture.

I barely understand Earthling culture.

Not everyone is as walled-off as I am, and maybe I should take a leaf from Teyra's tree.

Or whatever.

"Right. The completeness," I manage awkwardly.

"Teyra." Hadeon begins to fiddle with a glass vial full of bubbly red liquid. "Emmy would like to . . ." He lowers his voice as though we're standing in a crowded room where anyone might overhear us.

The only danger I can discern is if Teyra's tincture bottles somehow have ears and are interested in our business.

"Emmy would like to know about the Silvarum. Can you help us?"

Teyra draws back. She closes her eyes and inhales a deep breath. "Silvarum." Her eyes slowly open. "I get many of my ingredients on the outskirts of the Silvarum. I'm not allowed to cross the threshold, same as anyone else. But I have . . . seen things."

"What kinds of things?" I press.

"I know, perhaps better than others, why the Silvarum is forbidden." Teyra shares another look with Hadeon, and something unspoken passes between them.

Hadeon turns to me. "Teyra will take us to the outskirts."

"To the outskirts and no farther, for that is all I can offer." She wraps her long fingers around my face and tilts my head upward so she can look me straight in the eyes. "Oh, but how you favor her."

My heart kicks. "I never thought we looked alike. Our hair—"

"Is different, to be sure. But the rest." Teyra shakes her head, then turns to Hadeon. "The ghosts of our past have come to haunt us at last."

THIS WAS A MISTAKE.

I'm picking through the back alleys of Castramore with two near-strangers, trying to avoid notice. Ignoring the librarian's instructions, flouting my friends' advice. Breaking laws, probably.

What happens if you break a law in Rivenlea? Do they have due process? Rights to a fair trial by one's peers?

I glance at the two superheroes leading me, one literally green and making flowers bloom as we pass, the other producing a pleasant breeze to cool us as we walk.

I don't even *have* peers in Rivenlea.

"All well, Emmy?" Hadeon says over his shoulder.

"Just wondering if Rivenlites practice capital punishment."

"Oh, dear, what an odd musing." Teyra plucks a leaf from a plant growing between two cobblestones in the path. She holds it to her nose and inhales deeply. "There will be three more weeks until fall subsides."

And they think I'm the odd one.

"Don't worry, Emmy." Hadeon offers his hand as we step off the path and down an embankment, headed toward part of the forest I don't recognize. "We are not breaking any codes or statutes. But it's wise to remain discreet if you don't wish to answer questions."

I do not wish to answer questions, so I scurry along after my two coconspirators and wish I had listened to Wistlee.

Teyra is leading us through a maze of brush. There's no path, so I have to watch my step and follow closely, lest I end up sprawled on my face in the dirt, as per usual.

But after a while of picking our way toward the Silvarum in silence, I get bored and ask Hadeon, "How did you two meet? Did you know each other before you moved in above Teyra's shop?"

"I should say so," Teyra answers, flashing a smile. "Hadeon and I were in Novem VI before we retired."

"Really?" I look at Hadeon. "So you did missions together?"

"Many." He smiles. "Do you remember *Dr. Jekyll*, Tey?"

She flings up a hand. "I'd like to forget, sir."

Hadeon laughs. "Jekyll and Hyde somehow managed to split into two characters, and it was a nightmare trying to convince Jekyll to take Hyde back into his mind."

"That sounds . . . intense."

"In the end, Teyra was the one who convinced him, but it took all her skills as a Harmony."

My eyes go wide. "You didn't drug him?"

They both laugh.

"Not her skills as an apothecary," Hadeon explains. "Her relational skills. Harmonies are peacemakers. The bleeding hearts of every Novem."

"Excuse me." Teyra makes a good effort to project annoyance, but I can tell she's faking.

Not for the first time, I wonder what Camille would be if she were born a Rivenlite. Not a Dragon like me, surely. Maybe a Harmony. Though it's hard to imagine my sister with green locks instead of blonde. Emerald eyes instead of blue.

Maybe a Muse?

I don't know too much about them, but they seem to be positive, friendly people. That sounds like Camille. Plus, they're humanoid, so it's a little easier to imagine her in that role.

"You said you'd tell me about your most memorable mission," I remind Hadeon.

Teyra stops for a moment but doesn't turn. Almost like my words have struck her.

Or pierced her.

But then she carries on as if nothing happened, inching us closer to the tree line.

"Another time," Hadeon says gently.

I'm left to wonder what kind of trauma that "memorable" mission produced for these two.

A few minutes later, Teyra stops suddenly. "Here," she says. "It's just in through here." Her lips purse. "Are you sure, Emmy? You are quite sure you want to see?"

"I think so." I don't know how to answer, since I don't know what I'm about to walk into. What if it's horrible? What if I *don't* want to see?

Too late now.

But as we tiptoe together into the trees, it's not immediately horrible. Only strange.

Much like in the other forests, the evergreens tower above us. Fragrant green needles block out most of the sunlight, and a blanket of underbrush covers the forest floor, creating a soft carpet of decomposing leaves and damp earth.

Teyra is paused just outside a break in that underbrush. A line glows faintly across the ground. It almost appears as though the brush has burned away around it, though surely that's not the case. Instead, perhaps the brush is repelled by some magical force.

"The border of the Silvarum," Teyra says. "This is the threshold we cannot cross without permission from the council."

"What would happen if we did?" The question surprises me, even though I'm the one who asked it. I definitely don't want to find out what would happen.

At least not from firsthand experience.

"If that threshold is crossed, the Elder Council would be alerted immediately," Teyra answers. "I've done it accidentally, I'm sorry to say."

"Twice." Hadeon grins.

"Strictly an accident!" Teyra insists. "I was collecting a rather rare herb and noticed a large patch just inside the Silvarum. I did not realize I was crossing the threshold until it was too late."

"Twice."

Teyra casts a glare at Hadeon I'm sure is meant to be fierce, but it's like a friendly squirrel trying to be fearsome.

"In any case," she says to me, "council had mercy on me. I'm known to them, and of course they understand about my livelihood and the service I provide to the community of Castramore. I was not punished."

"But maybe third time's the charm?" Hadeon's eyes glint mischievously.

"Do ignore Hadeon, Emmy. Laughter only encourages him."

I clear my throat and do my best not to encourage him.

"I do not think the Elder Council would look kindly upon us right now." Teyra frowns at the barrier. "We really ought not be here without permission."

Suddenly it isn't so difficult to hold in my laughter.

"But I would like to show you something." Teyra traipses deeper into the woods, carefully avoiding the glowing barrier.

Hadeon and I follow, and Hadeon becomes unsettlingly quiet and sober. Every step ties the knots in my stomach tighter.

"Here," Teyra says finally. She faces the Silvarum.

As I do the same, I gasp.

Within the trees, nestled among trunks of towering evergreens and graceful deciduous varieties, iridescent bubbles undulate. They hover just above the forest floor and stretch about eight feet tall. Some are even taller, a few smaller, but most measure the same size and shape.

As if a giant has blown bubbles with a massive wand and left them floating in this strange forest.

But as I begin to wrap my mind around these bubbles, I notice what's inside.

And just about lose my mind.

In fact, I think I've already lost my mind and somehow poured it into these bubbles.

"These are . . ." I can't finish what I'm thinking. My thoughts no longer feel safe. Or like they belong to me at all.

Because these bubbles are filled with them.

I see, trapped within, creatures I tinkered with in my imagination as a child. A winged cat I thought would be cool, until I realized having cat claws flying through the air would be awful.

And beside it, suspended in one of the largest bubbles, is the porcupine-giraffe combo I thought would be so funny when I was seven. Now I feel terrible for the poor thing.

There are human characters too. Half-formed ideas or poorly conceived side characters or redshirts I didn't give much thought to—I only needed them to fill out a battle scene so we could have some bodies hit the ground without losing any of my *real* characters. The redshirts are frozen in suspended animation.

It's grotesque and disturbing, and I want nothing more than to sprint back home to the safety of the cabin.

Instead, I finally find my words. "These are my ideas. My thoughts from childhood. They're . . ." A sick realization hits as I think about Princess Brielle Song and Queen Veronica in Ambryfell, the story sphere that shouldn't exist. I stare at the bubbles in the Silvarum. "These are half-formed spheres."

I look almost imploringly at Teyra. "I don't understand." At the impassive, albeit sympathetic, look on her face, I switch to Hadeon. "Why are these here? Why are my half-baked ideas *here?*"

"Emmy, the Silvarum has been a mystery in Rivenlea for almost twenty years. This used to be a normal part of a regular forest, and suddenly strange things began to occur."

A thought strikes me. "Almost twenty, as in . . . nineteen? Eighteen?"

I'm not sure I want to hear the answer.

"No, seventeen. I suspect"—he glances at the idea bubbles—"the Elder Council will be the ones asking *you* to explain."

THE ENTIRE TREK BACK TO

the outskirts of Castramore is spent mentally running through explanations I might give the Elder Council.

My brain somehow accidentally connected to Rivenlea through . . . the stars? The internet? I'm accidentally plugged in to the sphere grid so that my thoughts become reality in the Rivenlea Sphere?

I picture the sphere map in Ambryfell—with the Rivenlea Sphere at the center and spokes connecting to smaller story spheres.

Am *I* somehow the Rivenlea Sphere?

The sphere is supposed to be like a planet, but instead, if it's a person and that person is me, perhaps all my thoughts end up trapped in bubbles in the forest or else in glass spheres in the official library.

But no explanation comes close to making sense, let alone satisfying the many questions swirling around in my head. I try to employ my best world-building tactics to figure out what could possibly explain the ever-growing list of strange occurrences.

And all I can come up with is that I'm literally insane and this is a delusion.

None of it is really happening.

If I've fallen into the "it's all a dream" cliché, I quit.

"Here we are," Hadeon says, making me jerk to a halt.

I look around and realize we've reached the edge of the city and the darkness of night is fast approaching.

"We're currently due north of Castramore," Hadeon explains, "and the barracks are east. If you follow the edge of the trees, you'll run straight into them."

I nod, my brain still flicking through what I might say to the council, if I even get the chance. "Thanks." I gather myself and turn to Teyra. "And thank you for showing me the Silvarum. At least what you could."

Teyra takes both my hands in hers, her green eyes glittering again. "I wish I could bring you across the threshold and lead you to the answers you seek. But it is, at least, a start." She wraps me in a hug that smells like fresh-turned earth and the snapped ends of fluid-filled stems.

I feel as though I'm being embraced by an affectionate bean sprout.

After Teyra and Hadeon head into the city, I wait a few moments, a sense of aimlessness and confusion settling over me like a dense fog. But then I shake myself free and force my feet to obey, stepping along the path that will eventually lead me home.

Most of the journey is filled with vaguely troubling thoughts about those poor creatures caught in idea bubbles—how I'm basically an unwitting animal abuser and human enslaver for suspending them there—and before I know it, I'm standing at the front door of my cabin.

My cozy little home, nestled in the trees. The dying sun casts green, leaf-filtered light across the door.

Acute dread washes over me as I turn the knob.

Wistlee is sitting on the couch with Phen. They both swivel to look at me. I close the door gently into its frame, as though being very quiet will allow me to sneak in unnoticed.

Even though they're both staring at me.

My gaze lands on a very conspicuous pair of boots—new boots. Ones that appear to be just my size sitting by the front door. The boots from the shoemaker. The ones I lied to my friends about, saying I was picking them up after training.

The boots accuse me—try me, convict me, sentence and execute me.

My friends know I've lied, and now it's time to come clean.

"Hey," I begin.

"And so I might as well be running a dog-fighting ring," I finish, "because those poor things are trapped in bubbles and have been for years, so I'm basically the worst."

The crease that has parked itself between Wistlee's brows since I began spilling everything grows a fraction deeper. "I do not know what a dog-fighting ring is."

"Just as well," I say dejectedly. "There's people in there too."

Wistlee rises and begins to circle the room. I suppose she's pacing while she thinks, but it looks more like a graceful glide, because Wist just can't stop being ethereal and gorgeous, even when she's anxious.

"I'm sorry," I say for the fortieth time. "I shouldn't have done any of it. I don't know what's wrong with me."

"You just want answers," Phen says. "It's understandable."

He's been making excuses for me the whole time. And while his loyalty is admirable, I wish he would just admit I made a stupid choice.

And that I'm the worst.

I glance up at my roommate. Wist has stopped circling.

"You are clearly connected to Rivenlea in a way that is . . . unique," she says.

"Clearly."

"And we don't know why or how."

"I guess it started with your sister?" Phen offers.

"But it didn't. I had thought so, too, but some of those ideas in the bubbles were from years before Camille disappeared." I raise an eyebrow at him. "Flying cats? A porcupine-giraffe? I was very young."

He grins. "Okay, that's fair." Then the humor falls from his face. "So it started earlier."

"Much earlier. The flying cats were my first attempt at a story."

"At what age?" Wistlee asks.

"Maybe kindergarten?" I can't recall for sure. "And besides, Hadeon said strange things started happening seventeen years ago."

"When you were born," Wistlee observes. "You are intrinsically connected to this place."

"But why? Why in the world would I be? Hadeon and Teyra kept implying the answers I seek are in the Silvarum, but we can't get in. Not until we cut through a mile of red tape with the Elder Council. And even then, I get the impression from Rizak they may very well deny my request to enter."

I pause and bite my lip. "Maybe I could fly Frank into the forest?"

Wistlee shakes her head. "It would still sound the alarm. The barrier appears on the ground, but it extends up infinitely."

Of course. Makes sense, otherwise I could just hop right over it. A little leap, and I'd be in the Silvarum, and what kind of security is that?

Phen jumps to his feet suddenly. His hands twist together, and beads of sweat break out across his upper lip. "Oh, no."

Wistlee and I watch him for a moment, waiting for him to continue.

But he doesn't speak again. Instead, his chest rises and falls rhythmically, and after about twenty beats, I realize he's counting his breaths. Trying to calm himself. Stave off a panic attack.

"Phen." The astonishment is clear in my voice. "You have anxiety."

He wipes sweat onto the back of his hand and blows out a long breath. "Is it that obvious?"

"Probably only to someone else who has it." I've used

controlled breathing techniques to quell a panic attack more times than I can count.

"I'd appreciate it if you could keep that information to yourself, though." He takes another slow breath.

"Why? I mean, not that I would tell anyone, anyway," I amend quickly. "But why the secrecy? There's nothing to be ashamed of."

He snorts, but it's filled with derisive self-loathing. "A Sentinel with an anxiety disorder? A guardian who panics at the drop of a hat—sometimes for no reason at all? Have you ever heard of anything more ridiculous?"

"A Gryphon who can't fly, perhaps," Wistlee says with a small smile.

"And a Dragon who . . . isn't." I indicate my human-skinned arms.

The warmth returns to his face, and his eyes crinkle at the corners. "Okay. Maybe that."

But then he starts to twist his hands together again.

"What's bothering you, Phen?" I say, rising to get him a glass of water from the kitchen.

"It's just . . . we had a visitor during training today. Stacia Chasvoy." He glances at Wistlee. "Do you know of her?"

"I don't think so." Wistlee thinks a moment. "She is not a current Novemite?"

"No, retired Sentinel. She was showing us some things about creating gateways, but I think it was mostly for me. Since I'll be doing it for the first time for real when we head to Oz. But she said something that came to mind just now."

"What?" I encourage him.

"Well, she said something about gateways allowing us into story spheres. Then she corrected herself and said they allow us to circumvent barriers. I thought the phrasing was strange, so it stuck with me."

"It is strange," Wistlee agrees. "I've not heard spheres described as barriers before."

"But I suppose it's true," I chime in. "They're like glass bubbles, sort of. So we must have to cross a barrier to get into them?" I look back and forth between the two actual Rivenlites in the room. "I mean, right? It makes sense?"

"I suppose," Wistlee says slowly. "It's still a strange way to say it."

"But it's a good thing she did, because it's given me an idea." Phen's hands twist all the more. "I mean, maybe it's a good thing. Or a very bad thing, because this idea could get us in loads of trouble if we're caught."

"Tell me more." I don't even recognize myself right now. The phrase "loads of trouble" is not something that would usually pique my interest.

"Well, Hadeon and Teyra said crossing the barrier would sound the alarm, right?"

"Yes."

"What if we didn't cross it? What if we made a gateway inside the Silvarum?"

"And circumvented the barrier," Wistlee says softly.

Phen is sweating again. "It's a bad idea, right?"

"Depends on what you mean by that." I hold out my hand. "Brilliant idea. Definitely could work." Then I hold out the other. "Might get us exiled from Rivenlea if we're caught."

"Stars." Wistlee starts pacing again.

"I mean, you guys could always come back to Earth with me. We'd have to deal with my mom, and that would be . . . Yeah, never mind. Better to face the dungeon here."

My friends chuckle, but the room fills with tension again almost immediately.

"I'll do it," Phen says abruptly. "Emmy, if you want me to try, I will make a gateway for you."

Something swells in my heart, and I jump up and throw my arms around him, then let go before it gets weird. Right now, I'm 68 percent sure this is *not* a YA novel, and even if it is a novel, I'm not about to create an Emotional Dilemma for the sake of it.

Some bonds really are just about friendship.

Before I can squash it, a thought pops into my head: would

Laramie create a gateway and maybe get exiled for me? I roll my eyes at myself. What a cliché I've become.

Putting my hands on Phen's shoulders, I meet his gaze. "Phen, I can't let you take that risk for me. It's not worth you getting in trouble. I appreciate your willingness. So much, truly. But I can't let you."

But then Wistlee's quiet words surprise me. "That is for Phen to decide. For Phen and me. We have all the information. We know the risks. You must allow us to decide whether we feel they are risks worth taking."

Boundaries.

"But I can't let you do this. We . . ." I'm about to remind them we just met. Seventeen days I've been here. They shouldn't be taking such risks for me.

Yet it doesn't feel true that we just met. Maybe it's the overall strangeness of the situation we find ourselves in, but I already feel bonded to these two for life.

Maybe they feel the same.

"Getting caught would be bad," Phen agrees. "But we won't get caught." He tosses me a smile. "I know how to do this, and I'm sure it's going to work. The more I think about it, the surer I am. You deserve to find answers, Emmy. If those answers could be in that forest, then I want to help."

Tears sting my eyes. "I don't know what to say."

"Say we'll make a gateway tomorrow after training." Phen's smile grows wider. "We'll be back in time for supper, probably."

I can't help but smile back. "Thanks, Phen."

"I will go too," Wistlee says, and Phen and I both turn to her.

"Wist, seriously?"

"I am not much inclined to bend the rules, let alone break them. But, as the proper channels have proven somewhat ineffective, and as we will be leaving any moment for Oz, I think this is . . . permissible. Perhaps this once." Now Wist is smiling too. "I can make peace with it, anyway."

She crosses our tiny living room and takes my hand. "You will have my wings. Well"–her eyes twinkle–"the functional one, at least."

28

LARAMIE'S WOODEN TRAINING

sword is stayed a hair's breadth from my throat, the clunky "blade" threatening to leave a splinter in my trachea.

I glare up at him, irritated that he's managed to sweep my legs out from under me and land me flat on my back in the dirt. "Do you mind? I'd like to stand."

He eyes me, holding me captive a half second longer. Then he gets to his feet and offers me a hand. "You're distracted today."

"No, I'm not," I lie. Defensive, even though he's right.

"Yes, you are. You're doing worse than you did on your very first day."

"Thanks."

"No offense," he says congenially. "But usually you at least give me a decent workout."

"Again—you are too kind."

"Hey, I think it's saying something for how new you are to this." He glances at me. "If I have to shift to get the upper hand, you're doing something right. You know?"

Neither of us mentions that he hasn't had to shift once today. Because my mind is far away, thinking about the gateway Phen will create in just a little while. My thoughts are trapped in bubbles in the Silvarum, and I can't free them long enough to figure out where Laramie plans to smack me next.

The mildly pulsating welts on my arms and legs bear witness.

"Do you want to talk about it?"

The offer surprises me so much, I almost do. I almost spill everything about the Silvarum and my plan with Phen and Wistlee to gateway into it this afternoon.

But he'd tell Rhyan, surely, and then I would get my friends in trouble without finding any answers.

Except his chocolate eyes are right in front of me, inviting me to be honest. Assuring me I can trust him.

"It's nothing. I'm fine."

He holds my gaze a moment longer than necessary. Always longer than necessary.

"Well, if you care to be open for a minute, I'm here." His words are a little harsh, but his tone is light.

Teasing me and calling me out in one breath. How does he do that?

"I'm fine," I insist, then I notice Phen doing a terrible job of being subtle, waving me over toward the back doors of Ambryfell.

Rhyan has dismissed Novem XVII, and it's time to see what our Sentinel can do.

"I've got to go."

"I'm sure you do." Laramie hasn't missed Phen's gesturing, and he's surveying us both with keen eyes. "See you later."

He shifts into a hawk and launches himself into the sky.

And only then does it occur to me that in Rivenlea, one might have an Echo spying on them at any time—an inconspicuous hairbrush lying on a dresser, a plate of sandwiches on the dining hall table, a friendly alley cat trailing one through the streets.

Or a hawk, soaring above it all, observing whatever deviant behavior he wishes.

"Would he break your trust in that way?" Wistlee asks after I've shared my Echo concerns with her and Phen.

"It's Laramie. We don't have trust. We hate each other."

Phen doesn't even try to control his laughter. "Right. Deep hatred. Clearly can't stand each other."

"It almost sounds like you're mocking me."

He merely grins.

"Shall we begin in our cabin, then?" Wistlee suggests. "It's private, at least."

I nod. "That'll work. The only way he would see us in the Silvarum is if the trees aren't thick enough to provide cover and if he already suspects that's where we're going. And how could he?"

Unless he's already been spying on me.

But he wouldn't . . . would he?

I still haven't decided whether that's something consistent with his character when we reach our house. I don't know him well enough to know his heart. I know his arrogance, his flirtation, his confusing moments of tenderness, his embarrassing . . . frankness.

But do I know his heart?

No more time to think about it now.

Phen is warming up his hands and wrists like he's preparing to enter a cage fight. I've only ever seen Sentinels acting as guardians, turning themselves to stone during training. I've not witnessed gateway creation, so I have no idea what to expect.

"Here goes nothing," Phen says, voice shaking slightly.

His eyes drift closed. He inhales a deep breath. His right hand lights up. He crouches low and begins to draw an arc in the air—from the ground up to the midpoint of the curve, like half a rainbow. Then he takes another breath, and his left hand begins to glow. He mirrors the movement on the other side, completing the full archway.

Because that's what it is. A glowing archway—like the one I followed Frank into, but more visible. In the park back home, the gateway shimmered like heat waves, there from one angle, gone from another.

This arch is lit up like a supernova happening underwater—glowing a shade of blue, bright and deep.

I catch a breath.

Phen opens his eyes and seems to be a bit startled himself. I'm not sure that bodes well. "Well, I guess it worked."

"Appears so." Wistlee inspects the gateway from every angle. "Shall we?"

"I've never gone through one I created." Phen eyes the gateway tentatively. "Only those created by far more experienced Sentinels."

"Well, I jumped through one that appeared out of nowhere in a world where it's not supposed to exist," I say. "Surely this will be safer?"

There's only one way to find out.

Before one of my friends can volunteer to do the deed, I leap through Phen's first proper gateway.

And tumble into the forest of my childhood imagination.

IT SEEMED LIKE A GOOD IDEA

at the time.

When I was seven, the thought of trees made entirely of glitter was enchanting. How sparkly they'd be. How magical! How fun!

But now, as I've just tumbled out of Phen's gateway and rolled to a stop beneath what appears to be a glitter tree, I'm rethinking my life choices.

Because this tree sheds glitter like a deciduous tree sheds leaves, and I'm lying in a pile of sparkle that's never going to come off my clothes. How will I explain this? I'll have to burn them.

Wistlee arrives next, using her feathered wing to glide to a stop gracefully, one eyebrow arched in my direction. "Are you quite well?"

I hitch onto my side and heave myself out of the glitter pile. "Just dandy."

Phen stumbles through the archway but manages to keep his footing, so I'm the only one covered in glitter.

Which is just as well, but kind of embarrassing.

"Wow." He looks up at the towering grove of sparkling nonsense—magenta, aqua, gold, an opalescent white that doesn't match the others but felt like the most magical color to me when I was seven.

Phen turns toward me, an unasked question on his face.

"I was a strange child," I say, brushing as much of the hot-pink glitter from my pants as I can.

"Halt!"

I whirl at the intruding voice, nearly having a heart attack.

The owner of the voice is sprinting toward us, and I half expect to see him pull a sword from a scabbard. We're dead—absolutely toast. Caught glitter-handed. Probably about to be executed by some guard.

But as he gets closer, I realize he is definitely not a soldier. At least he's not dressed as one, and he's not brandishing a weapon. Instead, he looks like a middle-aged guy who works in tech and is on vacation. On his way to a safari, probably.

His sleeves are rolled up past his elbows, and slung around his hips is a utility belt of some sort. Tools and glass vials stoppered with corks dangle from the belt.

The contents of the vials glint in the sunlight, and I realize they're full of glitter.

What in the world of sparkles . . . ?

"Don't touch anything!" the man shouts, holding out his hands like we're velociraptors he's attempting to clicker-train.

His warning comes a second too late.

Phen has reached up to examine the lowest-hanging branch of a golden glitter tree. The moment his fingers make contact, the branch explodes in an impressive shower of shimmer.

If Phen ever wondered what he'd look like gilt, well . . . now he knows. His hair is no longer inky black but sparkly gold. His fawn-colored skin? Sparkly gold. Clothes? Sparkly gold.

The stranger sighs. "I told you not to."

Phen spits out glitter. "Not fast enough!"

"What exactly does 'halt' mean to you?" The man huffs, then he turns to me and Wistlee. "What are you doing here?"

My brain cycles through a hundred lies we could tell, but I don't particularly want to lie. We're busted anyway if he turns us in. "We were just . . . collecting information."

"Fellow scientists?" He eyes Wistlee, his mouth pressing into a tight line. "You look like Novemites."

My heart lifts slightly.

He nods to me. "Except you."

I deflate.

"We are," Wistlee acknowledges. "We're investigating some strange occurrences in this forest—and Rivenlea at large."

The man snorts. "Well, for strange occurrences, you're in the right place. The Silvarum is full to bursting with those. And thank goodness, else I'd be out of a job."

He approaches Phen, initially appearing like he's going to help Phen de-glitter himself. Phen holds out his arms, obviously grateful for the assistance. But then the man whips out an empty glass vial and begins collecting a small sample off Phen's forehead. When he steps back, our poor Sentinel is no less golden than he was before.

"I'll take this back to my lab for cataloging, even though I didn't actually need it," he says with a sharp look at Phen.

Phen's only response is to spit out another wad of glitter.

"Council should've told me," the stranger mumbles, tucking the vial into a pouch on his belt. "They usually let me know."

Phen's eyes widen under the glitter, and Wistlee looks like she's about to say something, but I quickly signal her.

Keep quiet.

The man is scribbling in a field notebook, glancing repeatedly at Phen, then scribbling more every few seconds.

I can see Phen's annoyance under the thick layer of glitter, and I bite my lip to quell a laugh.

"So, you're researching these trees?" I say to the stranger.

"Yes, have been for years." He scribbles some more. "Supposed to be figuring out how they work, exactly. Where they came from. Why they exist." He glances up from his pad. "Dr. Vid Kalin, by the way. Sparkophytologist."

I stare blankly. "You're a . . . glitter botanist."

His brows crinkle. "Sparkophytologist."

"Right."

"Council tasked me with studying, cataloging, researching, and dissecting these trees many years ago."

"About ten?"

"Yes, about ten years." He looks at me sideways. "Council told you?"

"Something like that." I could answer one of his questions for him—where these trees came from. Because they most definitely came from my childish imagination.

The how is another matter entirely, and that's what Wistlee, Phen, and I are here to find out.

But I decide not to hand this poor sparkophytologist more questions than he's already piled up.

"We won't keep you," I say. "And we promise not to touch any more trees."

Dr. Kalin hands me a cloth from a pocket on his belt. "Here. Use this for your trousers."

The cloth seems like it's charged with a special sort of static electricity that collects glitter. My pants are cleaned with a few careful brushes.

Phen waves a gilded hand. "Hello?"

Dr. Kalin sighs. "There aren't enough collection cloths in the world, son."

But he does pull another two clean cloths from his pouch, and we do our best to at least clear Phen's face so he can breathe without inhaling glitter.

"It will fall off somewhat as you move about," Dr. Kalin assures Phen. "Sort of."

"Great."

"I did try to warn you," Dr. Kalin says, then addresses me. "Good luck on your quest. Whatever it is."

"Thank you. Good luck with . . . this." I gesture toward the trees. "I hope you find all the answers you're looking for."

He nods. "Likewise. If you find anything you think might be pertinent, report to the Elder Council, and they will inform me."

Then he snorts and shakes his head. "At least they're supposed to. Anyway, they know where to deliver my mail." He vaguely indicates the forest.

"Thank you, Dr. Kalin." Wistlee bows her head. "Might you be able to direct us northward?"

"The northwest part of the Silvarum," I clarify. "I think."

Dr. Kalin nods. "Head this way." He points. "You'll hit a small village shortly. From the village, head west." He shows us which way is west.

"I'm sorry, village?" Wistlee's eyes are wide. "Others live in the Silvarum? I've not heard this before."

"One other researcher and one . . . er, caretaker. But the village is—well, you'll see. Due north." He points again. "It's very small. Mind your steps. Cheers."

He wanders off, field notes in hand, scribbling every twenty paces.

Phen shakes his head. And is rewarded with a small cascade of glitter from his hair. He makes a face.

I pat him on the back as we begin our trek north. "Just think of it as really fancy dandruff."

THE SILVARUM IS LIKE ANY

other forest—most of the time. Fragrant evergreens have been keeping us company since we left Dr. Kalin and his glitter trees.

Or my glitter trees, I guess.

And since the sparkles faded into the distance behind us, the Silvarum has been quite normal.

Until this moment.

I'm currently staring at what can only be described as a mushroom cottage. Literally. A door is cut into the stalk. The large cap serves as a roof. The gills underneath the cap are as long as my arm, and still, it's a small dwelling.

"Is this the village?" Wistlee's brows knot. "Surely when Dr. Kalin said to mind our steps, he did not think we would step on this?"

"Only if—" I stop as a man climbs from the mushroom door, unfolding his massive frame from within the fungus dwelling. "Only if we were giants," I say.

And at first, he really seems to be. But when he clears the underside of the mushroom cottage and draws up to his full height, I guess he's about seven and a half feet tall. Huge, though not like a mythical giant.

But almost.

He sees us and starts. "What're you buttons doing here?"

His gaze lands on Phen, and the surprise melts from his face, replaced with sharp annoyance. "Vid sent you? Tell him to stay *off* my turf. I don't need his nonsense here. I do serious research. Serious!"

Phen shakes his head. "No one sent us. We—"

But the mushroom man takes one long stride and grabs Phen by the shirt. He gives him a good shake—probably meant to be gentle, but it knocks Phen's teeth together—and a glimmering shower rains down around him.

"*Seeds!*" the mushroom man bellows.

"Stop!" Wistlee sails between them and uses her forearm to knock the man's hand from Phen's shirt. "Hands off him."

Mushroom Man lifts his palms in surrender. "I'm sorry." He shakes his head. "But Vid needs to stay in his own part of the Silvarum. That's the agreement."

"Dr. Kalin didn't send us or the . . . seeds." I raise a brow at the sparkles on the forest floor.

"Ooh, *Dr.* Kalin." He wiggles his thick fingers and rolls his eyes. "Fancy. You know, my research is important too!"

"Look," I start, taking a step toward Mushroom Man, hoping to calm him. But I don't get a chance.

He bellows and scoops me up before I can blink.

Wistlee is trying to intervene again, both wings unfolded in panic as she beats against Mushroom Man's back. But he barely seems to notice.

"You almost killed them!" His big green eyes fill with tears. "How could you?"

"I . . ." Honestly don't know what to say. But then I look down, right at where I was about to step.

A collection of mushrooms sits just beneath us. And looking at them now, it's a wonder I missed them. The bright red caps make them fairly obvious.

And then I remember.

"Talking mushrooms," I say softly.

Mushroom Man sets me down, well away from the cache. "Of course."

Wistlee and Phen are staring at me with matching quizzical expressions.

"I thought it would be funny," I say weakly.

"You're a small giant," Phen says, casting a wary glance at Mushroom Man.

"Or a large man, thank you very much." He shakes his head. "Buttons. And anyway, what're you doing here if Vid didn't send you to scatter seeds on my turf?"

He doesn't wait for us to answer as he lowers himself to the forest floor, getting on eye level with the red-capped mushrooms. "Hello, littles. How are we today?" His gaze swings upward to us. "Well? You didn't answer my question."

"Are you talking to us or the mushrooms?" I ask as I watch him scoot on his belly to get a different angle.

"I'm Topher," he says, ignoring my question. "Topher Rys, and these are my crimcaps. Watch your step there. That's the jellis patch." He points to a fallen log covered in mushrooms. "My shiitakes. Do please, if you can be bothered, watch your steps. To them, *you're* the giants." He shoots Phen a look.

"We'll be more careful," I say.

"Good. You gave them quite a fright."

Wistlee darts a glance at me. "So you . . . speak to them?"

"Of course. What else is a fungalinguist supposed to do? It's my life's work. To learn the language of the mushrooms." He climbs slowly to his feet. "It *is* serious scholarship. I don't care what Vid says, and don't you listen to him either. I'm a scientist too!"

"Oh—of course you are," I offer.

"They have many different dialects, you know, and it's just as much an art as a science. Language is that way. I've finally got the crimcaps' written alphabet well in hand. They can't write it, of course, on account of not having hands or mouths or brains, but I'm really onto something here. Sporroglyphics—huge breakthrough."

"You must have them dictate an oral history of their kind," Wistlee suggests, and Phen has to hide his guffaw under a phony cough.

"That actually is my next project!"

I look at him, torn between bewilderment and guilt. I created this bizarre area of study for this poor man, and I can't help feeling sorry for him.

"I don't hear anything."

We all turn to the sound of Phen's voice. His ear is pressed against a cluster of shiitakes popping out from the log.

"Spores!" Topher moves faster than a man his size ought to be able to, diving toward Phen and pulling him away from the mushrooms. "They're *sleeping*," he scolds, as though this were completely obvious and Phen is the rudest person alive.

"Mr. Rys, sir, which direction is west?" Leave it to Wistlee to stay focused.

He waves a meaty hand. "Thataway." He's brushing glitter off the shiitakes, glaring at Phen. "Seeds," he mutters.

"We shall continue on our quest and leave your, ah, village in peace." Wistlee gracefully gestures to the clusters of mushrooms, and I now realize there are dozens of them.

"Yes, yes. Good to meet you. Enjoy your questing. Watch out for the cats. It's autumn already."

"We . . . Okay, thanks," I say. Does he mean flying cats? What does autumn have to do with anything? But it doesn't seem worth it to ask.

We gingerly pick our way through the forest surrounding Topher Rys's mushroom cottage, careful to avoid patches of fungus. Questioning our sanity the whole way.

Or maybe that's just me.

But I only have about five minutes to think on it. The Silvarum isn't large, and it's not long before I see a glint up ahead. The shimmer and sheen of large bubbles.

We've reached the grove of my unformed ideas.

"I saw this from the outside," I say softly as we get closer, again struck by the strangeness, the grotesqueness.

And the embarrassment.

Some writerly thoughts ought never see the light of day. Strange imaginings better left trapped in spiral notebooks. Random musings we self-edit into oblivion.

And here mine are, sitting out in the open for all to see. For all to judge.

The first bubble that comes into clear focus is a frog-shaped creature that looks like it's made of liquid glitter.

"What's with you and glitter?" Phen asks.

"I was a child," I say, face reddening.

"A sparkly child, apparently."

I throw a halfhearted glare at him and trudge forward. "These are more recent ideas."

"Maybe they are organized by date of creation," Wistlee muses.

"The ones along the outer edge of the Silvarum were from when I was really little. So that might make sense."

"Which means the glitter frogs were recent." Phen grins.

My face is now aflame. "I said *more* recent. I stopped writing a long time ago." I push ahead a little faster, just to escape glitter-frog judgment.

But I freeze almost immediately. Stunned into stillness by the shock of what's before me.

I've longed for this moment for so many years. Wished on so many stars. Prayed, even, unsure if God could hear me. Convinced that if he could, he definitely wouldn't want to listen to me or help me. Or turn his face toward me and my family and our suffering.

And yet, here she is, just as I'd hoped. Golden hair pulled into a ponytail, summer-tanned skin just as I remember.

Camille.

My Camille. My dearest, truest friend.

My sister.

I feel an arm at my back, and I realize my knees have given out. Phen has caught me. Wistlee's leathery wing is out, supporting me. Trying to right me, to steady me.

They can't know, of course, but I'm sure they've guessed.

The blonde-haired, blue-green-eyed twelve-year-old girl standing before us is my yearned-for Camille.

And she's suspended in time inside one of my bubbles, her mouth frozen open in a surprised *O*.

31

SURELY WE'RE LATE FOR

supper already.

I don't know how many hours it's been. I'm not Rivenlite. I don't measure time by the position of the sun in the sky, and how do seasons work here, anyway? Where on the planet are we? What sun are we circling?

Who knows. Who cares.

I need to find Rhyan, and the only place I know she could be is the dining hall.

Wistlee and Phen hurry after me, throwing words of caution ahead, as though they could rein me in and slow me down, but my blood is on fire, and I need to find Rhyan.

"Emmy, let's talk about this," Phen calls.

"Please, Emmy. Let's not get you banished from Rivenlea," Wistlee pleads.

But what does it matter?

What sort of place is this? My sister—my flesh-and-blood sister—has been trapped in a bubble, suspended in time, for seven years and . . . no one noticed? No one cared?

More than ever, I'm not sure I want to be here. Banish me. Send me home. At least the Earthly police were trying to find Camille.

This place may be the cruelest of all.

I ignore my friends' cries and burst into Ambryfell, storm down the hallway, and thunder into the dining hall.

It's full. Every Novemite is here, it seems, working on dinner. I spot Rhyan's silky black hair almost immediately. She's sitting between Canon and Laramie, their heads down, deep in conversation.

At least, they were, until I blasted into the room and startled them.

Now their heads, along with everyone else's, swivel toward me.

For once in my life, I'm too angry, too distraught, to shrivel beneath unwanted attention.

I halt behind Rhyan, vaguely noticing the whole Novem—except my delinquent crew—is nearby, and I begin to wonder if we missed a meeting.

Doesn't matter. Focus, Emmy.

"Did you know?" I blurt.

Rhyan's eyes pop. A hush descends. Everyone stares.

Don't care.

"Did I know what?" Rhyan's brows knit together in confusion.

"I was just in the Silvarum. You know, the bizarre forest of strange happenings that are somehow tied to my imagination."

Rhyan rises, face taut. "You were where?" Her gaze bounces to the sheepish Gryphon and Sentinel shuffling in behind me.

"It's not their fault. It's mine." I force myself into her line of sight. "I did this, and now I understand why everyone wanted me to stay out."

Rhyan draws herself up to her full height. "It's not that anyone wanted you to stay out. But there's a procedure—"

"To the abyss with your procedure!"

Her eyes flare. "Careful, Dragon."

My fists curl. Oh, that they had Dragon claws. "No. You can't tell me to be careful. Not after what I just saw."

"What did you see?"

I'm not sure her bewilderment is real. "As if you don't know."

"I don't. I haven't been in the Silvarum for years. I'm not allowed in either."

"From the moment I arrived in Rivenlea, you've dodged my questions about Camille, been cagey about your answers," I point out. "You knew I was looking for my sister, and you had to know she's right here—in the Silvarum."

Rhyan draws back as if slapped. "What?"

I hesitate. My voice gets trembly. "You're telling me you didn't know?"

She shakes her head. "I didn't know. I knew you had a special mental connection to Rivenlea—and because of that, you might know this place. I knew the Elder Council had information about your sister." She takes a quick glance around the room.

Everyone is watching. Laramie's gaze is fastened on me as if by bolts, and his mouth is slightly open.

Rhyan lowers her voice. "Are you telling me your sister is physically here? Where is she?"

"Trapped." Tears rise, and they choke my words and sting my eyes. "She's trapped in a . . . bubble." It sounds stupid. Ridiculous. But I don't know how else to describe it. "Frozen in time, stuck at twelve years old. I don't know if she's really alive."

"She is." Canon's voice startles me.

I slowly turn my head to him. I allow his declaration to sink in to every fiber of my being. "*You* knew?"

My only satisfaction is that Rhyan looks just as surprised—and at least half as betrayed—as I feel.

"I've been doing research for the Elder Council," he says as though it excuses him. "It's been a matter of utmost secrecy. I was not permitted to share with anyone, not even you, Captain."

"Oh. The Elder Council. Great." I want to throw things. "What else do you know? Fungalinguist is out of the bag now, might as well tell me everything."

Canon's eyes dart around the still-silent room. I've made it awkward for him, and I'm not proud of the satisfaction that brings me.

Well. I'm a little proud.

Canon clears his throat. "Camille is alive. Attempts to extract her from that enclosure have been unsuccessful. We believe she's trapped in stasis somehow."

"Stasis? You mean like Earth's 'happy stasis'?"

Everyone looks confused. At this moment, I'm angry enough to tell them just how broken my planet is, how colossally filled with darkness and suffering and wrongness. But I can't collect my thoughts into one coherent stream. If I could, I'd fire away.

"Great, so"—I tick off facts on my fingers—"I tell a story to my sister in a park on Earth. Somehow it creates a bubble of horrors here in Rivenlea. She ripples away, shredded to ribbons on my planet, and lands in one piece here, trapped in said bubble of horrors. She's frozen at twelve years old, alive but . . . aware?" I look to Canon for confirmation of that statement.

He shrugs. "Unclear."

I close my eyes and attempt to draw a full breath. "Canon, why did this happen?"

His face is serious. He seems slightly moved by the situation, but it's honestly hard to tell. Maybe it's a good thing that the Novemites equipped with lasers in their hands and eyes aren't prone to external emotional displays.

But right now, I need him to act like a human being. Or humanoid being. Or whatever.

My head hurts.

"Miss DuLaine, I know this is a difficult situation."

"Difficult?" For some reason, my gaze lands on Laramie.

He is a difficult situation. Potentially complicated—the swoony story boy who seems bent on turning my heart inside out at every opportunity when I'd much rather focus on other things. That is difficult.

My sister held captive and frozen in time, possibly aware all the while, is something else entirely.

"Forgive Canon for his pathetic, unfeeling choice of words." Rhyan glares fire at her friend, then tamps it down and turns back to me. "Emmy, believe me when I say I understand. Not from experience, perhaps, but you certainly have a right to be upset about Camille. I would be, were I in your place."

"Stop being reasonable and saying nice things!" I'm almost yelling. I want to keep my flames burning because the moment I allow them to be snuffed out by compassion and kind words, the grief will swamp me.

By the look on her face, Rhyan knows it. She pulls a long breath. "You have a right to be upset," she repeats quietly. "We will demand an audience with the Elder Council when we return."

"When we return?" I echo mindlessly, but I already know what she means.

"Yes," Rhyan says. "We leave for Oz in the morning."

We leave for Oz in the morning.

I don't know how I'm supposed to feel. Excited, I suppose. How many times did I imagine traveling to Oz as a child, thumbing through the magnificent corners of Baum's imagination as I read the Oz books?

Now that I've seen the quirky corners of my own imagination come to life, I'm not sure I want to step down this yellow brick road.

But I'm standing here, in front of every active Novemite, in front of my team. My friends. A spotlight is shining onto my insecurities. My fears. My shame. My otherness. I don't belong here, and neither does Camille, but this is where we are. For better or worse. And somehow it's my fault.

So, yes, I will go to Oz in the morning like I'm supposed to. I will try to help Novem XVII fix whatever's broken in Dorothy's world. Even though I'm not a real Dragon.

But, I silently promise Camille, *I will not give up. I will find a way to free you. Or I'll die trying.*

32

I GAZE DOWN AT MY
comfortable boots. The shoemaker did an excellent job. They're
fitted perfectly to my feet. I can move around in them, walk in
them, outmaneuver Laramie in them.

Well, maybe.

"Frank," I say, stroking her scaly neck with one hand while
she nibbles wyvern treats out of my other. They feel meaty and
gross, and I try not to think too hard about what I'm holding.
"Why is everything so messed up?"

Frank puffs a cloud of white smoke from her wide nostrils
as she slurps the final treat from my palm, leaving behind a
glistening puddle of wyvern spit.

I wipe my hand on my pants with a shudder. "Was that
absolutely necessary?"

She grunts and nuzzles my shoulder. I glance around the
mouths of the caves. All is silent at the hive—it's pretty early still,
and I just stole away for a minute while the rest of the Novem
was packing their bags. Wistlee and I packed last night, at her
insistence.

"Preparedness is the ultimate weapon against disaster,"
she'd said.

"Dramatic," I'd replied.

"An old Gryphon proverb," she'd responded with a smile, and I'm sure that's true, but it's also Wistlee's life motto, I think.

Since my only company besides Frank is a tiny sparrow winging its way toward the caves, I nuzzle Frank back. "I'm going to miss you, my beastly girl."

She responds with a love bite to my bicep that nearly draws blood.

"You could bring her with us, you know," says a voice from behind me.

I scream and spin around in time to watch as the sparrow expands, morphs, shifts into a tallish boy with dark gold hair, hot chocolate eyes, and the most obnoxious grin.

"Stop doing that!" I whisper harshly, as if I hadn't just screamed and disturbed anyone within earshot. "That should be illegal."

"You think I should be outlawed?" He holds a hand to his chest as if he is shocked, scandalized, and hurt by my words. "Emmy, how could you?"

I roll my eyes. "Not you. But—" I stop and glance at his jaw—take in the way he needs to shave and yet somehow that makes him look more perfect. I adjust. "No, I was right the first time. You should be outlawed."

He laughs. "I'm going to take that as a compliment."

"Don't."

"Too late." He nods to Frank. "May I?"

"May you what?"

"Say hello to Frank. I didn't want to interrupt your . . . conversation."

My cheeks heat, and I glare at him, but before I can respond and absolutely forbid him to get anywhere near my pet, Frank trots over to greet him.

Traitor.

She nuzzles up to him at least as affectionately as she was just nuzzling me, and I try to dismiss my irrational jealousy.

"What are you doing up here, anyway?" I ask as I pat Frank's flank. "I didn't think you had a pet wyvern."

"I don't. I visit Frank sometimes." He shoots me an impish glance. "Hope that's all right."

"And if it's not?"

He merely shrugs, and Frank gives me a look over her shoulder like I'd better not forbid her favorite person from coming to visit.

Backstabber.

"I bet you shift into a wyvern so you and Frank can share all your collective secrets with ease," I say, watching Frank nuzzle Laramie's shoulder.

"No way," he says immediately. "Wyverns are the sacred protectors of Rivenlea. It would be very offensive for an Echo to shift into one. I would never do that to Frank."

"Oh."

"You can bring her," Laramie says again. "To Oz with us."

I purse my lips. "What if she gets hurt?" A thought strikes me. "What if we get hurt? Can we get hurt in spheres? Can we *die*?" I suddenly realize I've signed up for this task without asking nearly enough questions.

I must have left my good sense, if I ever had any, back on Earth.

"It doesn't happen often, but yes. It can happen. More often Novemites get trapped in spheres where they don't belong."

The image of Camille trapped in her bubble pops into my mind and sends a pang through my gut.

Laramie winces, as though he understands my thoughts. "Oh." His voice quiets. "I'm sorry, Em."

"Don't be. You didn't trap her there. That was all me. You've got no reason to be sorry." My gaze shifts back to Frank's claws clicking against the stone in delight as Laramie strokes her chin.

He just keeps petting Frank as though he and I can exist in comfortable silence together. Like we're friends, or something.

As though he knows when to respond and when to let me sit with my twisted forest of thoughts.

After a moment, he says, "Rhyan sent me to find you."

"And what made you think I'd be here?"

He looks like he's stifling a laugh. "Well, you were here."

"That's hardly the point." But my cheeks heat again, because it sort of is the point.

"We should head back," he says. "Will Frank be joining us?"

I frown at two sets of hopeful eyes. Suddenly, I feel like Laramie and I share joint custody of my wyvern. I can almost hear Frank plead, "But Dad says it's okay!"

I sigh. "Only if Frank promises to stay tiny unless I tell her she can stretch her wings." I need to keep her safe. "And only if you help me take care of her." Because they will both enjoy that.

"Not keen to help her hunt?" Laramie grins.

There's also that.

As though she understands every word we're saying—likely she does—Frank shrinks down to pocket-size. She climbs up Laramie's boot, then glides the short distance over to my pants and wiggles her way into my pocket. One claw pokes through the material and stabs my thigh. I swallow a yelp.

"Em?"

There's a hand on my shoulder, and I freeze. Laramie gives it a sympathetic squeeze. Of course, we come into physical contact all the time during training, and this is no different.

Except it is, because his eyes are filled with understanding and sympathy, and my knees respond by turning to pudding.

That doesn't happen during training. Melting into pudding is not part of the deal. Not even for Laramie, who could probably shift into pudding if he wanted to. The thought makes a word escape from my constricted throat before I can stop it. "Butterscotch."

He blinks a few times, but then that sympathetic look is back. "I'm sorry about your sister."

Tears sting. I will them away so hard, I'm almost sure the veins in my forehead are popping with the effort.

"We'll—" He clears his throat. "I'm sure you will find a way to help her."

I try to say thank you—because I mean it, and even though it's Laramie and I spend half my life convincing him and everyone else he's the worst, he's kind sometimes. Often. I actually do see and appreciate it. He should know that.

But I can't make my tightened throat obey. The words won't scratch out before he throws his smile my way and blinks into a sparrow again.

Laramie glides back down to Castramore, and my unspoken, overdue thanks stays locked inside me.

"Got enough stuff there, Phen?" I lift an eyebrow at Phen's bag, set at his feet in the yard. It rivals the largest hiking pack I've ever seen. He looks like he's about to ascend Everest.

Phen glances down at his massive pack. "It's good to be prepared."

"That is true," Wistlee says, but I can't help noticing her own bag is tiny. Lightweight and filled only with essentials.

Phen notices too, his gaze shifting between his pack and Wist's, and he frowns. "I think I'm doing it wrong."

Wistlee smiles and checks her gear one more time—Gryphon armor in place, her rope and whip slung from her belt, her golden helmet tucked under one arm.

Rhyan strides up, decked out in her usual don't-catch-her-in-a-dark-alley outfit, plus an extra layer of tactical gear. A sword is strapped to one hip, and special gloves cover her hands. I have no idea if it's true, but I imagine they amplify her fire powers somehow.

I try my hardest not to wilt in her formidable presence.

I'm still mad at her. I think. I'm mad at someone, anyway,

and as the first Rivenlite I met, maybe Rhyan gets to bear the brunt of it.

Her flickering gaze dances on me for a moment, then she addresses our group at large. "We don't know what we're walking into, XVII. Best to be prepared."

This is becoming a recurring theme. "How can we be prepared if we don't know what we're walking into?" I want to know.

"Prepare for every circumstance. Expect the unexpected."

"There's plenty of 'unexpected' going around lately." I lift my chin and force myself to meet her gaze.

She sighs softly—almost like she's not interested in having a standoff with me in this moment. She steps closer, and I resist the urge to step back. Resist the urge to eye her sword, which she could probably use to cleave me in two.

"Soldier," she says quietly.

How did I become a soldier? If you want to talk about unexpected, that takes the magical cake.

"Are we going to have a problem?" Rhyan asks, voice still quiet. It's not a threat. Not really. She sounds tired. Grieved. Like maybe what's happened to me and Camille is bothering her, too, and it wasn't her intent to deceive me.

The sincerity in Rhyan's voice thaws my iceberg of anger. At least the one I'd been deep-freezing on her account. There's probably another one or two tucked away in there, but in this moment, even I can admit it shouldn't be directed at Rhyan.

None of this is her fault.

"No," I say finally. "We aren't going to have a problem."

She looks at me intently. "If this is going to work—if we're going to successfully complete our mission and return safely to Rivenlea—I need you to trust me. I'm your captain, and you need to trust me."

I could lie, but the basis of trust is honesty. So I opt for the truth.

"I'm working on it."

She nods. "Okay." Then she reaches into the bag slung over

her shoulder and pulls out three objects, then tosses them to me, Phen, and Wistlee. "Masks," she explains. "We don't know exactly what's gone wrong in Oz, but the sphere in Ambryfell is filled with smoke. These should help."

Fabulous.

"White and gray smoke?" I ask.

"Black. Very black." Rhyan narrows her eyes. "Why?"

I can't explain why I asked that question. Except . . .

"Oz shouldn't have tech or certain kinds of fuels. They are"—I rack my brain, trying to remember all the stories I'd read during childhood—"kind of steam-powered? There shouldn't be plastic or stuff like that."

"So black smoke is potentiality concerning." Rhyan presses her lips together.

"I guess it depends on what's burning. It could simply be a forest fire out of control. Or maybe they do have coal. But they really shouldn't have large fires in Oz."

"Good to know," Rhyan says. "Good thought, Emmy." She strides off, headed for Canon.

And Laramie, I don't fail to notice. He's not a sparrow anymore, and I choose to ignore the fact that he somehow looks twice as attractive in tactical gear.

"Well done, Dragon," Wistlee whispers.

My attention on Laramie snaps like a cut cord. "Oh. Thanks." I force a weak smile.

It may be the only insight I have to offer my Novem on this entire mission, and that thought gives me more dragonflies than—

I glance at Laramie.

Well, anything.

33

PHEN LOOKS LIKE HE'S ABOUT

to lose his breakfast.

I can't blame him. The entire Novem is staring at him, as is one stranger I don't recognize. The small man with round glasses, white hair, and a robe that would be at home in any school of wizardry is standing next to Rhyan.

We're just outside Ambryfell, gathered around a stone arch I'd noticed before but hadn't thought too much about. It looks a bit like a place where someone might have a wedding. Slap some flowers on it, and it'd be downright pretty. Romantic, even, if you're into that sort of thing.

But then I realize this must be the place where Sentinels create the gateways through which Novems jump into spheres. Perhaps it's more ceremonial than anything. I've seen Phen make a gateway into the Silvarum with no stone arch, and I jumped through a gateway into Rivenlea that didn't even seem official. But maybe it's different when jumping into spheres. I still know next to nothing about Rivenlea.

I wonder who created that gateway on Earth—the one I followed Frank into. The question has poked at my brain more than once.

That question, and at least a dozen more. Maybe the Elder Council will help me when we return. But if I'm being honest, I think it's likelier they'll just toss me in prison.

I turn my attention back toward Phen, because even though he looks like he'd rather be anywhere else, this is his big moment. Sentinels are guardians all the time, the Novems' faithful lookouts and constant protectors, but getting us into the spheres is the absolute most important thing they do.

Without them, our missions wouldn't happen.

My heart flies out to Phen as he wipes his sweaty palms on his trousers. I can see him counting his breaths. The anxiety is probably crushing.

You can do it, I send him the silent message.

If only he could hear me. But maybe the silent support does something, because a second later, he draws a deep breath. His right hand lights up, and he traces a half arc with it, following the path of the stone arch.

Then he mirrors the process with his left.

The next moment, I realize the stone archway is actually important. Because the arc of light Phen has created looks much like the one he made to jump into the Silvarum, except it's sinking into the stones of the arch. Lighting them up and making them glow.

Emerald green, of course.

I almost laugh. I wonder if anyone else gets the reference.

But of course they don't because they don't have actual books here. Just spheres, which tell the story, but not quite the way a book does.

A dart of regret pings me. I could have at least told them the story—what I could from memory, anyway. I agreed to be part of this Novem and convinced them I wasn't useless, even though I'm not a biological Dragon.

But have I really done everything I can to help the team prepare for this mission? Or have I been too distracted with my personal problems?

The answer is clear, and I'm not sure how guilty to feel. They do have my sister trapped in a bubble in a forbidden forest, after all. The Rivenlites aren't innocent bystanders. But for now I have to set aside everything related to Camille and be the best Dragon I can. Otherwise, I could be putting my team and all of Oz in danger.

"Captain Doyle," the robed stranger is saying, "you have our prayers for the success of your mission, for the safe return of your team, and for the complete restoration of balance to the sphere grid."

Rhyan bows her head. "Thank you, Elder Lytero."

The word "elder" brings me to high alert.

Elder as in Elder Council? Is this one of them—the people who kept the truth from me? The villains in my story?

But my brain is bouncing around in too many directions to think straight. "What happens to Novemites left behind in spheres accidentally?" I ask no one in particular.

Oddly, Marella turns. She looks down her nose at me but answers my question. "They're stuck until we can send a team to rescue them. And that's if we can even find them. Sometimes they get folded into the story."

"Folded into the story?"

"That's right." Rivit's dark brows rise. "If they're folded in, they usually end up in Earthly movie adaptations."

While my brain is busy with this startling tidbit, Novem XVII moves together through the gateway into another fantasyland altogether. Just before I follow them down the rabbit hole, through the wardrobe, off to the second star on the right, I lock gazes with Elder Lytero, noting his reflective Bolt eyes.

He nods. An acknowledgment of . . . something.

I try to read his mirrored gaze. I can't discern what he's thinking or feeling. Does he recognize me? Does he know my sister? My story? Can he answer my questions?

But all I get is that brief glance, the small nod, before my body begins to shred.

And whether I'm ready or not, I'm careening headfirst somewhere over the rainbow.

MY BODY HAS NOT KNITTED

itself back together, and I'm starting to get concerned.

How long does it take to get to Oz? And where are we, exactly? We can't be flying through space—the spheres aren't like planets. At least, I don't think they are. I should have asked about the physics of intersphere travel.

If anyone even knows. Rivenlea is a fantastical dream world full of many questions and few answers, so it probably wouldn't have mattered.

Still, as I careen through the nothingness, feeling my body, my soul, my very essence stripped to bits and flying uncontained, it seems it might have been prudent to ask.

Poor Phen—I hope he's okay.

And Wistlee. Has she traveled like this much before? Is she accustomed to this strange, unstitched feeling?

I briefly hope Laramie is put back together exactly the same as he started out.

Before I have a moment to get lost in more thoughts of Laramie, the ribbons of me—my essence and my person—begin to weave themselves back together. Pain lances through my seams—fiery trails of sutures lacing up and down my body. I don't recall that being part of the process before, but this is the first time I've jumped into a story sphere, unless Rivenlea counts.

I land more gracefully than I've yet managed when jumping through a gateway. I'm prepared for the tumbling feeling, the upside-down disorientation. I direct the arc of my body as it reforms itself and force my feet downward.

They pound into the ground harder than I'd like, but at least I'm on my feet, not my back. Not tumbling across the earth and crashing into a glitter tree or some parallel Ozlike feature.

Pinpricks of fire shoot through the nerves in my feet, but I hold my ground. Don't topple or cry out. The rest of the Novem has landed similarly, though it seems they are not feeling traces of fire like I am.

Maybe it's because I'm an Earthling. Maybe I'm cellularly different—scratch that. I definitely am, a fact confirmed as I watch Faela alight on the ground, her green Harmony skin looking oddly faded and sallow.

Weird. It was vibrant and lovely in Rivenlea. I noticed because she had wrapped a scarf around her yards of hair in preparation for our journey. The scarf was a rosy pink color that complemented her many shades of green.

Now she looks . . . yellow-gray-green, at best.

Wistlee's wings are out, and she glides to a stop next to me. She, too, looks wrong. Grayish-brown, not golden and shimmering in the sunlight as she normally is.

And maybe that's part of the problem. The sunlight is a hazy orange-brown mess, not clear and bright like in Rivenlea. It reminds me of smoky sunsets during wildfires back in California, the rays fighting through an abundance of particulate matter, trying to light the world, to do the work with which they were entrusted.

The smell hits me one second after that remembrance.

Acrid. Choking.

Rhyan said black smoke filled the Oz sphere, and she wasn't kidding. I pull on the mask she gave me back in Rivenlea.

As I do, I catch sight of my hands. Greige. It could simply be the light, the smoke casting strange shadows and hues all about.

But something is poking at my brain. A nearby garden—or what was once a garden—jolts my memory.

The remnants of plants are drab. Not dead and dried out, the black-brown hue of neglect. But actually gray like my neighbors' flowers back home. Like my bedspread.

"The color is draining," I say aloud.

Wistlee is gazing around, nose scrunched. "One wonders what it looked like before. Surely more beautiful than this?"

I follow her gaze and take in the landscape at large for the first time.

My heart drops.

Oz—my beautiful Oz, the world I escaped to when I was a lonely child with her nose in a book—isn't just faded and drab. It's ruined.

A sky that ought to be sapphire blue is gray brown with pollution in the breaks between clouds of smoke and ash rising from who knows how many fires.

The rolling grass hills that should be kelly green, dotted with the dwellings of Munchkins or Winkies or other Ozites, are scorched. Razed. Some of the smoke is rising from what once must have been a cluster of villages. The earth is blackened. Nothing seems to be standing. No dwellings or towns or farms. Only piles of refuse and rubble. Some of which are still flickering with heat and flame.

Far in the distance, I see some sort of truck. A diesel-powered beast. Then I notice another. And another, each belching more dark smoke into the air as it trundles along the roads that ought to have been traveled on foot by a contented party of misfits. Instead, it's like Mad Max has coughed on Oz, and the spheres have gotten jumbled.

This is not my Oz.

Marella is taking in the same sad scene. She wrinkles her nose before pulling on her mask. "What a dystopian dump."

"That's not how it's supposed to be," I shoot back, defensive on behalf of this world only I truly know. "It's . . . broken."

Marella shrugs. "Obviously. That's why we're here."

"I mean . . ." But what do I mean?

Only that she shouldn't judge this world based on its brokenness.

I see Rhyan nearby, deep in conversation with Canon. Laramie is beside them listening, mask in place. But it can't conceal the concern on his face.

Dieselpunk nightmare Oz is clearly not what anyone was expecting.

"Captain," I say and try to take a step. But the needles shooting through my legs make me draw up short with a wince.

Wistlee catches my arm. "Emmy!"

The pins and needles are restricted to my lower legs now, no longer shooting all the way to my torso. I nod. "I'm okay. Just a little . . . weird from the journey."

My gaze is drawn to my left, and I nearly cost Wist her balance as I stumble away from the creature looming beside me.

Not a creature. A . . . statue?

But in the next second, the stone carving morphs into the flesh-and-bone version of himself.

"Phen!" Relief floods me. "You're all right! But why did you go into guardian mode?"

Though his usually tawny skin is looking ashen and faded, it's clearly flesh, as compared to the stone he was a moment ago. Even in this warped and faded world, I can see a bit of a blush creeping over his cheeks.

"You were in pain, and I kind of panicked." He grins sheepishly. "Sorry. I'm on edge here."

"Perhaps with good reason." Wistlee's gaze is riveted to one of the large trucks. It appears to be headed our direction, though it's still a good distance away.

There's time.

"Captain," I say to Rhyan. I'm prepared for the strange feeling in my legs as I walk toward her, and I manage not to wince. "The color."

She gestures to her clothing, usually black as pitch, now faded to the color of ash. "I've noticed."

"It was happening on Earth too," I say.

It's the second time this week I've shocked the unflappable Rhyan Doyle. "It—what?"

"Maybe it wasn't happening everywhere," I amend. "But it was happening around me."

Gazes fix onto me. I'm starting to feel like I'm some kind of curse, bringing destruction with me everywhere I go.

Maybe that's true.

But I shove these thoughts away and embrace my role as Dragon. Marella and probably half the Novem are already suspicious of me. They don't think I can perform the duties I'm supposed to and believe I'll be a drain on the team.

And they're right, in a sense. I don't look at this world and see the invisible structure of the story unfold before me. The invisible scaffolding supporting *The Wonderful Wizard of Oz* is as hidden to me as it is to them. I can't say immediately what's gone wrong and what needs fixing.

But I do have something to offer. Especially in Oz. A world I've traveled to in my imagination many times before.

I block out the curious, judgmental eyes upon me and focus on Rhyan. "The color drained from my neighbors' flowers. Then I noticed it in my bedroom too. My bedspread faded to blah the day I left."

Rhyan frowns. "Did you notice this elsewhere?"

She means in Rivenlea. It's the only other place I've been.

"Perhaps her vision is going," Marella suggests lightly, creating a jet of breeze to cool those standing beside her. The smoky air is stifling.

I don't bother allowing my anger or embarrassment to rise at her dig. I gesture around us. "This all looks normal to you? Perhaps you're the one who needs a trip to the optometrist." Okay, maybe they rose a little bit.

Marella spares me half a sneer but no more sharp words.

The shriek of an engine revving comes from behind us, startling me. A moment later, an ATV of some sort skids to a stop.

A person the size of a typical adolescent but clearly much older hops off, moto boots crunching in the loose gravel. Her white hair is buzzed short. Goggles cover her eyes, and a gas mask protects her airways.

I would have expected her to be in a white gown and polished shoes and a pointy hat instead of the leathers she's wearing. And that gown ought to be covered in stars that glitter like diamonds.

If we're starting at the beginning of Dorothy's story, this ought to be the Good Witch of the North. If I squint, maybe it could be her? Maybe she's just been corrupted by the story turmoil like the rest of this place. But her face looks so hard, so unkind, it's difficult to imagine this is the benefactress of Oz, the fabled Witch of the North.

And even so, I half expect her to welcome us in her sweet voice and call one of us "noble sorceress" or perhaps hand us a pair of silver shoes.

Instead, she's pointing an automatic rifle directly at my head.

35

EMLYN DULAINE, AGE SEVENTEEN,

*from Castramore via Earth, died unexpectedly early Thursday morning.
Ms. DuLaine was attending her first mission as a Novemite and had
worked for approximately three and a half minutes before she was
accosted and shot by a deranged pretender Witch.*

"She is survived by . . . no one, really."

Wistlee turns to me. "Pardon?"

"I was just writing my obituary," I say, gaze fixed to the muzzle
trained far too keenly in my direction.

"Oh!" In my periphery, I see Wistlee shake her head at my dramatics.

Two more ATVs scream into the clearing where we stand, depositing
two small men before us. They draw their weapons.

Munchkins.

A pang shoots through my heart at the absence of their curled
shoes and pointy hats. Ridiculous, I know, given the circumstances.
But somehow, this Oz—this hardened, smoke-filled, diesel-stinking
Oz—feels like losing a friend.

Rhyan holds up her hands. "We mean no harm. Please, lower
your guns."

The little woman cocks her head to the side but does not lower
her weapon. "And what manner of sorceress are you?"

Rhyan hesitates a moment. Then her hands flare. "A fire sorceress."

The two men scramble backward, away from Rhyan's magic, but

the woman only swings her weapon away from me and toward our captain.

"A Wicked Witch!" one of the men cries out in a strangled voice.

"Off with her head!" the other shouts.

My heart stills. Off with her head?

Rhyan snuffs out her hands. "No, I'm not a Wicked Witch, I assure you. We're here to help."

"Help?" the woman scoffs, narrowing her gaze through the scope of her rifle. "Do *you* know where the Witch of the North has gone to?"

Against all reason, I edge forward, concern winning out over good sense. "She's missing?"

"Probably murdered." The woman glances at me but keeps the gun on Rhyan. "Was it you?" Her gaze slices through our crew, strange by any standard and probably deeply suspicious to the Munchkin woman. "Surely it was you."

"It was certainly not." Rhyan's hands are still up in a gesture of peace, and somehow she keeps her voice steady. There's no shake, no tremble, as she tries to defuse the situation.

I'm very glad she's the captain and not me.

"Please, listen to me," she urges. "We are here to help you."

"Your story's gone wrong," Canon adds. "We are here to help set it right."

"I'll say it's gone wrong." The woman doesn't lower her gun, yet she seems to be considering their words. "Everything's gone to pot since the Witch of the North vanished." Then she shrugs. "Least these showed up." She nods to her weapon.

"All the better to kill you with," one of the Munchkin men adds.

Another dart of ice shoots through me at his words. His terribly, terribly wrong words.

"The stories," I whisper, the thought beginning to weave itself together. Wistlee and Phen are watching me, waiting.

Before I can fully grasp what my brain is trying to tell me, the woman is signaling her comrades to lower their weapons. I guess she's decided to trust Rhyan for now.

"Do you have the shoes?" She's raised the gas mask to rest atop her head, eyeing Rhyan's hands warily, clearly concerned they might ignite at any moment.

"Shoes?" Rhyan's confusion is genuine, but I immediately know what the woman means.

"The silver shoes?" I ask. "Have they gone missing too?"

"Aye. The silver shoes, the Witch of the North. The Wicked Witch of the East is dead, at least, and thank the stars for that. That confounded house fell on her, and good riddance."

She nods vaguely behind us, and I turn to see a smoldering pile of ash and rubbish. With a start, I realize the smoking pile of ruin was once Uncle Henry and Aunt Em's farmhouse.

The woman shrugs. "We burned it. The body didn't disappear and it was starting to stink."

Ugh.

"Though, perhaps the Witch of the North got trapped under there somehow too, but there are no extra bones. Just the one set." She slings her rifle across her back, pulls out a rolled cigarette, and pops it into her mouth. She shoots Rhyan a look. "You mind?"

Rhyan hesitates, frowning, but then she creates a tiny flicker of flame across her finger and lights the woman's cigarette.

It seems almost heretical even in this ruined Oz land. I'm doubly thankful for my mask.

One of the men is openly gawking at Faela, her stunning, willowy green form towering over him. "Mirror, mirror on the wall," he mutters under his breath, shaking his head in something like amazement.

My disjointed thoughts snap into alignment. "The stories," I start again. Louder this time so those beyond Wistlee and Phen will hear me too. All heads turn to me. "The stories are communicating with each other."

I'm not sure what I expect. Maybe I'm hoping for lights of realization to ignite in their eyes. Maybe I'm expecting a few mouths to drop open as comprehension dawns. Maybe I'm even hoping against hope that someone will say, "Well done, Dragon."

Instead, I'm met with blank stares.

"Communicating with each other?" Rhyan's tone pitches to incredulous.

"Impossible," Canon says flatly.

Marella rolls her eyes and whispers something to Rivit.

A bucket of anxiety douses me. And I suddenly wish I had been smashed by the farmhouse.

But I try again anyway because it's supposed to be my job. It's the whole reason I'm here. To provide insight. "These things they're saying—they're lines from other stories."

"Emmy, we don't have time for this," Rhyan says with an impatient sigh. "We need to help these people *now*."

I'm trying to help them, can't she see that? I attempt to steady my voice, but I feel it shaking before I even speak. "This is . . ."

What? What is it, Emmy? You don't even know. Why are you opening your big mouth and proving correct those who think you're a fraud?

I swallow my mortification and blurt, "I think this is important."

Rhyan sighs again. "Emmy, let's focus on what's going on with *this* story."

Like a child who's been scolded, I shrink back. I want to disappear, but instead I swallow and nod.

I can help this way too. I know this story, and the others clearly don't.

"Okay." My eyes close as I draw every detail from my memory. "Dorothy should be here. The Good Witch of the North is supposed to meet her." I glance at the Munchkin lady. Definitely not the Witch. "The Wicked Witch of the East kind of . . . shrivels up, leaving behind her silver shoes. They take those and give them to Dorothy."

"Morbid," Marella mutters.

A bit.

"The Good Witch takes off her magic cap, and it gives Dorothy instructions—she's to go to the City of Emeralds to find the Great Wizard. Perhaps he will help her get back to Kansas."

"Kansas?" The Munchkins and Rivenlites all look confused.

"It's an . . . Earth state in the Earth country the United States. Where Dorothy is from." I wave my hand. "Never mind."

"We didn't prepare for Kansas," Canon says to Rhyan.

I take a deep breath. "Kansas doesn't matter. Forget Kansas. It's just where Dorothy is trying to go. It's not a sphere." But honestly, for all I know, Kansas *is* a sphere. Maybe everywhere is a sphere.

I'm starting to get that familiar what-is-reality headache.

"Anyway," I say, trying to rein back around to the story at hand, "the Witch of the North tells Dorothy where to go and gives her a protective kiss." I look around at the graying, dystopian nightmare landscape. "I guess in the absence of those magic shoes and protective kiss—and with no idea what she's supposed to do or where she's supposed to go—Dorothy has fled."

"I don't know this Dorothy," the Munchkin lady states. "All I know is that the terrible Witch of the East who used to rule over us is dead."

"Good riddance!" the men shout in unison.

"And neither the Witch of the North nor her sister in the South nor any other witch has come to rule over us." She places a warning hand on her rifle and glares at Rhyan. "And if you're the sorceress who's come to try, it won't happen easily. I promise you that."

"Aye!" the men shout.

"I'm not here to rule over you." Rhyan is sounding weary.

"Like you could if you tried!" one of the men spits.

The Munchkin lady pulls a long drag on her cigarette. "The Munchkins are loyal to me," she says. "We need no witch to rule us, nor wizard to guide us. Finally, we make our own way in this brave new Oz."

"Does the Emerald City still stand at the center of Oz?" I ask.

The Munchkin lady merely shrugs. "We don't travel there. Never have."

"And the shoes. You're sure they're gone?"

She shrugs again. "If a Munchkin had taken them, I'd know. I know all that happens here in the East."

Phen leans in to me and lowers his voice. "Are the shoes important?"

"In the story? Yes. They help Dorothy get back to Kansas. So we need them if we're going to have a proper ending."

"But first and foremost," Canon inserts smoothly, "we must rescue the Witch of the North, if she lives still, and find Dorothy." His eyes travel from me to Rhyan. "Correct?"

"I suppose so," I say. But I can't seem to let go of the shoes. Did the Witch of the North run off with them? She wasn't interested in them in the original story—except to give them to Dorothy. To help her.

"The shoes," I begin.

But Rhyan stops me. "No. We need to focus on finding Dorothy. She's the protagonist. That's the key here."

It feels like a slap. It probably shouldn't. She's our captain, after all. It's her duty and her right to make those kinds of decisions. But isn't it my job to discern what's story-important? What information is mission-important?

But, of course, I'm not a real Dragon.

"Rhyan," I say, trying to keep my voice down so I won't be overheard by the likes of Marella and Rivit and Faela and the others. Laramie.

"I know I'm not a real Dragon," I start.

"This isn't about that. This is about the fact that—" Her gaze drops to the ground. Gray and desolate and scalded. Then she looks me dead in the eyes. "The fact is you behaved rashly when you snuck into the Silvarum. You broke laws and put your own needs before that of the Novem. No matter what was happening with Camille, the fact is . . . I can't trust you anymore."

THE SHAME STILL BURNS

acutely as Rhyan rallies the troops. Giving directions. Issuing orders. Preparing the details of our search and rescue mission.

But all I can hear is her declaration, ringing over and over through my head: I can't trust you anymore.

And she's right.

How can she possibly? I defied her and forced my way into the Silvarum, my curiosity stronger than my desire to respect the process.

You were desperate for information about your missing sister, a small voice reminds me.

And that's true. But does it justify me? I'd thought so. Now I'm not sure.

She wouldn't tell you anything useful, the same voice says.

Also true. Rhyan was frustratingly opaque when I asked for information. But . . . does that justify me?

You're used to looking out for yourself. How can you be blamed for that?

I squeeze my temples between my palms.

"Emmy?" Wistlee places her hand on my arm. "Are you well?"

I shake my head. "Rhyan is right. She can't trust me. I'm too self-centered."

"You were just looking for answers," Phen says quietly.

Which only reminds me I dragged two perfectly trustworthy, innocent Novemites into my schemes, and now she probably doesn't trust them either.

Also my fault, and probably the worst of my offenses.

As if sailing through the years, all the way back from my childhood, my mother's voice reminds me: Two wrongs don't make a right.

No matter what secrets council kept from me, it did not justify betraying my captain and withholding information from her.

"We'll get a safe distance from Munchkin territory and set up camp for the night," Rhyan is saying to the group, "then begin our journey in the morning."

Rivit looks at the blackened sky. "It was early morning when we left Rivenlea."

"It's nearly nightfall in Oz." Rhyan glances up. "That's what they tell me, though how they can see through all this smoke, I don't know. Anyway, time is inconsistent across spheres, and the sooner we adjust, the better." Her gaze skims off me like a skipped stone. "Let's go, everyone."

"That way," I say. Shame and disappointment and frustration have squashed my voice. A voice that wasn't very strong to begin with.

"What?" Rhyan asks. "Speak up, Emmy."

I point in the direction that must head west. "I think that's the yellow brick road. Hard to say for sure, but those bricks look at least slightly beige. So that's the direction Dorothy ought to have gone in the story."

Rhyan gazes that way. "We might as well follow the path of the story, until we have a better lead."

Canon nods his agreement. I make a point not to look at Laramie, but he must have agreed as well. Rhyan seeks counsel from Laramie and Canon on many of her decisions, I've noticed.

But didn't Canon break her trust too? Didn't he withhold from Rhyan the fact that he knew more about my sister than even she did? Why isn't he being punished like I am?

I'm being petty and immature, because of course Rhyan and Canon have many years of relationship to withstand some bumps. Rhyan and I are practically strangers. It doesn't totally subdue my desire to nurse the sense of unfairness. But close.

The only way forward is to try to earn back her trust.

The Novem makes its way down the beige brick road, and I try not to notice the Munchkin dwellings. The other Novemites don't react, of course. These homes look perfectly normal, given the disintegration of Munchkin society. The little barricades surrounding each home, the bars on the windows, the razor wire fences—it all looks as expected to the Novemites who don't know this story like I do.

But I know these should be quaint homes—round with domed roofs. I know that Dorothy was charmed by the neat fences and the fields of grain and vegetables surrounding each homestead. All those fields lie scorched.

The houses should be blue, the favorite color of Munchkins, but any color that may have still remained has been drained away.

Does the color just get erased? Or does it go somewhere?

It's odd to imagine a giant pool of color filled with the yellow of Oz's bricks, the blues of the Munchkins' homes, and the blues, purples, and pinks of my galaxy bedspread. And the reds, oranges, and yellows of my neighbors' flowers.

But I think of the sphere map in Rivenlea—the way those orbs are meant to hold reality in place—and I realize a big tub of all the color in all the worlds isn't such an insane idea. Maybe it does exist.

Either way, if we can figure out what's going on, hopefully it will somehow set the colors right. Then we won't all be doomed to live in slowly graying spheres.

As we continue through Munchkin country, grief pressing on my heart at each ruined or fortified home, I still naively hope Boq or some other friendly Munchkin will appear. Invite us to a little neighborhood celebration. Offer us pies and fruit and nuts for dinner.

For some reason, I think of Mokah Snick and her lovely little bakery. Which makes me think of Hadeon and Teyra, and for the first time, I wonder.

They said they knew my sister. My sister in a bubble. They knew where she was trapped, what she was like. They led me near to where she was. Why didn't they just tell me? Maybe prepare or warn me?

There are no answers here. No friendly faces or kind offers of hospitality. Only angry yells, boarded-up doors, and a couple of well-aimed rifles, followed by threats.

"It's not supposed to be like this," I say to Wistlee and Phen beside me.

Oz, yes. But also . . . everything.

"I know, Emmy," Wistlee says. "This is quite desolate."

She means Oz. But it feels broadly applicable.

"Rhyan?" I call ahead.

Rhyan stops and turns around—but only halfway, which is probably due to the heavy gear she's carrying yet somehow feels symbolic. "Yes?"

"Munchkin territory is mostly farmland. That little copse of trees up ahead is probably our best bet for cover for the night. If that's what we're after."

She looks into the distance at the stand of trees I've noticed. "Right. Thanks."

Her words are clipped, but her tone is neutral.

I'll take it.

Once we reach the trees, Novem XVII puts its training to use and sets up camp in ten minutes. Our record is eight, but it's hard to breathe through these masks.

Faela has set a ring of stones at the center of camp and filled it with good kindling and the driest wood she could find. Marella and Rhyan have the cookfire blazing in seconds.

Control of flame and wind helps with that.

Our tents are simple—just enough to keep the elements away, and I hope Oz doesn't have bugs that are very large.

Or very poisonous.

Rivit, Rhyan, and Laramie set out to search for food, and I pull out the bread I tucked into my pack just a few hours before, back in Rivenlea, contenting myself with the thought that this is what Dorothy packed in her basket when she set out through Oz.

And if she's out there somewhere now, I try to send my thoughts toward her, hoping somehow she can hear and be comforted.

Hang on, Dorothy. We're coming.

Sleep doesn't come easily.

I'm sitting on the fallen log outside my tent, staring into the darkness. A fire burns somewhere in the distance, throwing an eerie glow on the horizon and casting strange shadows. But that's the only light able to fight its way into the trees. Our cookfire has been doused.

Sort of like my hopes.

I had not fully admitted it before this moment of solitude, but I had wondered if maybe—just maybe—I had found something like a family in my Novem.

Or at least a place to belong.

I knew it would be a battle. I would have to prove myself a useful member. The uphill climb would be steep with those like Marella, but I would win them over eventually. Oz would be my chance to do it.

And as much as I wrap myself in impostor syndrome like it's a comfy blanket, deep down, I really believed I would prove my worth. If given the chance, I would be able to show I have strengths I bring to the table.

But now I've made a mess of all that. I've lost the trust of my captain. I'm probably in trouble back in Rivenlea. I dragged my friends into my selfish choices. And no one will listen to me about what's happening in Oz. Dorothy is in danger. Hadeon has—betrayed me? Maybe that's too strong a word, but I have a few questions for him.

The Witch of the North has vanished.

"The shoes," I say aloud to the smoke-obscured stars.

"The shoes you've got on match your outfit just fine," a voice says lightly beside me, and I startle.

Laramie shifts from the form of a toad I have just noticed, and he's not even trying to hold in his laughter. "Sorry," he says, seating himself beside me.

"That's creepy, you know. Hanging around when people don't know you're there."

"I literally just hopped over. I was keeping watch."

"As a toad?"

He grins. "It's excellent cover. You can't argue with that."

No, I can't. But I want to. "You shouldn't sneak up on people."

"I wasn't trying to sneak. You're supposed to be in bed."

"Yeah, well." It's the wittiest comeback I have at the moment. My gaze drops to my boots. "I wasn't thinking about my outfit," I say, remembering his dorky quip that startled me.

"I know." His eyes look black in the night. He pulls a mask from one of his pockets and places it over his face. "This smoke is awful."

I frown at my boots for a moment in silence.

"The shoes," he prompts me.

"They're important," I say. When he doesn't respond, I continue. "But I don't blame Rhyan for not believing me. Why should she?"

"Because you're our Dragon."

"But I'm not really. I'm just . . . pretending." I shove my sleeves up my arms to show my human skin—completely unremarkable—and thrust my forearm in front of him. "See? Not a Dragon."

He takes my forearm and gently turns it over to show the underside. "You've hurt yourself," he says quietly.

He's right. There's a wound there, midway between a scrape

and a gash. "I think it happened when we jumped the gate." I frown at the cut. "I thought I'd cleaned it."

"It's still bleeding a little. You should've wrapped it. Faela will have some tinctures and salves to help."

Do they have antibiotics in Rivenlea? I should probably be more careful about cuts and scrapes.

"I need to check my penicillin privilege."

"What?"

I shake my head. "Nothing."

He's still holding my arm, examining my scratch like a medic. But the moment before he releases me, his thumb grazes my skin. Brushes across it, as if to wipe away the sting of the day. It's not the touch of a medic. It's a gesture of affection.

I yank my arm away. My emotions too tangled to pull them apart and figure out what that gesture meant, how I feel about it, whether or not it even matters.

Laramie folds his hands in his lap. As if determined to keep them to himself.

And why wouldn't he, after I snapped myself away from a simple brush that was probably platonic or accidental. And who even wants to touch Laramie anyway?

Not me.

A little bit me.

"No," I say aloud.

"What?"

"Nothing. Just . . ." I wave my hand as if that provides any sort of explanation.

And he nods. Nods like he understands all the things I've not said.

He rises to his feet. "I won't keep you. We should both get some sleep."

"Yes. Frank has probably abandoned my sleeping bag for Wistlee's by now." I stand too. "Maybe you can shift into a bear so you can hibernate."

"Not quite the season for hibernation."

"And I'm sure it wouldn't be at all startling for Canon to wake up next to a bear in his tent."

Laramie grins. "He's used to me."

"If he ever gets eaten by an actual bear because he didn't think to escape, it'll be your fault."

"As if Canon has a shot against an actual bear anyway."

"Laser hands?" I suggest. "Or he could try lecturing it to death."

Laramie's grin widens. Then dims. "Hey, Em?"

The nickname doesn't make me bristle anymore. "Yes?"

"For what it's worth, if you say the shoes are important, I believe you. And I'll speak up for you with the captain."

"Oh." I mean to say thank you, and instead "Oh" is all that comes out.

"I'm just one person," he says, trying to minimize the magnitude of what he's said, what he's offered to do. "And how important can one person be, really?" He smiles. "But I'll try."

Before I can tell him exactly how important one person can be, he slips away and disappears into his tent.

I'm left alone with my tied tongue, my sharp self-loathing. And the tiny flame of hope that comes from being believed.

37

I CAN'T BRING MYSELF TO

make eye contact with Laramie the next morning, and I'm not sure why. Why is it harder to look him in the face after he's been nice?

I begin shoving pieces of our tent into my pack. Then I pull a groggy Frank from my pocket and feed her a small piece of Wistlee's morning bacon.

"We need to follow the yellow brick road," I say to Rhyan as she replaces her mask. She's just polished off the last of a rather questionable cup of coffee Rivit brewed over the morning campfire.

"Yellow?" She scrunches her nose.

"Beige brick road," I clarify. "Oz is . . . not itself."

"I know." She smiles, but the brightness looks forced. "But that's why we're here."

I bite my lip. I know we're here to supposedly help the characters, but I still can't shake the feeling we're doing a larger harm, somehow.

"Where are we headed, Dragon?" Marella's words slice, even when they appear benign on the surface. It's probably the way she says *Dragon*, with just a little too much emphasis to be genuine.

"As I was just telling the captain, we need to follow the brick road." I gesture ahead to where the road is barely visible through the trees. "We may even meet some help along the way."

We can't expect the story to be exactly as it is in the book I know so well. But if it's remotely similar, I know who we're likely to meet today.

And despite what he says, he's full of ingenious ideas and plenty of helpful thoughts.

My secret hope is that he'll have some notion of where we can find Dorothy. Heading toward the Emerald City with no reason to expect she's there doesn't sit well with me. It's not much of a plan, and I prefer a solid plan.

Even if I'm not a real Dragon.

It's nearly midday when the smoke begins to thin. We're still in Munchkin country, but it's less populated here. Fewer farms and fields burning. Fewer trucks and ATVs and motorcycles belching pollution into Oz's atmosphere.

Most of the Novem removes masks, stuffing them into packs. Though it's not like taking a breath of sweet, clean air, pulling in a breath without a mask on still feels refreshing.

But a moment later, I sort of wish I had my mask back on. Because I want to hide behind it. Escape from what I think I'm seeing—and smelling—just ahead.

The Munchkin farmer's field should be off to the right. And it is, exactly where I expected it to be. Within the field, our friend, the Scarecrow, ought to be positioned on a wooden pole, keeping watch over the corn, scaring off the birds.

It had occurred to me the Scarecrow might be hostile. Like the Munchkin folk who were friendly to Dorothy in the story and not so much toward us, I did wonder if the Scarecrow might try to attack us, maybe light us on fire in an ironic twist.

I did not expect to find a scorched patch of earth where the farm ought to be. Nor did I expect crows picking at the ruined field, searching for morsels of dead things. But most of all, I did not expect to find the blackened, charred remains of the Scarecrow in the exact spot I hoped to see his painted-on face.

My gasp sticks in my throat. I choke.

Wistlee is at my elbow, brow furrowed in concern. "Emmy, what is it?"

The rest of the Novem has paused at Wist's alarmed tone. We'd been trudging in relative silence for some time.

I point, unable to force out the words.

Rhyan follows my gesture. Sees the pile of ash. The remnants of straw. The tattered bits of fabric.

Given the state of the field, I wonder how long he was able to hold off before the fire reached him, pinned as he was. He was terrified of fire. How awful must his last moments have been?

Bile crawls up my throat.

"What was it, Emmy?" I can't tell if Rhyan's concern is for me or the mission. Probably a little of both.

"Who," I manage. "Not what. Who."

"Oh." Rhyan's face falls. "An ally?"

I swallow. "The Scarecrow. Dorothy's friend and companion. I had hoped . . ."

"That he might know where she would go."

"It's silly, really. In this version of Oz, I guess they never met, since Dorothy isn't following the plot." My gaze skims across the land, and my mind goes to the most un-Ozish thing possible. "Unless she's the one who set this fire."

As much as I hate to think it, we can't rule it out.

Rivit is crouched down, his hands to the ground. "It's cold. This was burned a while ago."

I had figured as much, since there was no smoke or heat. No smoldering like you see when a fire's still alive but low on fuel.

Yet I can't help feeling like we just missed the chance to help him. "Maybe if we hadn't stopped for the night," I say, dismay taking hold. "Maybe if . . ."

But I stop. I know it's not true. We just got to Oz the previous day, and this fire's been dead for a while. Which means the Scarecrow's been dead for a while too.

Could we have saved him if we hadn't spent those last few days in Rivenlea? Maybe if we'd had more urgency . . .

"All will be set right, Emmy." Rhyan places a bracing hand on my shoulder. "When we fix the story, he'll come back."

I can't pull my gaze from the pile of the Scarecrow's remains. "I always wanted to meet him. He was my favorite."

Wistlee loops her arm through mine. On my other side, Phen drapes his arm across my shoulders. I rest my head against him as my tears rise, then fall. But I'm a little ashamed at the ridiculous display.

The Scarecrow isn't even real.

But that's just it, isn't it? When you love a story person, they feel real. And standing here, inside the Oz sphere, it's more than a feeling. These people are just as much flesh and blood as the rest of us.

Well. Not in the Scarecrow's case.

I almost smile at that—he always made references to his lack of a real body, so I indulge myself in thinking he might find it amusing too.

A nearby presence draws my attention, and I see Laramie hovering about. Almost as though he wants to reach out. Even if just verbally. Tears are still dribbling down my face, and I must look extremely pathetic.

Laramie doesn't make a move to comfort me, no matter how pathetic I look. Instead, he offers a pained, sympathetic smile, then rejoins Canon, Marella, and Rivit by the edge of the farm.

"Emlyn?"

I turn to see Faela's green eyes trained on me. "Yes?"

"I would like to bury his remains. Would you help me?"

Her kindness makes the tears spring forth again. I manage a nod.

She takes my hand and leads me to the ashes of a good friend I never met.

With Faela's Harmony-born connection to the earth, it's no time at all before she's opened up a little space in the ground. There isn't much left of the Scarecrow, so it's more than enough for a grave.

I pick through the pile of ashes, collecting everything that's probably him. It's gruesome and yet not, somehow. It feels right to honor him and the friend he would have been to Dorothy.

"Thank you for doing this," I say after a moment. A few buttons from the shirt go on top of the pile of ash. "I know they probably think it's silly." I tilt my head vaguely to the others waiting on the brick road.

"It's never silly to honor something—or someone—that mattered to you. Whatever form that takes." She smiles again, then presses her fingers into the ground.

Green seedlings begin to sprout up, poking their heads out for air and sunshine.

If there's any to be found behind the smoke.

"Marella would scoff," I think aloud, then wince. They are roommates and friends, and I don't want to offend Faela. Not after she's been so kind.

And really, she always is. I'm not sure how she and our snooty Zephyr have become so close.

But Faela merely smiles. "Marella is not as cruel as she'd have you believe."

"Why does she want me to think she's cruel at all? Wouldn't it be better to be friends?"

"Yes," she says, scooping dirt into our makeshift grave. "Marella can be a very loyal friend. But she's wary of you."

"Me specifically?"

"New people in general. But yes, you specifically." Faela sits back on her heels and absently runs a hand over her seedlings, helping them grow taller. Buds begin to form at the ends of the stems. "We have waited a long time for our Dragon, and you are not what we expected."

I hold back a weary sigh. "Believe me, I never expected to be here either."

"Marella only wants Novem XVII to succeed."

"That's what I want too."

But as soon as I say it, I'm reminded of all my misgivings

about the Novemite missions. I'm reminded of the fact that I'm not sure we're actually helping anything by resetting stories.

Then my gaze is drawn down to the burial mound before us. If resetting the story will bring back those who were lost, perhaps it's not a bad thing.

"Well," Faela says, wiggling her fingers so the flowers she's growing burst into bloom, "perhaps there's hope you and Marella will be friends, after all. A common goal is a good place to start."

I brave an uncertain smile. Faela moves to pluck her new flowers, but I place my hand on hers. "No, leave them." The white blooms streaked with pale blue look perfect just where they are, in the ground beside our makeshift memorial. "That way they'll last longer."

She nods. "Aye." She rises and helps me up after her.

We rejoin the others waiting for us on the brick road, ready to continue our dreary journey without the one who might have been our strongest ally.

But then, in a moment of strangest irony, the second we step onto the path, Faela is gripped around the waist and hoisted into the air. It takes a couple seconds to process what I'm seeing.

Faela has been picked up by a murderous tree. And there's a whole forest of them barreling down upon us.

38

WHEN A HARMONY SCREAMS,

the plants shudder. As though the frequency pains whatever receptors they have to perceive sound. Or perhaps like the pain and fear of these delicate earth-loving creatures can be felt in the cells of all nearby flora.

Whatever the reason, Faela screams, and the tree holding her shivers like a chill runs up its trunk. The spindly branches wrapped around Faela's waist quiver, and then she's falling to the ground.

Marella is there in a flash, creating a cushion of air to buffer Faela's fall.

"Behind me!" Rhyan calls, and her hands ignite. She lifts the flames, clearly about to light up this ferocious tree.

"Please, don't!" Faela cries, still struggling to her feet.

The captain casts a sideways glance at her Harmony, irritation evident. "Fae . . ."

"The land is already destroyed." Faela places a hand on Rhyan's arm. "Please, no more fire."

Rhyan hesitates, then her hands blink out.

And the tree takes advantage. Rhyan barely has time to duck beneath the swipe of a large branch. She pulls Faela out of the way of another advancing tree. "Back!" she orders as we scramble away from the trees.

All except one of us.

"Phen!" I call, seeing he's standing frozen in front of Faela, Marella, and Rivit.

Not frozen. Turned to stone. Protecting them like a good Sentinel.

Except one of these rabid trees is about to smash a thick branch into him. What happens if Phen is smashed to bits while he's turned to stone? Does he die? Will he get stuck in some weird movie adaptation of Oz?

I don't want to find out.

But before I can make a move to rescue him. Canon lifts a steady hand, deploys a laser, and slices the branch clean from the attacking tree.

Faela yelps, but she doesn't rebuke Canon.

The tree can live with one branch cut, and this fighting forest isn't messing around. We must be allowed to defend ourselves.

"They're not supposed to be here," I try to explain. "This doesn't happen until later, and they're in the wrong part of Oz entirely."

"We grow where we wish, and we fight where our king sends us, thanks very much." It takes me a heartbeat to realize it's the tree talking to us.

"Your . . . your king?" I say, mostly to buy time. "They're not supposed to talk either," I whisper to Rhyan.

"The Lion, of course," the tree answers. "Formerly cowardly. Now beastly. Very royal. King of the trees and the beasts within." The tree inclines its leafy head. "Since we made him our king, we've expanded our territory."

"Ah, the Imperialistic Lion." Phen, back in the flesh, raises an eyebrow at the tree.

The tree shrugs its bark-covered shoulders. "More importantly, our king has given us orders."

"To do what, exactly?" Rhyan asks.

Someone nudges me. I turn to see Laramie, nodding subtly

to the sword strapped at my hip. Rhyan had told us to lay off our weapons when possible, given our reception by the Munchkins.

But when I glance back at the forest, I see why he's signaling me. Why his fingers are wrapping around his grip.

The trees are slowly clustering behind their spokestree. Preparing for a strike. Laramie and I will need to hack at some branches, and soon.

Faela is right that a wildfire is probably a bad idea. But there are so many trees closing in on us, I wonder if our swords and Canon's beams will be enough.

"Why," the tree leans down toward Rhyan, a leer on its bark-constructed face, "to kill the intruders, of course."

"Em!"

I'm still in the motion of pulling my sword from its scabbard, but I duck in time, and Laramie hacks at the branch swinging toward me. Every tree on the front line is attacking, reaching for a different member of the Novem.

Laramie is at my back now, and I can almost imagine we're in the training yard at Ambryfell. We've practiced this—fighting together—as many times as we've practiced fighting each other. And it feels comfortable. Natural and familiar.

There's a metaphor in there somewhere, I'm sure.

But right now, I lean back on him to escape the swipe of a branch, then push against him to leverage my position and launch a counterstrike.

But it's nearly impossible to hack away limbs with a sword. I inflict the equivalent of a gash, and the tree is offended, at most. We will never win a fight like this.

Canon does his best to Bolt through the attacking limbs. Whether intentionally or not, I see him slice clean through a trunk. Faela has the good sense not to flinch too hard.

I'm all for conservation, but these trees are trying to kill us.

"We've got to get out of here," I shout.

The Cowardly Lion's gone feral, apparently, so that's another ally we can count out. The next friend we're supposed to meet is the Tin Woodman. I would rather not meet the Lion himself. His minions are quite enough.

"Where to?" Rhyan calls back. She uses her hand to burn an imprint in the tree reaching toward her. "There's too many of them."

The Tin Woodman's house should be close—at least as the crow flies.

Flies.

I glance at Wistlee. She's using her rope to lasso branches as they snap toward her and Phen. She seems to feel my eyes on her, and when our gazes meet, I realize a moment too late she's discerned what I'm wishing for.

A Gryphon who could fly would be very helpful right now.

Wistlee grimaces and I wince. Why did she have to glance over at that moment? Why does she always guess what I'm thinking? I take a breath, berate myself. It was my glance, my thoughts that were the problem.

I try to send my brainwaves toward her—to tell her I think she's perfect just as she is, and who needs two working wings, anyway?

Laramie stumbles into me, knocking a bit too hard against my side.

"Careful," I say, nodding down to my pocket. "Frank's in there."

Frank.

"Frank can fly us out of here to the Tin Woodman's house!" I exclaim, hope rising inside.

"I don't know who the Tin Woodman is." Laramie gashes another branch. "But I'm in."

Frank is still sleeping when I yank her from my pocket. She starts awake, blinks twice, then turns her tiny reptilian eyes on me in a glare.

"Not now, princess," I tell her. "We need your help."

Her blue-black ears perk up, and she's sitting on her haunches in my palm a moment later, ready for her orders.

"Frank, can you fly us out of here?" I show her the attacking forest. "We're in a bit of a jam."

My wyvern may be mischievous and occasionally traitorous, but she doesn't need to be asked twice. She leaps from my hand, already double, triple, octuple in size before she hits the ground.

Her scaly body swells until she's large enough to hold three of our group on her back without hindering her wings. That's only three trips. We can make it.

"Frank, I need you to find a cottage that direction somewhere." I point toward where the forest is supposed to be. "I can't give you much more information than that, except you might find a man made of metal there."

Frank tilts her head at me.

"I need you to take three of us at a time. Can you do it?"

Frank snorts, sending out a puff of smoke. At that, a few of the nearby trees shrink back.

"Rhyan, you should take Faela and Marella," I say. "I'm not sure what you'll find at the cottage."

"All right," she agrees. "Then Rivit, Phen, and Wistlee."

So Canon, Laramie, and I can keep hacking away at the trees. The idea of going last knots my stomach.

"You got it?" Rhyan eyes me expectantly, but it's truly a question. I have the option to say no.

I watch Faela and Marella scramble onto Frank's back. Then I force steel into my spine. "I've got it."

Rhyan nods once, then follows the other two onto Frank. With one powerful burst from Frank's wyvern legs, they're in the air, searching for the Tin Woodman's cottage.

I can only pray he's alive—and hasn't turned against his Ozite self too.

39

"CANON!" WISTLEE'S SCREAM

pulls my attention.

She's deeper in the trees than she should be, but it doesn't take long to see why. Phen has turned to stone again, and she's trying to make sure he doesn't get smashed to pebbles. She's up in one of the trees, clinging to a branch while it swings wildly.

"I can't." Canon's face is contorted in concern. "There is too much movement. I could hit her."

I'm already running before I have a chance to collect Laramie to help me. But it doesn't matter. I feel him at my heels and silently thank the stars for him—for his bravery and intuition, the way he anticipates needs and responds to them selflessly.

I mean, he's still the worst. Obviously. But thank goodness he's here.

Laramie sets to work slashing at the trunk. I'm hacking at the thin branches reaching for Phen like menacing fingers. Wistlee is still awkwardly trapped on a larger branch flailing through the air.

"Wist, you have to jump!" I shout. "Canon can't take a shot while you're up there."

Wistlee inhales a deep breath, then she spreads her wings and jumps. Her body lists awkwardly, her uneven wings throwing her off-balance. She tumbles to the forest floor the same as I would. As if she had no wings at all.

I rush to her and help her get out of the way. Laramie ducks, then Canon fires his shot. Splits the leafy beast in two. That tree won't move again.

Don't tell Faela.

Phen transforms back into flesh again, and I throw an exasperated glance his way. "You've got to stop doing that, Phen. You're going to get turned into ground cover."

He blows out a frustrated breath. "It keeps happening accidentally. Whenever I get"—his voice drops—"scared."

My heart goes to him, but I don't have more than a moment to spend on compassion.

"Frank will be back for the next group any minute," I say, hoping it's true. Surely they've found the Woodman's cottage by now . . .

Unless it's not visible from the air.

Rhyan will sort it out. Despite our fractured trust, I respect Rhyan as our captain. She's a good leader, and she'll find the cottage.

"Rivit?" I call. I've lost track of our Muse, and he's supposed to be in the next group out. "Where are you?"

He appears a moment later, tiptoeing from the darkness of the forest that shouldn't exist. A wide grin splits his face, and then I notice his pockets and backpack are absolutely bulging with . . .

"Apples?" Laramie has stayed in a readied stance, just waiting for a branch to try to snap at us. One eyebrow arches at Rivit's pockets.

The Muse holds a shiny red apple aloft, and I see now that, indeed, these fill his pockets too.

Rivit tosses the apple to Wistlee, who nets it in her feathered wing, batting it up so she can catch it in her hand easily.

"Fresh fruit!" Rivit proclaims. "Who doesn't like fresh fruit?"

Laramie shakes his head with a short chuckle. But I remember what Rhyan first told me about Muses, the keepers of story magic. They're all tricksters and pickpockets.

It would not have occurred to me to pilfer an attacking forest for food, but Rivit's not wrong. Who doesn't like fresh fruit? And he made it out in one piece, so it can't have been the worst idea.

A shadow passes over us, and I glance up to see Frank circling for a landing. No one is on her back, so I assume Rhyan, Marella, and Faela made it to the Woodman's cottage.

Safely, I hope.

The ground quakes when Frank touches down, and I'm once again glad she doesn't usually walk around at her full size. I would miss my pocket dragon.

Wyvern.

Whatever.

"Rivit, Wistlee, and Phen," Canon calls out. "You're up."

Wistlee looks my way. "You'll be all right?"

I nod. "Will you?"

She folds both wings behind her back. Flashes a pained smile. "Of course."

Frank blows a puff of smoke toward the trees, pushing them away while we settle the next crew onto her scaly back.

"Hold on tight," I say to Phen. He's looking slightly green.

He wraps his arms around Frank's neck, and Wistlee wraps her arms around Phen's waist, then spares me half a wink.

She's got him. In case he turns to stone again.

"I'll save you an apple, Emmy!" Rivit hops onto Frank behind Wistlee like he does this every day. Like bareback wyvern riding is his hobby.

"Thanks." I stroke Frank's neck. "You got them?" I ask her.

Frank bumps me with her snout—either a sign of affection or annoyance. How dare I question her competence? Of course she's got them.

A laugh escapes. "Good girl. Don't forget to come back for us."

She bumps me so hard this time, I almost lose my footing.

"Okay, okay." I pat her flank, and Frank catapults into the air once more.

With just the three of us left, it's easier to make sure no one dies via tree branch. We're all armed, and the goal is simple. Stay alive until Frank comes back. Keep the branches at bay. Don't die.

"This is killer on our blades." Laramie has just landed a hard swipe. He shakes his head. "We'll need to spend the rest of the day sharpening them."

I slice several tiny branches and about a hundred leaves from an attacking tree. "Look on the bright side. At least you're winning against this opponent. Unlike when you and I spar."

It's a ridiculous boast and we both know it. But he laughs, and that was the point—to make him smile.

Not that I like his smile.

"Ah, yes. We have finally found an opponent I can beat," he remarks. "A tree."

"Well"—I slice another branch—"when I retell this story, these trees will be stationary. And you will have only just bested them."

"Fair enough," he says. "That'll paint quite a picture— swordsman versus tree."

"Solider versus windmill. Downright quixotic."

He laughs. "What?"

"Never mind." I really have to get these Rivenlites some books.

Several minutes later, Frank touches down nearby, and it's our turn to get away from the homicidal foliage. Canon provides cover as we jog to Frank. But something in her eyes pulls me up short.

"Frank?" I place my hand on her head. "What is it?"

Her scaly brow is furrowed. Imagine a lizard looking concerned, and that's Frank's face right now.

Something is wrong, and we need to get to our friends as soon as possible.

And pray they're still alive.

FRANK WINGS HER WAY OVER

the forest of furious trees, now helpless to reach us even with their longest branches.

"Something is wrong," I say to Laramie behind me. "Frank looked upset."

"I know." His voice is tight.

The only thing we can do is get there as fast as possible. It can't be far. Frank made multiple trips relatively quickly. And if my mental map is correct, it should be just a bit west.

I try not to take in the scenery around us. Even if Oz had been resplendent in its full beauty, I couldn't enjoy the look of anything from this height. Unless I was safely tucked in an airplane.

But anyway, the only thing visible is miles of destruction and thick clouds of smoke.

After about a minute, Frank begins to descend toward a copse of trees that lies ahead, a small cottage just barely visible amid the leafy canopy. Thank goodness for Frank's keen wyvern eyes. I'm not sure I would have spotted it myself.

The trees appear to be still, as proper trees ought to be. No attacking branches or angry bark faces. But as Frank gets lower, I can see why she was concerned.

The cottage is under attack by a band of well-armed Munchkins.

Though Frank hasn't quite landed, Laramie jumps to the ground and sprints toward the fight.

But the Munchkins have guns.

Rifle versus sword—I don't like that match-up. Then it comes to mind that Laramie could probably shift into an automatic weapon, now that he's familiar with them.

The idea twists my stomach.

But he doesn't shift into a firearm. In fact, I blink and can't see him anymore. Because Rhyan and Marella have created a stream of fire, somehow avoiding the trees while holding back the attacking band. The flames are too bright to look at directly, and I imagine Laramie is somewhere behind them.

"You're in league with the Witch of the West!" one of the Munchkins cries.

"We're not!" Rhyan shouts back. "We're here to save Oz!"

"Save us?" another Munchkin scoffs. "We're finally free!"

I can't hold back a sigh. This is freedom?

"We don't want to kill you," Rhyan says loudly. "But we will if you force us." To prove her point, she causes the firestorm to swell. A nearby tree ignites.

"Fire sorceress!" a Munchkin cries.

But Rhyan accomplishes her goal. The Munchkin band—only six in all—seems to decide it's not worth it. They retreat, hopping onto several ATVs.

"We're watching you!" one calls back as they zoom away, kicking up dirt and fallen leaves in their wake.

After a long moment, Marella closes her hands, winking out the wind. Rhyan extinguishes her flames. Faela rushes to the tree that's still on fire, pressing her hands against it, whispering words under her breath, and somehow pulling the flames down. It's damaged, of course, but it'll live. Just a few scorch marks.

Canon looks at Rhyan. "Everyone whole?"

Rhyan wipes ash from her forehead with the back of her hand, succeeding only in smearing it. "I think so. We were looking for Emmy's ally, and they sprang from the trees."

The cottage appears to be the Tin Woodman's, though description in the book was sparse. Maybe it's not his . . .

"In the story, he's rusted nearby, but who knows." I frown at the door. "Did you go inside?"

"Poked my head in." Rhyan fixes her gloves. "It looked empty, but I didn't search."

I hesitate before the cottage door. Do I knock? Yes, I decide. Polite in any world.

Three raps on the wooden door. "Hello?"

"Go away," a small, miserable voice answers. "Just let me die."

I turn to Rhyan, eyebrows raised. She lifts a hand. "It looked empty. But I only glanced."

I turn the knob. No lock. I push my way into the Tin Woodman's cottage.

He's not visible at first, and I see why Rhyan thought the place was empty. No candles or lamps are lit, and it's surprisingly dark inside. Every corner draped in shadow. The darkness pressing in from the outside, pushing out from the interior. But scanning carefully, I can see a glint of silver in one corner.

The Woodman has folded himself up into a ball. And he's weeping, almost silently.

"Let me rust here," he whispers. "Just let me die."

"Mr. Woodman, sir?" I'm not sure how to address him. He is called Nick Chopper in later books, but only the Tin Woodman in *The Wonderful Wizard of Oz*. "It's okay. You can come out. The Munchkins are gone."

His quiet sobs are his only answer for a moment. "You should have let them come for me. I deserve it."

Wistlee sidles up beside me, her wings tucked tight so she can fit through the cottage door. She glances at me. "Is he well?"

"Apparently not." I look at the piteously miserable tin man. "The Munchkins are gone. Will you come out and see us?"

He sighs, his breath catching on another sob. He doesn't unfold himself from the corner, but he does lift his head off his metal knees. "I only wanted to help."

Before I can think better of it—after all, he could have an axe—I cross the cottage and lower myself to the floor. "I'm sure you did," I say, recalling every beat of his character. Every moment of his story that made me love him so.

"It wasn't supposed to be like this." He turns watery eyes toward me. "Let me rust here. Please. This is all my fault."

"Of course it's not." I put a hesitant hand on his arm. I'm startled by the cold metal, even though I knew it was there. It's strange all around to be talking to a metal man.

"It is my fault! It wasn't supposed to be this way. They promised it would make things better, not worse. And now look at Oz. Look what's become of the Munchkins. They were such a peaceable people." He drops his head onto his arms with a clank.

I glance helplessly at Wistlee, but she doesn't know the story, so she's even more lost than I am.

"Who promised you?" I have no idea how to comfort him, but perhaps he can provide some information that will help me do so.

Or help us figure out how to fix Oz.

"She's probably dead by now," he whispers into his arms.

Alarm spikes. "Dorothy?"

"The Witch of the North." He lifts his head. "Dorothy is another matter entirely. Surely she's lost forever too."

"We're trying to find her." The words sound feeble.

"Where could she have gone?" The Tin Woodman sniffles. "She hadn't her protective kiss, nor the instructions of the Good Witch. Nor," he wails, "the silver shoes!"

My breath catches. He's very aware of the proper story—more than he should be. "Do you know something about the shoes?"

The Tin Woodman's empty chest rises and falls. Finally, he drops his voice to the faintest whisper. "He's taken them."

"Do you mean the Wizard?"

The Woodman shakes his head. "No. But he promised me. He promised revenge against the Witch of the East for what she did to me."

"But Dorothy accidentally killed the Witch of the East with her house."

"I didn't know." His eyes are glistening. "Things had gone a bit wonky after the last time. We were supposed to reset, but it didn't quite work. Something had gone wrong. We were starting to remember." He turns toward the one small window of the cottage, staring out at nothing.

I'm struggling to understand what he means. But I need him to keep talking. "Then what happened?"

"Dorothy hadn't arrived yet. I guess she'd gone back to Kansas?" With that uncertain question, I imagine he'd be screwing up his face in confusion if he weren't made of metal. As it is, his expressions are pretty limited. I don't answer and he continues. "I knew the Witch of the East had wronged me."

You could say that again. In the book, she'd enchanted his axe to cut off his body parts one by one. Not the kind of backstory that would make it into a children's book today.

"I wanted vengeance, so I stole her silver shoes."

My heart leaps. "You have the shoes?"

"Oh, no." His tears start again. "I gave them to him."

"Him who? Do you know his name?" Desperation crawls through every word.

"My dear girl." He looks at me and shakes his head sadly. "It hardly matters anymore."

Dread settles in my stomach. "Why?"

"The silver shoes are no longer in Oz."

My heart stops. "Where has he taken them?"

"I'm sure I don't know. But everything has only gotten worse. The silver shoes are not in Oz, and we'll all die for it." He casts a forlorn glance at an axe propped in the far corner of his cottage. "Off with their heads, indeed."

Maybe he heard it from one of the Munchkins. Maybe it's not actually a separate data point. But the impossible truth that struck me yesterday hits again today.

Worry swims in Wistlee's gaze. "What is it?"

"Somehow, the stories are communicating with each other— and it might be the key to everything."

41

"THIS IS *NOT* YOUR FAULT," I say for the fortieth time.

The Tin Woodman has given up trying to convince me. He doesn't even answer, just shakes his head. Stares listlessly at the wall.

My tangled feelings are crashing into each other. Like emotional gridlock. It's a multi-car pileup in my brain, and I don't know how to clean it up.

"Come with us," I blurt.

The Woodman lifts his gaze. I've finally said something that surprises him. "What?"

"Come with us. The shoes are gone, but we still need to find Dorothy and the Witch of the North, if she lives. You could help us."

He seems to consider it for a moment. But then he balls himself tighter into the corner. "I just ruin everything. If I'd had a heart, maybe it would've been different. But I'm useless. Worse than useless. I ruin everything."

"But you were always the kindest one. That was the whole point! You had a heart all along. You just didn't realize it."

He shakes his head, and the metal grates dangerously. He's already beginning to rust.

I look about for an oil can, but I don't see anything. Where did Dorothy find it in the book? On a shelf in the cottage. I rummage through the cupboards in the kitchen and find nothing. No food, because what does a tin man need with food?

But no oil can either.

I slam a cupboard door, unsure whether to scream or cry in frustration.

"I buried it." His voice is quiet again. "You'll never find the oil can."

"But why?" Tears prick my eyes. "Please, let me help you!"

"Allow me to rust."

Rivulets of tears start down my cheeks. We have to be able to help *someone* here. Surely.

Wistlee's comforting presence appears at my side. "He'll be reset if we can rescue the story," she reminds me softly.

If we can rescue the story. But can we? I don't know how that works. Do we need the silver shoes in order to rescue the story? Or would finding the Witch of the North and Dorothy be enough?

A headache pulses behind my eyes.

I need to tell Rhyan about the silver shoes.

The Tin Woodman was my last real hope that one of Dorothy's allies would become one of our allies. I can't imagine setting Oz right—can't imagine Oz *being* right—without any of them.

"Emmy?" Wistlee says. "Let's leave him."

I have to try one more time. I cross the cottage and lower myself down to the Woodman's level again. "You always had a heart," I say. "That was the whole point. You spend the entire story showing kindness and caring about everyone. You never needed the Wizard to give you anything."

He blinks slowly through the rust collecting around his eyes. "That's a nice thought, dear girl. That what we needed was inside us all along."

Then he leans his head back against the wall, closes his eyes, shudders a weary breath.

And completely gives up.

I'm starting to feel like I'm leaving chunks of my heart all over Oz. Exiting the cottage, I'm half the person I was going in. Wistlee is practically holding me up, and I can't stop crying.

"Oh, spheres." Rhyan rushes to my side. "What happened?"

It feels ridiculous to put into words. Could these Rivenlites possibly understand why this is hard? Why it's traumatic to watch the Tin Woodman let himself rust?

"He won't come with us," is all Wistlee says by way of explanation.

And it's enough for empathy to ignite in Rhyan's eyes. "I'm sorry, Emmy."

"I just wanted one of them to be real. I mean, really themselves." Then I blurt, "Rhyan, the silver shoes are gone."

Every Novemite turns toward me. If they weren't listening before, they are now.

"Gone?" Rhyan stares at me blankly. "What do you mean, gone?"

"They're not in Oz. At least that's what the Woodman said."

"Perhaps they've gone back to . . . Kanziz?"

"Kansas." I pause, mulling this. Could it be possible Dorothy took them back to story-Kansas?

But it can't be that. Unless the mysterious "he" gave them to Dorothy and told her to get out of Oz. Somehow this doesn't feel right, but I suppose it could be possible.

"Maybe," I say. "But the Tin Woodman made it sound like they'd left. Fully left. As in, left the sphere."

If it's possible, her stare gets blanker. "Left the sphere. That isn't . . . You can't . . ."

"I know. Nothing should be able to leave, right?"

"Right, except through a gateway." She frowns. "What else did he say?"

"Off with their heads."

"What?"

"The stories are communicating with each other," I remind her.

Rhyan shakes her head. "That's also not possible."

"I know, but . . ." I bite my lip. "Well, I'm not possible either, am I?"

Rhyan's eyes bore into me, demanding I elaborate.

"I shouldn't be here, theoretically. I'm from Earth. I shouldn't have been able to come to Rivenlea at all. My unfinished draft certainly shouldn't be in Ambryfell. My sister shouldn't be trapped in a bubble in the Silvarum. And yet . . ."

"And yet all these things are happening." Rhyan blows out a long breath. "So what does it mean?"

Rivit surprises me by piping up. "It means the rules are breaking."

"Emmy is breaking them," Marella inserts, somewhat unhelpfully.

But she's not wrong. Who can fault her for pointing out the obvious?

Even so, Laramie rounds on her. "It's not Emmy. She's not causing it."

"She's at the center of it," Marella counters.

"Can't you see she's as much a victim as anyone?" His voice rises. "These things are happening *to* her. Will you back off?"

I stand in stunned silence. Behind Laramie, fully in my view, Phen grins. If he says something smart, I'll never forgive him.

Or I'll give him the silent treatment for at least an hour.

But Phen doesn't get a chance to make any kind of remark, and I don't get a chance to recover from Laramie's defense of my virtue, or whatever. Because, at that precise moment, a low growl sounds from within the forest.

Frank, still full-size, bounds toward the growl before I can stop her. Her tail whips into a tree trunk as she squeezes into a space too small to accommodate her. The tree nearly cracks in two.

"Frank!" I shout after her. I move to follow—unwisely.

But I don't get far before Frank bursts back out of the trees, her reptilian eyes abnormally wide, her expression seeming to shout, "Run!"

We all scurry backward, but not fast enough to escape the beast at Frank's heels.

It takes me three full heartbeats to process what I'm seeing. The mangy, tangled fur. The tawny head twice the size of Frank's. Paws as big as Volkswagens.

At least it seems so.

Because somehow, though I can't explain it, the Cowardly Lion is as big as a semitruck.

And he's barreling straight toward us.

RHYAN'S SHOUTING ORDERS,

but I'm standing there, barely hearing. I can't seem to move.

The Lion is enormous. He takes out several trees as he crashes into the small clearing, attempting to eat my wyvern.

He's trying to eat Frank.

The thought is enough to jumpstart my frozen self. I draw my sword, as if it would help. I'm a little comforted to see Laramie do the same.

We duck behind the Woodman's cottage to escape a swipe of the Lion's paw. "How is he so huge?" I gasp. "He's supposed to be the size of a normal lion."

Laramie peeks around the corner to assess the Lion's current location, then glances back at me. "When things start breaking, all bets are off. Stories can evolve in strange ways."

I hadn't considered it too deeply before, but of course that's true. Otherwise, how did Munchkin technology evolve to include vehicles and weaponry overnight?

Still it's strange to see that the Cowardly Lion—Dorothy's friend—has turned into an actual monster of sorts.

Rhyan and Frank are each attacking him with streams of fire from different angles. They seem to mostly succeed in burning off patches of fur and not much else, but at least they're keeping him busy.

The smell, though, is pretty brutal.

Canon misses with a laser from one of his hands. He lands with his next try, and the Lion lets out an enraged roar. He doesn't seem able to speak anymore. He's gone wild, and I see now why the trees obey him.

Of all the dangers we've faced in Oz so far, I've never felt so certain about our impending demise.

On the other side of the Woodman's cottage, a female voice cries out.

"Captain!" Rivit calls. "Faela's down!"

My stomach drops as I imagine the giant paw crashing into gentle Faela, felling her like one of these trees.

Next to me, Wistlee is struggling as she tries again to take off. Attempting to scale the beast's back to subdue it from above is my best guess.

But her wings fail her again. She mutters in frustration, then pulls her rope from her belt. I expect her to lasso the neck of the Dastardly Lion, but that's not her plan. Instead, she catches a branch above the Lion's head, looping her rope over it, then holds tight to the ends and scrambles up the trunk of a nearby tree.

From her new vantage, Wistlee swings across the open space and lands on the Lion's back with admirable grace, considering the awkwardness of her makeshift rope setup.

The Lion flinches but takes little notice of her otherwise, busy with Rhyan's and Frank's fire streams assaulting him from the ground. Wistlee deploys her wings, spreading them wide for balance, then gingerly unfastens her rope from the branch above her head after two unsuccessful attempts.

She's pulling something from her belt, and I can't see what at first. But after she ties it to the end of the rope, then uses it as weight to swing the rope around the Lion's neck, I can tell it's some sort of hook.

Wistlee has the rope-and-hook mechanism secured tightly around the Lion's neck before he even seems to remember he's got someone on his back. She glides down, landing somewhat off-balance, but not enough to stop her from sprinting the moment she hits the ground. Before the Lion can collect his wits, Wistlee has the other rope end tied around the trunk of a tree.

"Emmy!" she calls, tossing something my way.

I catch it without hesitation. It's another rope. I turn to Laramie. "Help me."

Wistlee is tossing ropes to others in the Novem and directing traffic. Her plan begins to unfold as she positions us, tells us what to do with her ropes. Soon we're lashing the Lion to the ground, Gulliver-style. Rhyan, Frank, and Canon keep him distracted enough that he doesn't rip the ropes away from the trees until there are too many.

He falls to one knee when Laramie and Rivit pull a rope sharply to the ground. Then he takes two more knees and finally crashes all the way to the ground, letting out a monstrous roar of frustration.

The sound waves hopscotch down my spine, and I steady myself. "Laramie, do you think you could shift into a tranquilizer gun?"

He casts a confused glance my way as he secures the end of another rope. "A what?"

"Never mind."

But Faela seems to be on my page. She's mixing tiny bottles of substances from her pack, and I can only assume she's creating a sedative of some kind. When she turns my way, the gashes down the side of her body come into view. I gasp.

"Oh, Faela."

She gives me a small smile as she hands the finished tincture to Rivit. "Don't worry."

She must have balms and salves to help her wounds, but I'm still going to worry. The Lion took quite a swipe at her.

Rivit edges toward the thrashing creature, then somehow

dodges every snap of the Lion's jaws with precision to drip Faela's precious tincture into the salivating mouth.

It seems too small an amount to do anything useful to such a large creature, but almost as soon as the liquid hits the Lion's tongue, he begins to blink. His eyes cloud and the thrashing subsides.

The Lion stretches his mouth in a yawn and curls up as much as the ropes allow him. His eyes close, and within seconds, he begins to rumble like a giant house cat, purring through its afternoon nap.

Marella is already dabbing medicine on Faela's wounds. Rhyan is patting Frank, telling her she's a very good girl, indeed. Everyone looks to be okay.

Relief washes through me, followed immediately by exhaustion.

I look for Wistlee to congratulate her on a well-executed plan. But I turn just as she brushes past me.

"Hey, Wist?"

She stops and swivels so our eyes meet. She forces another smile. "And you thought you were the one who wouldn't measure up."

Any argument stays lodged in my throat as she turns back around and continues toward the captain.

She just saved us, and yet she's still bothered about the wings. How do I convince her flying doesn't matter, especially when she's so brilliant? Not to mention talented and clever.

My eyes collide with Phen, who was also watching her. "I've been trying to tell you both," he says with a shrug.

I'm ready to explain why my situation is completely different, but the ground rumbles. The leaves above us quake as the forest floor shakes.

"The trees," I realize aloud, whirling to Rhyan. "The trees!"

She's already got it. Not these trees surrounding us, but *the* trees—the sentient ones who were attacking us before.

The ones who avow the Lion as their king.

They're coming for us.

"We've got to get out of here." Rhyan's face is grim. "Which way, Emmy?"

I try to get my bearings, try to remember what comes next, which way lies the Emerald City.

"There." I point. "I think. We should reach the edge of this forest soon."

"We'll just hope those attacking trees aren't heading in from that direction." She raises her voice. "Let's go!"

Frank's scaly flank gets a generous rub as we skirt through the trees. "You've been very helpful."

She snorts, but she looks spent. Exhausted.

"Shrink down," I suggest. "You can ride in my pocket."

She obeys immediately. A moment later, I'm scooping her off the ground and tucking her into my pocket.

Novem XVII hobbles out of the woods a bit later, a little worse for wear but without further incident from rabid trees. Finally, a stroke of luck.

Except, the moment we break from the tree line, my stomach sinks. Up ahead is the ravine that comes next in the story, just as I expected. What I somehow forgot was that the Tin Woodman got Dorothy and company safely across.

And the poor Woodman is back in his cottage, probably paralyzed with rust.

My brain begins constructing ideas for how we might get to the other side, weary and beat up as we are, but then fear ripples through me.

In the story, the urgency to get across the ravine was created by the rumbling of a pack of Kalidahs coming from the forest.

And I'm pretty sure I hear their strange growls now.

KALIDAHS ARE DESCRIBED IN

The Wonderful Wizard of Oz as beasts with the heads of tigers and the bodies of bears. I tried vainly to picture it as a child, and even my illustrated copy didn't help much. The drawings looked odd—goofy, even—and reading about the harrowing escape of Dorothy and her friends didn't carry quite the bite it was supposed to. The creatures seemed too ridiculous.

But now that I'm fighting back-to-back with Laramie once again, barely avoiding the swipe of a bear's paw, only just dodging the snap of a tiger's jaws, I can see how this weird hybrid creature is, indeed, terrifying.

Plenty of bite. I recant my childhood testimony. Kalidahs are ferocious and not at all goofy.

The Kalidah before us rears up onto its bearlike hind paws, and Laramie takes the opportunity to run his sword through its chest. I wince away from the blood spatter but feel no regret.

There's nothing kind or nostalgic about these creatures, and if we need to dispose of them, I feel just fine about it.

"Emlyn!"

I look over at Rhyan, whose arm is covered in blood. I quickly realize it's not hers. She's cleaning off a dagger.

I suppress a shudder.

"Can Frank take us across this ravine?"

I reach into my pocket and withdraw my sleeping wyvern. "She seems exhausted. Should I try waking her?"

Rhyan shakes her head. "No, I expected this. I just thought I'd check. She'll need time before she's able to grow again. If she's able to grow again while we're still in Oz. Only Rivenlite air is ideal for wyverns."

Panic spikes my heart. "What do you mean? Does it hurt her to be here?" I curl my hand over Frank's sleeping form, careful not to crush her scaly little body. "And the air quality has been bad on top of everything."

Rhyan's smile quirks—the first true smile I've seen from her in a while. "She'll be all right. She's just going to tire quickly. And she fought well today."

Irrational pride swells through me. It's not like I had anything to do with it. But she's my little traitor, and I love her.

Rhyan openly smiles now, and I know she can read my feelings plainly. But the warm moment fades quickly, and she's back to business as captain. "So, this ravine . . ."

"The Woodman is supposed to make a log bridge," I say, as Laramie fends off another Kalidah.

Rhyan nods once. "Got it."

Then she takes off toward Canon and Faela, presumably to enlist them in the work of felling a tree. Laramie and I are on the defensive again.

"Was hoping we wouldn't have to fight off anything else so soon," Laramie puffs between strikes. "I've had enough for one day."

"Me too." I jab at the Kalidah, but it's not quite enough force for a mortal strike. "Though you could shift into a sparrow or something and take a break up there." I nod vaguely to the sky, finally beginning to darken.

Some days seem eternal.

"Yes, but I wouldn't leave—" He only just blocks a bear-paw swipe.

"Pay attention!" My voice pitches oddly, panic constricting my throat. I finally land the deadly wound I've been aiming for.

I fight the urge to close my eyes as I retrieve my sword. This is a bloody business, and I'm not a fan. "I'm a pescatarian," I say aloud.

Laramie ignores my random comment. "Thanks," he says instead, noting my kill. He shakes out his shoulder, and I wonder if he's been hit.

"A bit distracted?" I raise a brow at him.

He flashes a smile, eyes on me. "Always."

My stomach cartwheels. But before I have to think of something to say, Wistlee calls us. "Emmy, Laramie!"

We turn in unison to see that Faela and Canon have made a crude bridge, on which half the Novem currently stands.

"Come on," Phen beckons.

Another group of Kalidahs is bolting through the trees, heading for us, so we don't waste time. We sprint to the log just as Faela climbs down on the other side. Laramie covers me as I step onto the log, my boot skidding on the bark.

I squash down my perfectly rational rising terror.

There is no choice. The ravine must be crossed, and right now, this is the only way to do it.

Rhyan hops down on the other side and draws her bow. "Laramie, go! I'll cover you." She withdraws an arrow from her quiver and pulls the string taut.

My feet slip again, and I stop.

A second later, I feel Laramie at my back, holding me steady. Helping me balance.

An arrow sails past my left ear. I have to move, or I'm going to get us both killed. I scoot one foot a little forward, then the next.

"Good," Laramie says, following along after me as I creep forward like an inchworm.

Foot worm.

Yard worm.

Measuring tape.

"Tapeworm," I say out loud.

"Do you have much experience with those?"

I take another step. "Obviously. Never leave home without one." I take three steps in a row, Laramie's bracing presence still at my back.

"Good to know," he says. "Watch your step there," he adds

"Don't tell me what to do," I shoot automatically. But I heed his warning and step down from the end of the log carefully.

The end of the log.

I spin around and grin at Laramie as he jumps down from the log too. As he grins back, I'm lost in his chocolate eyes a moment before I remember the entire Novem is standing there. I turn around and clear my throat. "Canon, would you destroy the bridge, please? Don't need the Kalidahs following us across."

"Gladly." One exacting slice from our Bolt and the log bridge collapses into the ravine.

"At least I won't have to kill any more of them." Rhyan peers into her quiver. "I don't want to use the last of my arrows."

"Who knows what else lies ahead," Canon agrees.

"Emmy does." Wistlee pats my shoulder. "She's guided us well thus far."

My cheeks heat.

"I agree," Rhyan says as she looks at me. "And what does our Dragon think about that field as a spot to camp for the night?"

"I'd say we've had enough for one day." For a year.

The Novem follows Rhyan toward the field.

Laramie lingers a moment to spare me a courtly bow. "After you, Your Royal Hostess. I did not realize your subjects are apparently tapeworms, but the more I learn about you, the more intrigued I am."

For once, I play his game. I incline my head like a queen, wave graciously, then whisk past him with utmost dignity.

Privately contemplating how he can make parasites seem enticing.

GENTLY, I REMOVE FRANK

from my pocket. If I listen closely, I can hear her quiet snores.

"She should eat." I turn to find Rhyan standing there with her bow. "Frank worked hard today."

"Yeah. She did." I scratch Frank's head with my finger. "Frank? Wake up."

Frank's lidless eye cracks open. Her snout scrunches in drowsy annoyance.

"I'll hunt for you," Rhyan says to her.

At that, Frank perks up. And expands to the size of a house cat.

I glance at Rhyan, bemused. "One squirrel should do."

She smiles. "Be back in a few."

Faela and Rivit have built a nice fire pit, and Rhyan lights it on her way out to hunt, Canon on her heels. Faela and Marella set to work preparing food for the Novem. The rest of us set up the tents.

The vast field seems peaceful enough, at least at the moment. The countryside here is less populated, so the odds of running into a raiding band of Munchkins is relatively slim.

Fearsome beasts? Who knows. But we have to sleep sometime.

By the time Rhyan returns with a dead rodent for Frank and two rabbits for dinner, we have camp fully set up and the beginnings of dinner simmering over the fire. Faela is kind enough to make a small pot of vegetarian stew for me.

"Hey, Emmy," Phen says when he, Wistlee, and I finally have a moment to sit and rest. "What were you and Laramie talking about?" He waggles his eyebrows.

"Tapeworms," I answer immediately, offering no further explanation, even as his eyes widen at my unexpected response.

Wistlee clears her throat, saving me from myself. "Emmy, tell us what you know of the silver shoes."

Faela is offering me my special bowl of stew, and after she's served both Wistlee and Phen, I speak. "Wist, you're a good friend. But you really don't have to pretend. It's all right."

She blows on a spoonful of steaming stew. "Pretend what?"

"That you think the shoes are important. I know Rhyan doesn't think so, and Canon thinks we just need to find Dorothy or the Witch of the North."

"Yes." Wistlee swallows her spoonful. "Our leaders believe Dorothy and the Witch are priorities." She stares into her stew as she stirs it for a moment. "But I was in the cottage with you."

I had nearly forgotten she heard everything the Tin Woodman said.

She cocks her head to the side. "I just got a . . . sense."

"I know that feeling well."

"Aye. Deep within. I could feel that the shoes mattered. I think you're right."

Wistlee thinks I'm right. The revelation triggers a swell of emotion, and I'm deeply grateful to her. For her.

I absently stroke Frank's head. She's already finished her food and curled up next to me.

"The shoes hold a charm," I say.

"A certain *je ne sais quoi*?" Phen waggles his brows again.

I laugh. "No, a magic charm. The Munchkins weren't sure exactly what the shoes did, but they knew they were important. Because the Wicked Witch of the East guarded them closely."

Laramie lowers himself down beside Wistlee. "Mind if I join?"

Wistlee is too fast, responding before I can protest. "Not at all, Laramie. Please." She scoots to the side to allow him more space.

I inch closer to Frank on my other side when Wist wiggles over, and now I'm sandwiched between *two* traitors.

But Wistlee turns to me calmly, pretending she doesn't know exactly what I'm thinking. "Do continue, Emmy."

My thoughts have scattered, and I try to collect them. "Dorothy wears the shoes for the entire story, not realizing they can carry her across the desert surrounding Oz. They are the way to get home to Kansas."

Phen rocks back and briefly closes his eyes. "So they are a means of transportation."

"Yes." My stomach stirs uneasily. "They can carry Dorothy away from here."

"Or anyone anywhere?" Laramie's gaze is on me intently, and for once, it doesn't make me squirm.

"Presumably."

"And now that the shoes have left the sphere—"

"But Rhyan says that's impossible," Wistlee reminds us.

"Pretend it's possible," Laramie proposes. "Let's suppose for a moment that the Woodman is right." His eyes go to me again. "What would it mean?"

"I have no idea. Would the shoes work outside the sphere?"

"Let's say they do," Laramie ventures. "What then?"

I think through the implications. "Perhaps they could be used for travel *anywhere*."

"That's definitely a valuable item," Phen observes.

"Like seven-league boots," I put in.

Three curious Rivenlite stares turn my way.

"It's an item from European—that is, Earthling—folklore." They may not know what Europe is. "You take one step wearing the boots and travel seven leagues. Helps you get places faster."

"So perhaps the silver shoes function like that?" Wistlee asks.

"But there's more." My intuition is spiking again. "They basically let Dorothy fly. These are storybook shoes."

"Imagine what they might be able to do outside of their sphere," Laramie adds.

My heart stutters. "We have to get them back."

The four of us sit around the fire brainstorming as long as is wise. But we still don't have any idea how to find the shoes. They could be anywhere in the universe. Anyone could have taken them. The only clue the Woodman gave us is that the thief is male.

That doesn't narrow it down much.

Wistlee's eyelids are drooping, and Phen has been patting the same spot on Frank's head for the last half hour. The rest of the Novem turned in at least ten minutes ago.

"We need to get some sleep." I bite back a yawn. "Tomorrow will bring plenty of adventure, I'm sure."

"Twist my arm." Phen pops to his feet—unsteadily, since he's only half awake. "See you all at sunup." He doesn't even remember to nod conspicuously to me and Laramie or wag his brows. He must be really exhausted.

"Goodnight, Laramie," Wistlee says. Then, "See you in the tent, Emmy."

I nod back. "Sure. Three minutes."

When Laramie and I are alone, I suddenly can't remember why I didn't leave with Wist. My mouth dries out like an old leaf. Words have fled, along with my good sense.

Laramie clears his throat. Then he moves toward me, closing the space where Wistlee just sat.

My brain explodes in forty-seven different directions.

He frowns and reaches toward my leg. Reflexively, I jump back.

"What are you doing?" My voice stays low, somehow, but the question is filled with an appropriate amount of alarm.

And surprise. Laramie has embarrassed me more than once, but he never struck me as the type to take this sort of liberty.

He draws back as if he's received an electrical shock. "Oh, I'm sorry. I didn't mean—" He gives his head a shake. "I just—I think you're injured."

"What?" I glance down and realize he wasn't reaching toward my thigh, like I'd originally thought. Instead, he'd been about to touch my ankle, folded beneath me crisscross.

I'd taken off my boots and socks at some point, easing the strain on my tired feet. A three-inch patch of skin around my left ankle is visible, and it's strange. I lean closer, frown at it. Try to take in what I'm seeing.

Frank huffs in her sleep and stretches. And then it clicks. I comprehend what I'm looking at and speak it aloud.

"Scales."

45

I SAY IT. I SEE IT. BUT I CAN'T

fully grasp it. "Those are . . ."

Laramie pulls in a sharp breath. "Scales. You're right." He runs his hand over my leg. "May I?" He gestures to the hem of my pants.

I nod mutely, brain working a thousand miles per hour without landing on anything helpful—like explanations or the ability to engage in verbal communication.

Laramie rolls up my pants, exposing another inch or two of my leg. The scales extend to the edge of my calf, then fade into normal human skin.

The fire is burned down to embers, glowing softly in the velvety darkness. I twist my leg, marveling as the opalescent purple scales catch the light. They seemingly absorb it, causing the scales to glow from within.

It's the exact color of my stone in the Taenarum.

"Laramie?" The weakness—fear, confusion—in my own voice is such that I want to banish it. To disallow it from telling on me, projecting exactly how I feel.

And the fact that I'm turning to Laramie for reassurance and explanation.

But the strangeness of the situation overrides my emotional hangups.

He runs his thumb over the scales. "Maybe a rash?"

In spite of myself, I laugh. "From the tapeworm, probably."

He smiles, but he doesn't look up. He's checking my other leg. Because if this is just in that one spot, confined to one ankle, perhaps it *is* a rash or maybe an infection. Something explained by infestation or contact from something.

The semi-reasonable explanations that have begun to bloom in my mind are immediately squashed. Identical opalescent scales are on the other leg too.

Laramie slowly shakes his head. A deep crease pinches between his brows. "I don't understand. Unless . . ."

"Please, out with it," I say nervously. "It couldn't possibly be more disturbing than my thoughts."

· "Do you think it's possible you're . . ." His gaze drifts to my wyvern, still curled up like a kitty beside me, totally oblivious to the fact that her human is—

"Becoming a Dragon." My heart hiccups. I stare down at my newly purple skin. "I'm turning into a Dragon."

"Or maybe you always were one."

Part of me believes that when I wake in the morning, my ankles will be returned to normal. I will have fully human skin again. Maybe I'll even ask Laramie about the scale situation, and he'll have no idea what I'm talking about because the whole thing was just a bizarre exhaustion-induced dream. Just a dream.

Quite appropriate for an Ozian adventure.

I don't even check my ankles in the morning. As I put on my socks and boots, I still don't look, gripping onto the possibility that everything is completely fine. Normal, even. Mundane, if you will.

Except for the fact that I'm traipsing through an actual storyworld, trying to rescue characters and fix plots.

But when I exit my tent, Laramie is already up, sipping

something steamy from a camper mug. His eyes meet mine, and I know immediately I didn't dream it. Those scales were real, and we both saw them.

Okay. Plan B.

"Hey," I say quietly.

"Hey." He pours another cup of coffee and hands it to me.

I wrap my chilled fingers around it and allow the hot liquid to practically scald me before I reposition. "About last night . . ."

I wait for this to be like a YA novel. For him to know exactly what I'm going to say and to wave me off. Tell me he's got this, don't worry about it.

But he doesn't. He just waits for me to go on.

"Could we . . . I mean, maybe it's best not to tell anyone just yet?"

His brows rise, but he doesn't respond, which forces me to say more.

"Until we know what it means?" I say, and it sounds more like a question than I wanted it to.

But I'm not sure if it's the best course. What's the protocol, really, when one discovers scales on her legs?

He takes a sip of coffee. Then another. Painfully slow. Now I'm the one waiting.

"You don't think we should tell Rhyan?" he says after forever.

I'm not sure. We probably should tell Rhyan and Wistlee and Phen to get their takes. Maybe even Canon, because he's such a know-it-all. Maybe he'll have some clue what's going on.

But I'm still mad at Canon and don't wish to discuss my ankles with someone who knew about Camille and didn't tell me.

"I don't know," I admit. "I don't know what's the best strategy."

"Some Dragon." His eyes twinkle over his mug.

I shoot him a glare. "Cute. Real funny."

"People tell me so." He winks. The humor falls from his expression. "I don't know, either."

"So maybe we should keep it to ourselves for a little while? When it makes some sort of sense, we can tell them then."

Uncertainty crosses his face. Eventually, he nods. "If that's what you want. For now," he adds.

"Thanks." I take a sip of semi-muddy coffee.

"Emmy." Rhyan's crisp voice nearly makes me drop my drink.

"What? No, I didn't," I blurt.

She pulls up short, confusion on her face. "What?"

"Nothing. I don't know. No."

Laramie snorts and then hurriedly sips his coffee.

Rhyan's eyes dart between the two of us, then she shakes her head, obviously deciding it's not worth it. She addresses me again. "Which way, do you think?"

Oh. I scan the horizon.

It's easier to get my bearings now in the full light of day.

"We need to find the formerly yellow brick road. I think that's it up ahead." I indicate the direction of what appears to be a brick path.

The bricks aren't even beige anymore. They're more of a warm gray.

We break camp and reach the drab-brick road before the sun has fully burned off the nighttime chill. These bricks have seen better days, and it's not just the fact that they're draining of color.

They appear to have been laid centuries ago and the land has settled unevenly beneath them, creating a lopsided patchwork of stone. Many of the bricks are cracked, some missing altogether, and weeds have found a happy little paradise to call home.

"We might be better off walking beside the road," I say to Rhyan, nearly tripping over a crooked brick for the fourth time.

"No kidding."

The weeds are choking out the bricks in some places, and I gaze at one patch for a moment before my vision fuzzes. I blink and shake my head. Everything returns to normal.

With a frown, I keep on beside the rest of the Novem.

Three more times, my vision blurs, and once I become so dizzy, I have to grab Wist's arm to keep upright.

With a pang, I wonder if my body is short-circuiting because of my Dragoning.

Drongoning. Drangonging. Dragoninning.

A giddy giggle floats up around me, and I'm vaguely aware it's my own laugh.

"Emmy?" I feel Wist throw a glance over my head to Phen, but I don't bother to assure them I'm fine.

"Dragoninning," I say instead.

It isn't until we crest a rise and the meadow ahead comes into full view that I understand.

The countryside has fallen into disarray. Many fields have been burned, and the thick patches of wildflowers Dorothy and her friends ran across in *The Wonderful Wizard of Oz* are gone, those weeds the only plants left standing.

And yet the field before us is untouched, and I realize with a start those weeds weren't weeds at all. Those plants were just not in bloom yet, their buds closed tightly in odd, fuzzy pods.

"Poppies."

A crimson meadow stretches before us, poppies in full bloom as if enchanted to remain perpetually open, no matter the season.

They probably are. Enchanted.

"Poppies." I turn to Rhyan. "The flowers will make us fall asleep." My mind floats. Fall, then sleep. Fall to sleep. And turn us a little loopy too, apparently.

I hear Faela giggling oddly nearby. At least I know I'm not the only one.

"Masks," Rhyan orders, whipping off her pack and pulling the drawstring loose. "Everyone, grab your masks!"

Yes. Good idea. I pull out my mask and strap it to my face. Check the seal. I draw two deep breaths and immediately feel less fuzzy.

"This is working," I tell Rhyan through the mask. "It's filtering out whatever causes the drowsiness." The scarlet poppies sway enticingly in the breeze as if beckoning us forward.

A shiver tiptoes down my spine.

"But we should probably hurry anyway," I caution.

Novem XVII plows through the meadow at Rhyan's command. Normally, I'd be careful of flowers—no need to destroy beautiful things as you move through the world.

But not today. These flowers are trying to harm us, so I don't feel bad charging through and trampling them.

They'll probably magically spring back as soon as we're through, anyway.

Frank's snores boom from my pocket, and I realize she's probably being affected by the poppies too. But it doesn't matter because she's tiny again, tucked safely beside me. As long as I get through this field as quickly as possible, we'll both be fine.

I think.

I'm about halfway through the field when Faela lets out another weird giggle. "Oh dear. Dear, dear. What lovely red lips you have."

I turn to see her bent over toward one of the tallest poppies. Possibly preparing to kiss its red petals.

"Fae?" Marella is pulling at her arm, trying to get her to move again. "Come on. Let's go!"

"Just a wink and a nap and a snooze and a kiss. One moment. Thank you, bye." She giggles and begins to lower herself to the ground, despite Marella's efforts.

I drop beside her, looking closely. "The seal. Something's wrong with the seal on her mask." The rubber that should be making an airtight lock around her nose and mouth has been damaged somehow.

"Faela!" Marella's voice pitches, tears sparkle in her eyes. I imagine the desperation I'd feel if Wistlee or Phen went loopy and collapsed in this field.

And maybe it would have been as simple as carrying her out, but maybe these poppies cause brain damage. Who knows?

I don't take the time to consider any of this. I just pull Faela's useless mask from her face, whip off my mask, and place it on our fallen Harmony.

"She'll be okay," I say to Marella.

Faela's already stirring, and her eyes are starting to clear.

"Emmy." Wistlee stands stock still a few paces behind me, staring at the three of us on the ground. "What did you do?"

"It's fine. I just need to—" I sway on my feet as I try to stand. "Oh."

Then I take off at a loping, wild run. I fall thrice, skin one of my palms, and only just stop myself from smashing my face into the dirt.

The poppies multiply. They stretch on endlessly. Then they swell up, and a crimson tsunami crashes over me.

Or maybe I just fell down.

I was so close. Or maybe I was extremely far. Same difference.

Scarlet petals envelop me from above. A sliver of blue sky peeks through the scarlet canopy. But I only see red. I breathe deeply.

This is fine.

A face blocks out the sliver of blue. Interrupts the calming blanket of crimson.

"Cherry. Scarlet. Claret."

The face shakes. As if I'm weird. Or I've done something silly. That can't possibly be true.

My body lifts from the ground, and I'm pretty sure I'm levitating. But then I realize arms have wrapped around me. I'm being scooped.

"Like ice cream. Mashed pertayters." I giggle. "Po-tay-toes."

"Help me out a little, will you?" the face says, and I feel my arm being swung around a pair of broad shoulders.

I fight to keep my eyes open. Fight to stay upright so the face doesn't have too hard a time carrying me the rest of the way through the ocean of poppies.

The corners of my vision begin to cloud, then fade to black. But I force my eyes open. They come into focus briefly on the face.

It's a good face. Even through the mask, I can see it's a good face.

I giggle, and it sounds like champagne bubbles. "You're so pretty," I burble.

Then I pass out.

46

STARS DANCE BEFORE MY

eyes. I crack them to slits, and punishing light assaults me. I groan and roll to my side.

"Morning, sunshine."

I know the voice, and I wonder why *this* voice is here instead of one of my friends.

Laramie is your friend, some traitorous part of my brain reminds me.

"Is not," I say aloud.

"Oh, yeah?" He places the back of his hand against my forehead, checking my temperature. "Tell me all about it."

"I will tell you nothing." I try to sit up, only to wooze back over. I resign myself to resting here.

"You had plenty to say before you lost consciousness."

Panic strikes me. Suddenly I'm able to sit straight up without getting too dizzy. "I did?"

"Oh, yes." He grins. "Plenty."

I claw back through my memories, trying to grasp an inkling of what I might have said.

The options are not appealing.

"I . . ." My gaze lands on my boots, and instantly all the embarrassing things I might have said to Laramie flee my mind.

A scarier option presents itself. "Did I say anything about . . ." I nod toward my ankles.

"No. Don't worry. It was far more entertaining than that."

Relief floods my veins, but then I consider curling up in the dirt for a while. "I don't even want to know."

His grin broadens, and he turns to Rhyan, who's hovering nearby with the rest of the Novem. "She's fine."

Everyone's masks are off. We must be out of the poppies.

A canteen appears before me, and I expect to find Wistlee or Phen on the other end of it, offering me water. Instead, Marella stands over me.

I stare at the canteen, too stunned to take it.

"It's not poisoned." A smirk quirks her lips.

"I didn't think—thanks." I accept the water gratefully.

She shakes her head. "That was dumb."

"Thanks."

"No, I mean . . ." She blows out a breath, and a puff of wind swirls around us both. "We could have carried Faela out. You didn't have to sacrifice your mask for her."

"I . . . I know." I sag a little. "I didn't really think through it."

"Right. And that was . . ."

"Dumb."

"Brave." She takes back the canteen I'm handing to her. "Thanks for helping her."

I'm almost too surprised to speak. "Sure," I manage.

Then she breezes away. Laramie raises his brows at me, and I respond with a shrug. Never thought the Ice Queen would melt, but I guess recklessly saving her best friend who didn't need to be saved couldn't hurt.

I'm steady enough to climb to my feet now, and Wistlee comes to my side, offering a balancing arm. "We need to get back to the road," I'm now rational enough to say. "The Emerald City isn't too far."

Assuming it still stands.

The closer we get to the Emerald City, the more cracked the bricks. The more stretches of road missing altogether. The more evidence that something very bad happened here.

Houses that might have been green once stand in ruin along the side of the road. Those who lived near the Emerald City had a strong preference for all things green, and this is where they once dwelt. But now these dwellings are charred piles of greenish rubble.

"They must have been attacked." We've stopped to examine the dozenth pile of ruins. "But who did it?"

"The Munchkins?" Rhyan lifts a charred board with the toe of her boot. "They seemed keen to take over the whole of Oz."

"Maybe," I say. "But Oz is so segmented. It's hard to imagine the Munchkins having much interest beyond their own territory. And didn't they tell us they'd never been this far?"

A weak cry from the far side of the rubble sets my heart racing. "Help?"

Marella gives a startled scream, and Laramie draws his sword. Everyone is backing away.

Except Faela who moves toward the distressed voice. "Where are you?" she calls.

"Here."

This voice is so feeble, Laramie sheaths his sword. The rest of us follow Faela to search for the distraught person buried somewhere in this pile.

He's hidden himself beneath a blackened plank of wood that probably belonged to the siding of this house.

The man is bleeding from a gash in his stomach. It looks like a handful of claws sliced through him. His skin is ashen, and he's shivering. He must have been lying there all night.

"Sir, were you attacked?" I ask as we clear away the debris around him. Obviously he was, but I hope the question will help him speak.

"This was my home once," he answers. "It was destroyed some weeks back."

He coughs as Marella and Rivit shift his position, and Faela pulls a series of bottles and tins from her utility belt.

"My family fled when they attacked. I thought to return to see if anything was left." He winces as Rivit pours water over the gashes. He then gazes at Faela curiously. "We were not known for our kindness to foreigners in this part of the country in ages past. Why are you helping me?"

"Because you're in need," Faela says simply. "Now brace yourself. This will sting."

As she and Rivit continue cleaning and dressing the man's wound, he goes on with his story.

"The raiders were gone, but there's nothing left, of course."

I glance at the gashes, looking ever more like claw marks now that they're cleaned of dried blood. Kalidah, maybe?

Rhyan tilts her head to his injuries. "Who harmed you?"

He winces. "Flying monkeys. Didn't see them coming, and they can be dreadfully quiet when they want to be, you know."

"I didn't know." She shoots me a glance, then mouths, "Flying monkeys?"

My heart sinks a little. "I had sort of hoped the flying monkeys would have disappeared somehow."

"Wishful thinking," Rhyan observes.

Definitely.

The injured man coughs, then winces again. "I was too weak to travel back to my family, so I stayed here overnight. But I'm afraid I was bleeding more than I realized."

Rhyan signals Laramie, and he begins to gather food and water for the man.

"Can we help you get back to your family?" Rhyan asks.

"That's kind, but you're doing quite enough," the man replies, watching Faela and Rivit, who have just about gotten his wounds dressed. Faela has slathered half a tin of antibacterial salve into his cuts.

"Sir," I venture, "do you know how the Emerald City fares?"

The man's face saddens. "I'm afraid it's not much better than my poor house here. It stands mostly in ruin."

More hopes dashed.

"It could be a trick," the man amends quickly, probably noting the despair on my face. "The Wizard is, after all, known for his great illusions. But I have seen the city for myself, and it was so beautiful once. But not anymore. And then . . ." He pauses. "Perhaps we best not mention that."

"No, please." I'm nearly begging. "It would really help us if you'd tell us what you know. We're searching for the Witch of the North." I don't mention Dorothy because he probably has no clue who she is.

"Oh, that you could find her." It's almost a prayer, and his face screws up as though he's fighting tears. "Yes, I will help you." He lowers his volume, and we all lean in to better hear his words.

"There are rumors," he whispers. "The Wicked Witch of the West has been sighted in the city."

WE STAND BEFORE THE GATES

of the Emerald City, and tears course down my face. It seems all I do in Oz is cry.

Because they're not gates anymore. There's no green man to greet us or strap green spectacles on our faces. There's no brilliant city to dazzle us. No green marble houses studded with emeralds.

All lies in ruin. Piles of jade rubble. A few rats scamper about, searching for scraps of food. But otherwise, the city seems lifeless.

Except, perhaps, the only building still standing.

I wipe the tears from my cheeks and try to collect myself.

I'm supposed to be the logical, strategic Dragon. Not a walking emotional meltdown.

But this is Oz. *My* Oz. The place I escaped to in my imagination when I was little. The place that inspired some of my own stories and creatures and concepts.

I can only take so much. I can only see it destroyed so completely and in so many different ways before I can't hold it together anymore.

Rhyan is near, waiting patiently. With a final big sniff, I turn to her, my voice crackly. "That's the palace there in the center of the city. The Wizard should be there—if he's alive."

Though I honestly can't imagine he is. If the Wizard was alive, surely he would not have let this happen to the Emerald City.

Surely.

Rhyan signals us forward, and the Novem picks its way through the rubble.

We are nearly to the palace in the center of the city when Rhyan suddenly shouts, "On your left!"

Instinctively, I draw my sword and whip to the left, noting that these new instincts are . . . handy and . . . strange.

Everyone else is also on guard as two people—a man and a woman—peer out from behind a mostly toppled wall. "We're not hostile," the man calls out.

"Who are you?" Rhyan calls back.

"Citizens of the Emerald City," the woman replies, grief troubling her features. "We lived here once."

"What happened?" I ask. The only thing I can imagine is bombers. What else could cause this sort of destruction?

The man shakes his head. "We hardly know. It must have been magic, for one day, all was well. Not for the Munchkins in that eastern country, but here, at least. We were happy and healthy. And the next moment, it seemed there was a . . . burst."

"An explosion?" I ask.

The man shrugs.

He would have no frame of reference, I suppose.

"The city crumbled." He takes the woman's hand. "Many were killed, many more injured. We survived, but only just. And"—he waves aimlessly to the rubble—"what now? Where are we to go? What are we to do? Now that the Wizard has turned against us—"

"Wait, what?" I interrupt him. "The Wizard did *what*?"

"Why, have you not heard? The rumor is the Great Wizard and Witch of the West have joined forces."

"That can't be true," I blurt immediately. I believed the Wicked Witch might have made it into the city, as the injured citizen suggested. But to conquer the Wizard, not join forces with him. "How could the Wizard turn against his own city?"

"It's only the rumor," the woman says. "But if it isn't true, where is he? Why hasn't he come to help?"

To be fair, I have a fuller knowledge of the Wizard than these characters do. I know he's a man from Nebraska who landed in Oz accidentally via hot air balloon. And that he's a bad wizard, but he's a good man.

Isn't he?

I turn to Rhyan and quiet my voice. "He can't have joined with the Witch of the West. They were enemies. He wouldn't have let her in this city, let alone join forces with her."

Rhyan looks unsure, like she's chewing on several possibilities.

"Emmy?"

I turn and squint in the direction Phen's pointing.

"Does that answer your question?" he asks.

Framed in one of the tall palace windows stands the Witch of the West, recognizable by the magical cap on her head—golden and encircled with a ring of diamonds and rubies. Around her swarm three flying monkeys.

And she's looking straight at us.

48

the Wicked Witch of the West had one eye, powerful as a telescope, and was generally depicted as hideous in the illustrations.

I'm not sure if the illustrations were unfair or if this bizarre Oz reboot has been kind to her, because the Wicked Witch doesn't look half bad. Her skin is not green. She's not getting the 1930s glam treatment Good Witches got in certain adaptations, but she looks elegant, cold and strong as steel. Like a proper storybook villain.

In the book, the winged monkeys only do the Wicked Witch's bidding because she has the golden cap, which grants her the ability to command them three times. She uses her wishes first to enslave the Winkies, second to battle the Great Oz and flush him from the west, and third to destroy the Tin Woodman and Scarecrow and bring Dorothy and the Lion to her.

The Wicked Witch is wearing the golden cap now, but these flying monkeys appear ready to obey, with or without the charm of the cap.

This story has gone sideways and inside out.

She shouldn't be here in the Emerald City.

I'm about to call out to her and demand to see the Great Oz, when suddenly he appears in the window beside her.

"Hello, strangers!" he calls. "Are you friend or foe?"

My mouth falls open. Rhyan is looking at me as though I'm supposed to have the answer to this question. But Oz has become a jumbled mess. Is the Witch still wicked? Is it true she and the Wizard have formed an alliance?

Does this make him wicked too?

Did they destroy the Emerald City together?

"That depends," I call back. "Why don't you tell us what's going on."

"Afraid not, my dear." Then he turns to the Wicked Witch. "Kill them." He casts an apologetic look down to us. "Sorry. I always was a bit of a coward."

Then he disappears from our view.

I'm left with the shredded fabric of my pathetic childhood in my hands.

How could he align with *her*, of all people? How could he let this happen to his beloved city? He always was a bit of a coward, yes, but never bad. Never wicked.

I don't have time to sort through my feelings. The Witch of the West signals to her three monkeys. "Destroy them!"

Rhyan whips out her bow and an arrow, taking swift aim at a monkey barreling straight at us. She strikes her target in the shoulder. He tumbles off course but doesn't completely go down.

"Emmy, where's Frank?" Rhyan pulls out another arrow and nocks it.

Yes! Frank!

I pull her tiny form from my pocket. She's rousing, blinking up at me.

"Frank, can you grow?" I glance up to the Witch in the window. "We need to get up there."

Frank squints up at the window. Then she seems to understand. She starts the process of growing, and before long, I have a kitten-size wyvern in my hand.

But changing size is obviously becoming more difficult for her. In Rivenlea, she can shift back and forth as fast as Laramie changes from sparrow to toad to circus rose to human. Frank is about the size of a beagle now and still slowly expanding.

As Frank grows, Rhyan's follow-up strike takes down one monkey. Wistlee has successfully roped another, which Laramie is about to finish off.

The monkeys are larger than expected, and somehow the thought of running one through with my sword flips my stomach. Probably because in the book, they speak. They aren't wild beasts like the Kalidahs. They're thinking, feeling beings.

Laramie's blade drives through the chest of a monkey, and I flinch.

The third monkey dive-bombs Faela, and Marella sends it swirling into the air with a burst of wind. Canon slices it in two.

The pit in my stomach rises in revulsion. I'm not sure we had another choice, but still.

The Witch shrieks and disappears from view.

"Emmy, you and Laramie go ahead." Rhyan acknowledges Frank, who is now the size of a large horse. "Canon and I will cover you in case more of those monkeys show up. Then I'll be right behind."

I hesitate, unsure about separating from the rest of the Novem.

"I'll be right behind you." She looks me squarely in the eyes. "Get her talking, see what you can find out. I trust you."

I stare. "You do?"

She chuckles. "Just go, will you?"

Right.

I grab Laramie and pull him toward Frank. He must have overheard Rhyan because he doesn't resist, no questions asked. He climbs on Frank's back, ready to pull me up in front of him.

Maybe he trusts me too.

I refuse to allow the warmth spreading through me to pull my attention from the task at hand. We need to catch up with the Wicked Witch. For all I know, she's escaping down some palace staircase or calling forth another fleet of monkeys.

"She doesn't actually have much power," I tell Laramie over my shoulder. "The golden cap grants her some wishes, assuming we didn't just kill the last of her monkeys, but mostly all she does in the book is trick Dorothy."

"Then why are we afraid of her?"

"Because the books tell us she's very powerful and wicked."

"Okay. Uh, sure."

I'm uncertain how to explain why classics can get away with this. But they can, and we love them.

Unless . . .

Just as Frank reaches the window and Laramie and I tumble from her back, it occurs to me that the Wicked Witch might be extremely powerful at this moment. She might be holding the one thing we need to set Oz right.

She might have found the silver shoes.

THE WICKED WITCH OF THE WEST

is glaring down at us.

Laramie and I are on our feet, swords drawn, before she's able to speak. The Wizard is nowhere to be seen.

My attention snaps to the Witch's feet, and I almost expect to see those glittering silver shoes winking at me, mocking me, telling me the most obvious answer has been in front of my face the entire time. That of course the villain stole the thing I want to find.

But I don't see silver glinting back at me. Instead, I see sparkling green heels entirely encrusted with emeralds. Emeralds pulled from the ruins of the city, probably.

The Witch is holding a long, thin silver sword. "Well. I suppose we ought to have expected this," she says.

I dart a glance at Laramie, then look back at the Witch. "Oh?"

"I know exactly what you are," she says, an ugly sneer twisting her features. "Which Novem is it this time?"

My heart stops. I can feel the color drain from my face. Even Laramie, usually unflappable, jolts at this question.

She knows about Novems.

"How do you . . . ?" is all I can manage.

She holds the sword steady, anger directed at me. Anger and . . . pain. "Do you have any idea what it's like?"

I lower my sword, but only just. "Tell me. What's it like?"

"You swoop in here with your self-righteous missions, resetting us again and again." Her sword hand trembles now. "Do you know how many times I've been melted into a puddle? Six hundred thirty-two times!"

"But you're not supposed to remember that." Laramie eyes her warily, as though she might burst into flame. "When your story is reset, so is your memory."

The Wicked Witch switches her glare toward him. "Whoopsie."

"Are you saying you can remember everything that happens?" My sword lowers another inch. "Every divergence, every reset, every alternate Oz when your plot's gone rogue?"

She scoffs. "A conscious memory is not the only way to hold on to your experiences, useless child. Even if the mind does not remember, the bones do."

"And yet your mind does remember." Laramie's sword is ever ready.

Which is probably just as well, as I'm too taken aback to be of any use.

"I've had the benefit of being reminded." She glowers at each of us in turn. "We were promised something better. When will he make good on his promise?"

My nerves spark. "Who made that promise to you?"

If the Witch was going to tell me, she doesn't get the chance. Rhyan, Phen, and Rivit tumble into the room next. Phen immediately spins back toward the open window and turns to stone, just as a flying monkey tries to enter.

The monkey smacks against the stony Sentinel, the force sending him spiraling down to the rest of the Novem. I hear Canon's laser hand fire, and I can only assume the monkey met a grisly end.

Rhyan spots the Wicked Witch's sword, and her hands light.

The Witch laughs. "Ah, have you come to kill me, fire dancer?" Her smile drops, and she leans forward menacingly. "Try it."

Then she lunges.

"Rhyan, the fire won't hurt her!" I yell as Laramie deflects a strike that was aimed for our captain.

The Witch shrieks and turns on Laramie. They cross blades over and over, the Witch surprisingly agile in those heels. Have to respect that, if nothing else.

Phen flips back to flesh and bone, allowing Marella and Faela to jump off Frank's back through the window.

"Fire hose," I say suddenly.

Laramie is distracted for a moment, and he takes a slice to the shoulder. He winces, then pushes back into the Witch's space. "What?"

"Shift into a fire hose. Attached to a hydrant, I guess." It was a spur-of-the-moment idea. I haven't thought it through completely.

"Never seen one." He ducks under a strike. "Something else?"

"A bucket of water."

"That I can do."

He dances away from the Witch's next sword strokes, and I slip in to take his place. It's hard to give it my full effort, though. I can defend myself and the other Novemites. Give Laramie the space to shift safely.

But I can't escape that pain in her eyes. Because I know what she means.

I know how trauma seeps into your bones and your body remembers, even if your brain loses the details. What would six hundred thirty-two reboots, six hundred thirty-two times reliving the same trauma over and over, do to a person? To their heart?

"Emmy!"

Rhyan's shout snaps me back to reality and the fact that I'm barely blocking the Witch's strikes. She's gaining ground with every movement. Rhyan sends a stream of fire toward the Wicked Witch, but the Witch merely grabs it in her hand and winks it out with ease.

Still, it's enough to distract her for a moment.

And I know what Rhyan doesn't. We need water, not fire.

Laramie shifted into a bucket some moments ago, and he's probably wondering what's taking me so long. I drop my sword, grab the bucket. Whisper, "Sorry about this," to him.

Then I douse the Wicked Witch of the West.

Our gazes meet for a moment. She doesn't speak. Doesn't say something slightly ridiculous like in the book ("Look out— here I go!"). Instead, there's an unspoken understanding that passes between us. And I don't like it at all.

She's the villain. I don't want to understand her, sympathize with her. After all, she was truly wicked. The Wizard's assurances from the book ring through my mind. She was very wicked and had to be destroyed. It's okay to call evil what it is and not make excuses for people who do terrible things.

But I have to wonder.

Could it have been different? Could she have been redeemed? And if not, might there have been a better way to deal with her, rather than making her relive a watery death six hundred thirty-two times?

Thirty-three.

The Witch is reduced to a puddle before me. And I'm still holding bucket-Laramie in my hands.

I set him down so he can shift back to human form.

He pops into existence next to me and grimaces. "I feel dehydrated."

My pack, canteen included, is back on the ground. His must be too. But Faela comes through with a drink for him.

"We need to find the Wizard," Rhyan declares.

She's right. Who knows where he's skipped off to.

But as Laramie hands Faela's canteen back to her, I draw closer to him and lower my voice. "Laramie?"

He looks at me inquisitively.

I can't take my eyes off the pool of Witch at our feet. "I think we're torturing them."

WISTLEE AND CANON PLUNGE

through the window a moment later, and the alarm in Wist's eyes sends my heart thudding against my ribs.

Frank shrinks to the size of a ferret and alights on the windowsill. She looks woozy. I scoop her into my hands, and she shrinks to palm-size.

"Good girl. Rest now." I slip her into my pocket, then immediately turn to my roommate. "Wist?"

"Soldiers are coming," she says loud enough for everyone to hear. "They were descending on the palace as we made our escape."

"So we're surrounded?" Rivit clutches Marella.

Canon nods. "It would appear so."

"Then we'll fight our way out," Rhyan declares, as though this is simply another Tuesday.

Which it is.

I mean, maybe not Tuesday. I have no idea what day it is, but this is our job. What we train for. This is why I pick up my sword and ready it.

Although . . .

"Laramie, how do we nonlethally—"

But my question is broken off by a knot of several soldiers dressed in green tactical gear bursting through the door. It's a strange amalgamation of the old Oz and the new—the Emerald City where everything is green or appeared so due to the use of green glasses, and this dystopian evolution with technology and firearms and destruction at every turn.

Before I can fully reconcile these competing realities, Rhyan blasts one of the soldiers with a stream of fire, intensified by Marella's gust of wind.

"No!" I cry.

Several fellow Novemites swivel to look at me, a quizzical expression on each face. Canon blasts another soldier through the chest with his attack beam, and I feel like I'm going to faint.

"Emmy," Rhyan says urgently. "What's wrong?"

"These . . ." I gesture mutely to the bodies on the floor, just as Laramie adds another to their number. "These are people. We're supposed to use nonlethal methods on people."

Rhyan's laugh startles me. As though she's been silly, forgotten to tell me something. "Oh, of course. Don't worry." She pats my shoulder. "The mission is just about complete. We'll reset the story, and these men will be just fine."

"But . . ." I don't know how to explain my suspicions. How to approach the idea that the characters aren't magically whole when the stories are reset. How to tell her that they are remembering.

"Early in the mission, we don't want to cause heartache with human death," she explains to me. The room is clear of soldiers for the moment, and the rest of the Novem is collecting gear and prepping weapons. "If we killed the Munchkins when we first arrived, for example, their families would have suffered, even if only for a short while. We're not trying to inflict pain, though it'll be forgotten shortly."

Words fail me. I know she's right, in one sense. These people—these friends and colleagues I've traveled with and fought beside—would not intentionally cause suffering. They care about the stories and the characters, and they're truly trying to help, even by putting their own lives at stake.

The Munchkin rebel leader with her automatic rifle comes to mind.

But Rhyan is also fundamentally wrong. If the characters can remember, if their minds or bodies are holding on to everything that happens to them, we *are* causing suffering. And inflicting pain. We are agents of heartache, bringers of death.

Again and again and again.

"I know where he'll be," I say suddenly. "At least I think I do. Let's get there as quickly as possible."

To avoid killing anyone else, if we can help it.

Rhyan casts a strange look my direction, but after a moment she signals everyone out the door.

We meet up with several more knots of guards, searching the palace for us, presumably at the Wizard's orders. I try to make my body obey my brain—force myself to follow my training, take the kill strikes when they're presented.

But I can't seem to do it. I can't claim ignorance like the others, I can't bring myself to kill a man.

Instead, I focus on defending Faela, Rivit, and Phen, our Novemites who are not combatants. I focus on supporting Laramie's efforts. I pray for a way to understand all this—to put the pieces together. Because that's my job. I'm the Dragon.

The scales appearing on my legs pop to mind for the first time in hours.

Right. There's also that.

"It's too much," I say aloud.

Laramie nods at me sympathetically. "It's a lot, I know."

He thinks I'm talking about the pile of bodies we leave in our wake. And I guess I am in a way. But it's so much more. It's everything.

"The throne room should be this way," I say abruptly. "At least I'm pretty sure. I think the Wizard will be there."

It's where he met Dorothy and her friends. Where he was finally unmasked. Where he "gave" them courage, a brain, and a heart. Surely he will cloister himself there, let his soldiers attempt to dispatch us, and hope he never has to face us.

Anger boils in my veins.

The large double doors just ahead surely lead to the throne room, and we've worked our way through so many soldiers, it's hard to imagine others are following us. This is our chance to confront the Wizard.

Oz, the Great and Terrible.

I slam my hands into the doors hard enough to sting, but I hardly care.

Oz has not bothered to conceal himself behind a screen or create an illusion to terrify or dazzle us. He appears as his true self, a little old man with a wrinkled face.

Except this Wizard doesn't look meek. He looks smug. Cold.

"I suppose you've dispatched the Witch, then?" He shakes his head. "Never could keep herself dry, that one."

"I thought you'd be more upset," I say. "She was your ally, wasn't she?"

He shrugs. "Recent alliances are easily broken."

I glance around at my fellows. Is that what I am? A recent alliance?

My neuroses can wait. The anger in me doesn't leave room for much else.

"How could you do this?" I'm almost yelling. The depth of the betrayal I feel surprises me. But this is off script. This is not the Wizard I know. "How could you let this happen?"

"Let what happen, my dear?"

"Oz is ruined! Have you not seen what's going on? You formed an alliance with the Witch of the West, the worst of them all. The eastern countryside is burning. The Emerald City is in shambles, and you did nothing to stop it. Nothing to help."

He doesn't react. He shows no emotion, save that smug look he favors.

And then I realize.

"This was your doing. Not an unforeseen consequence." I gape at him. "You ruined Oz on purpose."

"Very good, my dear. You are starting to see the big picture."

"I don't understand." I rub my temples. Try to make sense of it. "Why would you want to destroy your home?"

"It isn't truly my home, now is it?"

No, I suppose not. He's from Nebraska.

"But you made a home here. And you get a happy ending. You travel back to your true home in a balloon. Why are you trying to destroy your story?"

"Ah, but the book doesn't really tell you what happens when I get back to Nebraska, does it?" He clucks his tongue. "It hardly matters. I see now you are still missing too many pieces of the puzzle. So I'll just tell you this: not every interference breaks or fixes us. Some interferences simply cause us to remember."

My stomach pinches. "Who was it?"

The rest of the Novem turns to me, but I ignore them.

"Who came here and interfered? Who caused you to remember?"

"The one who took the silver shoes." He tilts his head to one side. "You'd know him better than I."

"Enough," Canon says sharply, and he unleashes a bolt. It zaps the wall behind the Wizard, just to the left of his head. "Where is the Witch of the North? Do you have Dorothy?"

"I do not have Dorothy. She's truly lost. If you want to see the others, well . . ." He eyes the scorch mark on the wall behind him. Swallows. And there I see the cowardly man who posed as the Great Wizard. "I can take you to them."

"Them?" Realization strikes and I gasp. "You have Glinda too."

"Glinda?" Rhyan's brow furrows.

"The Good Witch of the South. She would have had to be kidnapped, too, for him to destroy Oz. Otherwise, she and her people would have fought back."

The Wizard sighs. "Indeed, they tried." He climbs to his feet heavily. "Shall we, then?"

He leads us to the dungeon underground in this palace, the only piece of the Emerald City to retain its former beauty. The point of Laramie's sword at the Wizard's back encourages him not to try anything.

"It won't work, you know," the Wizard says to me.

"What won't?"

"Reuniting with the Witches. You won't really be able to reset the story. Not anymore."

"If we find Dorothy—"

"Not even then, I'm afraid." He seems more giddy than fearful. "The story can't be fully reset."

I know he's right. It's what I thought before.

We can't reset Oz without the silver shoes.

51

TWO CRYSTAL-BLUE EYES

peer out from a decrepit cell. Dank, despite being made of polished green marble. Red ringlets cascade over her shoulders, down her back. Her dress was obviously shimmering white once, but now it's filthy.

How long has she been locked in here?

Glinda, the Good Witch of the South, gazes at me and smiles. "Are you a good witch or a bad witch?"

Yes. No.

"Neither," I say.

"Both?" Phen suggests under his breath, earning a shushing from me.

"We're here to rescue you." Rhyan pulls the Wizard of Oz into the torchlight. "And maybe lock him in here in your place."

"Oh dear." Glinda's beautiful forehead creases. "This is troubling, indeed."

"Hello?" a voice a few cells down calls out. "Who's there?" The kind, wrinkled face of the Witch of the North appears behind her cell bars.

I look at Rhyan. "The Good Witches, North and South."

She shoves the Wizard forward. "Give us the keys."

The Wizard, outnumbered nine to one, doesn't have much

choice but to allow himself to be placed in Glinda's cell, and I'd be lying if I said I felt sorry for him.

"We shan't leave him in there long, surely," Glinda says with a gentle frown. "He was once our friend."

Which makes his betrayal of her all the worse.

The Witch of the North looks down at her dress, which is still glittering through the dirt and grime. She sighs. "I'm afraid this dress is ruined. It was my favorite."

"Glinda," I say to the Witch of the South, "have you met a little girl named Dorothy?"

"Ah, Dorothy." Glinda hangs her head.

The Witch of the North sighs again. "Sweet Dorothy."

No, no, no. Their tones say "dear, departed Dorothy," but I'm praying that's not what they mean.

"We have not met Dorothy, no," Glinda continues. "But I can see all that happens in my realm. That poor child is very lost."

"She's gone south?"

"Indeed. She went south until she could go no more, and there she's sat. All this time."

Rather than easing, the dread gets spikier. "She could be starving to death out there," I worry to Rhyan. Dorothy very much relied on the help of her friends and strangers in the original story. Could she possibly survive in this hostile Oz?

"Oh, yes." Glinda nods. "If you wish to find Dorothy, you should hurry."

I reach into my pocket. "Maybe Frank could take us." My wyvern blinks up at me sleepily.

"Yes." Rhyan pulls a few items from her utility belt and hands them to Canon. "Just you and me. We can travel faster that way." She addresses the rest of the Novem. "Look after the Witches. Get them some decent food if you can find it. Collect the packs and anything else we shed along the way, and keep a sharp eye for more soldiers or those monkey creatures. Canon is in charge until I get back."

Wistlee takes my hand. "Be careful."

I give her hand a squeeze and look over at Phen. "You too."

I spare Laramie a glance. He nods.

Time to go rescue Dorothy.

Glinda's instructions are detailed and specific. It's hard to miss the little girl sitting on the edge of barren desert, her knees tucked close, forming a tiny ball. The basket beside her is empty of bread, save a few crumbs. Toto is curled at her feet, looking forlorn and dehydrated.

And Dorothy is completely gray. Her dress is white-and-gray checkered. Her skin is ash. Her hair is slate. Her eyes like graphite.

She glances up as Frank glides to the ground. But she doesn't look nearly as startled as one might expect a person to be when they see a giant wyvern for the first time.

"Hello," she says. "Who are you?"

"I . . ." I'm trying to conceal my surprise at her condition. "I'm Emmy. This is Rhyan."

She looks back toward the desert stretching before us. "I'm Dorothy." She pauses a moment. Tilts her head. "I landed . . . somewhere. It felt familiar, somehow, but I didn't know where I was. I thought Nebraska, maybe. Or even a Dakota. So I headed south."

I glance out at the lifeless desert. Definitely not a Dakota.

"This isn't Nebraska *or* South Dakota, is it?" Tears fill Dorothy's eyes. "I'm so confused."

"No." I crouch to her eye level while Rhyan pulls out her canteen for Toto. "This is Oz. A land totally different from the one we come from."

Dorothy scrunches her nose. "Oz."

"Do you know it?"

"It . . . feels familiar. But how can it? I don't know it. Do I?"

Poor girl.

"It feels familiar and yet very not." She sighs. "Have you seen the terrible things happening all over the countryside?"

"We have. We've traveled through a lot of it to find you."

She musters what I think is supposed to be a smile. "That's kind."

"We need to take you to the Emerald City." I point to Frank. "You can ride that wyvern with us."

Dorothy glances at Frank. "Toto too?"

For some reason this makes me want to both laugh and cry. "Toto too."

She nods. Begins to gather up her dog and her basket. Then she sighs deeply and turns her watery gray eyes on me. "Must we really do it all again?"

The question steals my voice. I don't know what to say. She doesn't realize she remembers, but . . . she does.

"Traveling to the Emerald City will be easy with the help of the wyvern," Rhyan says, misinterpreting her question.

Dorothy doesn't explain. I'm not sure she could, even if she wanted to. She slowly climbs to her feet. "Well, then. I suppose we should go."

And we do.

We will reset the story, as best we can. We will do what we came to do.

But I vow silently to help Dorothy and the others even more. I *will* figure out some way to save them for good.

WHEN WE LAND IN THE

Emerald City, the Novem is clustered outside around the doors to the palace. They don't appear to have had any additional trouble, and they've collected all our things.

Glinda and the Witch of the North stand with them.

"Oh, there's Dorothy!" Glinda exclaims, her blue eyes sparkling. "At last."

"Dorothy!" The Witch of the North helps Dorothy off Frank, then enfolds the girl in her arms.

Dorothy is a shell of a character. She doesn't even question these two strange women or wonder why we've brought her here.

"I miss Aunt Em," she says.

"We'll get you home soon enough." Rhyan promises, then turns to Phen. "Ready?"

This is the part I've yet to see. Resetting stories involves a Sentinel building a gateway, just like the one we use to travel to and from Rivenlea. But this gateway is different somehow, and if we've completed our mission, it will tell us.

At least that's what Phen has said. Frank shrinks small enough to fit in my palm, and I gently place her in my pocket, my gaze locked on Phen.

He steps forward, looking less nauseous than he did the first time he had to do this.

He draws the half arc with his glowing right hand, then mirrors it with the left. The emerald-green arch doesn't have any stones to sink into this time. It simply creates an archway of light. Three empty rings rest along the top of the arch, as though waiting to be filled.

"What's that?" I whisper to Wistlee.

"That's how we'll know if we completed our mission." Wist nods to the empty rings. "Watch."

Rhyan ushers the Good Witch of the North toward the archway. "We found the missing Witch," she says. Her posture is formal and her voice official.

The Witch of the North touches the green arch. The first of the empty rings begins to fill with glittering silver light.

"Oh, beautiful!" The Witch of the North applauds. "Most lovely." Then she takes Dorothy's hand and pulls her close. Plants a kiss upon her forehead.

At that, Dorothy receives the protective mark she should have had in the beginning of the story.

Rhyan gestures Dorothy forward. "And we found our lost protagonist."

Dorothy hesitates. Then she grazes her fingers across the green arch. The empty ring in the middle fills with pale blue light, the exact color Dorothy's checkered dress ought to be.

If it wasn't drained of all life.

The archway is pulsing now. I turn to Rhyan to find her frowning.

"What's wrong, Rhyan?"

She purses her lips. "I'm not sure about the third light."

But I am.

"It's the silver shoes," I say. "The shoes that have been taken from Oz."

"We can try it with just two," Canon says quickly. "Many stories have been reset without all the missing pieces in place. Sometimes it's impossible to collect everything."

"That's true," Rhyan agrees. She gestures to Phen. "Let's do it."

Phen's right hand lights up purple, startling me back a step.

He starts at the bottom left side of the arch and draws his hand all the way across. The arch changes from emerald green to ruby red in a blink.

Rhyan nods, satisfied. "Well done, Phen. We can get back to Rivenlea."

"And Oz?" I can't quite take my eyes from our grayscale little girl. "It will be reset?"

"Should be. When a Novem is able to create a gateway back to Rivenlea, it means the story mission is complete."

Everyone is bustling around, getting their packs strapped to their backs. Saying goodbye to the Witches.

I take Dorothy's hand. "I'm going to find a way to help."

She gazes up at me again, her eyes two gray pools. "Promise?"

I swallow. "Promise."

Her face is too serious. She doesn't smile. Barely nods. It only strengthens my resolve to keep my word.

"Through the gateway, everyone," Rhyan calls out. She pats my back. "Let's go home, Emmy."

I follow her to the edge of the gateway, then step into the red light.

Turning back to wave at Dorothy, I watch Oz begin to reform. The Emerald City rebuilds itself, stone by stone, marble block by marble block. Emeralds reset themselves into the building exteriors.

There is now green pavement, green glass in the windows. Green candy in the candy shops. It's reforming into what was described in the book. The Oz of my childhood.

But it only holds for a moment.

No sooner are the streets of the Emerald City put back together than they begin to drain of color. Bleakness trickles down from the peaks of the roofs, the tops of the towers, washing over every building, every tree.

Every person.

Glinda and the Witch of the North are starting to look the same hue as Dorothy—ash, graphite, silver, smoke. They wave at us, apparently unaware they're losing their vibrancy by the second.

The yellow brick road glows golden for one more moment. Then it winks into slate.

Maybe it's supposed to be this way. Maybe this is what happens when a story is reset.

But I can't make myself believe it. My heart knows this isn't how it's supposed to be. Everything is going wrong. Something is sucking the color out of Earth and now Oz.

Where else is it happening? And who—or what—is doing it?

Glinda and the Witch of the North seem to have realized something is wrong. They're looking down at their dresses. Examining their arms and hands. Panic lances through their expressions, but I can't hear what they're saying. The wind whipping through the gateway is roaring in my ears, pulling me backward, forcing me to return to Rivenlea.

For a moment, I lock eyes with Dorothy.

And then, to my horror, she shreds to ribbons. Unravels. Disappears.

A scream rips from my throat. Gets caught on the wind and pulled to pieces. Scattered. Lost.

A strong hand grips me from behind and yanks me back into the gateway.

As Dorothy vanishes from Oz, so do I.

53

I HIT THE GROUND

in Rivenlea, knees smacking into the grass of the yard outside Ambryfell. Dry heaves rack my body, rattling through my bones, blurring the world around me.

The air hits me, and I know right away. The smell is familiar. The atmosphere comfortable. We're back home.

But I've just witnessed Dorothy Gale ribbon away like Camille. And I'm replaying both incidents in my head over and over. First Camille is in Oz, her blue-green eyes popping against the gray backdrop. Then Dorothy is in California, shredding away in a neighborhood park.

Then they're both together, their ribbons twisting, dancing together, disappearing together.

Screams echo around me. Dorothy's? Camille's?

No. They're mine.

Several hands are on me. Someone is shouting.

I swallow bile. Pull deep breaths through my nose, force them out my mouth. Flip onto my back.

Several faces hover above.

Wistlee. Phen. Laramie.

The knowledge that I must look like the worst drama queen washes over me, and I'm embarrassed. A little ashamed. Why can't I keep it together?

Because you have PTSD, the voice of my therapist Katelyn reminds me. You have triggers.

Watching people shredding to ribbons being chief among them.

"It's all connected," I say.

There is a pause.

"I'm fine."

The three faces share doubtful glances, as though I can't see them.

"I'm *fine*," I insist. "But did you see Dorothy?"

"No, I saw you standing in the gateway, almost left behind," Laramie said, irritation edging his words. "Do you know what happens if you get stuck between spheres?"

"No idea."

"Me neither. I don't think we should find out."

"Laramie, it's all connected. Dorothy ribboned just like Camille."

His face screws up. "She what? Slow down."

I shoot him a look. When have I been known to slow down?

That prompts a half smile. "Okay, explain it to me, then."

"My sister, Camille. She unraveled seven years ago at the park near our house. Disappeared off the face of the Earth."

"And ended up here."

An unpleasant jolt spikes through me. "Yes. And Dorothy just ribboned in the same way. Right as we were leaving Oz."

Laramie's brows draw together. "Is it part of the story resetting, maybe?"

"I don't think so," Phen speaks up. "The story is supposed to return to its former glory. Not break down."

"And Oz was becoming drab again already," Wistlee adds. "I saw it too."

A thought strikes me, and I shrug my pack off my back, then dig into it. After a moment of rifling, I pull out my notebook. I'd brought it for journaling, but I hadn't taken the time to write in it while we were in Oz. Exhaustion hit me too hard each night after a full day of adventuring and story-fixing.

But I open it now and start sketching the sphere map as it appears in the Ambryfell library.

Phen peers over my shoulder. "What's this?"

"The sphere map." I stop sketching and examine my work— Rivenlea is one large sphere in the middle with spokes shooting out from it, connected to smaller story spheres. "Looks more like a coronavirus."

"A what?"

"Nothing." I flip the page around to show everyone else. "Where is Earth on here?"

Laramie tilts his head to the side. "It's sort of here." His finger draws a circle that encompasses Rivenlea and all the story spheres.

"How is that?"

He gives a simple shrug. "It exists on a different plane, I guess."

So I draw the Earth circle surrounding everything. "How is Earth connected to what's happening here, in the realm of story? The story spheres are connected through these gateways." I point to the spokes. "But how is Earth connected to Rivenlea?"

All three Rivenlites examine my paper for several moments.

"Aside from holding Earth in place or keeping it in its happy stasis. Or whatever," I add.

Laramie shakes his head. "It's not."

"Then how am I here?" I point to the overlapping but disconnected spheres. "How did Camille get from Earth to Rivenlea? How did I get from Earth to Rivenlea? And why is Earth draining of color, just like Oz?" I glance down at the pack by my feet. At the grass that looks . . . wrong. My breath catches. "Just like here."

It's still autumn in Rivenlea. The trees are aflame with crimson, orange, gold, amber. The final breath of vibrant life—a deep, rich inhale—before the world exhales the frost of winter.

Except the grass.

The grass in the training yard isn't green. It's not yellow or brown, turning in season with the trees.

It's less than beige, devoid of its color. Like the yellow brick road. Like Dorothy's eyes. Like my neighbor's flowers and my galaxy bedspread.

"It's all connected," I murmur. But how? My brain feels on the edge of grasping something important, but I can't make it click. "Look at the grass."

Wistlee looks down and starts. "Oh dear."

"Your notebook," Phen says suddenly, eyes on the object in my hands. "Isn't that how Frank got into your bedroom?"

"Yes," I say slowly.

"And weren't you writing in it when your sister disappeared?"

"Yes. But . . . how?" I hold up the notebook. "My mom bought this at a regular store. How is it a link between Rivenlea and Earth?"

"It's not the notebook." Wistlee turns to me, her eyes wide. Afraid.

Her unspoken revelation hits me full force. "It's me," I whisper.

"Everyone cross through in one piece?" Rhyan jogs up to us. "Marella hit her head on landing, but she's okay. They're taking her to rest in the infirmary, just in ca–" She stops short at the expressions on our faces. "What is it?"

"Rhyan, the grass."

She drops her gaze. Purses her lips. And I wait for vindication by her ensuing freak-out.

It doesn't come. "Looks a little drab," she comments. "But the light is bad out here. Sun's setting."

"The . . . light is bad?" I look at her like she's sprouted another head. "Rhyan, the grass has no color!"

She sighs. Rubs her temples and closes her eyes. "Emmy, I'm exhausted."

"Yes, I know, but–"

"Stop. Give it a rest, okay?" Her tone isn't cruel or harsh, but still it feels like a slap. "We're all tired. We've just had a successful first mission, completed in excellent time. We've earned a break."

"Successful? Did you not see Oz turn that weird gray-beige? Did you not see Dorothy disappear? Did you hear anything the characters said? Rhyan, they're remembering. Every version of the story. All the reboots. They have to live it over and over. We're not helping them. We're hurting them."

She suddenly looks a decade older. More tired than I've ever seen her. "Emmy, stop. We are the good guys. Okay? We're the good guys."

What I have to say next nearly lodges in my throat. I take a deep breath.

"I don't think we are."

Now flames light in her eyes. "We completed our mission. We did what we went there to do. Must you question it?" She huffs a sigh. "You know, this is the problem with Earthlings. Everything is messy and complicated for you—never simple. You have to make everything difficult."

I suddenly feel stripped of all my clothing, standing naked in front of these Rivenlites in the yard like I'm some sort of tiresome oddity. A freak. A complication.

But what else is new?

"Please listen, Rhyan. Everything is that way for us because *we* are that way. We're not storybook characters—all good or all bad. Every Earthling is capable of immense good and depraved evil."

Rhyan watches me for a moment. Chews on my words. Perhaps senses the truth of it. But it doesn't move her. "Well, maybe that's not the way it is here in Rivenlea. It's not that way in the story spheres. Things aren't so complicated there."

"Yes, Earthlings write stories in black and white. Good guys versus bad guys. We write tidy heroes and hopeless villains. But real people? We are both hero and villain. The struggle of good versus evil resonates with us because it's *in* us. I can't help but see things as complicated. And I'm sorry if it's frustrating—but it doesn't mean I'm wrong. Does it?"

The flames in Rhyan's eyes blink out. But I haven't won. She has the look a mom gets when she knows she should continue the argument, teach her child something about adulting or correct their wayward thinking, but she's just too tired. So she'll send them to their room or their therapist and hope they figure it out eventually.

Except I'm not wrong.

They should be listening to me on this—if for no other reason than because I'm the only Earthling in this far-flung sphere of impossibilities. I'm the one who knows about the brokenness and beauty of my world, the hardship and the glory of the human condition.

And yet, somehow, I've lost the argument.

Rhyan's announcement is weary. "Get some sleep, everyone."

That's it. She turns and rejoins the rest of the Novem, heading toward the back doors of Ambryfell. She casts a look over her shoulder at Laramie as if to say, "You coming with us, or are you staying at the kids' table?"

Indecision shadows his face as he glances at me. Then he holds my gaze. Meaningfully. Reminding me of his words back in Oz: I believe you.

I acknowledge him with a nod, and he catches up with Rhyan, where she waits for him by the door. I frown at them— Rhyan most of all.

She doesn't mean to mess with my goals. She doesn't mean to stifle me, squash my revelations. Stand in the way of my progress.

"She's an accidental contagonist," I say aloud.

I freeze as my mind jolts. Jumps. Jumbles.

I watch as the door closes behind my contagonist captain and my obnoxiously perfect story boy. I stare at the gray grass and slowly turn to my faithful friends. I think of my sister trapped in a bubble—and her disappearance that started it all.

I lick my lips. "This is the plot I'm supposed to fix."

Wistlee looks at me—brows raised, mouth slightly open. "Pardon?"

"This. What's happening here." I gesture to everything around us. "This is why I'm in Rivenlea. This is the story that is breaking, and I need to help fix it. If I can figure it out, I might be able to set things right—with the stories, with Earth." My voice drops to a whisper. "With Camille."

Phen and Wistlee now share that dumbfounded look. Who could blame them? I've become the shocking, embarrassing conspiracy theorist friend, gesturing frantically at all the supposed connections scribbled on Post-its and tacked to the corkboard of my insanity.

But I'm not wrong. At least, I don't think I am.

I snatch up my pack to head inside Ambryfell. "I need to see Rizak."

54

BUT RIZAK ISN'T IN AMBRYFELL.
The person patrolling the shelves says he's gone home for the evening and to try again tomorrow.

I'm approximately three seconds from exploding.

But Wistlee politely asks when Rizak is expected tomorrow, and we're told he'll be in after his coffee and pastries, just like always, and there isn't so much a time when Rizak comes in. More a feeling of when he's due to arrive.

I am two seconds from exploding.

Wistlee thanks the man kindly. Inquires after Rizak's favorite morning hangout.

Mokah Snick's, of course, the best pastries in Castramore.

When I'm one second from exploding, my friends pacify me with a plan. We will meet in the morning in Castramore. We'll catch Rizak at his morning coffee and pastries and talk to him then.

I breathe deeply and work to defuse the bomb in my brain. Yes, this is a good plan. And yes, if I collect every shred of willpower I have, perhaps I can wait until then.

Not like I have a choice.

But this plan allows me to let go for the evening. I walk back to the cabins, bid Phen farewell, and go home with Wist.

The plan allows me to set aside my spinning thoughts and fall into a deep sleep minutes after my head hits the pillow.

Or else I'm just that tired. Who knows what intersphere travel does to one's brain anyway.

I awake in the morning with a jolt and with mingled excitement, anxiety, and dread.

Slipping into truly clean clothes never felt so good. My boots need a solid brushing and polishing, but I'll get to that later. Right now, it's time to find Rizak.

Wistlee is already dressed and waiting for me in the common area. "I thought to make tea, but then I figured you'd want to get going."

"Yep." I make a beeline for the door, grabbing her arm to pull her with me on my way.

"I am glad I divined your intent correctly." There is a smile in her voice.

When does she *not* read me correctly?

Phen is waiting for us in the agreed-upon spot. He doesn't even try to cover the yawn stretching his entire face. "It's early."

"It's not that early," Wistlee counters.

"Maybe for you, but I'm not a Gryphon. You all get up with the sun. And I didn't sleep well." He rubs his bleary eyes.

"You should try turning yourself to stone for the night," I suggest. "That ought to give you some good rest."

"That's weird." Then he pauses. "It might actually work."

As we pick our way through the back alleys toward the heart of Castramore, my attention is pulled by the kaleidoscope of progressing fall colors. The backdrop of tall evergreens only serves to highlight the changing colors of the other leaves. A tree so red it's nearly pink almost makes me stop in my tracks.

It's the only thing that could distract me from my mission to speak to Rizak. Autumn is my favorite season.

Imagine if this all faded to gray, drained of life.

The idea quickens my steps, firming my resolve.

"Emmy DuLaine!" a cheery voice calls as we approach the bakery service window. Mokah Snick's bright gaze snags on Wistlee and Phen. "And you brought friends, just like I asked!

Wistlee the Gryphon and Phen Fydell." She smiles broadly. "Welcome back to Rivenlea."

Mokah doesn't wait for responses before she starts stacking breakfast pastries on plates for us. "Coffee?"

Yes, I do want coffee. But I also see two men sitting at a bistro table on the stones outside Mokah's shop, enjoying their breakfast and coffee over light conversation.

One of the men is Rizak.

"Be right back!" I'm already in motion, heading toward the table.

I hear Wistlee making apologies and ordering for me, but I hardly register the words.

"Rizak," I blurt. Mannerless and intruding.

My mother would sink into the ground in shame.

But Rizak looks up, showing only mild surprise. "Oh, hello, Emmy. I'd heard the news Novem XVII was back."

"But I bet *The Wonderful Wizard of Oz* sphere in the library is already wrecked again."

His surprise transitions from mild to stark. "How did you know that? What happened? I have not had a debriefing with Captain Doyle yet."

I'm vaguely aware I might get in trouble for beating Rhyan to the punch. Oh well.

I turn to the other man, finally acknowledging how rude I'm being. "Oh, I'm sorry. I'm interrupting."

The other man—tall, early thirties maybe, with sandy brown hair and keen eyes—smiles. "Not at all. I'd be interested in what you have to say." Then he bows his head. "I'm Hew Breon, by the way. Deciduous cat herder of the Silvarum."

"Decidu—what?"

Hew nods down to the leashed animals at his feet. Only then do I realize they are not small dogs as I'd originally thought. They are three cats tethered to the legs of his bistro chair. One orange, one reddish-brown, and the other golden.

"Deciduous cat herder." He reaches down to scratch the

ears of the golden one. "Hydee, Bea, and Traysea are just about ready to turn, and getting out of the Silvarum for a bit helps the transition along. Oh!" A chilly breeze kicks up, and Hew smiles. "Watch!"

The breeze ruffles the cats' coats. The orange one shudders. And then its fur falls out.

All at once.

I nearly jump back in surprise.

The reddish one is next. With a little shiver, she drops her entire coat. Last, the gold one sneezes, and his fur hits the stones beneath his paws.

Three completely naked cats huddle behind Hew Breon's chair, looking up at him like this is all his fault.

"Oh, Hew." Mokah is bustling from her shop, carrying a tray full of mugs and plates of pastries. "Look at that mess."

"Have a broom? I'll sweep it up." He catches Mokah's gaze and throws a different sort of smile her way. "I promise."

Her face flushes crimson and she giggles. "I'll get it." She pauses and looks down at the cats. "Mrs. Nima dropped off sweaters for the herd yesterday. I'll grab something likely to fit."

"You're the best," Hew says, not taking his eyes off her until she's disappeared into the bakery. Then he turns back to the rest of us with happy eyes. "My fiancée."

Between the adorable Castramorian couple, the naked cats, and the idea that some Mrs. Nima knits sweaters for them every year, my heart fills with affection for Rivenlea. This place that's become my new home.

We have to save it.

Wistlee, Phen, and I take chairs from nearby tables and squeeze in with Rizak and Hew. Mokah has returned with the cat sweaters, and Hew has busied himself beside her. They wrestle the garments onto the naked cats, despite their mewling, vociferous protests.

"So," Rizak says as we sip our coffee and select sticky buns, "tell me about Oz."

I swallow a bite. "We weren't even through the gateway, and it was already breaking again," I say. "Oz was fully vibrant for half a second, then the color drained. Which is something I observed on Earth just before I came here. And now . . ." I pause. There's no grass around here, only shrubs and trees. "The grass in the yard is turning drab too. Something is sucking the color out of all the worlds."

To my great satisfaction, Rizak looks severely startled.

"There's more," I tell him. "Dorothy shredded."

Now Hew looks alarmed. "That sounds . . . messy."

I take a moment to explain the ribboning process—what little of it I understand, anyway—and the fact that it happened to my sister before she showed up here.

"Heavens." Hew shakes his head. "Those of us living in the Silvarum know about the bubbles, of course. But it's a closely guarded secret."

"So I've gathered." I try to keep my tone level. "Even Rhyan didn't know Camille is trapped there."

"Nor I," Rizak confesses. "I knew of the strange happenings, of course, but nothing of your lost sister. Even if I'd known there was a girl trapped there, I don't think I would have drawn the connection."

"Does this mean Dorothy is trapped somewhere?" Wistlee asks, her sticky bun paused midway to her mouth, this disturbing thought obviously having just occurred to her.

"I think it's possible," I say. Then I turn to Rizak. "Would we be able to see her in the sphere in Ambryfell if she's still in her story?"

He looks thoughtful. "Likely, yes. As the protagonist, she is usually visible. Unless the blasted thing has completely filled with smoke again."

I chew my thoughts and my sticky bun. "I think there's a good chance she's still in Oz, though I can't really explain why. Just a gut feeling. It was the same as when Camille shredded, yet different. Camille looked like she was being whisked away.

Dorothy looked like she was losing herself. Like her identity was unraveling as much as her body."

The thought that this also happened to Camille occurs to me, but I don't voice it. I don't even want to entertain it. If I thought I couldn't restore the sister I lost, I'm not sure I could keep going. She's a person, not a story character. She can't simply be reset.

"Don't forget about the shoes, Emmy," Phen reminds me.

"Right." This is starting to feel like a ten-thousand-piece puzzle, itty-bitty pieces scattered all over my brain. "The silver shoes are missing from the story."

Rizak's eyes pop. "You mean missing *in* the story."

"No. Missing *from* the story. The characters told us the shoes had been taken from Oz by some mysterious man. I couldn't get much else out of them. And there's one more thing."

Rizak and Hew lean forward.

"The characters seem to be remembering."

Rizak frowns. "That's not possible."

"And yet it's happening."

Rizak leans back in his seat and blows out a slow breath. He looks to his friend, as though the answer might be written on Hew Breon's forehead and we all just missed it.

"I don't know what to make of any of that, Miss DuLaine," he says finally.

"Me neither. Except . . ." This next part makes me feel weird. Like I'm casting myself as the hero, and it's a bit awkward. "I think this is the plot I'm supposed to fix. Not Oz. Or whatever mission Novem XVII gets called to next. *This* one."

I'm vaguely aware that I've said nothing about the scales forming on my legs. But I haven't even told Wist, though they were still there this morning when I dressed.

I had half expected them to disappear once we left the Oz sphere.

My attention shifts back to Rizak, who nods in agreement. "I think you're onto something there."

"Really? You do?" I've gotten used to authority figures dismissing me.

"Yes, though I can't pretend to have good advice." He smiles. "Hew?"

"Let's noodle it."

What a dork. I love him.

"If there's an overarching plot happening," he says, "one that connects Earth with Rivenlea and the spheres, where do we start? What's the first piece to address?"

The pieces of the puzzle now feel like streams that don't want to come together.

"It started with Camille," I reply. "She's where this started, at least for me. I don't know what was happening in Rivenlea that might have caused it." Here I go with the main character energy again. "But if I'm supposed to fix this story, it makes sense to start where it began in my world. Right?"

They all seem to agree, and Rizak knocks his knuckle against the bistro table. "Right, so let's focus on how to rescue your sister."

Tears rise. *Finally* someone other than my friends cares about Camille's predicament. And actually wants to help solve the problem.

"The Elder Council won't be keen to let anyone into the Silvarum without great reason," Hew says. "I live there because I'm a deciduous cat herder."

I elect not to tell him I had the idea for deciduous cats one fall when I mused it would be awesome if cats' fur changed with the seasons. I didn't call them "deciduous cats" or fully think through the implications that their fur would, of course, fall out with the seasons too. But, like Topher Rys the fungalinguist and Dr. Vid Kalin the sparkophytologist, I'm afraid I've inadvertently created a very ridiculous career for this man.

But he doesn't seem to mind. "The cats are allowed out from time to time, obviously, but generally they stay close to the Silvarum. Which means I do too." He raises his brows meaningfully.

I catch his drift. "And that means you have free access to the places we're banned from."

He taps a finger to his nose.

"Which gives us some freedom to experiment without running aground of the council." Rizak consumes half a sticky bun before he speaks again. "The bubbles, as you call them, in the Silvarum. These are ideas you had in childhood?"

"Yes. Half-formed ideas that never really made it into stories."

"Camille obviously ended up there by accident."

"Right. I was imagining . . . a new character when it happened." Mortification washes over me at the idea of saying, "I was imagining Laramie Shayle." Maybe it's something I should mention, but at this point, it feels impossible that I could have created Laramie.

I don't want my allies to think I'm completely nuts.

"So Camille is trapped inside a half-formed thought," Rizak muses. "But what if we could bridge that bubble to another bubble? Or, better yet, to a sphere?" His eyes light. "If we could get her into a proper sphere—"

"We could create a gateway to rescue her," Phen interjects, his Sentinel instincts kicking in.

"Precisely." Rizak pushes his glasses up onto his nose.

"But how?" Wistlee asks. "How can we build a bridge into this bubble? There are supposed to be rules about how spheres are created, after all."

"Supposed to be, yes," I point out. "They don't seem to apply to me."

No one argues with this.

But I still don't know exactly how to carry out Rizak's plan. Until suddenly I do.

I turn to Phen. "The notebook."

55

TWO DAYS LATER, WE'RE
huddled together in a cool, comfortable corner of the Ambryfell
library. Under Earthly circumstances, I would have a book in
hand and be curled into a ball in one of the squashy chairs,
perfectly content with my life.

As it is, anxiety sweat is making my shirt stick to my back.
My journal is sitting on my lap, pen poised over it. Wistlee is at
my right elbow, Rizak at my left.

Phen is stationed just outside the Silvarum, waiting for word
from Hew. He's said he might try to enlist Dr. Kalin and Topher
Rys to help, but it sounded like a dicey proposition. There's lots
of drama between those two, and Hew wasn't sure he could
convince them to work together.

"Are we ready?" Rizak glances around, then nods to the
page. "Seems to be all clear for the moment."

Aside from Phen hanging around the Silvarum without
permission, we're not doing anything wrong. Or explicitly illegal.
But we decided as a group it would be best not to broadcast our
activities. Just in case.

"Yes, I'm ready." But then I just stare at the blank page,
empty lines mocking me. "I don't know what to write."

I've taken a seven-year break from writing, and I *still* don't
know what to write?

"It can be anything," Rizak prompts. "The first test is to see what happens when you write anything down. Will it create another bubble? That's what we need to determine first."

Right.

I've outgrown starting my stories "Once upon a time," but I haven't written anything since I began every story that way. I press the tip of my pen to the paper.

I sit in a darkened cell, plotting my escape. Imagining freedom so vivid, so sharp and detailed and dimensional, I could reach out and brush my fingers upon it.

"Okay, stop." Rizak places his hand over my paper. "That's good. Now we wait."

Yes. Now we wait. For Hew or Phen or someone from the Silvarum to tell us if anything happened. Did my random musing about—I check back at what I wrote—a prisoner, apparently—create an idea bubble? Does the notebook still work like some bridge between my brain and Rivenlea?

Partway down the nearby aisle of spheres, a gateway suddenly flashes into existence. So much for keeping a low profile. Phen was supposed to get word from Hew, then sprint back to Castramore.

But when he stumbles through, I see things didn't go according to plan.

Every square inch of our Sentinel is covered in bright aqua glitter.

It takes several minutes to get Phen cleaned up enough that he can speak. "I don't want to talk about it," he mutters, spitting glitter.

Wistlee and I make a valiant effort not to laugh. And mostly fail.

Phen makes a face. "Those three forest-dwellers are impossible."

"You did not go in the Silvarum, did you?" Wistlee frowns.

"No." Phen spits out more glitter. "That's all you need to know."

Rizak is brushing aqua glitter from several nearby spheres. "But the bubbles?"

Phen's eyes light at this, and he seems to forget about the glitter for a moment. "Emmy, did you write something about a dungeon?"

"A prison, but yes. Close enough." My heart begins to pound. "Does that mean . . . ?"

"Yes." Phen grins through the glitter. "The notebook still works the same way. You can make new idea bubbles."

"And therefore," Rizak chimes in, "you can probably create another sphere like the one that shouldn't be here but is. The Impossible Sphere, I call it."

I shoot him a look, and he gives a mild shrug. "I'm just thrilled to finally have some context for it. Maybe that mystery will be solved yet."

"There is one thing, Emmy." Phen's expression becomes somber. I brace myself. "When your new bubble showed up, Camille . . . she . . ."

My stomach drops. "Just tell me."

"She started to lose some color."

I try to quell the rising nausea.

"Hew said it was just her hair and around her face a little," Phen offers weakly. Trying so hard to make it not terrible.

I take his hand to reassure him that one more hard thing isn't going to break me. I look at Rizak. "What's happening to the color? It's everywhere now, draining from everything. I wouldn't be surprised to find it affecting these spheres." I gesture to the shelves filled with glass balls. "Why is this happening?"

Rizak draws a deep breath and exhales. "I've not heard of anything like this in all my years as librarian. Never has anything like this been mentioned to me. Except . . ." He taps a finger to his chin as he trails off.

I force myself to count to twenty. Then I can't stand it anymore. "Except what?"

"Well, there's *Somnium Comedenti*."

Phen's face remains blank, but Wistlee gives a start, then shudders.

"What's *Somnium Comedenti*?" I dread finding out.

"The Dream Eater," Wistlee answers, her voice trembling. "How could that be?" she asks Rizak.

He shakes his head. "I'm not sure. But it's the only thing I can think of that remotely resembles what's happening." He looks at Phen and me. "It's a legend of the ancient Novems."

"Is it a monster?"

"It's an idea." Rizak squints. "Like a force or a . . ."

"Vacuum," Wistlee supplies.

"Yes, a vacuum. The Dream Eater was said to suck away hope and goodness and charity from Earthlings. It was why Novems were created in the first place. If the stories—which, in those days, were mostly myths and oral histories from every culture across Earth—could be kept intact, it would block the draining force of the Dream Eater. And the beauty and goodness of the world would remain untouched."

The happy stasis. Well, there's plenty of darkness on Earth. Is this evidence the Dream Eater had actually been successful over all these centuries? Immense suffering is endured by millions every day. Does this mean the Dream Eater has been draining the world since the beginning? Did the ancient Novems simply get it wrong, thinking that holding the stories together would stop this force?

But the color only just started draining from Earth, at least as far as we're aware. Something changed, otherwise the worlds would have been diminishing in color for millennia. But what changed?

"If it is the Dream Eater draining beauty from the worlds, why now?" I ask. "Why is it able to do that?"

"It's almost as though holes are being punched through the spheres," Wistlee says slowly.

"Like whatever protective barrier exists around the spheres is breaking down," Phen agrees.

Rizak frowns. "And the Dream Eater is draining at will, through those holes."

"Like holes in the ozone layer," I add. Curious eyes turn toward me. "Never mind. Rizak, is it safe to say, then, that the Dream Eater is exploiting the holes but not causing them?"

He considers this. "The Dream Eater was somewhat passive, at least in the legends I've been told. Wistlee, what say the Gryphons?"

She must notice my puzzled expression and explains. "Gryphons are meticulous in their preservation of history, especially mythologies and other belief systems."

I decide not to tell her that, on Earth, gryphons are mythological creatures, so this seems perfectly fitting and wonderfully ironic to me.

"From what I know," she continues, "*Somnium Comedenti* is a passive force. But do not confuse passive for innocuous. The dangers are significant. Imagine a world drained of all beauty, goodness, kindness, hope, and, greatest of all, love." She wraps both arms and both wings around herself. "If the Dream Eater is real and present in our age, and if it is exploiting the dark work of someone else, it must be stopped."

The dark work of someone else.

My eyes graze over the hundreds of spheres within view. Then they land on Phen, and I stare at his aqua sparkles—stare without seeing. Thinking.

Finally, I look at my accomplices. "I need to see Earth."

56

"YOU NEED A WHAT?"

Laramie is looking at me like I've fallen through the ceiling.

"An enchanted mirror." I scratch behind Frank's ears.

Much to my annoyance, it took me an entire day to come up with a plan and work up the nerve to execute it. Frank is a very convenient excuse to spend time with Laramie, so I asked him over breakfast if he was up for a visit.

It's early afternoon, and we're seated near a ledge outside the hive. Frank is curled between us, our joint-custody daughter.

Laramie pats her head absently. "I don't know what that is."

"It's pretty much what it sounds like." This is totally awkward, but I have to keep going. "I know it sounds silly, but it's a mirror that allows the holder to see into other places. Other worlds, I hope. I need to know what's happening on Earth for more context. I'm trying to make sense of what's happening here and in the spheres."

"You want me to shift into a mirror so you can . . . hold me."

"You make it sound even weirder than it is."

He grins. "I'm not sure that's possible. But also, I can't shift into an enchanted mirror. I've never seen one."

"I know. But what if . . ." I chew my bottom lip. "What if you read about one?" Surely there's an adaptation of "Beauty and the Beast" with an enchanted mirror somewhere in Ambryfell. "Or if I tell you the story of one? It would have a detailed description of the mirror." I'd be sure to add one, anyway.

He cocks his head. "Maybe. It could work."

"Then we have to try," I say. "Will you do it?"

"It's quite a favor you're asking." He leans back on his elbows, and Frank immediately shifts and curls up with her front legs on his chest. He grins at me. "What if you break me while I'm in mirror form?"

"That would be very bad luck."

"And I might shift back into human form with a broken face."

"Truly unfortunate." He looks far too pleased by that remark, so I glance away. "Will you try?"

He doesn't answer right away. Just watches Frank as she gets comfortable and closes her eyes for a nap. After several long moments, he asks, "How is your leg?"

"It's . . . the same. I don't think the scales are spreading." I look at Frank's blue-black scales and wonder what it would be like to be covered in them.

I would need to find entirely new shades of makeup.

"Em?"

Oh. "Sorry, what?"

He laughs and shakes his head. Doesn't repeat his question, whatever it was.

We sit in silence a few moments longer. Then he speaks again. "I have one condition."

My stomach pinches. "Which is?"

"You have to tell Rhyan what you see."

My stomach positively puckers. "I can't. She doesn't want to know."

"It's important that you tell her."

"But why?" I sound whiny, but I can't help it.

"Because she's our captain. You and she have disagreed on this, yes, but you still owe it to her."

"Do I?" I huff. "Because I feel like she owed it to me not to dismiss my concerns in the first place."

"You're right. She did, and that's exactly what I told her."

My stomach unpuckers a little, and heat spreads through me. The pleasant kind, like I might be curled up in front of a fireplace, wrapped in a favorite blanket while the autumn wind whips outside. "You stood up for me?"

"Always." He flashes a knee-melting smile. "Except when you're wrong."

"Convenient, since that'll never happen."

He snorts.

"But also not true."

Genuine confusion ripples across his features. "No? When did I not stand up for you?"

"When you left me sprawled across the table my first night here." I shrug. "I guess it's not fair to say you didn't stand up for me, but you did disappear pretty quickly. I got the message."

The confusion only deepens. "And what message did you get, exactly?"

"That you didn't want to be associated with me. I get it," I rush to acknowledge. "It was a ridiculous moment. But . . ." I pause, at first unable to say the words. "It hurt."

His eyes widen. "I had no idea you'd taken it that way. I was trying to make it less embarrassing for you. You seemed really flustered, and I felt bad. I'd been flustering you on purpose. I thought it would be better if I stopped. I was trying to be respectful."

"Oh." Suddenly, my first few days in Rivenlea are reframed in an entirely different context, and I'm not sure what to do with it.

"I will try it," he breaks into my thoughts. "I'll try to shift into an enchanted mirror, as long as you tell Rhyan afterward."

I draw a deep breath and pat Frank's rump. "Deal."

I'm curled up in that cozy corner of Ambryfell, my Impossible Sphere visible on the shelf nearby. But that sphere is not the one currently holding my attention. There are a dozen or so other spheres collected on the ground before us.

A red rose is visible in one. A fleet of sinking merchant ships in another. A hideous beast roars silently in another.

Laramie's gaze is locked on that one. "What's this story again?"

"These are different versions of 'Beauty and the Beast.' It's a fairy tale."

"About our relationship?"

"Yes. I may be the beast."

He laughs. Then he picks up one of the spheres. "So, are you going to tell me this story?"

And I do. As I tell pieces of the old tales, their respective spheres light up, the imagery inside changing in response to my words.

I know these tales by heart, of course, and I take the liberty of condensing the story, cutting out extraneous characters from some versions, editing out parts of the tales of yore that don't translate well for a modern audience.

Like the part in Villeneuve's version where Beauty is only allowed to marry the prince because she's secretly of noble birth.

Lame.

But I make sure to include the bit about the magic mirror from an Italian version. One of the spheres glows as I add this part, and—thank heavens—the enchanted mirror appears in the sphere.

Laramie's eyes meet mine. We actually have a shot at this. He's seen a magic mirror, even if only a tiny one inside a small sphere.

"And so they married in a lavish, ridiculously expensive royal wedding."

"And lived happily ever after?"

"Obviously."

Laramie leans back and nods. "I like that story."

"Me too. It was a favorite when I was a kid."

"It's nice to think that first impressions can be wrong, isn't it?" He wags his eyebrows meaningfully.

"You look like Phen."

"Do I?"

"Just your eyebrows." I purse my lips. "Wait, am I seriously the beast?"

He laughs, then jumps to his feet and offers me a hand. "Shall we?"

"Live happily ever after? Please, sir. I barely know you."

He shakes his head, but he's still smiling. Putting up with my humor.

Laramie might actually be a saint.

I clear my throat. "Ready?"

He doesn't respond. Except to suddenly pop into a perfect replica of the enchanted mirror we saw in the sphere. I lunge forward to catch him and only just manage.

I grunt in frustration. "You did that on purpose. If I do drop you when you pull something like that, it's your fault. I won't feel bad in the least."

The mirror glints in the light of the glowstones, and I swear he's winking at me.

"Oh, sure. It's all fun and games now. But when you're a bunch of shards, don't come crying to me." I hold the mirror at an angle, slightly away from me. Anxiety zinging across my nerves.

What if I ask to see Earth and it's a disaster?

What if I ask to see Earth and it's completely fine and I'm wrong about everything?

I take a deep breath and angle the mirror toward my face. "I'd like to see Earth. Show me . . . my house."

An electrical pulse misfires in my heart. It's not that I haven't thought about my family since I came to Rivenlea. I have. Every time I think of Camille, a remembrance of my parents skips across my brain.

But I've made a point to smash down those thoughts. Reject them. Rebuke them like they're unhealthy, unwanted.

Because it's too complicated and too painful. And I didn't think I could get back to see them, in any case, so why did it matter? Better to ignore thoughts of the ones I left behind, right?

I'm rethinking all those choices as the mirror surface clouds. As images begin to take shape in the fog of the glass.

The first thing that shows up is my mom's face, and I choke a cry. Shadowy rings encircle her eyes. Her cheeks are sunken, cheekbones more visible than usual, like she hasn't eaten for a week. She has a hand at her temple, massaging it the way she does when she has a headache.

Though I had thought of my mom, I hadn't fully considered what this would be like on her end. Or my dad's. What their experience would be if I suddenly disappeared.

They've lost both their daughters now.

And—foolishly, callously, selfishly—I didn't expect them to care that much.

I want to flood apologies through the mirror, but I can't, of course. I can't hear what they're saying either, but Dad shows up behind Mom for a moment. Panic is written across his face, and I grip the mirror handle tighter.

Something is wrong. Aside from his daughter vanishing, I mean.

He's trying to get my mom to move. He gently tugs at her shoulder. Pleading with her. But she just keeps rubbing her temple. She shakes her head and says something. His panic turns to desperation, then he's disappeared from the image. It's just my mom, looking so tired she could fall asleep and never wake up.

I can't watch her anymore. It's too much.

"Show me . . ." I'm not sure what to ask for. Then I think of my dad's panic. "Show me what's happening outside."

The image explodes into chaos.

The pavement of my street is cracked. People are running

by, carrying bags, children, pets. It seems they're screaming, but I'm watching a silent movie, the audio muted, their voices lost to me.

Black clouds fill the skies, whether smoke or storm, I can't tell. I gasp when I realize one of my neighbors' houses is gone. The ground has opened up and swallowed it, like we've had a massive earthquake or a sinkhole.

I jump up as though I might cross worlds—dimensions, spheres—and hop into my old world to help them.

But it's impossible.

I can only watch in horror as something shadowy barrels from the sky and slams into the sidewalk, nearly striking a family who lives up the street. The father jumps out of the way just in time, shielding his wife and two small sons from the blast's shrapnel.

A cry escapes my constricted throat. Because it's perfectly still and completely serene in this library, I probably sound like a crazy person.

"Laramie!"

The mirror in my hands transforms back into the Echo from Novem XVII, and I'm not holding him anymore. He's holding me, his arms wrapped around me as I tremble like a wintry branch in his embrace.

"What happened?" He smooths my hair. "Em, what did you see?"

I allow his touch to comfort me without being embarrassed or haughty for once.

After a moment, I pull back, tears streaking down my face, and meet his eyes. "Earth is breaking."

57

RHYAN AND CANON SIT IN

the study. I had assumed this was Canon's office when I first met him here, but the study actually belongs to Novem XVII and is technically Rhyan's office.

She sits at the desk now, eyes bored into me. Occasionally dancing hot glares Laramie's direction. "You did what?"

I feel like I'm in the principal's office. Which I pretty much am. Though it occurs to me it would be far worse to be seated before the Elder Council, and I'll probably have to do that eventually too.

Maybe this is more like being at the teacher's desk after class, and the Elder Council will be like the principal.

"Or the firing squad," I say aloud.

"What?" Rhyan doesn't even try to hide her irritation.

"Nothing. Sorry."

Appropriate remorse pools in my gut. I *am* sorry for disobeying Rhyan. "I didn't want to," I say. "Disobey you, I mean. But you wouldn't listen."

She rubs her temples and looks ever like my mother.

That reminder spurs me on. "But this is too important. I had to test my theories. I had to see what's happening on Earth."

"Impossible," Canon says. "You can't just *see* what's happening on Earth."

"The Elder Council has its ways," Laramie cuts in. He's staring directly at Canon, and his expression isn't friendly or easygoing for once. There's steel there, and I can't say I dislike it. "So do they know, Canon?"

Canon doesn't pull his strange, reflective eyes away from Laramie's stare. But he also doesn't answer the question.

For the second time in as many weeks, I see betrayal spark in Rhyan's expression as she turns to Canon. "You've got to be kidding me, Egbert."

"I'm not at liberty to share confidential matters the council has entrusted to me." Canon's voice is unyielding. Unapologetic.

Rhyan slams her hand on the table, and Canon jumps.

It brings some satisfaction.

"All right," Rhyan says. "What is it you've discovered that the council apparently already knows?" Her glare darts Canon's direction.

No need to bury the lede. "Earth is breaking."

I'm met with a completely blank stare. Blanker than blank. Like an untouched slate. A fresh piece of notebook paper. "Breaking."

"Earth is starting to look as bad as Oz. I saw it myself."

"How?" Canon actually has the nerve to look at me with suspicion. "How can you possibly know this?"

"I'm not at liberty to share my own ingenious solutions when I don't feel like it."

Laramie's mouth twitches.

But Rhyan isn't so easily diverted. "What do you mean Earth is breaking? Explain, DuLaine."

Uh-oh. She last-named me. And rhymed. "It's falling apart like a broken story. You know, when the stories go rogue? That's happening on Earth."

"Actual Earth?"

"Yes." I try to keep the impatience from my voice. "I saw my parents. It wasn't a story version of my world. It was my *actual* world."

"*This* is your actual world." Canon gestures vaguely, apparently indicating the entirety of Rivenlea.

"Honestly, I've had about enough of you." I ignore the look of utter indignation on his face and focus on Rhyan, who seems a little taken aback by my sharpness. "Rhyan—Captain Doyle—please. Please, listen to me."

Her gaze flicks up to Canon. "You say council already knows about this?"

His face turns stonier than a Sentinel, and he doesn't respond.

"There has to be a mistake," she says after a moment. "Earth can't just break like a story. It's not a sphere—not in that way. It's . . . Earth."

"I'm only telling you what I saw," I persist. "It was like the apocalypse. And it's connected to everything else that's been happening."

"*Somnium Comedenti*," Laramie says. Bless him for remembering.

"Yes." I turn to Canon, even though I just told him I was done with him. "Surely you're familiar with that?"

He spares one curt nod.

"Rizak believes that could be why the color is draining. From Oz and Rivenlea and Earth."

"The Dream Eater?" Rhyan blinks. "This is getting weirder and weirder. That's an ancient idea, a myth."

"Something is draining the color from the worlds. We think it's like holes being punched in the spheres for some reason, and the Dream Eater is exploiting them."

"But what's causing them?" Rhyan leans forward in her chair. "If you're right, what's causing the holes?"

"I don't have that part figured out yet," I admit. "But I'm telling you—the situation is dire. We have to do something immediately. Earth will go the way of Oz if we let it."

Rhyan drums her fingers on the desk. "I can't understand how any of this is happening. And yet . . ."

"Council confirms it." Laramie is watching Canon. "Even if only by their silence."

Canon is still unmoved.

"And yet, you are our Dragon," Rhyan finally finishes. She studies me for a moment, her eyes softening. "You were right about the silver shoes. You were right about almost everything in Oz."

An embarrassing cascade of emotion threatens to break through my defenses.

"Perhaps you can see something the rest of us can't." She almost smiles. "Like a proper Dragon." Then she stands, decided. "We'll take it to the Elder Council. I'll place another urgent request immediately."

My heart that had been so buoyed by her belief sinks into my toes. "A request?"

"It's how things are done," Canon states, and I valiantly resist the urge to punch him.

"But it could be too late by the time they accept the request. I have to speak with them right away to tell them what I saw and what it means." I beg Rhyan with every cell in my body. "Rhyan, *please*. It's my home. My family."

She takes a couple slow breaths. "I'll do everything I can. Okay? We will see what they say. Maybe we can reset Earth, though I've never heard of such a thing."

Reset Earth? No. It'll never work. She doesn't understand. She said herself that Earth isn't like the spheres. There are far too many stories, too many narratives and characters and lives unfolding on that planet to ever reset it.

Imagine the collective trauma.

But I don't say this aloud. "We have to plug the holes in the spheres before it's too late."

"I'll do what I can," she promises.

Laramie and I each spare Canon a sharp glance as we leave the study. Then we trudge down the hallway of Ambryfell. We stop near the front doors, and I turn to face him.

"We won," he says.

"It feels like we lost."

"I know." His hand moves like he's going to reach for me, then it drops suddenly.

A moment later, Wistlee and Phen appear from behind me. Wist's eyes are wide. "Well? What did Rhyan say?"

Laramie and I give the full recap as the four of us walk back to the cabins.

"What!" Phen's exclamation startles a bird into flight. "Earth is falling apart and the Elder Council knows?"

Laramie's face is grim. "Seems so. But Canon didn't give us any useful information about that."

"In other words, he said nothing at all." I get that Canon thinks he's doing the right thing—keeping his sworn confidences, or whatever. But surely he understands the gravity of the situation.

Then again, maybe he doesn't. We are in uncharted waters, after all. Maybe he doesn't realize that by clinging to protocol so tightly, he—and the Elder Council—may be dooming us all.

We pause at the split in the path. Laramie's and Phen's cabins are one way, mine and Wistlee's the other. We stare at each other for a minute, and the meaning in our collective gaze is clear.

Now what?

I sigh and look at them helplessly. "I honestly don't know, guys."

Phen indicates my pocket, where my journal is safely tucked away. "You work on that."

"And what is my goal, exactly?" It's all become so complicated, so fuzzy, I can't even remember what I'm trying to do. Except save the world.

"Focus on Camille for now," Laramie suggests. "There's nothing we can do about Earth until we get the Elder Council involved."

"Yes," Wistlee agrees. "Focus on creating something to

rescue your sister from the Silvarum. A bridge between her bubble and a new sphere."

Yes. My original goal—rescue my sister. I almost want to cry at the thought that this was my only goal when I first landed here. How messy things have become.

With that flimsy plan in place—flimsy, because it depends entirely on me creating something brilliant to rescue my sister from a giant bubble—we bid the boys goodnight.

Wist and I continue in silence for a moment. Then she reaches out and wraps her feathered wing around my shoulders. "All will be well, Emmy."

"Will it?"

"Well . . . I'm not certain," she admits. "That is the truth. But even when all is not well, the worlds turn on."

"But will they?" I stop and look at her. "If we can't stop whatever is happening, couldn't it be the end?"

But Wistlee knows my question is rhetorical. She just squeezes me tighter in her wing. "All will be well."

I'm with you. We will walk through this together. That's what she means.

I'm still thinking of reasons I'm thankful for Wist when she pushes open our front door and steps into our cabin. I follow after her, my nerves prickling when I realize she's frozen in place three feet into the common room.

"Wist?" I peer around her shoulder so I can see her face.

Mute shock. Concern. Confusion.

Fear.

I track her gaze to what she's looking at.

And I nearly lose my dinner.

Neatly positioned in front of the fireplace are Dorothy's silver shoes.

58

"WISTLEE." I SWALLOW HARD.
"What . . . ?"

She shakes her head, mouth slightly open. "I . . . Those are them, correct? Those are the silver shoes?"

"Yes."

We stare at them in silence. I don't know about Wist, but I'm not sure what to do. I'm almost afraid to touch them. Partially out of awe. Dorothy's silver shoes.

What in all the worlds are they doing *here*?

"Do I tell Rhyan?" I ask Wistlee, desperate for some advice. "Will she even care?"

Wistlee's gaze is still stuck on the shoes. "Yes, she will care. But who could have put them here?"

"And why?"

Both are valid questions. Maybe it's time to invest in an alarm system for the cabin. Or a smart doorbell.

"Exterior cameras, maybe."

"What?" Wistlee breaks her gaze away from the silver shoes to glance at me.

"Nothing. We could at least do with a lock on the front door."

"A lock?" She cocks her head to the side, and I don't actually have the heart to explain to her why anyone would want a lock on their front door.

"Whoever brought these here took them from Oz," I say instead.

"That seems a reasonable deduction."

"Which means. . . it has to be someone from Rivenlea."

I suppose this should have been obvious from the outset. When characters in Oz began using terms and phrases and lines from other stories, I thought perhaps they were speaking to each other. But was it someone from Rivenlea communicating with them instead?

Someone who had been in other stories, knew the language, spoke the lines.

"Who could have done it?" I ask Wistlee.

A small crease comes to her forehead. "I don't know. Why would anyone steal from a sphere? I don't understand, Emmy. We are sent to stories to fix them. Not meddle."

"The fixing is a sort of meddling," I begin. But she shoots me a disapproving look, and I decide not to pull at that thread right now. "Okay, so it's a Rivenlite."

"Someone who has the ability to get into the stories."

"A Sentinel?"

"Or someone who is working with a Sentinel."

A thought hits me. "The silver shoes carry the wearer wherever she wants to go."

"Yes . . ."

"Like into a sphere, perhaps?"

Wistlee's mouth drops and she stares at me. "Or back to Earth."

Those words hit so hard, I shudder from the impact. Could I use these to go see my parents? Is that why they've been given to me? I could rescue my parents from whatever is happening on Earth. Or maybe use the shoes to rescue Camille from the Silvarum?

But no. They only carry the wearer. Dorothy did have Toto when she went across the desert out of Oz and back to Kansas. But I couldn't exactly scoop up my mom and dad, put them in a basket, and bring them back to Rivenlea. And even if I could, to what end? So they would be safe a little while longer while the rest of Earth perished and we waited for Rivenlea to follow suit?

And even if these shoes could transport me into Camille's bubble, what good would it do? I could put them on her feet, but she has to wish herself out. And I don't think she's able to. She's been frozen for seven years.

I grit my teeth in frustration. "Why are these here? Is someone trying to torture us?"

"Torture via shoe?" The smallest of smiles cracks Wistlee's lips.

"Torture via unanswered questions."

"You sound just like a Dragon."

At that, I smile too. And then it reminds me. "Wistlee, I have to tell you something."

"Oh dear. Is it something more shocking than Dorothy's shoes sitting in our cabin? I'm not sure how much more shock I can weather tonight."

"Well." I hesitate, then simply sit down on our couch, unlace my boot, pull off my sock, and roll up my pant leg.

Wistlee's eyebrows rise. "What—"

"I know."

"This is somehow more shocking than the silver shoes, and I was being entirely sarcastic, Emmy."

"Sorry," I say sheepishly and examine the opalescent purple scales. "It started in Oz."

Wistlee tears her gaze away from my leg to my face. "In Oz?"

Guilt whacks me over the head. "I should have told you."

"Did you tell Rhyan?"

"No. I only told . . . That is, he saw . . ."

Wistlee doesn't provide an easy out by finishing any of my mortified fragments. She just waits for me to complete a sentence, her look of shocked amusement deepening by the second.

"Laramie and I were sitting by the fire, and I had my boots off. He noticed it on my ankles." The words come out squished together somehow.

"I see." Wistlee crouches to get a better look. "May I?"

I nod, and she runs her hands over the scales.

"They truly are scales, then."

"I thought . . ." I don't want to speak it. It sounds too silly. "I thought maybe I was becoming a Dragon."

"This is my thought as well."

"Really?" I feel marginally less stupid. "Do you think it's possible?"

"I have never heard of such a thing." Her eyes twinkle. "Then again, I have never heard of such a thing as an Earthling or a human who is part of a Novem."

I give a nervous laugh.

She brushes the scales with her fingers again. "They're lovely. You'll make a beautiful Dragon."

I can't help but snort, imagining myself with empty Dragon eyes and a face full of scales like Salem and the others. "I doubt that, but thank you. They haven't spread farther since we returned to Rivenlea."

Will Laramie think I'm hideous if I turn into a full-fledged Dragon?

"Stop," I say aloud.

Wistlee knows me well enough to know I'm talking to myself, not her, and her kind smile wraps me in reassurance. But then it disappears, and all the worries of the past hour surface on her face again. "Emmy."

"I know." We both look at the silver shoes. "What in the worlds is happening?"

59

GLASS SPHERES FILL MY

entire field of vision. Countless characters and magical objects and fantasy worlds and important plot moments dance before me.

But I see the cracks too.

Not literally. At least not yet.

But I see the breakdowns beginning in some of the spheres. Like when the Oz sphere filled with smoke. I can see characters running through tiny streets silently, distressed and open-mouthed. Fires burn, shadow creatures fall from the tiny skies.

Dorothy's silver shoes are wrapped in a scarf and tucked away in one of my drawers. Last night, Wistlee and I decided to leave them there until we can collect more information. Until after our appointment with Rizak this morning. If someone in Rivenlea stole those shoes from Oz, it means there's someone here that can't be trusted.

A member of the Elder Council?

I definitely don't trust any of them.

"Hello, Emmy."

I nearly part from my skin. "Rizak. You scared me."

He smiles. "My apologies."

Could Rizak be the thief? I watch as he pushes his glasses

up on his nose and frowns at the distressed spheres, looking genuinely distraught at the havoc inside.

It could be him, but I would be shocked if so.

He turns to me and flashes a thin, worried smile. "Are you ready?"

I nod. "Ready as I'll ever be."

Wistlee and Phen have already scoped out a quiet back corner of the library. Rizak and I join them there, and I pull out my story notebook.

I stare at the closed cover. "I don't know what to write." Again.

"To make the leap from bubble to sphere, we need a real plot," Rizak says. "Correct? That was the difference between Princess Brielle Song and the bubbles in the Silvarum?"

"That's my theory, anyway. But . . ." I run my fingers along the notebook cover. "I don't know what story to write for Camille. Will it really pull her from the bubble, or will it just create a story-character Camille?" It's becoming so complicated I just want to give up.

Let someone else save the world.

But right now, I'm not trying to save the world, I remind myself. I'm just trying to save my sister, and no one else is going to care about that as much as I do. This is my job, my calling—and I know that.

I scrape every last brain cell together. Reaffirm my resolve to rescue Camille, no matter what it takes.

I open my notebook to a blank page.

Once upon a time, I begin, because suddenly I'm ten again and telling Camille her own story. I always began with "Once upon a time." Her eyes would sparkle, ready to listen to whatever outlandish thing I'd dreamed up this time. So if I'm writing a story for Camille, I can't start any other way.

Once upon a time, there was a girl named Camille DuLaine. She never saved the world, but she did save my world more than once. This is what happened.

The story of Camille, me, our parents—our childhood, the

shared jokes, the silly games, the places where we used to go adventuring, the sisterly language we shared that no one else understood—it all spills from my pen onto the page. The ten years we had together. Too short. And yet so full.

I write a scene from my fourth birthday party. Mom wasn't big on parties, but she had invited a few kids from my preschool class to come over. At the last minute, a nasty flu swept through the class, and no one showed up.

Camille saved the day. She dug into her dress-up trunk and pulled out all my favorite clothes—the ones she usually hesitated to let me wear because my hands were always sticky and I couldn't seem to not fall down and get everything dirty.

She dressed me up in all my favorites at once, placed a tiara on top of the mess, and called me Princess Emlynalinn. We played hide-and-seek around the house for hours. Then she oohed and aahed with delight as I opened my presents and snagged an extra piece of cake for me when Mom wasn't looking.

I flip the page and start a new scene. This time I'm in second grade, and Brandon Boyce is following me home from school. The elementary school is right down the street from our house. I should be able to walk home in peace. But this boy isn't content to torment me in class and on the playground. He has to make the bullying last as long as possible—every second counts.

He's throwing pebbles at my back. Then one hits me in the back of the head, whether or not he meant to. Sharp tears sting my eyes, and I speed up. But the next moment, I'm sprawling forward, shoved from behind, the weight of my backpack adding to the momentum.

The sidewalk has met me before I have time to right myself. Knees and palms shred on the rough concrete, and I let out a cry.

Brandon Boyce's laughter rings out behind me, but it's cut short with a strangled shriek. I turn around to see what's happening.

Camille and three of her friends have Brandon by the back of his shirt. They're holding him in place as he kicks out frantically.

He's doing his worst, running in place like a cartoon character, but the four older girls have him tight.

My sister towers above everything like a golden pillar. Her eyes flicker with blue-green fire. "Don't ever touch my sister again, do you hear me?"

Brandon squeals, and I'm almost certain he's about to cry. Serves him right.

"Promise it!" Camille booms.

"I promise!"

The bigger girls release Brandon, and his own flailing nearly makes him crash to the sidewalk. He rights himself just in time, flashes a rude gesture at Camille and her friends, then takes off down the street before they can make him pay for it.

But Camille has forgotten all about Brandon. She's crouching beside me, examining my scrapes, brushing dirt and tiny bits of rock from my hands and knees. "Are you okay, Emmy?"

I nod, biting down on the tears. Willing them to stop trickling over my face, dripping from my chin.

She pulls the sleeve of her hoodie down to cover her hand and uses it to dab my tears. Then she smiles. "Let's go home and get you cleaned up." She waves to her friends.

"See you tomorrow, Camille," one of them says.

"Bye, Camille!"

Then her friends disappear, continuing their journeys homeward.

"That was embarrassing," I mumble.

Camille shakes her head. "That boy is the one who should be embarrassed. I bet he grows up to be terrible."

My pen pauses above the notebook. Camille didn't actually say that. But I imagined it because Brandon Boyce grew up to be pretty decent, as second-grade bullies sometimes do. And the irony would be a nice thing to include in the story.

I try to picture him as he is now in high school, but it's difficult. Some of my Earth life has become shrouded in fog, while other bits remain etched in sharp relief. Brandon and I aren't friends by any stretch, but he does sometimes acknowledge my existence if we pass each other in the hallway.

My pen finds the paper again.

Camille is twelve. One week before she disappeared. She's preparing for her first junior high school dance. I'm sulking on the corner of her bed, glaring holes in the back of her head as she leans toward her vanity mirror and puts on shimmery clear lip gloss.

She sighs. "Emmy."

I shrug. "Whatever."

"Not whatever." She turns on her vanity stool to face me. "What's the problem?"

"There's no problem. I'm fine."

"Then why are you glaring at me?"

I shrug and look past her to the wall like any mature ten-year-old would.

"It's just a dance." She turns back to the mirror and smooths her hair.

I purse my lips, mostly to keep them from trembling. "I don't . . ."

"You don't what?"

"I don't like feeling left behind."

She crosses the room and sits next to me on the bed to put her arm around my shoulder. "No one likes feeling left behind."

"You never get left behind. You get to do *everything* first."

"Well, I'm older."

"That's not fair."

She laughs—not *at* me, exactly. But a little. I'm being ridiculous.

"You're going to get to do everything someday too."

I huff. "Mom won't let me do anything. I'm always going to be left behind."

"Hey, just because I'm doing new things, it doesn't mean I'm leaving you. I'll always be here."

I feel my chest constrict. "Do you promise?"

"I promise." She squeezes me tighter. "You'll always be my sister, no matter where I go. And you're going to have so many adventures of your own someday. You're going to have to tell me not to be jealous when those days hit."

In a rare moment of openness, I wrap my arms around Camille's waist. "Okay, I will."

"Emmy, stop!" Wistlee's voice yanks me from my memories. Pulls me from the page.

I shake myself back into Ambryfell, back to the library, back to the secluded corner. Phen, Wistlee, and Rizak are standing around me, and someone else is here too.

Hew Breon, no deciduous cats in sight, is holding a hand to his chest and wheezing. Sweat runs down his temples. He draws hard, shallow breaths, leans against the wall, trying to catch his wind.

"What is it?" I hop up, alarmed.

Hew holds up one finger, sucking in another long breath, then speaks. "It's breaking everything."

I startle. "What's breaking everything?"

"Your new story. First a bubble formed, much as the last time with the dungeon."

Prison. But yes.

"And then," Hew continues, "the bubble with the young girl began to be drawn into the new bubble."

As hoped . . .

"Along with everything else." Hew looks meaningfully at Rizak, then me. "*All* of the other bubbles began to get suctioned into the new story."

"How is that possible?" I stare open-mouthed at Rizak. "How can a new story that doesn't contain any of those elements take old ideas into itself?"

He shakes his head, his mouth pressed into a tight line. He pales, his skin tinging slightly green. "I don't know."

"That's not all," Hew says, inhaling deeply again. "The forest itself began to crumble."

We're all like stone. Stunned.

"Cracks are appearing in Castramore too." Hew shakes his head. "I didn't slow to gather details. I came as fast as I could. But there's panic in the streets."

"But, Rizak, how can this be?" My gaze lands on the story spheres.

No.

I rush to the shelves. Rake my gaze over the delicate storyworlds.

And see cracks everywhere.

"No!" I spin around to the others. They've followed me to the shelves, and their faces tell me they've seen it too.

Even as we stand there, another sphere cracks, the sound like melting ice splintering.

What have I done?

60

I RACE THROUGH THE HALLS

of Ambryfell, Wist and Phen clipping at my heels.

Rhyan. We have to find Rhyan.

The hum of panic and confusion reaches us from the streets, but I tune it out. Pretend it's not a factor. Because we have to find Rhyan before we can help anyone in Castramore.

We burst out the back doors and into the yard. It's disturbingly peaceful here. The chaos from the streets, the Silvarum, and the library, hasn't touched this place yet. A few Novemites are out here training, and they turn at our sudden arrival, curiosity scribbled on their expressions.

I don't fail to notice the haughty raised eyebrows of a few Dragons.

But I'm past caring, focused only on where Rhyan, Canon, and Laramie are standing in a knot near the back door.

Thank goodness.

Rhyan turns, something I can't identify in her expression as Wistlee, Phen, and I stop at her side. "We have been granted an audience with the Elder Council in two days," she says.

I jerk my head up, trying to process her words. "Two days."

She sighs. "It was the best I could do, Emmy."

"No, I know that, Rhyan," I say quickly. Though I'm struck by her words. "You mean they know Earth is breaking and the spheres are falling apart, but they're going to make us wait two days to discuss it?"

"It's how these things are done, Emlyn." Canon shrugs, and I can't help but wonder who invited him into this conversation.

I wave the words away. "I don't care about the Elder Council."

Laramie's brow furrows as he reads my face, the faces of Wistlee and Phen. "What's happened?"

"I tried to write a story to save Camille. Our idea was to pull her from the bubble by making a sphere for her." The concept sounds especially odd when I say it aloud. "My new story created a bubble that I suppose could have become a sphere like we intended, and it pulled Camille into it like we'd hoped. But then it started sucking up everything else. Castramore is fracturing. The spheres are actually cracked."

I meet Rhyan's gaze and beg her with my eyes. "Captain, please. We have to do something."

Laramie steps to my side. "Earth?"

Dread washes over me from head to toe. "I . . . I don't know." But deep inside somewhere, I do.

Whatever I've accidentally done here, it will have made the situation on Earth worse.

"But why?" My voice is abnormally loud. "I don't understand why my actions would have such dire consequences. Who cares what I write?"

"Obviously someone does." Canon has his keen ears perked, and I suppose he can now hear shouts from the streets, though they're still lost to me.

"*Somnium Comedenti*?" Wistlee asks. "Could that be who cares?"

The Dream Eater?

I puzzle through it. But no, not if I understand the concept correctly. "It's a passive force, really, isn't it? It's exploiting the cracks."

"So it would want more cracks in the worlds, if it had a vote," Phen points out.

"But it doesn't have a vote," Laramie counters. "Does it?"

Canon and Wistlee both shake their heads, and Canon speaks. "It's not a sentient being."

"It's a black hole." I bite my lip and ignore the puzzled expressions surrounding me. A fresh wave of dread swamps me. "Rhyan, if the Dream Eater sucks all the hope and kindness away from Earth, what's left will be . . ." The horror of it steals my words.

But Rhyan prods me on. "What will be left?"

"All the terrible parts. Hatred, abuse, persecution, selfishness, unkindness, deceitfulness. Evil. All that's left will be evil."

Rhyan's mouth opens then closes as she studies my face. But Canon shakes his head. "No. Not true. When we fix the stories, it keeps Earth whole. What you describe is . . . not wholeness."

A rare moment of compassion for Canon flashes through my heart. He truly doesn't get it—they both truly don't get it. They've honestly believed all this time that the work of the Novems has been preserving some sort of utopia on Earth.

"You're right," I say to him. "It's not wholeness. Earth has always been broken but not without hope. If we're going to save it, we must act quickly."

"Emmy," Rhyan says, then hesitates, "don't take this the wrong way. But if Earth is as you describe, if it is full of such darkness and evil, is it even worth saving?"

I recoil as if slapped. "It's . . . it's eight billion people," I say numbly. "You can't write off eight billion people." I look around the circle. "Can you?"

No one says anything—not even Laramie—and I'm struck with the possibility that maybe they *can* write off eight billion people.

If so, then Rivenlea is no better than Earth.

Desperation tinges my voice. "You told me stories hold us together, Rhyan. Isn't that what you and Rizak said? Stories bind us, help us see the universe more clearly?"

She nods.

"And what do the stories show us? That evil exists, yes. But good can triumph over it. Selfishness may be the human default, but we can choose to sacrifice for others. Good *can* win. Don't you believe that?"

Again Rhyan nods, but it's Laramie who speaks. "I do."

"As do I," Wistlee says.

"And me," Phen adds.

Suddenly, my notebook is burning a hole in my back pocket. I pull it out. Flip to the blank pages.

There are only a few left, and all at once, I know what I must do.

And it's going to cost me Camille.

Again.

61

WE'RE ALL RUNNING BACK

into Ambryfell, and I'm shouting over my shoulder. "I need to use my last pages to write something to fix the spheres!"

"But what?" Wistlee calls back. "What can you write?"

Honestly? I have no idea.

It brings me to a halt. "Some kind of structure to fix the cracked spheres?"

"Plot structure?" Rhyan asks.

"Literal structure?" Canon throws in.

I press a hand to my forehead. "I don't know!"

"A magic system?" Laramie suggests.

I lower my hand and look at him. Tears are threatening, and my fingers grip the notebook so tightly they hurt.

I always have an idea. A thought about where to turn next. But not today—not when it matters most. I'm willing to do what I need to, give up what I must. But I have no idea what comes next.

Wistlee is beside me now and hooks her arm through mine. "How many pages are left, Emmy?" Her voice is gentle.

The tears break free. "Only a few."

Wist draws a deep breath, then looks at Rhyan. "She won't be able to save her sister. Not with this notebook, anyway. If she writes something to save the worlds, she'll be out of pages."

"And we have no idea if it'll work with another notebook," Rhyan realizes.

"But Earthlings are capable of goodness and self-sacrifice." Laramie offers a half smile. Maybe like he's proud. "So Emmy's going to try to save the worlds instead of her sister."

Even Canon looks like he feels a bit sorry for me, so I must be extra pathetic right now.

I wipe my tears with my sleeve and sniff. "We don't have much time."

"Right." Rhyan is all business again. "Canon and I will convene with the other Novem leaders. Maybe the Elder Council will be more interested in what we have to say now." She turns her gaze on me. "We'll meet you back here shortly. Don't get lost. You hear me?"

The tears threaten again. "I hear you. We'll stay close."

"And . . ." Her eyes go soft and she swallows hard. "Be safe. Please."

With that, she and Canon head down the hall, toward an ascending spiral staircase. Only then do I realize I've never been upstairs in Ambryfell. I never explored beyond my little corner.

"The senior Novems' business offices are on the second floor," Laramie says, noticing my gaze. "Then the next few floors are apartments for Novemites. At the very top—Elder Council."

I stare. "They've been up there this whole time? Just sitting there and overlooking Castramore, ignoring all the problems crashing down on Rivenlea? The spheres, Earth?"

Laramie spreads out his hands with a small shrug.

"Well, say what you will about Earth, but in some ways Rivenlea isn't so different. Bureaucracy abounds." The desperation of the situation triggers my nerves again. "I'm not sure what's next," I admit.

"The library?" Wistlee suggests. "Might you get an idea of what to do there?"

"Let's try."

We take off down the hallway again, cutting corners a little sharply, but we don't meet anyone else. Not until we round the last corner near the front doors, just a few skips from the doors to the library.

I crash into a man, and my notebook goes flying.

Laramie reaches out to grab me, and Wistlee deploys her feathered wing to catch Phen as he stumbles back.

"Apologies."

I know the voice.

I yank myself away and straighten, forcing the face to come into focus. Make sure it reconciles with my remembrance. "Hadeon?"

Hadeon Exan is holding a finger to his lips, shushing me. "Keep your voice down, please."

"No," I say flatly—a bit rudely, but I don't really care.

He sighs. "Very well."

And then I see it. The bundle in his arms. I might have assumed it was a purchase from one of the clothing shops in town. Maybe a small treasure of some other sort—a teacup and saucer wrapped up to protect it, or a collection of dried herbs and tincture bottles from Teyra's apothecary that she'd bundled in a scarf she just pulled from her head.

But I know better.

The scarf belongs to Wistlee, and wrapped inside are Dorothy's silver shoes.

62

MY GAZE IS GLUED TO THE
bundle. Surely Wistlee sees it too. "Why do you have that?" My
voice sits a breath above a whisper, and for a moment, I'm not
sure he heard me.

"I've been waiting for you."

My stomach drops. "Why? Hadeon, what is going on?"

"I had hoped you would use them the moment you
discovered them."

Instinctively, I retreat a few steps. But then the shoes lure me
back toward him. One tentative step. "Use them?"

Pieces are clicking together, but nevertheless, I ask, "How
do you know anything about what's in that bundle, Hadeon?"

He meets my gaze, and his eyes sharpen. Harden.

But he remains silent.

So I speak for him. "You put the silver shoes in my cabin."
And then the final piece clicks into place, the awful realization
strikes the core of my heart. "*You* stole them from Oz."

"Shh." He looks up and down the hallway. "Keep your
voice down."

In my periphery, I see Laramie's hand touch his hip—but his
sword is not there.

"Why . . . why would you—" My head feels like it's filled

with cotton balls instead of a functional brain. "Why would you do that?"

He's quiet for several moments that feel like hours.

Days.

Weeks.

Then he pushes the bundle of shoes into my arms and looks me dead in the eyes. "Return to your cabin. Take the shoes with you. And use them, for heaven's sake."

I back away from him out of instinct. Surely he wouldn't try to hurt me—not here, not outnumbered four to one.

Except I know him even less than I thought I did. If he's capable of stealing the shoes from Oz, what else might he do?

I thought he was harmless.

"Emmy, please," he says.

The desperation in his voice only makes me angrier. I'm unable to get past the sense of betrayal and alarm ringing in my ears. "Please what? Why do you want me to use the shoes? Do you really expect me to trust you after you stole them from Oz?"

He draws a sharp breath. "Without the silver shoes, you will not be able to help your sister."

It's the last thing I expect him to say, and it punches me in the gut. No. In the heart.

"My sister? That doesn't make any sense." Images of Camille trapped in her bubble, Camille on the playground, Camille laughing and dancing and squeezing me tight flash through my mind.

My heart cracks open, revealing the empty space she left there and the gaping chasm losing her again will create. It zings with pain like an exposed nerve or a hot wire.

I would do anything to get her back.

Anything.

My eyes burn holes into Hadeon like I'm a Bolt. "What do the silver shoes have to do with Camille?"

He looks right back at me. "Not that sister."

63

I STAND IN AN AMBRYFELLAN

hallway as my world unravels.

My brain tries to process what Hadeon is saying to me, but the words don't belong together.

Other. Sister.

It does not compute.

Wistlee has her arm wound tightly around one of mine. Phen is at her other side, on the verge of turning to stone. Laramie is at my back, and I can practically taste his yearning for a weapon.

A shout from just beyond the doors brings me back into the present.

"Hadeon, I only have one sister. Camille. The one who is trapped in the Silvarum." Maybe he's losing it and simply doesn't remember. Just has me confused with someone else. Or has taken leave of his senses.

But his eyes look clear and focused when he speaks. "Emmy, I think it's time you learn where you truly come from."

My heart trips. "Hadeon . . . this isn't funny."

"You've never wondered why you're at the center of it all, Emmy? You've never wondered how you're connected to Rivenlea?"

Of course I've wondered. I haven't stopped wondering since a sassy little wyvern showed up in my bedroom and beckoned me through a portal into this place. Anomalies swarm around me like flies. Of course I've wondered.

But now that the possible truth is standing here in the form of a person, presumably ready to tell me something real, I'm not sure I want to know.

How can that be?

Maybe because I sense my world is about to upend completely. As if it hasn't already.

"It was Teyra, really," Hadeon begins.

"Teyra the apothecary?" Confusion permeates Laramie's question.

"Teyra the retired Harmony," Hadeon corrects. "She couldn't bear it. You were such a sweet baby, Emmy. A tiny pale thing with a load of dark curls. When Teyra learned you were meant to die, she couldn't stand to let it happen."

I stare at him, aghast. "Meant to what?"

"Spheres are fully formed worlds. You understand that now. Oz wasn't just filled with things that made it onto the page of the book in your world, correct?"

Well, a lot of things were happening in Oz that didn't come from a book. But I understand what he's saying. The Oz sphere exists as a complete world, not only a reflection of what's on the page in L. Frank Baum's story. Just because a particular house isn't mentioned in the book doesn't mean it won't appear in the sphere. The world is round, full. Fleshed out.

"Yes," I say hesitantly.

"You are a character, Emlyn. A character that didn't quite make it onto the page. And your story was set to be a tragic one. Teyra and one of your story sisters couldn't let it happen. They were determined to save you. So we . . ." He doesn't finish, although this sentence absolutely begs a whole essay's worth of explanation.

"You . . . *stole* me? From a sphere?" Suddenly, the silver shoes feel hot in my arms. My voice pitches. "You just swiped me like a pair of shoes?"

I look at Laramie, whose mouth is open in shock. Then I glance at Wistlee and Phen, standing beside me wide-eyed.

Wide, surprised. But not disbelieving.

"No," I declare firmly, because I can't reconcile this. "That's ridiculous. I was born on Earth. In a hospital, to my parents. I have one older sister who looks like my dad—our dad. I look like my mom. What you're saying is absurd. It cannot be possible." I punctuate each thought, every word.

Hadeon doesn't respond. Another shout from outside reaches us, and my patience has expired.

"I look like my mom, Hadeon!" I'm practically yelling at him.

He tilts his head. "Do you, though?"

My mind is spiraling out of control. Yes. I do look like her. Of course I do. We always said so. Camille looks like Dad. Emmy looks like Mom.

Except . . .

We said that because Camille is blonde and Dad used to be. They have the same nose. The same smile. The same golden skin tone.

Mom and I are both dark-haired. She has straight hair, mine is curly. She has olive skin, I'm pale. Her aquiline nose is regal and filled with character that my narrow, straight nose doesn't possess. Our mouths are different. Our teeth, our smiles. The shapes of our eyes.

"But my parents—" I falter.

"Believe you are their daughter. Only thrice in all of recorded Rivenlite history has a portal been created on Earth. When you crossed back to Rivenlea with the wyvern, when your Earthling sister accidentally crossed through and landed in the Silvarum, and when Teyra, Stacia, and I smuggled you out of Rivenlea. Your Earthling mother had just given birth to a baby girl."

"Eight weeks premature," I say numbly.

"Their baby daughter didn't make it."

I step back until I hit something solid, then realize it's Laramie. I'm thankful for his support because I'm not sure my knees are up to the task at the moment. "I'm a changeling. You swapped me for their Earthling daughter."

My recovery had always been called miraculous. That was what my parents said, though the whole "miracle baby" shine wore off pretty quickly.

The doctors couldn't believe my NICU journey—such a small, sickly baby seemed to rebound overnight, and it was not what they had expected. But they rejoiced with my parents. Said sometimes things happen that medicine just can't explain.

I try to choke past my sawdust-filled throat but have no words.

"We couldn't let anyone know what we'd done. Until now, only we three have known—even all these years later." He draws a deep breath. "We could be imprisoned, exiled, or worse. Even now, the Elder Council would not look kindly on the choices we made."

The disintegrating worlds come to mind. "I wonder why," I say dryly.

"Indeed. Our decision to remove you from your sphere had unintended consequences. Things have been falling apart ever since."

"This is how I'm connected to everything—to Earth, Rivenlea, and the spheres. This is why my stories break the rules. Why Camille got sucked into my thoughts when we were children. And why my soul remembers this world, even if my mind doesn't."

I'm struck speechless when I realize I didn't create Laramie. I didn't make up that story boy. I knew him already. And knew Castramore and some of these story people because I'm like a bridge between all these worlds.

I'm supposed to exist in a book—a fictional world—and my presence in reality is what's fractured everything. Created the holes that have allowed the Dream Eater to suction the life from everything.

I belong to the realm of story.

This is all my fault.

"Your story sister—the one who sought to save you as a baby—her story is falling apart, Emlyn. She's in great danger."

Two sisters in danger.

"She needs you to rescue her, and we must do it beneath the notice of the Elder Council."

My gaze drops to the bundle in my hands. "The shoes."

"Yes."

"Their magic carries the wearer where she wants to go."

"No gateway required."

I stare at him a moment. "But you stole these from Oz. You lied to everyone. You broke that world so I could travel to my original story and save my sister. You harmed an entire storyworld of characters. You withheld information from me and now this." I gesture wildly toward Castramore, the sounds of panic from the street still buzzing in the distance.

Hadeon has the decency to look chagrined. "I've been partly responsible for harming characters for seventeen years, Emmy. I'm trying to undo the damage, to right what I've wronged."

I huff a sigh. "You and me both." Then I'm quiet for a moment. Thinking. Deducing.

"I belong to a story, should have stayed there, but now I'm connected to Earth, Rivenlea, and the spheres," I ponder. "So I'm the one."

"The one?"

"Yeah." I force some steel back into my knees and stand on my own power, then give a mirthless laugh. "You took a random side character who didn't even make it into the book and turned her into the Chosen One. Lame, Hadeon. Really lame."

"I . . ." He shakes his head.

Numbness has shrouded me.

No, not numbness. Strength. Cold determination to do what I have to. To save what can be saved, to finally set things right.

For real this time. Not like a story reset. A true righting of past wrongs.

I bite away the panic and doubt creeping in and draw myself

up. "I'm the only one who will be able to stop the Dream Eater and plug the holes in the spheres."

Hadeon's brows rise. "How?"

"I'm the bridge." I turn to my friends, ready to forget Hadeon Exan ever existed, even as I work to restore what he's broken. "Let's go."

64

WE'RE STEPS FROM THE LIBRARY

when a small boy bursts through the Ambryfell doors, a fluffy, squirming bunny clasped under one arm.

"Joshua?" Laramie immediately drops to one knee to meet the boy at eye level. "What's wrong, buddy?"

Does he know absolutely everyone in Castramore?

The little boy sniffles and wipes tears on the back of his sleeve. "Please, help us! They're trying to take Mama."

I consider shoving the shoes back into Hadeon's arms before we follow Joshua into Castramore at top speed, but I have no trust for the old Zephyr. I clutch the bundle of magic shoes to my chest and run with the others.

Joshua leads us to the heart of downtown Castramore, where three-story brick buildings line the street. The same place I saw Jason and Denica and those other story people when I first arrived.

No, not story people. Actual Rivenlite people I only thought I'd made up. Rivenlites who had unwittingly invaded my consciousness through the connection I have to their world.

Of all the explanations, this is one I never would have guessed. Remember when I was convinced I was merely insane? Those were the good old days.

"Watch out!" Laramie shouts, throwing an arm in front of Joshua to protect him.

A vaporous shadow creature hovering in the sky collects itself into a missile and dives toward the building in front of us. It explodes against the exterior wall, shattering brick and eliciting screams from within.

"Mama's inside!" Joshua wails. "Please help her!"

The shadow creature spills down the side of the wall, pooling into itself on the ground near our feet.

Laramie again reaches for his empty hip, then curses under his breath.

Hadeon sends a blast of cold air toward the shadow creature, spinning away some of its smoky tendrils, delaying but not halting its formation into something more solid.

Both of Wistlee's wings are spread wide as she scales the exterior of the building, aiming for the window where Joshua is directing her. Phen instructs Joshua to hide himself, then turns to stone to protect the little boy.

"Em." Laramie's tone is desperate. "I don't have my sword."

I stare at him helplessly. Should someone run and get it? Is it in Laramie's cabin or the yard?

I begin to offer a suggestion, but then Laramie blinks out of existence, and something clatters to the stones at my feet.

A sword.

My sword.

Laramie has shifted into my sword. I pick him up—no, it, not him. I will never be able to do this if I think of my sword as "him."

The shadow creature before me has solidified into something corporeal, and it's moving toward Phen and Joshua. Where the little boy cowers behind the Sentinel. Phen makes an excellent wall, but he can't move when he's made of stone. So I have approximately three seconds to act.

I lunge forward with a stabbing thrust, aiming directly for the creature's shadow chest. At least, I think it's the chest.

The creature hisses and slows its progression toward Phen,

but otherwise my strike doesn't seem to have been very effective. An annoyance more than anything.

I spin away, twist around to gain momentum, then launch a downward strike aimed at the creature's arm.

With an unearthly shriek, the creature's arm parts from the rest of its body.

Before it can recover its wits—if it has wits—I spin again and repeat the process on the other side. The second arm falls to the ground, then wisps away into nothingness.

So we just have to do this piece by piece.

The armless shadow creature darts toward me, and I duck just in time. But the spindly shadow tendrils breathe an icy line down my spine. A shudder racks my body.

Before I can fully turn and launch another strike, the shadow creature forms its head into a missile-like point again and propels itself toward me. I dodge, but not far enough. The shadow darts through my left bicep.

Frost shoots through my veins. A gasp punches from my lungs. I reel back several steps and nearly lose my grip on my sword.

Well. I definitely don't want one of these creatures to punch through my organs, that's for sure.

Shadow Thing is collecting itself for another attack, but I decide not to give it the chance. I hack at the head, then cut piece by piece through the torso.

This is much less disturbing an exercise to do on an amorphous shadow than it would be on a flesh-and-blood creature.

With one final scream, the shadow creature fully disintegrates. A few ribbons of black smoke curl around the stones, but then Hadeon blows them away with a flick of his hand. Phen turns back to flesh, then scoops up Joshua. Wistlee has her golden rope anchored in the window of one of the upstairs apartments. Her feathered wing is partially covering a woman climbing down the rope beneath her, but the angle is such that she can't fully protect the woman, who I assume is Joshua's mother.

A new shadow missile dives toward the woman, but she pulls her leg up just in time. The bricks behind her explode.

"Hadeon!" I shout.

He sees it now, too, and he directs a blast of wind their way, careful to avoid hitting Wistlee and Joshua's mother and risk knocking them from the rope. The cover gives Wistlee the extra few moments she needs to help the terrified woman to the ground.

"Mama!" Joshua squirms free from Phen and runs to his mother.

She crouches and wraps both her little boy and his bunny— which is somehow still alive, despite the boy's stranglehold—in her arms.

One moment I'm standing there, sword in hand, watching a touching family reunion, thankful we could help. The next, I'm staring into Laramie's hot cocoa eyes, holding his face like I'm about to reach onto my tiptoes for a kiss.

I yank my hands away and step backward so suddenly, I almost lose my balance.

A grin slowly spreads across his face. "Sorry."

I collect my feet beneath me and do my best to glare at him. "Somehow I feel like you're not. Some warning might have helped," I huff.

"Hard to say much when you're made of steel."

"Strong silent type?"

"Something like that." But then his grin fades into a grimace.

A thought occurs to me. "Did it hurt you? Going through the shadow creatures, I mean."

"It's not my favorite."

A shriek from above snags our attention, and I look at the sky for the first time since we ran outside. Fending off specific shadow creatures has made me oblivious to the big picture problem here, but I see it now.

Oh, do I see it.

It's like a giant has poked his fingers through the atmosphere of Rivenlea. Pulled the invisible barrier apart, torn holes in it. Opened up cracks.

The shadow creatures are spilling through the holes.

The cobblestone street a short distance from our position has split down the middle. Shadow creatures crawl from the ground, reaching out for the fleeing Rivenlites as they run past.

"Dream Eater, phase two," Laramie says, face grim.

Great.

"We'll never be able to fight them all," I say. We duck from a shadow barreling down the street at chest height, looking for any warm body to pierce. "Even if we had every Novemite out here, active or retired, I don't think it would be enough."

Laramie turns to the woman and her son. "Rayleen, run to Ambryfell. Urge anyone else you meet to go with you. Barricade yourselves inside. We have a better chance of protecting everyone with only one structure to defend."

She nods, eyes full of tears and determination. She grabs Joshua's hand and they take off.

I send up a silent prayer they make it safely.

An unfamiliar voice booms nearby. "Novemites, on me!"

We look over and watch a burly guy with a beard turn himself into a human torch, chasing away three shadow creatures with his flames.

"Kimball Brand," Laramie notes. "Novem XIII captain."

Captain Brand's flames blink out, then he spies us. "Shayle, what are you doing? Let's go!"

"We're telling the civilians to gather at Ambryfell. Easier to defend one stronghold."

Captain Brand nods his approval. "We're releasing the wyverns."

A thread of panic ribbons through me. "The wyverns?" I say under my breath to Laramie. "Frank?"

"The wyverns are defenders of Rivenlea, Em." He says it

calmly, but I see the worried crease between his brows. And that confirms it.

Frank is in danger.

"Novem XVII!" Rhyan's voice.

We turn to see Rhyan's hands aflame, Canon, Marella, and Rivit flanking her, fighting their way through the streets. A moment later, the ground beneath us darkens, and I look up to see a giant wyvern pass overhead, claws extended, ripping through several shadow creatures.

I get it now. Frank truly is still a baby. This wyvern is at least twice Frank's fully extended size.

Rhyan and the others come up next to us. "Emmy?" She doesn't voice it, but she doesn't need to. The entire question is in that one word—my name.

Or the name my parents' daughter was supposed to have. Nausea rises. I don't even know who I'm supposed to be.

But I steel my nerves. Pick up the bundle of silver shoes I'd dropped to defend Rayleen and Joshua. Then I answer Rhyan's unspoken question.

"We're going back to the library. I know what I need to do."

65

"EM, WHAT *ARE* YOU GOING
to do?" Laramie asks as we race through the streets toward
Ambryfell.

"The only thing that might fix this."

"Em . . ."

I don't have time or breath to answer more fully. "We have
to get back to the library," I repeat.

We rely on Hadeon's Zephyr wind and Wistlee's whip to
protect us from shadow creatures as we work our way through
Castramore. We don't need to vanquish them now—only get past
them to reach the library as quickly as possible.

Because if we can do that, I might be able to put a tourniquet
on this situation and at least give the Novemites a finite number
of shadows to battle. As it is right now, more pour in from the
skies, crawl up from the ground, spill from the cracks by the
second. An inexhaustible supply of darkness.

The only way to stop it is to close the holes in the worlds.

And, thanks to Hadeon and Teyra, I'm the only one who
can do it.

"I'm the bridge," I pant to myself, just as we reach the doors
of Ambryfell.

Civilians are pouring into the building, and some Novemites

I vaguely recognize from the yard are defending the doors and windows.

"Library?" Wistlee asks.

"Yes."

We maneuver through the knot of people, pushing our way forward. I don't allow myself space to think about what I'm going to do. It's become clearer with every step we take toward Ambryfell, and if I think too hard about it, I'll lose my nerve.

Retreat and let someone else figure it out.

But I know this is the answer. It has to be me, and the worlds, real and fictional, can't afford for me to lose my nerve.

"Emmy!"

Wistlee's voice whips my head around. The distress, the panic, sets my heart racing before I even know what's wrong.

"Wist?"

But she doesn't need to say it because I'm tracking her gaze up toward the sky.

And there's Frank—my baby wyvern—battling two shadow creatures at once. The bottom drops out of my stomach.

I stare helplessly as Frank uses her claws to pull apart one shadow creature. But the second circles around, somehow able to move freely throughout the air with no restrictions, no boundaries, just an amorphous blob of trouble gaining the advantage over my baby dragon.

Wyvern.

Whatever.

Frank flips into a rolling dive, trying to shake the creature from her back. The smoky tendrils of shadow fingers loosen from Frank's neck. She rolls into another dive, then cuts sharply into a steep climb. The shadow loses its grip.

But two more scream from the sky just above Frank.

I turn to Wistlee, feeling numb. Impotent.

How am I supposed to help Frank way up there? How can I keep her safe?

It takes me only seconds to realize my mistake, but Wistlee's eyes say it all. I can hear exactly what she's thinking: "If only I could fly."

My soul splits into exactly two pieces—one that wants to comfort Wistlee, and the other that wants to save Frank.

Because now Frank needs saving. The two new shadows have latched onto her back, fingers hooked beneath the ridges of the scales along her spine. I can see Frank's reptilian face contort in pain.

Fire races through my veins and ignites every nerve.

That's my wyvern, and I want nothing more than to rip to shreds the shadow creatures who are hurting her.

Radiant heat appears suddenly to my right as Rhyan pulls the string on her bow, a flaming arrow nocked and ready to loose.

She releases it and finds her first mark. One of the shadow creatures attacking Frank shrieks as it's propelled backward, spinning into nothingness.

Rhyan pulls another arrow from her quiver, lights it with her hand, then nocks it. Pulls the string tight. Looses.

This one hits its mark and a little more. Frank flinches and pulls back, smarting from the burn across her spine. Then she's spiraling into a dive that looks like it could be intentional—or it could be caused by the grazing hit she just absorbed.

Frank crashes to the stones before us and shrinks to the size of a pony.

"Frank!" I rush to her side, examine her wound, take her floppy ears in my hands, and nuzzle her face. "Are you all right?"

She chuffs. Bumps me with her forehead. Snorts smoke into my face.

I give a relieved laugh. "Good girl."

Rhyan utters an exclamation and releases another flaming arrow into the sky, and the screams of shadow creatures tell me others are probably doing the same.

I gape as I watch a full-grown wyvern succumb to the pull of at least a dozen creatures on its back. The beautiful forest-green scales flash through the sky. Its pearly cream-colored underbelly peeks into view as it spirals toward the earth. Then it winks out of view behind the buildings and towering evergreens in the distance.

The ground shakes on impact. I dart a panicked glance at my captain. I can't voice the terrible question—is that beautiful wyvern dead?

Rhyan's expression answers the question anyway. But all she says is "Go."

LARAMIE. I NEED TO FIND LARAMIE.

While I've been distracted with Frank, he's fought his way to the front doors of Ambryfell and is helping Castramorian civilians into the building. He's acquired a sword from somewhere—not his own, but at least it's something. Castramore is safer when Laramie's armed.

I push toward him with Frank at my heels, losing track of Wistlee and Phen but hoping they can see me in this crush of people. I've also lost track of Hadeon, and this sits in my stomach like curdled milk. Where is he? What's he doing? Do I need to be concerned about him?

For the moment, I decide to let it go. I don't need his help to do what I'm about to do. And once I do it . . . Well, I won't care about where Hadeon is or what he's up to. Someone else will have to tie up that plot thread.

"Em." Relief fills Laramie's voice as I slip my way through the crowd and land at his side.

A moment later, Wistlee and Phen draw up next to us. Laramie nods, and that's our cue to try to head inside. We leave defending the building and ushering in civilians to other Novemites and enter the foyer of Ambryfell.

Those Novemites can look after the Castramorians, but no one else can seal the holes. Just me.

"It's so tropey," I say aloud.

The others glance at me, but no one asks. They're used to my mini outbursts.

Leaving these friends will be the hardest choice I've ever made.

"Library," I say, picking up cat-size Frank, shrunken down for my convenience.

Such a good girl.

A dozen or more Novemites are leading Castramorians through the hallways that branch to the left and right off Ambryfell's foyer. Those hallways lead to many rooms and offices, as well as the spiral staircases connecting to the higher floors and down into the subterranean levels. Lots of places to hide. Lots of room to squirrel away the innocents so the Novemites can defend the building—the heart of Castramore that has become a fort.

I send up a prayer that they'll be able to do just that. A prayer that they will buy me the time I need.

It will only take a few minutes.

Conveniently, we need to go straight ahead and the Novemites are directing everyone away from those double doors, behind which rest the precious spheres and their sacred home.

Upon entering the library, we immediately meet Rizak, armed with . . . a broom.

"Emmy?" His brows rise, eyes widen behind his spectacles. "Laramie?" Then his gaze drops to Frank in my arms. "Oh dear."

Laramie eyes the broom. "What are you doing, Rizak?"

"Defending the spheres, if those creatures breach Ambryfell." He glances down at his weapon. "It was all I could find."

Sweet man.

"Rizak, we don't have much time," I say. "But I think I know how to fix the worlds. To fix the spheres and Earth and Rivenlea all at once."

His eyes grow wider.

"Phen." I turn to our Sentinel. "I need you to make a gateway."

"Okay." He looks at me warily. "Into what?"

"The sphere map." We all shift to look at the glowing grid of pillar stories, the delicate spokes tethering them to Rivenlea, the story gravity that holds them all in place.

"The sphere map." Phen looks blankly at me, then Rizak. "Is that . . . a thing?"

Rizak opens and closes his mouth a few times, but no words surface.

"I can make it a thing." I set down my wyvern and hand the bundle of silver shoes to Rizak. Then I pull my notebook from my pocket. "I can make whatever we need."

"Emmy," Wistlee says, placing a gentle hand on my shoulder, "remember what happened last time you created something new in your journal?"

Of course I remember. And I know what I'm risking. Creating what I need to save the worlds is likely to make the damage worse at first. It's likely to destroy Camille's bubble—or else take her into some other world. Either way, she'll be lost to me.

Again.

Always.

"There's no other choice." I force confidence and strength into my voice, neither of which I actually feel. "I don't know what will happen in the Silvarum when I do this, but we have to risk it."

"Em."

I don't turn to him. Won't. Can't.

"I'll make whatever we need in here," I continue. "Write some short fiction about the sphere map—whatever we need."

"Em?"

I still don't turn. "Then Phen will create the gateway."

"Emlyn." Wistlee moves aside, and I feel his hands on my shoulders. He turns me around, and there's an entire world—a whole sphere's worth—swimming in his eyes. "What are you going to do?"

I hold his gaze but don't answer directly. "And then it'll be time. I'll do what I have to."

"Which is what?" The concern sharpens. His gaze becomes more urgent.

A smile creeps onto my lips, because it's either that or start crying. "I'm going to jump into the sphere grid."

"You—what?" Laramie's voice pitches unsteadily. "No. Absolutely not."

I look around at my friends. They're all gaping. No one seems to feel the resignation I do, and I can tell they're going to fight me.

But we don't have time.

"I'm the bridge," I say, eyes back on Laramie. "Don't you see? I broke the worlds, punched holes everywhere I traveled because I'm not supposed to exist here. I'm a story. A figment of someone's imagination." My small smile widens just a bit. "And all this time I thought *you* were the imaginary one."

Laramie shakes his head. "But you can't—"

"I must. I created these cracks. I'm the piece that connects it all, and the only way to put everything back together is to—"

"Bridge the gaps," Rizak finishes. His words are edged in grief, colored with sadness, and I know he's reaching resignation.

He gets it. I'm the bridge.

"There's no other way," I say to Laramie. "I'm begging you not to argue. We don't have time to—"

I never get to tell him how short time is.

Because at that precise second, the doors to the library burst open, and a wave of shadow pours into the room.

AMBRYFELL HAS BEEN BREACHED,

its heart filling with darkness.

Laramie shoves me behind him, and Wistlee pulls out her whip. Frank grows to pony size again and faces the oncoming threat, though I see the raw burn across her back and know it must still hurt.

And Rizak, bless him, stands between the shadow monsters and his beloved spheres, a broom in one hand and a bundle of shoes in the other.

I have no weapon. No way to fight. I only have a notebook in my hand.

Before I can stop her, Frank launches herself into the air. Her wings unfold, and she banks sharply to the left, heading toward the massive shelves filled with spheres. With unearthly cries, the shadow creatures follow her. And only then do I understand.

She's drawing them off me. Loyal little beast.

"Frank!" I cry, knowing she's not going to come anywhere near me. Knowing but refusing to accept that she's putting herself in danger to give me a shot.

But Laramie knows. He draws his sword, then tugs my arm in his free hand. "Em, run." When I don't respond right away, he nods to my notebook. "Go!"

Get somewhere safe. Write the shortest piece of microfiction about the sphere map. Frank is sacrificing herself to give me a chance.

I force my feet to work. Gripping my notebook, I dart toward the large desk where Rizak likes to hang out. I duck under, concealed—at least for the moment.

Frank's huff reaches me, even here, and I try to block out the sounds. Wistlee's shouts, Phen's cries. Laramie's commands.

My hands shake as I open the notebook and pull out my pen. I stare at the blank page. I try to clamp down the river of adrenaline coursing through me to allow my brain the space to think through what to write.

I suit up. Strap on my boots. Prepare for the journey. A constellation of options unfolds before me, speckling the space between with worlds upon worlds, stars upon stars.

An intake of breath. A steeling of nerves. A jump into the unknown.

An astronaut launching into outer space?

No. A reader entering the library.

I spare a few sentences to describe the actual sphere map, just to make sure my intent is clear. To ensure the grid is included in the story—the sphere.

My mind is starting to fold in on itself thinking through the particulars of this idea. It's a complete story, created in my notebook, so the sphere should exist in Ambryfell somewhere now. At least in theory. Phen can create a gateway into the sphere map, and I can plug the holes.

It's going to work. It's got to.

I tuck the notebook into my back pocket and emerge from behind the desk, only to discover a horror story playing out before me.

Frank is being attacked by five shadow creatures. And she's much smaller now than when she was being attacked outside, so five creatures is enough to completely consume her. In fact, she's down to the size of a Border Collie and shrinking by the second.

She's struggling to stay in the air, fighting not to crash onto the shelves near where she hovers, but any second she'll lose that battle.

My friends have already noticed.

As Laramie cleaves shadow creatures on the ground, Wistlee has taken to the air. She's climbing the massive shelf near Frank, her whip gripped in one hand.

I strangle my cry just in time. I nearly called out her name, drew attention, gave away my position, undoing all their work of distracting the shadows.

Instead, I watch with clamped lips as Wistlee tries to assist Frank. When Wistlee is nearly level with Frank and her shadowy assailants, Frank finally loses her battle. The creatures rip her from the air, sending her plummeting toward the stone floor.

"No!" Wistlee cries, and with that, she takes a flying leap after the falling wyvern.

Laramie shouts something. Phen, too. I'm running toward them, watching Frank and Wistlee and a knot of darkness tumble toward the floor.

And then it's as though the world freezes, goes silent as a wintry morning. All I can see is Wistlee as she unfurls both her wings with a sharp snap.

The snow-white feathers fall from her right wing. A leathery bat wing to match her left is revealed. The feathers catch the light of the glowstones as they float to the floor.

But I hardly notice that. Because Wistlee—my dearest Wistlee—has dive-bombed Frank's attackers, scooped the beleaguered wyvern into her arms just before they both hit the ground, then launched herself back into the air.

Wistlee is flying.

68

TWO WINGS. WISTLEE HAS

two leathery wings, and, no longer off-balance, now she can fly.

I want to stand there, doused in appropriate awe, watching Wistlee soar at last, even as the final few feathers drift to rest on the floor.

How did they fall? Why?

But there's no time to ponder that now.

"Phen!"

He's ready for me, waiting by the sphere map as Laramie defends them both against the shadows. He's already building the gateway.

Rizak catches my eye then. Beating a shadow creature with the broom, bless him.

"Rizak!" I call. He turns, and I point to the bundle still tucked under his other arm. "Keep those safe. Get them back to their owner, if you can."

I don't wait for him to answer or acknowledge me. Phen's gateway is almost done, and he glances up, shaking black hair from his eyes. "Emmy?"

So much is baked into that simple word:

Are you sure?

Do you want to do this?

Do you really have to?

I nod once, finding that steel again. Convincing myself—and maybe Phen—that it's going to be okay. Whatever happens, it will be okay.

But then there's a bump at my shoulder, and I nearly crumble to pieces. I turn, losing myself for half a second in hot chocolate eyes.

"Em." Laramie pauses, grasping his brief respite from fighting shadows.

I resist the urge to touch his face. To stand on my tiptoes and give him a kiss. Because that's not fair. It'll only make this worse for him, and in a few moments, it won't matter to me either, so there's no point, really.

"You're not as awful as I thought at first," I say instead.

His face pinches. "Please don't go."

I nearly lose my resolve.

Instead, I force a smile to bloom in full, even as my eyes well with tears. "Take care of Frank."

Then I jump into the gateway.

I'M UNRAVELING AT THE SEAMS.

Tumbling through space.

Floating into the void.

It's not terrible, to be honest. I had no idea what to expect, and it had occurred to me I might jump through that portal into fiery lava. I'd considered there might be shards of story glass or an eternal slide with no end that I'd have to travel on for the rest of forever.

Floating through space as a shredded-up person isn't too bad, considering some of these other options. The only pain is that burning sensation in my legs.

But the moment I begin to make peace with this existence—and the fact that I'll never eat another bite of food or sip another ounce of coffee again—I feel myself stitching back together. Reforming into a person with a real body and actual problems and some very serious emotional baggage.

I'm no longer tumbling through space. Now I'm catapulting. Rocketing.

Where, I couldn't tell you.

The atmosphere around me changes, and I inhale a breath. Feel the warmth enter my lungs, then I hit something solid.

My body tumbles over the hard ground, then smacks into something and comes to rest. My eyes open, but I'm dizzy and disoriented. I can't quite make out anything in front of me or get my feet beneath me to stand.

"Emmy?" Rizak's spectacled face appears over me. Then he turns away and shouts, "Phen!"

Boots thunder toward me. I still can't quite scrape myself together to stand, but I roll onto all fours and manage not to throw up.

"Emmy!" Wistlee's boots enter my vision as she alights from above, and then her arms are hooked under my armpits, helping me stand.

I look around at the shocked faces of my friends—Rizak, Wistlee, Phen, who appears too dumbfounded to breathe.

Somehow, I've been spat back into the library of Ambryfell, right where I started.

Pleased as I am to see my friends again, relieved as I am not to be dead or fused into the sphere grid forever, panic grips every cell in my body.

"It didn't work." My voice is small and weak. Defeated.

Because I'm out of ideas. This was our one shot.

But then a scream that could peel paint from the walls echoes through the library. A breeze kicks up, as if there's a whole team of Zephyrs blowing wind throughout the room.

It's not Zephyrs, though. Cracks in the flooring open up, and the shadow monsters are sucked into them. One screeches as it's pulled through a window, shattering the glass on its way out.

"It did work," Rizak shouts over the wind. "The cracks are closing!"

As he says it, I can see chaos swirling in many of the spheres on the shelves. Smoke pours from some, others have tiny shadow creatures being dragged out from them, then pulled into the cracks in the floor.

My hair whips into my face as I finally fight to stay on my feet. "We need to get out of here," I shout above the din. "Where's Laramie?"

Wistlee says something, but it's lost in the roar of the wind, the static of the suction. It's like the entire room—indeed, all of Rivenlea—is sitting underneath a giant vacuum cleaner. And if we're not careful, we'll be whisked up with the shadows.

Rizak is pointing down one of the rows of spheres. He shouts something, but all I hear is "went that."

That's all it takes.

Laramie went that way, and that's all I need to know. I take off toward the row Rizak indicated, ignoring whatever shouts of concern follow me.

I know it's dangerous. I know we need to get out. But not without Laramie.

And thank goodness, Rizak was right. I round the corner and see Laramie. He's got a kitten-size Frank in one hand, his sword in the other. Frank appears to be unconscious.

Please not dead.

But I don't let my mind rest there. We need to get out of here, then we can help Frank.

"Laramie!" I shout.

He glances up. Does a double take. I see his lips move but don't hear the word. "Em?"

I almost laugh, allowing myself to feel a whisper of true relief for the first time since I crash-landed back in Ambryfell. Yes. I'm here—not dead, not lost.

Laramie is motionless for a moment too long. A shadow creature bowling toward one of the high windows careens into him, knocking him into the shelf of spheres. Thank the stars Rizak isn't beside me watching this, because the shelf sways. Several spheres nearly lose their balance.

But Laramie rights himself. Remembers himself.

He sheaths his sword and takes off toward me, our shared-custody wyvern curled safely in his hand. The wind swells into a tornado, but Laramie puts his head down and fights through it.

I grip the shelf beside me, bracing my body, reaching out with my other hand. Fighting to find him in the gale. We're nearly close enough to brush fingertips.

At the last possible moment before he reaches safety, Laramie is knocked sideways by another shadow creature spiraling into a crack in the floor.

It's poetic. Cinematic. So close, yet we come up short.

Laramie loses his balance. Maybe instinct tells him what's about to happen, or maybe he's as surprised as I am. But I see his eyes go wide. He clutches Frank to his chest and curls over her protectively.

And then, in the space of one breath, one heartbeat, one gasp, they are both sucked into the sphere on the shelf beside them.

70

I FEEL LIKE I'M FLOATING

through space again. Spinning. Unraveling.

Screams vibrate around me. I know they're mine, but I feel disconnected from everything unfolding in Ambryfell. Like I'm watching it distantly, wondering how the movie will end.

A strong hand grips my arm. Pulls me away. Next thing I know, I'm folded into two leathery wings, hunched low, waiting for the tornado to subside.

The wind beyond Wistlee's wings eases to a gentle battering. Then a mere ripple. And finally it dies, though the echo still roars in my ears.

Wistlee unwraps me. She tucks her wings back and places her hands around my face.

I'm sobbing, and I don't even care to hide it.

"Oh, Emmy. What happened?"

I hiccup, feeling ever more like a toddler and still not caring. "They got sucked into a sphere. Laramie and Frank were pulled into a sphere and just . . . disappeared. How is that possible?"

Wistlee stares for a moment. Finally, she says, "I wish I knew. The rules feel rather . . . fluid right now."

That's an understatement.

An idea strikes, and I straighten. I mark off the few yards

that had been between me and Laramie. Just another couple of steps, a solid leap, and I would have had him.

I scan the shelves of spheres, several of which look like they've just been through a battle.

There. This one.

I pick it up and know it immediately.

My heart stops. "Oh, mercy."

Tiny story Laramie is visible in the sphere. Even tinier story Frank is still in his hand. He's looking around, taking in the rolling English countryside, the stone wall covered in dead vines. The hidden door only just visible when I look very hard.

Laramie's little face is creased in confusion. Then he strokes Frank's head, takes a few steps into the Yorkshire landscape, and disappears from my view.

When I look up, tears rippling my view, I see Wistlee, Phen, and Rizak gaping at the sphere.

"He . . ." I close my eyes and swallow. Try to fight against the grief. "He really wasn't half bad, after all."

Phen winces. "Can we build a gateway, maybe?" He looks at Rizak. "Surely we can just make a gateway and go find Laramie and Frank in this sphere, can't we?"

"Before we do anything, you better come look at this." Rizak beckons us back toward the front of the library.

I resist the urge to pocket the sphere in which Laramie is now trapped. Instead, I carefully replace it on the shelf, holding my hands on it a moment longer than necessary, then follow the others.

"Oh, my." Wistlee is gazing up at the sphere map, and a moment later, I see what she sees.

Golden, glowing Rivenlea still sits at the middle of it all, dozens of spokes fanning out from its sphere and connecting to the smaller silvery story spheres. But now, the story spheres are also connected to each other by opalescent purple pathways.

Oz is connected to Sherwood Forest. Camelot is connected to Neverland, which is connected to the Hundred Acre Wood.

Anne Shirley's Avonlea is linked to H. G. Wells's martian-infested Earth in *The War of the Worlds.*

I gasp. My mind thunders through the implications, each worse than the last.

"You were right, Emmy," Rizak says softly. "Only you were able to seal the cracks in the worlds. But it seems . . ."

"I'm the bridge," I say numbly. "I sealed the cracks, but now everything is connected."

My stomach crashes to my toes. Does "everything" include Earth?

I take a trembling step backward. "What have I done?"

Castramore is shell-shocked. We walk into the chaos of cleanup. Triage, damage assessment. Counting the casualties.

I jump out of the way as a stretcher whisks by, my heart seizing when I recognize the massive man splayed out on it.

It's Topher Rys, the fungalinguist. He has burns on one side of his body and appears to be rolling in and out of consciousness.

Mokah Snick is passing out cups of steaming liquid, but her head is bandaged and blood is seeping through.

Ambryfell is damaged, stones blasted out in places, rubble peppering the grounds beneath. But the building is standing, at least, and that's something.

"Emmy!" Rhyan shouts upon seeing me.

She jogs up beside us, panting. "Wistlee, Phen!" she exclaims. "You're in one piece." Her face floods with relief as she glances around. But it doesn't last long. "Where's Laramie?"

A wave of dizziness swallows me. I close my eyes, and after a moment, I open them to face my captain. "Rhyan, I need to tell you something. Some things."

Her eyes flash with alarm. "What did you do?"

71

NOW I GET AN AUDIENCE

with the Elder Council.

Apparently all one has to do is break the universe, then put it back together incorrectly, and they squeeze you onto the calendar within twenty-four hours.

So I'm standing before the double doors of the Elder Council chambers on the top floor of Ambryfell, staring out a nearby window, watching the rebuilding efforts down below.

Rhyan is beside me, dressed neatly in Flare attire that looks like it's never seen the dust of the yard. She has a silver brooch affixed to her cape, and I distantly wonder what the symbol means—curved branches entwined into a complicated knot.

Probably the insignia of a captain.

Professional Novemite wrangler.

"Expert babysitter," I say aloud.

"Indeed." Rhyan shoots a sideways glance my direction, then turns to the doors. "Are you ready?"

"Not really."

"Good, let's go." She pushes the doors open and strides in, chin up. Confident and assured, if not proud.

I shuffle after her, biting my lip. My eyes dart around the chamber, then nearly pop right out of my head when I look up and see the hole gaping in the ceiling.

As if we all needed a visual reminder of my catastrophe.

A bench of Elders sits at the far end of the room, up on a raised dais, almost like a courtroom or statehouse. And this is both, I suppose.

The nine Elders are dressed identically in long black robes. Most of them have white or silver hair, except the emerald-green Harmony man seated in position two and the violet-haired Dragon seated in position five.

The only person I recognize is Elder Lytero, who saw us off to Oz. He's seated in position one, peering over his round glasses at me as I do my very best to hide behind Rhyan.

She stops before the bench and steps to the right, subtly motioning me to stand at her left. I'd much rather stay behind her, but I scrape together whatever shreds of maturity I possess and move to take that place. I try to match the angle of Rhyan's chin and pretend I have her confidence.

The violet-haired Dragon stares at me with empty black eyes and speaks. "Miss Emlyn DuLaine."

Yes, Mr. Creepy Dragon Face?

I clear my throat. "Yes, sir."

"We have heard much of you and your movements." He looks down his straight nose and fixes those black orbs onto my face. "And now that I see you, I wonder at the fuss."

"Me too," I say before I can quite stop myself.

His haughty expression and rude words don't inspire restraint.

Still, Rhyan elbows me. "Your Honors," she says, "Novemite DuLaine is here to answer for her actions, but I beg you to indulge me as I remind you of her excellent service on her recent mission to Oz."

Good old Rhyan.

The Elder in position six, a man with very curly snow-colored hair, leans forward. "That's all well and good, Captain Doyle, but does this young Novemite have any idea of the chaos she's caused?" He glances at the Dragon to his right.

"However dismissive Elder Kalamar wants to be, we are sailing uncharted seas."

The Elder in position three, a woman with long smoke-colored hair, studies me. "Characters in several stories have already discovered the bridges. Have you any idea what this means?"

"Yes, ma'am," I say. "It means eventually the villains will become aware of the bridges too. Some likely already have. And then they will be able to move freely from sphere to sphere, wreaking havoc as they will. It could mean the end of countless storyworlds, should any one of them succeed."

The spiky-haired woman in seat seven raises her brows at Elder Kalamar, the Dragon. "However much you dislike her, she's definitely one of your Dragons."

He narrows his black eyes. "Debatable, Felia."

I ignore the disdain on Kalamar's face and raise my voice. "I'm not a Dragon, though. Not really. I'm not exactly sure how I got imprinted as a Dragon when I passed through Rivenlea seventeen years ago, but I don't come from here."

Raised brows, shocked whispers, frowning mouths.

"No," Elder Felia says. "You were born in Rivenlea."

"Was I?" I meet her gaze. "To whom?"

More frowns. More whispers.

"Your name appeared in the Taenarum nursery," Elder Lytero says. "This only occurs when the child in question is a future Novemite."

"And yet you know I come from Earth." I pause and let them think about that for a second. "I suppose you'd been watching me somehow. I'm told the Elder Council has ways to see what's happening on Earth."

This is met with a few scandalized expressions.

"If I'm from Rivenlea," I plow on, "and somehow appeared on Earth, where is my Rivenlite family? Why don't they miss me?"

The only thing I hear is my heartbeat pounding in my ears. Silence fills the council chambers.

I suck in a breath and let the last bit tumble out. "I was born in a sphere. I'm a character from a story, pulled through Rivenlea, then deposited on Earth. That's why I was able to create the bridge. Because I *am* a bridge, linking the spheres with Rivenlea and Earth. That's why I thought I could seal the cracks."

"Which she did," Rhyan reminds us all.

Bless her.

"But there were unintended consequences." My voice shrinks, and it brings to mind Frank morphing from minivan size to pony size to cat size.

"I'd say so," the Elder in position nine remarks. "Eight Castramorians were killed by those shadow creatures. Six civilians, two Novemites. Dozens more lie injured in the infirmary. No one can possibly measure the damage to the spheres, and let us not forget Novemite Shayle."

The room seems to sway. I want to close my eyes against the piercing pain in my heart. But I have to at least pretend stoic acceptance of this for the sake of Rhyan and the rest of Novem XVII.

"No," I say quietly. "I could never forget Novemite Shayle."

"He's been folded into that sphere," the Elder Echo continues, "and who's to say if we will ever be able to get him back."

The Elder in position eight, a woman with braided silvery hair, turns to the Echo. "Peace, Axel. Once we ascertain the facts of the situation, we can discuss what to do about Novemite Shayle."

"Your Honors," Rhyan says, "I would like to submit to the council that Novemite DuLaine may have inadvertently created the bridges between worlds, but she did so innocently. She did not anticipate that result."

"But *we* might have," Elder eight points out. "This is why we have procedures and rules. This is why petitions are brought forth for council to consider, relying on our centuries of combined experience and varying perspectives as seasoned Novemites."

"Indeed, Elder Calea." Rhyan bows her head. "And the council will note I submitted a petition for an audience shortly before the chaos erupted. And another days before, prior to our mission. Novemite DuLaine was attempting to follow procedure to share with the council what she had discovered about Earth and the Silvarum. She was trying to follow procedure."

Rhyan leaves off the implied *for once.*

"But then the world began to split apart." Rhyan looks up at the Elders. "This was an emergency situation, and Novemite DuLaine responded in kind, working to save lives. Lives were lost, yes. But that burden is not Emlyn's to bear. With all due respect, I suggest you consider your own delays in responding to her requests. Your indecision allowed this situation to escalate."

Rhyan bows her head again, as if waiting for their wrath to descend upon her, and I'm struck by how awful this must be for her. To defend me against the Elders, she has to stand up to authority figures she clearly respects.

I don't deserve her.

The Zephyr Elder ruffles in her own wind. "Well! Is someone seeking a demotion, perhaps?" She glares at Rhyan.

"Enough," the wizened Gryphon in seat four says abruptly and considers us both for a moment, his neatly tucked shimmery gold wings rising and falling as he breathes. "As chair of the council, I move to issue a continuance for Novemite DuLaine until such a time as Castramore has recovered from her wounds, the bridges between worlds can be investigated in depth, and evidence of her negligence—or not—can be brought forth."

"Elder Gable, do you mean to suggest she should be allowed to remain an active member of Novem XVII?" Kalamar scoffs. "After all that's happened?"

Elder Gable turns to his colleague. "I do not wish to act in haste, precisely because of all that's happened. Elder Sax suggests we sail uncharted waters, and I quite agree. Something strange is afoot, and now is not the time for haste and imprudence. Not until we better understand the times."

"Motion for continuance seconded," the Harmony Elder says.

"Elder Cordio seconds," Elder Gable says with a nod. "Shall we vote?"

Council splits five to four. Unsurprisingly, the Zephyr—whose name is Aura, apparently—and Kalamar vote against me. Sax looks pained and worried, but he ultimately votes against me too. As does Elder Axel, who looks like he will never forgive me for losing one of his Echoes in a random sphere.

But the other five Elders vote for my continuance. A reprieve that gives me a little time—and a little time is all I will need.

Elder Gable looks down at me and Rhyan. "You are free to return to your work about Castramore. But do expect to be called back for questioning." He focuses specifically on me. "Do not think I have forgotten what you said about being a character from a sphere, Novemite DuLaine. I do not believe this to be possible, but we will hear your explanation at a later date."

"Quite the claim." Elder Lytero frowns.

"Preposterous." Elder Kalamar shakes his head. "Even more ridiculous than a human Dragon."

"Yet it may explain some of the strange happenings," Elder Cordio muses.

Elder Gable nods to us. "You may go, as we shall enter closed session now."

"Thank you, Your Honors." Rhyan bows once more.

I can't exit the room fast enough. I only just restrain myself from sprinting toward the doors. We step into the hallway, and Rhyan closes the doors on the voices of the debating Elders. She keeps her hands pressed against the wood and leans her forehead against it.

Then she takes a deep breath and turns to me. "We need to go help the others. They're rebuilding a damaged part of Ambryfell."

I knew this—Wistlee told me. I nod. "Yes, of course."

"And, Emmy, please." She looks at me pointedly. "Try to stay out of trouble. I'm not sure how much goodwill we have left with the council."

I nod again. I really don't deserve her.

Especially because of what I'm about to do.

I DON'T KNOW WHAT AWAITS

me when I carry out my plan, but I decide not to say goodbye to Wistlee and Phen, as though I'm preparing to meet my death. But I plan to return.

At least, that's what I'm telling myself. Power of positive thinking, and all.

I tiptoe down the hallway in Ambryfell, having just excused myself from dinner. I'll be right back, I told them. Then I set out toward the library.

Rizak never questioned what was in my mysterious bundle. When I requested it back, he retrieved the wrapped silver shoes from behind his desk and handed them to me, no questions asked. He merely stated he assumed I would be able to return them to their owner myself, since I'd landed back in Rivenlea after jumping into the grid.

And I will. Eventually.

But right now, I need those shoes.

I grab my pack and sword from the front corner of the library where I'd hidden them earlier. Pull out my cloak and throw it on. Then I carefully unwrap the silver shoes.

Dorothy's slippers catch the low light of the glowstones surrounding the library. The broken windows have been boarded up, and it's darker in here than usual.

But that suits my purposes just fine.

The shoes seem to wink at me, daring me to make use of them.

I feel like a terrible person, and Rhyan is likely to kick me out of the Novem and turn me over to the council when I get back. She'll be absolutely correct in doing so.

But I have to try to make one thing right.

I stare at my boots, then at the silver shoes. How does it work? Do I just put them on and wish myself into the sphere? I have no idea.

So instead, I decide to find the sphere, then change my shoes.

I'll never forget exactly which row, which shelf, which sphere. I'll never forget exactly where I saw Laramie drain from this world into another.

There, the sphere full of the rolling dales of Yorkshire.

I begin unlacing my boots. Remove them and tuck them into my pack. And then I slip on the silver shoes.

They fit perfectly, as though little Dorothy also wears a women's size six and a half. But these are magical shoes, so surely they adjust their size to the wearer's needs.

I shoulder my pack and take a deep breath. Here goes nothing.

"Emlyn DuLaine, don't you dare!"

My soul nearly leaves my body at the sound of Rhyan's voice.

I whip around, expecting to see my very angry captain marching toward me. Possibly on fire. Maybe throwing fire at me, if I'm very unlucky.

Instead, I find my irritated captain marching toward me, flanked by Wistlee, Phen, and the four remaining members of Novem XVII.

Even Marella. Canon.

"Is this to be a public flogging?" I say, hoping the joke won't land me in hotter water.

"Have you not earned it?" Wistlee fires back. Her normally gentle eyes challenge me. Her wings move slightly.

Phen's mouth is pulled into a tight line, and I realize I'm in trouble for not telling them my plans.

But then I notice the Novem is dressed for travel. They're battle-ready, packs strapped on.

"Wh-what . . ." I stammer. "What are you doing?"

"You didn't think we'd let you go alone." Rhyan folds her arms across her chest.

Canon huffs. "A mission alone? What were you thinking, Miss DuLaine?"

"I was thinking I made a mess and need to clean it up."

"Without us?" Faela frowns and shakes her head. "We're your team, Emmy."

"Your allies," Rivit adds.

"Your friends." Marella glances away as soon as she's said it, and I do her the favor of not gaping.

Instead, I turn to Rhyan. "Did the Elder Council approve this?"

She purses her lips and doesn't respond right away. I can't help but wonder if I've been a bad influence on her. But all she says is, "We will deal with the Elder Council upon our return. For now, we need to rescue Laramie."

I quite agree.

And I can't help but take a deep breath, draw in the sense of a full family surrounding me. Something I've been missing since Camille disappeared from Earth all those years ago.

A pinprick of hope pierces my soul. Maybe we'll be able to do it. Get Laramie back before he's folded into the story for good, figure out how to deal with the bridges connecting everything. And maybe—just maybe—we will even find Camille again, wherever she's been pulled to.

"So." Rhyan's fiery gaze challenges me, a smile playing at the corners of her mouth. "Where are we headed?"

Carefully, I pick up the correct sphere. "Have any of you ever heard of Misselthwaite Manor?"

EPILOGUE

"HADEON?" SHE BREATHES OUT his name like a sigh and a song. "How are you here, my love?"

Hadeon crouches on the dock, brushes a dark, wet curl from her forehead. But he doesn't answer. Not yet. It's been so long since he's seen her face-to-face, he'd like to savor the moment as long as possible before shattering it.

Her enormous brown eyes look up at him, then close as she rests her cheek against his palm.

"It will be easier for me to come to you now," he says softly. "At least for a while."

"How?" She laughs, tears sparkling in her eyes. "I would not argue, of course. But how is this possible?"

"She's . . ." The words get stuck in his throat. He clears them and tries again. "She's come at last."

She gasps. Pulls back a bit. "Here? Now?"

"No, in Rivenlea."

She begins to shake, quivering in the water. "You must bring her, then. It's time."

"I have tried. I gave her the silver shoes from Oz."

"And?"

"She has used them for another purpose—for now," he adds quickly, seeing her distress grow. "I had to tell her more than I wanted to. It did not go to plan."

"Hadeon." Tears slip out. "You must bring her. Or else I will never be able to leave. We will not be together."

He looks over her head for a moment, watching the roll of gentle black waves. The ocean seems bottomless at night.

"It is difficult," he says finally. "She is not what I expected."

"Difficult?" She shakes her head. "I have endured many hardships, and the promise of our love has seen me through them all."

"Sørena . . ."

"Go. Bring my sister to me." The tears dry up as she pushes away in the water. "Or else don't come back again."

She dives beneath the surface, a flick of her iridescent aqua tail fin her final wave goodbye.

TO BE CONTINUED

ACKNOWLEDGMENTS

I feel like Emlyn, staring at her blank notebook page, unsure what to write, because this story has been such a long time coming, and I never could have gotten here without the help of so many people. Where to begin?

At the beginning, of course. To my dear husband, Dave, the inspiration for all my best story boys, but Laramie most of all. I couldn't pursue my passion for storytelling without your support, and you've been the most supportive, most amazing partner I ever could have asked for. I love you.

To my children, Shane, Jared, and Keira, who have put up with many years of many deadlines and continue to cheer me on. I love you more than the cats, I promise.

To my cats—

Just kidding.

To my sister, Genessa, and her husband, Travis. My very first readers. You fell in love with Emlyn nearly twenty years ago, reading my roughest, greenest drafts and liking them enough to spur me on—to write more, to keep telling stories, to imagine maybe I could even publish them someday. Quite fittingly, I have pulled Emlyn out of that first story and placed her elsewhere, but I know you will still recognize the story girl you knew all those years ago. I hope I've done you proud.

To Dana Black, my alphaest alpha reader, who willingly submits herself to my drafts nearly the moment I'm done writing them. Thank you for being there for me through countless seasons of my life and my career. But most of all, thank you for being you. I like her a lot.

To Chris Morris, for . . . everything. You're truly a blessing in my life, and I'm lucky to call you my friend. Thank you for smiling at all the weird ways I write you into my stories. Mushroom giants, for instance.

To Ashley Mays, for reading this story in its squidgy first-draft state. Thank you for the decade of friendship and life we've shared. It has meant the world to me. *In omnia paratus.*

To Sarah Grimm, Avily Jerome, and Catherine Jones Payne—I could call you guys my "writing friends," but it doesn't come close to covering it. Thank you for the years of friendship, the tears and laughter, the brainstorming and workshopping. For helping me think through the idea that became Emlyn's *Unraveling* in its earliest stages. Love you all so much.

To C.J. Redwine, for helping me wrap my mind around this story when I just couldn't seem to make the strands come together. Without you, I wouldn't have gotten here.

To the Enclave team—it's impossible to describe how lucky I feel to work with you daily and to place my stories in your expert hands. Jamie and Trissina—you are incredible. We are my favorite three-headed creature.

To my editors—Lisa Laube, Sara Ella, and Jodi Hughes. The time, attention, and love of story you pour into your work is wonderfully apparent. Thank you for making this book better than I could have on my own. Lisa, thank you especially for helping me navigate the waters of our mutually beloved storyworld, Oz. I'm so grateful for everything you bring to the table, on and off the page. ♥ Sara, for catching every single Easter egg and reference I buried in this story and delighting over them in the margins. That was life-giving! Jodi, for your eagle eyes and expert-level chaos-wrangling. This story is sparklier for your efforts.

To Steve Laube—thank you for believing in me and waiting oh so patiently (ahem) as I recharged my batteries enough to tell this story. And for putting up with all the unnecessary tea and faces in butter. I appreciate you deeply.

To the Oasis team—Steve Smith, Charmagne Kaushal, Lisa Smith, and the whole crew, thank you for all you do.

To Kirk DouPonce—I'm continually in awe of the magic you

create. Thank you for another brilliant, stunning, gorgeous cover. I know I say it every time, but this is my favorite cover yet.

To my faithful agent, Rachel Kent, for being by my side the last fourteen years (!!!). I am blessed to have your steady hand guiding my career. And I'm so glad you saw Emlyn's potential—and maybe mine too—when I was too green to have any business pitching to you. I'm grateful.

To the dear readers who have found my stories, reached out to me, left reviews, commented on my social media antics, taken the time to post about my books—I still pinch myself sometimes. Yes, you are real. Yes, this is really happening. Thank you for being willing to adventure with me. You make the struggle and stress of the publishing industry more than worth it.

All glory goes to the Lord, the Creator, Author, and ultimate Storyteller. Thank you for rescuing me and calling me yours.

ABOUT THE AUTHOR

Lindsay A. Franklin is the Carol Award–winning author of *The Story Peddler*, ECPA best-selling author of *Adored*, and Managing Editor of Enclave Publishing. She would wear pajama pants all the time if it were socially acceptable. Lindsay lives happily among the rain and evergreens of the Pacific Northwest with her scruffy-looking nerf-herder husband, their three (nearly) grown geeklings, and three demanding thunder pillows (a.k.a. cats). You can find out more about Lindsay and her books at LindsayAFranklin.com or connect with her on Instagram @ LinzyAFranklin.

SELLING STORIES IS A
DEADLY BUSINESS

Available Now!

The Story Peddler

The Story Raider

The Story Hunter

www.enclavepublishing.com